A
Quest
For
Skye

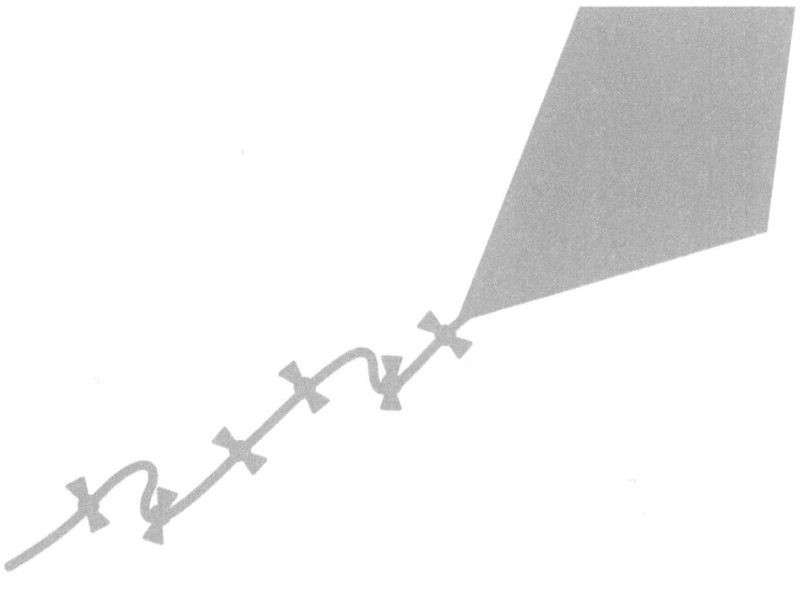

A
Quest
For
Skye

J. L. Rothdiener

NAVIGATOR BOOKS

SAN DIEGO, CALIFORNIA

A QUEST FOR SKYE

Copyright © 2012 by J. L. Rothdiener

Biblical references taken from the HOLY BIBLE, New International Version (NIV), New Living Translation (NLT), and King James Version (KJV).

Navigator Books

www.navigator-books.com

ISBN-13: 978-0-9852523-3-5

Printed in the United States of America

Acknowledgements

No book is written without the help of many people.

I would like to thank:

My wife, Joy, who put a great deal of time and effort into this project.

Burton and Sylvia Murdock for their time, support, and knowledge of the English language.

Madison Austin, the sweet girl adorning the cover.

Beyond Batten Disease Foundation, whose video inspired me to write this novel.

Tracy and Jennifer VanHoutan and their family, for whom I have the highest respect.

Jeffery and Maria Edwards, my publishers at Navigator Books, who never fail to give me honest, practical advice.

Melba Lackey, a friend whose expertise is invaluable.

Jane Murdock, whose medical knowledge was helpful.

Trans-Siberian Orchestra, "My favoritest group in the whole world."

Dedication

Dedicated to the children who are battling a disease for which a cure has not yet been discovered—specifically Batten disease.

May you remain steadfast in the Lord as you wait for that cure.

But those who trust in the Lord will find new strength.
They will soar high on wings like eagles.
They will run and not grow weary.
They will walk and not faint.

Isaiah 40:31 NLT

Chapter One

The fury of the restless waves pounded the cliffs as the scientists fought desperately for a cure. The salt tang of the ocean mist hung heavy on the air of the small island town. This was an important day for the island's residents, though most of them didn't know it.

Near the center of the island was a small hospital, a clinic with an experimental laboratory. To an outsider, the unusual nature of the lab's equipment might have suggested the lair of mad geniuses, bent on world domination, or the creation of some breathless monstrosity. But these were not characters in a horror movie. They were dedicated physicians and scientists, fighting against the clock—fervently searching for the cure to a certain disease before it stole more innocent lives... the lives of children.

Dressed in white protective biohazard suits, four well-known researchers were on the brink of a major breakthrough in the medical field. They were preparing to mix a pharmaceutical surrogate of their own invention, and inoculate it with a radioactive microorganism. Preliminary findings had shown great promise.

Watching intently from his shielded office through a shatterproof window was Doctor Layland Leontiou, a Greek billionaire whose sole purpose in life was to combat childhood diseases.

The four figures turned to face him.

Doctor Whitman, a top researcher in the field of nuclear physics, spoke. "Everything is in place and ready to go. Malinda will operate the vial transfer through her laptop in this room. Doctor Miller and Doctor Bowers will assist me. I don't need to remind you of how precise we have to be. We can't afford to make a mistake here. If the organism is released too slowly, it will be ineffective. If it's released too quickly, it could cause an explosion, and destroy years of work."

Raw fear flickered across Layland's face. "You're certain that you've done everything in your power to ensure everyone's safety?"

Dr. Whitman nodded. "We've taken every possible precaution, Sir. The vials are housed in a solid case. If the transfer fails and an explosion *does* occur, it won't be powerful enough to breach the enclosure. As an added safety measure, we're wearing the best protective gear available. If anything goes wrong, we can fall back to the decontamination chamber and escape."

The lone female in the group assured the concerned man. "Honey, everything will be fine. The computer is programmed to do all the work. It will mix the ingredients precisely, at the proper time. We've tested, retested, and then tested again. Layland, I truly believe this is *it*. My heart tells me that it is."

For a moment, the couple only looked at each other, the intensity of hope evident in their expressions.

Leontiou wiped the sweat from his brow. "Okay, doctors, I'm entrusting you with my wife's life, and the lives of many of the people on this island."

He took a deep breath, and exhaled slowly. "Go!"

The scientists turned and surrounded the isolation enclosure: a hollow cube of thick-walled Lexan, about four feet on a side, cast in a single seamless piece for airtight integrity. On three walls were built-in protective gloves that reached inside the box, making it possible for the scientists to handle the materials inside. On the other side was a small airtight door, programmed to be opened and closed by the computer.

The men, experts in their fields, inserted their hands into the gloves, ready to begin the process.

The woman stepped in front of her laptop to initiate the delicate procedure. She typed in a series of commands, ordering the door of the enclosure shut.

When the door hissed closed, she moved next to the others to observe.

A video camera was recording the entire process. Layland alternated between watching the video and the live action. The video gave a close-up view of the procedure.

The men placed the vials in the correct position. Then they cautiously extracted their hands from the gloves, and stepped back to watch.

The computerized arm took over, swinging the pipette containing the radiated micro-organism toward the vial containing the surrogate.

"Okay, this is the critical part," Malinda Leontiou said. "The organism is about to be released. It will take the form of a retrovirus, and attach itself to the defective genes. It should destroy all of the damaged gene sites, and begin the process of rebuilding."

She stepped back in front of the computer and hit the enter key. The laptop screen scrolled through thousands of commands.

Malinda joined the others, watching the vial as it was opened by the computer arm. The components began to mix slowly, precisely.

"So far, so good," Malinda reported.

The words were barely out her mouth, when the computer screen froze.

Immediately, a siren alerted throughout the compound, followed by a continuous announcement. "Warning! Warning! Computer shutdown! Warning! Warning! Computer shutdown!"

The woman rushed to the laptop, to try to restore the sequence. She quickly realized that her efforts were futile. The entire system had crashed!

Without precision computer control, the radioactive organism was indiscriminately dumped into the vials. Deprived of its electromagnetic signal, the lock on the enclosure door defaulted to the unlocked position, and the enclosure automatically began to open, slowly.

"Get out!" Dr. Whitman shouted. "Get Malinda out!" He stepped in front of the opening door, forcing it closed with his body. "If air touches the virus, it will explode."

Miller and Bowers pulled Malinda away from the laptop.

"My computer," she screamed, reaching for her life's work.

She was still protesting when the two doctors threw her into the decontamination chamber.

The men rushed to aid Whitman, the brave scientist who was using his own body to shield the others from the harmful rays.

Whitman's arms were wrapped around the enclosure, his chest shoved painfully against the door. "Go!" he yelled. "It's too late for me. Get out! It's going to blow!"

Muscles trembling violently, Whitman strained with every ounce of his strength to hold the door shut. He was rapidly losing the battle.

The other men could see that it was too late to save their colleague, so they reluctantly rushed toward the safety of the decontamination room.

They had barely reached the door when the explosion went off.

Dr. Whitman was killed instantly, his body thrown backwards across the room with the force of a freight train. A fraction of a second later, the entire laboratory burst into flames.

The door of the decontamination chamber was still open. Miller and Bowers were caught by the shockwave and slammed to the floor, the plasticized fabric of their protective biohazard suits beginning to ignite under heat of the growing fire. The two scientists lay unconscious and unmoving.

The blast tore Malinda's headgear off, exposing her to the harmful vapors released by the accident. She slammed her palm on the emergency button, shutting the door, and sealing off the contaminated lab.

The automatic sprinklers kicked in, quickly extinguishing the fire.

From the decontamination chamber, the terrified woman looked through the glass, directly into her husband's pained eyes.

Dr. Layland Leontiou cried out in horror, "Malinda!"

Chapter Two

Excitement filled the air of the 747.

The plane streaked through the cloudless, blue sky toward '*The City Beautiful.*' Every seat was filled, most passengers anxious for the start of a long-awaited vacation.

One family was going to Disney World—a mother, father, and three children ranging in age from seven to eleven. Their eagerness was obvious to all around, as the children had spent the early portion of the flight running up and down the aisle of the plane shouting, "We're going to Disney World."

The active youngsters had followed the chant with a comical version of *The Mickey Mouse Song,* bellowing it at the top of their lungs.

Needless to say, the other passengers were ready to feel the wheels of the plane touch down on the runway at Orlando International Airport.

One older gentleman was overheard whispering to his companion, "My kids were *never* that wild." He followed the comment with a broad grin.

Among the passengers was a couple on their honeymoon, their faces radiating love for each other. Huddled in their seats, they were oblivious to their surroundings.

Four would-be adventurers in their early twenties were discussing an upcoming scuba diving expedition—certain that they knew the location of a sunken treasure.

A pair of father-son duos was discussing the deep-sea fishing adventures they had planned. Within hours, they would be out on the water, hoping to catch that prize trophy to hang on the wall back home.

While nearly everyone aboard was consumed with his or her own thoughts and plans, one couple sat motionless, barely aware of the commotion around them. Occasionally, one of them would smile slightly at some amusing word or antic from one of the children. Mostly, the couple stared silently off into the distance, seemingly lost in another world.

Sometimes, the man would reach out and tenderly hold the woman's hand, a reminder that he was there for her, no matter what.

The man's name was Doctor Morgan Hamilton. He was a well-known pediatrician and the administrator of a pediatric clinic in Saint Paul, Minnesota. Sitting next to him was Tammy, his wife of eleven years, also a pediatrician, who served as the Chief of Staff at the same clinic.

The couple shared a common bond—a passion for children, and the desire to help them in any way possible. The past few years, they had dedicated their efforts to special needs children who suffered from rare diseases.

Their demeanor was subdued for a couple in their thirties who were getting ready to embark on a fourteen-day cruise through the Panama Canal. For them, this was not an exciting adventure, but a much-needed respite from their fast-paced lives.

Only weeks before, Tammy had suffered her third miscarriage. The doctor had confirmed their worst fears when he told the distraught woman that she could never have a child. She would never be able to carry a baby through the first trimester.

The obstetrician had been compassionate, but he hadn't sugar coated the situation. "If you and your husband want to have children, you should adopt. Unfortunately, that's your best option at this point. Or, to be more accurate, it's your *only* option."

Tammy's eyes began to fill as she replayed the doctor's words for what seemed like the thousandth time. She knew the doctor had been trying to give them hope, but still the pain was unbearable.

Tammy and Morgan had been struggling to start their family for ten years. Since their early conversations as an engaged couple, they'd shared the dream of someday having a household bustling with children. Now, that dream would never come true.

Childlessness didn't seem real to either of them, both yearned to wake up finding it only a nightmare. No, it was far *too* real. They would never have their own natural children to love. How could they ever accept that?

Glancing at his wife, Morgan fought the impulse to touch her cheek and wipe away a stray tear.

When he'd first heard the news, Morgan had wanted to take his heartbroken bride away... away from the pain, from the well-wishers who didn't understand her heartbreak... away from everything!

For years, they'd been talking about a Panama Canal cruise, but they'd never been able to fit it in their schedules. Now was the perfect time.

So far, the smiles were few and far between. Maybe when they boarded the new ship, the laughter and the forgetting could finally begin.

After a comfortable flight, the Orlando airport came into view. The plane touched down, and pulled up to the terminal. As the passengers deplaned, the children, as well as some adults, could barely contain themselves.

Well-dressed employees from popular vacation spots were holding signs, watching for their clients.

The family with the three youngsters sprinted to the sign that read, "Disney World."

Others hurried toward signs that read, "Treasure Hunters Scuba Diving," and "Big Catch Deep Sea Fishing Adventure."

The honeymooning couple strolled hand-in-hand to a young woman holding a banner which read, "Cruise Ship *Isaura.*"

Morgan and Tammy would be spending the next two weeks on the same vessel.

"Good morning, everyone!" the cruise representative said. "I'm looking for a honeymooning couple by the name of Billie and Billy Hill." She chuckled. "That's cute, same first name."

She smiled at the young couple who were holding each other tight. "I would suspect you're the Hills, right?"

The newlyweds beamed and nodded their heads.

"Welcome! You're about to have the honeymoon of your life, on our spectacular ship."

Glancing at her clipboard, she announced, "Now, I'm looking for Doctor Walter and Helen Leary, and Morgan and Tammy Hamilton."

A woman in her late-fifties spoke. "We're the Learys."

"Then you must be the Hamiltons." The young hostess eyed Morgan.

He grinned. "Yes, we are."

"Great. It looks like we're all here. Ladies and gentlemen, you're about to embark on the cruise of a lifetime. The *Isaura* is not the largest ship on the high seas, but she's one of the newest, most beautiful, and definitely the most extravagant. You'll be pampered with our top quality services throughout your cruise. Please follow me, and I'll take you to the baggage area to claim your luggage, and then we're off to the shuttle."

After all of them had gathered their bags, the young woman led them to the ship's check-in area. Each passenger was presented an identification card, which also would serve as a credit card and room key. When everyone was ready, they boarded a small van that would deliver them to their floating home-away-from-home.

During the transfer, the Hills clung close to each other in a world of their own, whispering only to each other.

The Learys were bubbling with anticipation.

Morgan and Tammy sat silently, staring out the window.

After a short drive, they sighted the ship in the distance. They could make out the large, glittering, sapphire letters spelling out, "*Isaura*."

"Oh, look," Helen said to Tammy. "Isn't she beautiful? I wish we could have been on her maiden voyage last year, but Walter's work schedule wouldn't allow it. Luckily, they're holding the convention on board this week, and he wouldn't miss *that* for all the tea in China. He's so excited!"

She laughed. "Me, I'm going to sun bathe and spend hours at the spa."

Tammy smiled.

"Are you here for the convention?" Walter asked.

"No. Just to get away." Morgan tried to sound polite.

"What do you folks do for a living?" Walter switched his attention to Morgan.

"My wife, Tammy, is a doctor. I'm a hospital administrator." Morgan hoped the answer would satisfy the well-meaning people, so they would be left alone.

"What kind of doctor are you, Honey?" The older woman persisted.

The young woman hesitated, taking time for the question to sink in. Slowly, she answered, "Pediatrics. I specialize in children's diseases."

"Then you should come to this convention. It's all about childhood diseases. Sounds like it's right up your alley. We had a special invitation." Walter crossed his arms, waiting for the couple's response.

"I don't think we would be interested. We just need some time to ourselves." Tammy's shoulders slumped forward, a defeated, nervous chuckle sounded in her throat. She was hoping the well-meaning couple would take the hint.

"Walter, let the young people enjoy themselves. This is a cruise," Helen scolded, sensing something was wrong. "For us, I guess I should say for you, it's all business. For me, it's doing nothing, but relaxing. Ah, fourteen days of bliss!" she sighed.

Helen patted Tammy's hand. "You must forgive my husband. It's been his lifelong dream to be invited to this convention. I think it makes him feel important." She chuckled lightheartedly.

Tammy nodded, agreeing with the talkative woman.

Morgan and Tammy shifted their focus out the window again as the shuttle pulled up alongside the magnificent *Isaura*. Its newness sparkled.

The vehicle came to a stop. Porters were quick to open the doors. With a friendly greeting they announced, "Welcome to your first day in paradise. We're here to make this the best cruise you'll ever have. We'll deliver your luggage to your stateroom."

As the three couples stepped out of the van, they were met by an attractive woman. "Good morning, everyone! Since you already have your key cards, you'll only need to go through security. If you'll follow me, I'll take you on board."

Within minutes, they traipsed across the gangway onto the magnificent vessel. Handing the security guard their identification cards, he scanned them. "Welcome aboard, Mr. and Mrs. Hamilton."

A pleasant young woman stepped up to greet them. The nametag on her colorful, flowered shirt read, "Via—Tahiti." Cheerfully she announced, "Good morning, Mr. and Mrs. Hamilton. Welcome aboard the luxury liner, *Isaura*. My name is Via, and I will be your personal attendant. I'll make sure your room is kept to the highest standard. My job is to make your voyage the best it can be. If there is anything you need, please let me know. Do you have any questions?"

The Hamiltons remained silent.

"Great. Then please follow me and I'll show you to your suite."

As Via led them to their accommodations, she pointed out the many amenities along the way—restaurants, pools, bars, entertainment areas, and the theater. "The buffet is on deck eleven—they're serving lunch, as we speak. If you want to work off all the delicious food you eat on this cruise, you can take the stairs." The young lady chuckled.

Finally, they arrived at their glamorous suite. Via opened the door, gesturing for the couple to enter. The comfortable sitting area looked inviting. On a table along the wall was a large bowl of fruit. A vase of exotic flowers welcomed the guests. Sliding glass doors opened to a balcony.

"Your bedroom is through this door. It leads to another balcony—your private one." She led them into another room with a king-size bed. In the center of the bed, a swan made from towels caught their attention.

While the Hamiltons looked around, the porters put their luggage on the stands.

"You can unpack now, or I can show you more of the ship. Whatever you want. You make all decisions the next two weeks." Via smiled.

"I think we'll unpack," Morgan stated decidedly.

"That will be fine. If you need me for any reason, push the star button on the phone. I have my phone with me at all times. I hope you enjoy your stay." Via and the porters exited the room.

"It's beautiful," Morgan said, trying to get his wife to smile.

Not saying a word, she began to unpack.

He wondered if he did the right thing bringing her on the cruise, her sadness penetrated every part of her being. He hoped she could unwind, come to terms with the devastating news.

When they finished unpacking, Morgan suggested, "Honey, let's go explore the ship."

"No, thanks. I think I'll sit on the balcony and read for a while, but you go ahead. I want you to enjoy yourself." She mustered a half-smile.

Morgan watched his wife stroll to the refrigerator to get a bottle of water. She grabbed the latest novel by her favorite author, and opened the door to the balcony that overlooked the Atlantic Ocean. She sat comfortably in a lounge chair, letting her eyes wander over the sea. The hot sun felt soothing.

"Would you like me to ask Via to get you an iced tea or something?"

Tammy sighed. "Sure, that would be nice."

"I'll tell her when I see her. I'll be back in an hour or two."

Stepping into the long hallway, he almost bumped into Via. "Excuse me, Miss?"

"Mr. Hamilton, please call me Via."

"All right, Via, please call me Morgan. Could you please bring my wife an unsweetened iced tea with lemon? She's on the balcony reading."

"Yes, Sir. I will get it immediately."

"Sir?" he said as a question.

She grinned. "I mean, Morgan."

"That sounds better. Now if you'll excuse me, I'm going to explore this luxury liner."

"Oh, that's fun. Make sure you stop by the buffet in the dining room upstairs. It's superb—the best food on the Caribbean."

"I may do that. Thank you for your suggestion."

With that, he was on his way to see the sights on the ship, which would be his home-away-from-home for the next two weeks.

Chapter Three

Morgan headed to the tastefully decorated multi-storied atrium. The grand staircase, a double curved marble architectural marvel, cascaded into the center of the lobby. Eight glass elevators were embellished by crystal pillars that ascended from the staircase landing. He stared at the magnificent mural on the ceiling. "Classy," he whispered.

Everywhere he went, a staff member greeted him with a smile. "Good day, Sir. Isn't it a beautiful day?" *Just like the brochure said, the employees on this ship want to make this cruise the best we've ever had. Very friendly,* he thought.

He started to pass up the buffet, but noticed the tantalizing food and opted for a snack. A waiter handed him a plate and silverware. "Enjoy yourself, Sir. This is the finest buffet on the Caribbean." The cheerful employee grinned.

Near the crowded buffet line, was a life-size statue of a lighthouse keeper holding a lantern. The intricate details caught Morgan's attention. *It sure is lifelike. Almost like a real person.* He fought the urge to touch it.

Morgan worked his way through the buffet. *Wow! I hope I don't put on an extra ten pounds!* Grabbing a few delicacies, he sat down at a table next to a window overlooking the ocean.

He enjoyed people-watching as he nibbled his snacks. He noticed the diversity of people on board—many nationalities were represented.

The Learys spotted Morgan. Waving to him, they strolled by, each carrying two plates loaded with food.

"That's enough to feed a platoon of soldiers," Morgan whispered under his breath, snickering.

When he finished eating, Morgan resumed exploring the massive vessel. He'd already seen the buffet and pool area. Next was the large convention center.

He glanced into a large conference room where a couple of workers were arranging chairs. *This must be where the medical convention that I keep hearing about is going to be held.*

He picked up a brochure from a display table and began thumbing through it.

A neatly-dressed man in his sixties greeted him. "Good afternoon, Sir. Are you attending the convention?"

Scanning the brochure, Morgan was startled. "What? Oh, no, my curiosity got me. I'm just here for a leisurely cruise with my wife." He smiled at the kind man.

"Glad you're here. I don't believe we've met."

"Hamilton, Morgan Hamilton."

Shaking Morgan's hand, the friendly man responded, "Well, Mr. Hamilton, enjoy your cruise." He turned and left.

Glimpsing at the brochure, he noticed the photo on the front was the same man he'd just met. He spun around and watched the man making his way down the hall, stopping and talking to everyone along the way.

Stuffing the pamphlet in his back pocket, he continued his tour of the ship.

Morgan walked by the specialty shops that were closed while they were in port.

He noticed the library and decided to see if there were any books that would interest his wife—she was an avid reader. Near the entrance, Morgan noticed four different books arranged neatly on a small table. The author's name was Doctor Layland Leontiou.

Morgan looked on a back cover and was surprised to see the picture of the man he'd met only moments before. Leontiou... That name sounded familiar.

Morgan studied the book titles: *Childhood Diseases*; *Facts about Bowman's Disease*; *The Child Must Live: A day in the Life of Batten Disease.* Then he spotted the sequel, *The Child Will Live.*

"Hello, there." A female voice indicated he wasn't alone. A striking, older woman, dressed in a bright sundress, watched him from the opposite side of the table.

"Hello," Morgan replied.

"Are you here for the convention?"

"No, Ma'am. Just to get away and enjoy myself."

"Are you here with anyone?" she asked, reaching her hand out.

"Yes, my wife." He returned her handshake.

"On your honeymoon, or anniversary?"

"No. As I said, just to get away from the hustle and bustle of city life."

"I hear you. Nothing better than a cruise for that. How long have you been married?"

"Eleven years."

"How many children do you have?"

After a long pause, he added, "None."

"Not in the picture yet?" she smiled.

"Not in God's picture," he answered weakly, feeling like the wind had just been knocked out of him.

She sensed his sadness immediately and quickly changed the subject. "Are you interested in these books?"

"No. Well really, I don't know. I think I just met the man who wrote them."

"That would be my husband. He's the writer. I assist him, researching information when necessary." She brushed the hair off her face.

Morgan noticed two of the books had the name Layland and Malinda Leontiou.

Holding one of the books, he asked, "You must be Mrs.—how do you pronounce it? Lee-on-tyoo?"

"Very good, it's Greek and pronounced the way it's spelled." She smiled. "May I ask your name?"

"Morgan Hamilton."

"Morgan Hamilton. I've heard that name. What do you do for a living, Mr. Hamilton?"

"I'm a doctor. Well, actually, I'm the administrator of a pediatric clinic in Saint Paul, Minnesota."

A curious look came over the woman. "Your wife wouldn't be Doctor Tammy Hamilton, would she?"

"Why yes, how do you know her?"

"Of course, Morgan and Tammy Hamilton. You wrote the article in *World Medical Magazine*: *Why We are Concerned about Rare Childhood Diseases.*'"

Morgan grinned. "That was almost two years ago. You have an excellent memory. I have to admit, it actually was my wife's article. I only helped. You see, I run the clinic, but my wife has the brains in the family. She is truly a genius."

"I was very impressed with the article. In fact, I showed it to Layland, and we adopted a few of your procedures at our clinic. Dr. Hamilton, you and your wife must come to the convention." She emphasized the word "must," raising an eyebrow, and waiting for his response.

"Thank you for the invitation, but I don't think we'd be interested. We're trying to get away from work. That's why we're here." Morgan blew out a lengthy breath.

"I understand. If you change your mind, the offer stands. Wait! I have an idea. Maybe the two of you would speak at one of our meetings."

"Thank you, but I think we'll have to pass." Morgan's voice sounded certain.

"Again, I understand. We doctors need time off, too. Please, take these books as our appreciation to you." The thoughtful woman handed Morgan a copy of each of the books.

"Please, let me pay for them."

"No, it's my gift to you." She whispered to Morgan, "Besides, I know the author." She smiled. "Come by here tonight, and he'll be happy to sign them for you."

"Okay. And maybe I can convince Tammy to come with me."

"That would be great. I'd love to meet your wife. I've heard so much about her."

"Thanks for the books. I'd better go. Still have some exploring to do."

Morgan packed the books under his arm and continued on his journey. *She was kind. Tammy will have plenty of books to read on the cruise*, he thought.

Soon he entered a spacious lobby. He stopped to study a replica of the ship in a glass case. *Isaura... That's an interesting name. I wonder what it means. Probably named after some queen or Greek goddess.*

Before he knew it, Morgan was on the crowded pool deck, the Caribbean music blaring. A movie was showing on the giant screen.

Strolling through the spa and sauna area, he found himself in the exercise room. He stopped long enough to try out the bike and treadmill.

A young woman with jet-black hair sauntered over. "You look like you're familiar with the equipment. My name is Kim. I'm one of the trainers."

"Hi, Kim. I'm Morgan Hamilton."

"Mr. Hamilton, you look physically fit."

"I'm a physician. I try to stay in shape."

"Oh, you're here for the big convention? That's great."

"Actually, no. I'm only here for a cruise, but it seems like everyone I meet is talking about the convention."

"I guess it's a big thing. Well-known doctors from all over the world are here for seminars on childhood diseases. Word on the ship is that some of the greatest medical minds in the world are gathering here for fourteen days of discussions and recreation. I'm all for it. I have a son with leukemia."

"I'm sorry to hear that. How old is he?"

Kim dropped her friendly tone and her voice grew sad. "He died, only seven months ago."

"I'm sorry. How old was he?"

"He was six. I talk about him as if he were here, because he'll always be in my heart. He's with the angels now in heaven."

The young woman was distant for a split second and then snapped back. "I'm sorry. I shouldn't be talking to you about my problems. You're here to enjoy yourself, not listen to me blubbering about myself."

"No. Please, if you need to talk, I'm here to listen. I wish you could talk to my wife. Maybe you could help each other." A sad smile played on his lips.

"You know, I was so caught up in my own problems that I didn't even consider that you probably have your own set of troubles."

Morgan lowered his head. "My wife, Tammy has had three miscarriages. The doctor recently told her that she could never have a baby. Her lifelong dream was to be a mother to as many babies as possible."

"I'm sorry. That has to be hard on her. Actually, on both of you. Have you ever considered adopting?"

"I have, but she'll have nothing to do with it. She's down on herself, and God."

Kim touched Morgan's hand, looking deep into his eyes.

"If it were not for God, I never would have made it."

"What do you mean?"

"I mean, during Colt's illness, the people from my church were there for me. I'm a single mom, and no matter what I needed, they were there to help. Clothing, food, sometimes they even paid my utilities when I couldn't afford to. And when Colt was dying, my pastor, and his wife stayed with me. They missed their son's championship high school basketball game because they were holding my hand as my little boy slipped into eternity. There were dozens of people praying outside the room. If not for God and my church family, I wouldn't have made it. There's no telling what I would have done—probably drank myself silly, got high on drugs, anything to get my mind off what was happening. There was a time in my life when something like that would have been my answer."

Morgan listened intently.

She continued with her story. "I was sixteen when I had Colt. I was a wild child. My parents prayed for me every night, but I laughed at them. One night I spent the night at my girlfriend's house and a bunch of people came over. I won't tell you what happened that night. I'm ashamed of it now, but the result was my little boy. When I found out that he was sick, I blamed God. I also blamed myself because of my sinful ways. Because of the persistent prayers of my parents, and because of Jesus and His love, I am where I am today."

"I take it there was no father in the picture."

"As far as I was concerned, there was no father at all. Besides, I was too drunk to know who it was. My life changed when Colt was born. I'm glad my parents lived to see the radical transformation of my life. They were killed in a car accident six months after he was born. I'm sorry for the hurt I caused them, but they forgave me. They loved me in spite of the things I did. I know they sure loved their grandson. That little guy made me a better person. Now he's gone, but I don't blame God. I had six wonderful years with Colt. And, without him, I would never have met Zack."

"And who is Zack?" Morgan studied her.

"See the young specimen of a man over there?" She nodded to a well-built young man who was demonstrating how to operate one of the exercise machines to an older woman.

"Yes."

"Just last week he asked me to marry him." She showed him the diamond ring on her finger.

"Nice! When's the big day?"

"We've decided to wait until we're stable financially. He comes from a wonderful family."

Morgan found Kim's story interesting and hoped Tammy could meet her.

She looked back at Morgan. "The thing I love most about Zack is that he loves me for who I am. So does his family. They know my past, but love me in spite of it; there are no secrets between us."

"Kim, I see how much you love him."

"We believe God has brought us together. He has blessed us in many ways."

"That's something that Tammy and I have to come to terms with. We both know about God's love, but it's hard for us to accept that truth now. Why would a loving God leave us childless?"

"That's a tough one. If Tammy ever needs a shoulder to cry on, I'm here. And Zack is here if you ever need a listening ear."

"Thank you. I appreciate you taking the time to encourage me. I better go. I've been gone for a long time, and dinner is in a little more than an hour. I've visited every part of this ship except the children's area. I don't know why I'm going there. I guess just to say I've visited every part of the ship." He laughed. "It sure is spectacular!"

"Yes, it is. By the way, the meals in the dining room are the best on the sea. I highly recommend the seafood. It's really good for your diet." She grinned and then lowered her voice. "I know I should not say it, but for dessert, the chocolate cream cake is out of this world. It will stick to your ribs and force you to work out for three hours, but I think it's worth it."

"I'll remember that."

They shook hands and Morgan went on his way.

Chapter Four

Morgan took the stairs one flight up to the children's area. *Any steps I take will be to my advantage,* he thought, with chocolate crème cake on his mind.

He entered a brightly colored hall with a giant rainbow stretching the full length. Children's laughter came from behind a closed door. *That's always a pleasant sound,* he thought. Standing by the glass door, he peered at several kids of various ages jumping on a large, bouncy inflatable. Three young employees were watching them.

The sight of the youngsters having fun brought a smile to Morgan's face. His mind drifted to what it would be like to have a child of his own, but his thoughts were disrupted by a voice behind him. "Hey dude, you're blocking progress. Either go in or step aside, please." She drew out the word "please" for emphasis.

Morgan looked down at a charming girl. Her blue eyes sparkled and blonde hair bounced as she talked.

He was stunned by the girl's boldness. "I'm sorry. I didn't know I was in someone's way."

She looked up at him, cocking her head to the side. "What is your name?" she asked, more like a demand than a question.

"Morgan. And what is yours, young lady?"

"My friends call me Skye, with an *e*." She spoke every word with precision, and loud enough that everyone in the area could hear. It was obvious she didn't have a problem with shyness.

"Well, Skye with an e, that's an unusual name."

"I know. When I was born, my father said my eyes were the color of the sky, so the name stuck."

"What should I call you?"

"I don't know. Are you my friend?" Her confidence took him by surprise.

"I can be." Morgan replied, stooping down to her eye level.

"I don't know... My father says I shouldn't talk to strangers." Her eyebrows sprang up.

"What is my name?" he asked in a soft tone.

"Did you forget? It's Morgan." The girl put her hands in her pockets, watching inquisitively.

Morgan snickered. "And yours is Skye with an e, right?"

"Right!" She angled her head.

"Well, you know my name, and I know yours, so I don't think we're strangers anymore. What do you think?"

Skye's grin took over her whole face. "No, we're not." She held her hand out to him. "Hello, I'm Skye."

Morgan reciprocated, softly shaking her hand.

"No, that's wimpy. My father said that whenever you shake a hand, do it firmly, not like a dead fish."

"Oh, right." He grasped her hand firmly, wondering about the bundle of energy standing in front of him.

"That's better. Now, you can call me Skye. And please drop the 'e' joke. That's getting old."

Morgan noticed a large bracelet on her wrist. "Wow, that's a nice bracelet."

"Isn't it nice? My father gave it to me. He said it gives me personality."

Morgan was astonished by the young girl's large vocabulary and wittiness. "How old did you say you were?"

"I didn't. You should know—never ask a lady how old she is," Skye scolded, shaking her finger at him.

"I'm sorry, you're right." *She's a live wire,* he thought.

"I'm nine," she shot back with a satisfied grin.

"Nine! You mean nineteen?"

She put her hands on her hips. "Do I look like I'm nineteen?"

"I was just kidding," he said. "Sort of. But you sure act older than nine."

"Do you want to watch me jump? I can jump today. My father said I could." Releasing Morgan's hand, she kicked off her flip-flops, and went skipping into the room.

Morgan watched from the doorway.

"See! Actually, I bounce," she shouted. Giggling, she grabbed another girl's hand and they bounced together.

"Her bark is worse than her bite," boomed a voice from behind.

Morgan turned to see the gentleman he'd met earlier—the doctor-author.

"She's something. Is she your daughter?"

"Yes. She's my pride and joy."

"Did you teach her to be so outgoing?"

"Me? Oh, no. She came about it naturally. Everything she does is instinctive, and she'll even tell you that. Wait till she tells you a story. She leaves nothing out."

The two men stood side-by-side watching Skye enjoying herself with the other children.

"Your name was Morgan, right?"

Morgan shifted his attention to Skye's father. "Very good. You must have a knack for names."

"Well, not really, only names of people who impress me."

Morgan looked surprised. "Impress you? In what *way*?"

"I sense you're a caring person. I generally can pick out a man's occupation and character after I first say hello."

"Oh, really?" Morgan raised his brow.

"Yes. I know it's sort of strange."

"What do you know about me?"

"You? Well, Mr. Hamilton, I believe that you're ambitious beyond your age. Let me guess... I'd say you're a doctor, here for a holiday with your wife."

Morgan laughed. "You're good. How in the world did you know that?"

They glanced back at Skye. "My wife told me that while she was in the library she met a gentleman and gave away four of my books." He looked down at the books Morgan was holding. "I guessed that since you were carrying four of my books, you must be the gentleman she was talking about."

Morgan laughed. "You had me going for a moment."

"Dr. Hamilton, I would be honored for you and your wife to sit at my table tonight."

"Well thank you, but I'm not sure that's a good idea."

"Nonsense, I insist. You'll be my guests. You can have anything on the menu you want. Price is no object."

"This is a cruise. The meals are free."

"Precisely."

Both men erupted in laughter.

Their amusement was interrupted by a small voice. "Father and Mr. Morgan, come and jump with me."

The small girl grabbed the men's hands, dragging them into the room where the bouncy inflatables were located.

"Honey, we're too big for that," the father argued with his persistent daughter.

Refusing to give up, Skye continued, "Mr. Morgan, come on, don't be a party pooper."

She released her father's hand and tugged on the younger man with both hands.

Seeing that he might as well concede, he removed his sandals. Morgan handed Dr. Leontiou the books to hold. He stepped onto the bouncer with Skye and began jumping. He looked over at the girl's father who stood smiling.

Dr. Leontiou laughed heartily. "I told you she's her own person. Very demanding, and she didn't get that from me."

"Are you going to eat with us tonight?" Skye asked, jumping.

"Would you like me to?"

"Yes, yes. Pretty please."

"I'll see what my wife says. It will be up to her."

"What is your room number?" Skye's eyes sparkled.

"9730."

"Good. I'll pick you up at six."

"Don't get your hopes up. I don't think my wife will come. She's sad these days."

"Just ask her." The girl wasn't backing down.

"Okay, I'll ask her."

"Bye." The livewire grabbed her flip-flops and took off running past her father. She muttered, "Later," disappearing down the hallway.

"My goodness." Morgan stepped off the bouncer. "She has more energy than anyone I've ever met."

"You don't know the half of it," her father responded. "The offer for dinner still stands. If you can make it, just ask for Dimitri. Tell him you're a guest of Dr. Leontiou. We'll be in the Emporia dining room at six. No tuxes tonight. I hate tuxes." He crinkled his nose.

He reached his hand out to Morgan who responded with a firm handshake.

"Ah, she taught you well," the father joked.

Both men broke out laughing.

Morgan wandered back to the room. On the way, he glanced at his watch, it was after five. *Dinner is in less than an hour—that should give me just enough time to shower and dress.*

When he arrived at the room, Tammy was sitting in the makeup chair applying the final touch of lipstick. She seemed to be in a brighter mood.

Maybe time relaxing in the sun has done her good, Morgan thought.

"You'd better get ready, mister. We have a big evening ahead of us." Tammy surprised him, her voice sounding like a command.

He noticed his clothes set out neatly on the bed. "Honey, what has gotten into you?" Morgan's tone sounded hopeful.

"We've been invited to sit with Dr. Layland Leontiou and his wife Dr. Malinda Leontiou. Do you know who they are?"

He laid the books in front of her.

She picked one of them up. "That's great! You have *The Child Must Live*. I've wanted to read this book."

"Honey, how did you hear about the invitation to dinner?" He peered at his wife, waiting for her response.

She stood up and kissed him on the cheek.

"You'd better watch out! Those younger women will trap you every time," she teased.

"What do you mean? Did you meet Kim?"

She rolled her eyes. "Wow! You mean there's more than one? No, I meant Skye."

"Oh, Skye!" His first instinct was to laugh, and he did.

"Yes, Skye with an 'e.' You know a real cutie—about four feet, sixty pounds, blue eyes, blond hair, and a firm handshake."

"She was here?" He blinked.

"She certainly was, and I couldn't stop her from talking. By the way, she said I had a firmer handshake than you."

"Why, that little imp. She said that, did she?" Morgan gave his wife a crooked grin.

"Yes, she said she had to ask me to dinner, because you told her to." Tammy ran the brush through her hair.

"Well, I didn't exactly say that." He blushed.

"It doesn't matter. We're her guests, so we must go. Get ready. Now!" she ordered. "I can't wait to meet Skye's father and mother. Malinda is a medical genius."

Morgan was thrilled. It was the most enthusiastic Tammy had been in weeks.

He showered and dressed hurriedly as Tammy waited by the door, excited to meet the people in her profession she had only heard about.

Chapter Five

The lowering sun and the right amount of clouds hinted a spectacular sunset.

The vacationing couple glanced around the elegant dining room. Like a jewel adorning the room with radiance, a crystal chandelier crowned the center of the domed ceiling. The dining room was tastefully decorated with rich woods, and hues of cream and gold, with cranberry colored accents.

Morgan's thoughts were interrupted. "May I help you, Sir?"

The doctor shifted his attention to a formally attired, tall, slender man. His nametag read, "Maître d' Dimitrrri—Greece."

Morgan looked closer at his nametag, "Dimitrrri? That's an unusual spelling with three r's."

With a thick accent, he replied, "Yes. I get a lot of second looks and questions. You see all the boys in my family were named after my father, Dimitri. Each boy that came along got another 'r.'"

"Well, that's interesting. I read once that the heavyweight boxer, George Foreman, named all his boys George."

Dimitrrri smiled, nodding his head, even though he had no idea who the man was talking about.

Morgan continued to make conversation. "What was it like growing up with an unusual name? I mean, what was school like?"

"It was interesting to say the least. Everyone always tried to correct the spelling of my name by taking out some 'r's.' At least, it wasn't as strange for me as it was my brothers."

"Brothers?" Morgan asked.

"Yes. I have three brothers younger than me." He broke out laughing.

Morgan and Tammy joined in.

When the laughter subsided, Dimitrrri asked, "How may I help you, Sir?"

"We're supposed to meet Dr. Leontiou for dinner." Morgan scanned the dining area looking for any sign of them.

"You must be the Hamiltons."

"Yes."

"The doctor is expecting you. Please, follow me."

Dimitrrri led them to a large table in the back of the dining room. It was bordered by floor-to-ceiling windows on three sides. The room was suspended over the ocean giving a breathtaking view of the ship's trail. A glass floor made it the best table in the house to view the swirling ocean below.

The picturesque scene of the sunset with its crimsons and oranges could have made a prize-winning photo.

Before Dimitrrri could seat the couple, the cute girl Morgan had met that afternoon hurried over to them. Dressed in a bright orange dress, and hair curled in ringlets, the boisterous girl took over. "There you are. I was afraid you were going to be a no-show. Father told me that I couldn't go and get you because it had to be your decision to come. 'Don't be a pest,' were his exact words."

She grabbed their hands, dragging them to their place at the table where two other couples were already seated with her parents. Directing them to their chairs, she ordered, "Now, Tammy, you sit here, and Mister Morgan, your place is over here. I want to sit between you." She smiled, sitting down. Plopping her hands in her lap, she finally quieted.

Morgan winked at his wife.

"She's sort of demanding, isn't she?" Layland kidded.

"She's a young woman who knows what she wants," Morgan said, still grinning.

Skye's father stood, reaching his hand out to Tammy. "I'm glad you could join us. I'm Dr. Layland Leontiou."

Tammy shook his hand readily. "You don't know how much I've always wanted to meet you."

"Oh, you know of me?" he replied, with wide eyes.

"Know of you! I've read most of your books and have used them frequently to help diagnose children at my clinic."

"Well, I'm both honored and flabbergasted, but I have to be honest. The real brain behind the operation is my wife, Malinda." He motioned toward his wife.

Tammy shook Malinda's hand. "It's a pleasure to meet you." Keeping her tone upbeat, she added, "You have a polite and energetic young daughter."

"Why, thank you. This is one of her good days." Malinda smiled at Skye, who sat listening to every word of the adult conversation.

Dr. Leontiou continued with the introductions. "You've probably heard of Doctor Samuel Roberts, and his wife, Doctor Elizabeth Roberts."

Tammy smiled, greeting them warmly. "Sure, I know their work well. It's a pleasure to meet you."

Her eyes revealed surprise when she glanced over at the other couple. "Oh my, you're Dr. Laurence Whitman! I recognize your picture from your book."

Dr. Whitman commented, "Oh, you're the one that bought my book." Laughing, he said, "Seriously, I'm the one who is honored to meet you."

"I heard there was a medical convention here, but I never realized to what magnitude. I mean, the four of you have rewritten the medical journals on many childhood diseases." Tammy shifted her position, and smiled at her husband, expressing her pleasure of dining with their new friends.

Dr. Whitman introduced his wife.

Mrs. Whitman shook Tammy's hand, and then Morgan's. "I'm the nobody in the group. I've never written a book, and I've never discovered a cure for anything. I'm just an ordinary housewife."

"Don't underestimate yourself, Stephanie. You're the mother of my three children." The proud husband was quick to reply.

"Your three children? I recall having a little bit to do with that."

They all burst out laughing as the assistant waiter filled their water glasses.

Dr. Whitman sipped from his water glass. "Motherhood is nothing to be frowned upon. It's the noblest vocation on the face of this earth. You have the task of raising three children to be presidents, or kings. Or perhaps paupers, or vagabonds. You've got your work cut out for you."

"Nicely put," Dr. Leontiou said.

"What do you think, Dr. Hamilton? Is motherhood that important?" Dr. Roberts asked.

"Yes, do you have any children?" Dr. Whitman pursued the line of questioning.

A solemn look appeared on Morgan's face as he pondered how to answer the question. After a pause, he reached for Tammy's hand, squeezing it for support. "Yes, I believe motherhood is absolutely important, if and when you have the opportunity to become a mother."

For a minute, an awkward silence filled the air. Then without thinking, Dr. Whitman blurted, "I take it you don't have any children yet. Being in your thirties, I'm sure you know it gets more dangerous to have children the older you get. We, as physicians—"

Suddenly, Whitman yelped when his wife kicked him under the table.

"Ouch! What did you do that for?" the clueless doctor asked.

Mrs. Whitman scowled at her spouse. "I'm sorry. My husband is such a dunce sometimes. He can equate 'pi' by using Archimedes' Constant to the tenth level—whatever *that* is—but he doesn't know when to keep his mouth shut, unless he gets kicked."

Morgan tightened the grip on his wife's hand. "It's all right. It's a question we're often asked."

He took a deep breath. "The fact is, Tammy can't have a baby; she's lost three. Her doctor recently confirmed that she'll never be able to carry a baby full-term."

Skye snuggled up to Tammy. "You can share me with my parents."

Tammy blinked, fighting the tears, and gave a half-smile to the vivacious girl.

"Have you considered adopting?" Elizabeth asked.

"We've talked about it," Morgan said, "but we're not ready for that yet. Frankly, I don't know if we ever *will* be."

There was silence for several seconds until Layland added awkwardly, "Right. Now, on the subject of this meal, what shall we eat?"

Skye continued to hold Tammy's arm.

Their four-course meal was ordered, and small talk followed among the four couples. Once in a while Skye would agree, or compliment someone for something.

Once the appetizers were served, the hungry guests started to enjoy their delicious food.

"Father!" Skye interrupted the diners.

He eyed her, "Yes, Skye."

"You forgot something! We haven't prayed yet." She folded her hands.

"Oh, right. Would you like to pray for the meal, Skye?" the father asked, obviously self-conscious.

She bowed her head, extending her hands to Tammy and Morgan.

The couple looked at each other blankly and then took her hands. It was a practice that Morgan and Tammy had once felt important, but it had been years since they held hands to pray. In fact, it had been a while since they'd prayed at all.

The rest of the group took each other's hands, some of them feeling uncomfortable, glancing around to see if anyone was watching.

Skye closed her eyes. Her tone became less bubbly, more thoughtful. *Lord, thank You for this food that we are about to eat. I pray for those in this world who only have rice to eat tonight or go to bed hungry. I pray for all the children without parents. Please show them Your love. I also pray for my new friends, Morgan and Tammy.* " She clutched their hands tighter. *Give them a special blessing! Amen.*

Tammy wiped away a lone tear, hoping no one noticed.

The others at the table stared at each other in silence—perhaps because of the content of the prayer, perhaps because they prayed at all.

Tammy and Morgan were amazed at the love this little girl showed others.

They'd rarely seen such compassion in an adult, even less in a child.

The group began to eat. Not a word was spoken for a few minutes as everyone reflected on the prayer, wondering about the small girl who had a way of capturing people's attention.

Skye broke the tense quiet by commenting on her tasty shrimp cocktail. "This is my favoritest food in the whole world, besides chocolate!" She dipped a shrimp in catsup, and devoured it.

"Dr. Hamilton." Layland looked directly at Morgan's wife.

"Please, call me Tammy."

"All right. Tammy, would you honor us Tuesday by speaking at the conference? We'd like to know what your American clinic is doing in the treatment of childhood diseases. We'd be thrilled to have you share your insight with us."

A sad smile played on Skye's lips. "Tuesday? Excuse me, Father, but that's the day we kiss the dolphins."

Immediately, the expression on her father's face changed, showing his disappointment. He had forgotten the promise he'd made.

The girl watched her father, waiting for his response.

He cleared his throat. "Skye, I'm so sorry. You know I need to be at that conference. Could we change the dolphins to Friday, when we reach Panama City?"

His wife chided him. "Panama is sold out. The plan was to visit the dolphin exhibit in Jamaica after we climb Dunn's Falls." She paused. "Honey, you *did* promise her."

"I realize that, but Tuesday is the most important day of the conference. I can't get away and the schedule can't be changed. You know that."

"Morgan can take her." Tammy said.

"I can?" Morgan asked. He stared at his wife in confusion.

"I mean, I *can*! In fact, I would *love* to." His voice sounded nervous.

"Would you? Could you?" Skye jumped up, squeezing Morgan's neck tight.

Mrs. Leontiou stepped in. "Dr. Hamilton, I don't think you realize what you're getting into. Skye is high maintenance, and quite frankly, she never knows when to be quiet. I'm sure you've noticed that she talks and talks. If you think you can put up with that, I have no objections. But please don't feel obligated."

She chuckled. "If you value peace and quiet, you'd probably have more fun at the convention."

Without further thought, Morgan responded, "Nonsense. I think we'll be just fine." He smiled at Skye, uncertain of what he was getting into.

Skye's mother continued speaking about her daughter almost as if she wasn't there. "Tomorrow is sea day, and the convention begins. May I suggest spending a little time with Skye around the ship, and then make the decision to go... how do you say it? Dolphin kissing. We want you to know what you're getting into!"

She smiled. "Quite frankly, the thought of kissing a slimy fish sort of disgusts me, but my daughter thinks it's something she simply *has* to do."

Skye sighed, sitting up straighter. "Dolphins are not fish, Mother. They're mammals, like us. It's perfectly natural to kiss another mammal. I see you and Father kissing all the time."

"Right," Skye's father said quickly. "Now, what do you think of this meal? Splendid, isn't it?"

Laughter erupted around the table.

"We'd love to spend some time with Skye tomorrow. Tammy and I can get to know her a bit. As for Tuesday, I know of no reason that I can't take her to kiss a dolphin."

"Yay! I can't wait." Skye grabbed Morgan and Tammy's arms, holding them close.

"Good! Then it's settled. Tammy will be speaking at the convention, and Morgan and my daughter will be romancing the dolphins," Dr. Leontiou kidded.

The pleasant conversation continued as the adults enjoyed coffee and dessert.

Skye took a few bites of her chocolate cream cake with chocolate ice cream on the side. "Oh, I'm full."

As much as she loved chocolate, she couldn't eat another bite! "Tomorrow night, I'm going to eat my dessert first."

When they finished dining, Skye hurried over and grabbed her father's hand. "Let's go to the show, Father. It starts in ten minutes."

"Not tonight, young lady. I have a book signing tonight. You're signed up with the children's staff, and you can go with them. It will be more fun than hanging out with me."

"Oh, Father! I don't want to hang around those kids. Can I go with the Hamiltons?"

"Honey, I don't think they want a shadow trailing them," Malinda commented.

"We don't mind taking her. I'm looking forward to the dancers tonight," Tammy stated. "Can we take Skye to the theater tonight?" Tammy eyed Morgan.

"It starts in ten minutes," the youngster begged.

"Well, then, we better get a move on, don't you think?" Morgan gave his typical crooked grin.

The three of them rushed to the theater.

Chapter Six

In the brief time they knew her, Morgan and Tammy were amazed at the politeness, to say nothing of the energy, of the young child. Just nine, yet they observed her addressing adults as Ma'am or Sir, opening doors for elderly people, and generally being friendly to everyone she met. They thought it was certainly a rare treat to spend time with a child so courteous, so genuine.

When they reached the theater, they found three seats near the front. A waiter came by and asked Skye how she was doing.

"Isaiah, are you going to be our waiter?"

"Yes. How was your day, Skye?" he said, laying a few napkins on the small round table.

"Super! I met Tammy and Morgan today. They're very nice." She motioned to the Hamiltons.

"Hello! I'm happy to meet you. Any friend of Skye's is a friend of mine. Would you like something to drink?"

"No, thank you. We're too stuffed from dinner." Tammy puffed out her cheeks, illustrating how full she felt.

"Skye, you want a soda, right?"

"Right, 'the real thing,' you know."

"I know. I'll be right back."

"Thank you, Isaiah."

"That was Isaiah. He works at the pool during the day. He's really nice." She twirled a ringlet of hair around her finger.

Tammy and Morgan looked at each other, unsure what to think. *How does Skye know so many people?*

The first part of the show, they were entertained by a comedian. All three of them laughed till it hurt. It felt good; laughter had been scarce lately.

Skye laughed so hard, she slipped off the edge of her chair, which set them into another bout of laughter.

Finally, the dancers came out, and Skye drew closer to Tammy, falling asleep against her shoulder.

Tammy and Morgan would occasionally look down at the sleeping girl, her long blond hair draped over her face. Tammy brushed a stray curl out of Skye's mouth, and gently stroked her head. Each of them imagined how wonderful it would be to have their own child, yet painfully realizing their dream was dead. They had so much love to share. Nothing made sense!

When the show was over, everybody exited the theater—except Morgan, Tammy, and the dozing girl. Neither adult said a word, watching the sleeping angel they'd only known for half a day.

Tammy straightened her in the seat, and then Morgan picked up the still-sleeping child with his strong arms.

Isaiah moved next to him, asking quietly, "Sir, do you need some help with Skye?"

"No, thank you, Isaiah. We can take her home."

The couple began walking up the aisle, and then stopped suddenly. "Isaiah, I just realized, I have no idea what her room number is!"

"9001. Take the elevator to the ninth deck, turn left. It's at the end of the hallway." The waiter smiled. "Take care of her, she's special to us!"

"We will, Isaiah," Tammy grinned.

Morgan added, "That's convenient, it's the same floor we're on."

"Have a great cruise." Isaiah waved.

"Thank you." Morgan carried the sleeping child to the elevator. Tammy pushed the button. The ride to the ninth floor was silent.

As they neared their suite, Tammy requested, "Can you get her from here? My feet are killing me. Remind me not to wear these heels again."

"Sure. I'll be there soon."

When he reached Skye's suite, he knocked quietly on the door. Her father opened the door, a broad smile covering his face. He took his daughter, kissing her gently on the forehead, and motioned the younger man to enter.

"Did you have a good time?" Leontiou asked.

"The best! Your daughter is an exceptional young lady."

The doctor drew a loud breath. "You don't know just how special she is."

Morgan thought about that for a few seconds as Malinda retrieved her daughter from her husband's arms.

The men watched the mother carry the child to her room.

Layland remarked, "Thank you for entertaining her tonight. And if I don't say it again, thank you for taking care of her the next couple days. Hopefully, she's not too much of a handful." He grinned. "By the way, kissing a dolphin is something Skye has wanted to do for years. I don't understand why, but she does. I wish I could take her, but Tuesday's meeting is too important." He emphasized the words "too important."

"To be perfectly honest, Sir, I'm looking forward to it. There is something special about that little girl."

"She's captured your heart, hasn't she?"

"Yes, and my wife's too."

"She has that way with people. She lives every day to the fullest. If you haven't noticed, she knows most everyone on this ship."

"We've noticed, and we're curious about it."

"She goes out of the way to meet people, and to help them."

Morgan nodded. "I know. There were times tonight when she rushed in front of me to open the door for an older person. And she must have said hello to a hundred people or more. She certainly has a servant's heart."

The doctor's eyebrows sprang up. "Yes, I guess that's one way to put it."

He rubbed his chin thoughtfully. "Has she *witnessed* to you yet?"

Morgan allowed a nervous laugh. "Witnessed?"

"Yes, you know, given you what she calls 'The plan of salvation.'"

Morgan wasn't quite sure how to respond. "Um, no. But she *does* talk about God quite a bit. And she seems to pray a lot."

Leontiou shook his head. "Please, don't be offended. She means well."

"Oh, believe me, I'm not offended. I find it refreshing to see a young person excited about God. We should all be like that. You've taught her well."

"No, no! Neither her mother, nor I taught her that. Actually, she did that all on her own. It all started about three years ago when we left her at a missionary's house for a short time. Ever since then, she's been trying to save the world, including us."

Morgan was not sure how much he should pry, but figured since the good doctor began the conversation it would be permissible to ask a question.

"Has she succeeded with that? I mean, have you been saved? Are you and Malinda Christians?"

The doctor took a step closer. "My wife has no religious affiliation. In fact, you may consider her agnostic. You probably noticed that my wife is much younger than me—fifteen years to be exact. I met her at a medical convention in Sweden where I was a guest speaker."

Morgan cast a look in the direction of Skye's room. There were no sounds. He was glad for a few minutes alone with the physician.

Leontiou continued. "As for me, I'm sixty-two years old. My parents were Greek Ambassadors, serving in Turkey. I lived there the first eight years of my life. Since I'm Greek, I belong to the Orthodox Church, but I don't practice the religion. Business and religion aren't a good mix."

Morgan recalled how involved he was in church a few years ago—a deacon, Sunday school teacher. Somehow the stress of Tammy's three miscarriages seemed to have affected his relationship with God. *What happened to me?*

He studied Layland intently, finally speaking. "I believe practicing is where the problem is. I don't think we should practice religion. Loving God is the answer." As soon as the words were out, his mind was filled with haunting thoughts. *Listen to me. I sure seem to know the answers. I'm nobody to talk about practicing religion, or anything else about God.*

Interrupting his barrage of thoughts, Leontiou countered, "Dr. Hamilton, I understand where you and my little girl are coming from. I would do anything for her, but when it comes to something like God, both my wife and I reject her beliefs, as well as the religions of our families. My wife deals with scientific facts. I deal in the business world. There is no time left to try to sort out religious beliefs. Who really needs it anyway?" He shrugged his shoulders.

"If I may be so bold, Dr. Leontiou. It has been a long time since I've talked about this, but by accepting Christ you're not rejecting your family, nor are you going against science. There are many businessmen who are Christians and many scientists, too." The words were out before Morgan even had time to process them.

"Dr. Hamilton, when I married Malinda my family was not supportive, nor was hers. We try to stay civil to them only because they're family. To be perfectly honest, the only reason either of our families have contact with us is because of my money."

"Then, you really have nothing else to lose." Morgan's tone held a certain resolve.

"I think I do. As a doctor I see misery every day. I see death, horrible death. For what reason? Why would a loving God allow such horrible things to happen, especially to innocent children, if He really existed?"

An ache settled in Morgan's heart. "I don't have all the answers. I believe as Skye does. God does exist, and He loves us. As far as bad things happening, I wish I had the answer for that."

Skye's father checked his watch. "I appreciate what you have to say, but you don't know the whole story. When you do, I think you'll understand where I'm coming from. Now if you'll excuse me, I have a very important meeting in the morning. And you, well, you'll have your hands full with a little pistol named Skye."

Morgan nodded, making his way to the door.

Leontiou touched Morgan's shoulder. "One more thing, Sir, please make sure Skye keeps her sunscreen on and drinks plenty of water."

"I'll take care of her as if she were mine. Trust me, she's in good hands."

"I know she is, otherwise, I wouldn't let her go. Good night." He said, closing the door quietly.

Morgan stood motionless in the hallway for a brief time. *What was I thinking, trying to witness to someone, especially someone so important? Besides, who am I to witness to anyone?"*

Chapter Seven

Tammy was on the balcony drinking her first cup of coffee, and preparing for her upcoming speech. A loud knock on the door shattered the silence.

Morgan was shaving when he heard the knock. Expecting to see Via, he opened the door.

A small, bubbly voice inquired, "Are you ready?"

He looked down. "Skye, what are you doing here? Am I ready for what?"

"We have an entire ship to explore and a whole day of fun ahead of us. I brought my camera because I'm going to make a special scrapbook album about my cruise. I thought we could start by hitting the pool, and I don't mean the baby pool, nothing but the big one!" She stretched her arms out wide, emphasizing the word "big."

Morgan, still in his robe, stammered, "Uh... Well, I need to finish getting ready. And don't you think we should get some breakfast first?"

Skye shot back, "I already ate. Breakfast bar opened at six."

"You've been up since six?" Morgan cleared his throat.

"No, got up at five. I had to work out with Kim and Zack first." She started running in place. "I need to keep them in shape, you know?"

"You know Kim and Zack?" Morgan made a strange face.

"I sure do. Zack's a hunk." She patted her heart.

Morgan rolled his eyes, grinning. "Zack's a hunk, huh?"

"Yup."

"I'm a hunk, too!" Morgan said flexing his muscles and realizing his face was still lathered with shaving crème.

Skye giggled. "You're a doctor. Doctors can't be hunks, silly."

"Oh, I see. Come in while I finish shaving. Tammy's on the balcony. Go and say hi to her while I finish getting ready."

The little girl hurried to Tammy. "Make sure you put on your swimming suit. We need to try out the wave pool today," she yelled back.

He finished shaving and put on his trunks under his shorts. He wasn't sure what the day held, but he wanted to be prepared.

Stepping out on the balcony, Morgan noticed Skye was playing the game— Rock, Paper, Scissors with Tammy.

"There's my hunk now." Tammy laughed.

"Okay, enough of the funny stuff. " Morgan rolled his eyes.

When the laughter subsided, Morgan touched his wife's hand. "Honey, do you want to get a little breakfast?"

"Via brought me grapefruit and oatmeal this morning. I think I'll go and work out. I want to meet Kim and see this hunk Skye told me about." She winked at Skye, who was still trying to stifle her giggle.

"I can see I'm not going to live this down." Morgan blushed. "Well, young lady, I need some company. Would you like to go and sit with me while I eat?"

"Sure, I want to have some more bacon and maybe another banana. Have to keep my potassium level up."

He shook his head. *What will that girl say next?*

Skye hollered, "Come on, let's go!"

"Morgan, don't overdo it. Remember, she's a little younger than you," Tammy warned, sounding like a mother hen.

"Don't worry about me. I'll be fine," he boasted. "Your hunk will be okay."

She smiled at him, sort of flirting.

"You're not wearing your high heels to workout, are you?" Morgan joked.

"Not this morning. Judging by what that child told us, I knew it was going to be a busy day. I totally went for comfort," she kidded back.

After her workout, Tammy caught up with Morgan and Skye in the main lobby.

Starting on the bottom deck, they began walking every floor. Of course, Skye led the way. Their goal was to make it to the top deck, participating in all the activities at least once.

The nine-year-old snapped pictures of everything and everyone she saw. She spoke to almost everyone. She told one middle-aged woman that she had pretty eyes.

It was hard keeping up with the energetic youngster. Just when Morgan and Tammy stopped to look at something, she'd be on the move again. "Come on, slow pokes, we have more to see." She waved her arm for them to follow.

When they reached the main deck, they saw Skye's father.

"Are you having fun?" He picked up his daughter, embracing her.

"We're having a great time, Father."

"I'm surprised to see you. What are the chances we would run into each other on this huge ship?" Morgan sounded surprised.

"Actually, the chances are very good. Skye has a GPS tracking device on her. See her bracelet? It tells me where she is at all times."

"Impressive!" Tammy replied. "I've read about GPS tags for animals, and I've often thought that every child should have one,"

"Well, in my position, I need to know where my daughter is every moment, so I designed and patented that bracelet."

"Does she mind?" Tammy asked.

Skye looked at Tammy, answering for herself, "Not at all. I feel like I'm on Star Trek. You know, 'Beam me up Scotty.'" They all laughed.

"Would you like to join us on our escapade?" Morgan queried.

"I'd love to, but I have to get to the convention. I need to borrow your wife for about thirty minutes. We're having a get-together to kick off the meetings, and I'd like to introduce her to the other guests."

Tammy glanced at her husband. "Is that all right with you?"

"Sure. We'll finish this deck and then meet you." Morgan noticed the girl was growing impatient.

Skye had a ready reply. "The game room is right above us. We can meet there. I want to play a game of checkers with Mr. Morgan."

"Ah, there's something I really enjoy doing." Morgan said sarcastically, trying to keep a serious look on his face.

"Before you get too excited, Dr. Hamilton, let me tell you, Skye has rarely lost a game of checkers," her father boasted.

"You're kidding, right?" Morgan crossed his arms.

"No, you'll see." Layland glared.

They went their separate directions.

Morgan was ready for their game of checkers, but before he knew it, Skye opened a door that read, "Crew only."

"Skye, I don't think we should go in here."

"We're only going to be here a minute. We have to do something, come on." She signaled for him to follow.

Reluctantly, he trailed her. *I hope this child doesn't get us both in trouble!*

In broken English, someone greeted them from the deck above, "Good morning, Skye."

Morgan looked up to see a distinguished looking man with a beard, clad in white.

"Good morning, Captain D. We've come to take a picture," Skye voiced.

"Of both of you?"

"Yes. I need a Titanic picture for my album." She giggled.

The elderly man responded matter-of-factly. "How are you going to do that if both of you are in it? I mean, who's going to take the picture, Skye?"

"I was going to set the camera on something or other, and take a delayed picture."

"That sounds complicated. Would you like me to take it for you? It would be a lot safer, and I can get a great picture from the side."

"Yes Sir, would you please?"

"Sure, toss me your camera."

"Mr. Morgan, will you toss my camera to the captain? Be careful, it's breakable."

Morgan had no idea what was happening, but he felt he better do as he was instructed by Skye and the captain. He carefully launched the camera toward the captain, who caught it, fortunately.

Morgan whispered, "Captain? Is that the captain of this ship?"

Skye dragged him by the arm. "Yes, of course. Now, hurry we don't have much time."

"How do you know the captain?"

"We ate lunch with him the first day. He looks just like the lighthouse man at the buffet," she laughed.

"Now that you say that, he *does*. That statue sure looks real."

"It sure does."

They walked to the furthest point of the ship's bow.

"What are we doing? Are you sure we should be here? We're awfully close to the edge," Morgan murmured.

"We're okay. Listen, and do what I say. I'm going to stand in front of you. We're both going to spread our hands wide and yell, "We're the king of the world."

"Oh, like they did in the movie?" Morgan's voice sounded jittery.

"Right! Trust me. It will be fun! I've always wanted to do this."

"Uh, Skye?" Morgan stammered. "If I stand behind you, I don't think you'll be seen very well in the picture. I have an idea, why don't you be in the picture by yourself?" He tried to walk away, but she tugged on his arm.

"No way, Jose. This is a once-in-a-lifetime photo. I know, let me get on your shoulders. That will look real cool."

"Um... um... I don't think that would be safe."

"We'll be careful. I promise. Don't you think you're strong enough to hold me?"

"Of course I am," he replied sounding hurt.

The frightened doctor glanced at the captain who was watching from the deck above, waiting for his orders.

Morgan was more than a little frightened as he carefully lifted Skye to his shoulders. He knew he'd been entrusted with Dr. Leontiou's child, and he wasn't comfortable with the entire idea. He glanced up at the captain, who had moved over to the small perch on the side. He didn't seem concerned at all, so Morgan continued, reluctantly.

"Stop shaking," Skye scoffed. "You're making me laugh."

"I can't stop shaking, I'm scared to death! That water below us is so close. And *deep*."

"Don't look down. Now, spread your arms out like you're flying," Skye ordered.

"We're the king of the world," she shouted.

Morgan was too frightened to say anything, but he quickly spread his arms and brought them back, holding her legs tight.

Skye gave him a doubtful look. "I didn't hear you say anything. Remember you're supposed to say, 'We're the king of the world.' And hold out your arms for a longer time, so Captain D can get a really good shot."

"We're the king of the world," Morgan said quickly.

"No. We have to say it at the same time, silly. Now together, and this time really yell it loud. Hold out your arms. Okay, on three. One... two... three..."

"We're the king of the world," they both shouted, and spread their arms out like they were flying.

With Skye still on his shoulders, he stepped back to the safety of the ship's deck, hardly believing what he'd done.

"Did they turn out?" Skye yelled to the captain as he scanned the images.

The captain smiled, giving her the thumbs up. "They came out great! Send me a copy. I want to put it on my desk." He carefully lowered the camera by the strap and Skye grabbed it.

"I'll do it, Cap," she said, saluting the ship's officer from Morgan's shoulders.

He saluted her back, obviously amused by the girl's antics.

Only after Morgan moved to the hallway and put Skye's feet back on the floor, was he able to breathe.

"That was fun!" the little girl shouted.

"That was crazy," Morgan replied truthfully.

"Did you think you were going to drop me into the ocean or something?"

"Or, something." He sighed.

"Relax. Now, let's go swimming. And not in the baby pool."

"Are you a good swimmer?"

"My father says I swim like a fish." She puckered her lips like a carp.

"So do I," Morgan muttered. "A *dead* fish."

"You can't swim?" She cocked her head to one side.

"It has nothing to do with *can't*. Don't is more like it. But for you, I'll get in the pool. Just promise that you won't splash my face, or do any more of that king of the world stuff, okay?"

"I promise. The rest of the day will be easy, except for maybe a little rock climbing."

"Rock climbing! Oh boy! That will excite Tammy." His lack of enthusiasm showed.

"And we can't miss going down the water tunnel on Splash Mountain."

"I was afraid you'd say that," Morgan grumbled.

"Let's go get Tammy," the girl said, pulling his arm.

They arrived at the game room before Tammy, so Skye ran over to get the checkers.

Morgan smiled, thinking he should probably go easy on the nine-year-old.

While they played, Skye chatted about what they were going to do that afternoon.

Tammy arrived just in time to see Morgan jump two of Skye's red checkers. "Wow, you're really not going to give her a chance, are you?"

"I can do fine on my own." Right then, Skye jumped three of his men. "King me." She beamed proudly.

Morgan sat still, his mouth open wide.

Tammy put her arm around her husband's shoulders. "Looks like I got here in the nick of time. Should we go to lunch before this child beats my hunk in a game of checkers?"

"No, no, no. We need to finish this." Morgan's competiveness took over.

Within minutes, Skye was victorious.

"I believe Dr. Leontiou warned you not to play checkers with her," Tammy teased, trying not to laugh.

"One more game. I was giving her a chance."

"Sure you were, Sherlock. Now let's head up to eat before you really embarrass yourself."

Tammy grabbed Skye's hand.

"I figured out what she was doing," Morgan insisted.

"What was that?" Tammy winked at Skye.

"She was taking my mind off the game by talking all the time. I just need to concentrate more."

Skye patted him on the back. "I'm sorry, Mr. Morgan. I guess I should've let you win, but my father says to do your best in everything you do, and one day it will come back to you."

Morgan was still dazed by the girl's actions, but he looked at her and smiled. "Your father is right, Skye. You beat me fair and square, but I still want a rematch."

"We have the entire cruise for a rematch," she said, giggling.

The day continued, full of activities.

The three of them stopped long enough for an enjoyable lunch at the grill.

Every time they went by an ice cream machine, Skye made a chocolate cone. "It must be very good for me. It comes from the dairy food group, and I think chocolate comes from a bean."

Morgan and Tammy laughed, which felt good to them, a pleasant change from their unhappy times at home.

The three of them rock climbed, which still didn't tire the child.

Mid-afternoon they played shuffleboard with two elderly couples and then a game of miniature golf.

They must have walked around the outside of the ship at least four times, each time stopping to watch the ship's propellers churning up the salty-water.

Next came what Morgan dreaded most—the water slide.

Standing at the entrance, Morgan looked at the top of the slide. He asked his wife, "Are you going to do this?"

"Are you kidding? That's why I didn't wear my swimsuit. I'm going to watch you make a fool of yourself. Again!"

"Thanks for the support," he sighed, without even a hint of a smile.

"Do you want me to hold your bracelet?" Tammy asked the excited girl.

"No. It's waterproof. Anyway, it doesn't come off, but you can hold my camera and take pictures."

"That's some bracelet. I guess your father really doesn't want to lose you," Tammy stated.

"No. He says he's going to keep me."

"I would, too."

Skye pulled Morgan's hand, dragging him toward the entrance of the giant water slide. "Come on, let's go!"

"I don't think I can do this." Morgan reached out to his wife, partly trying to be funny, the other part having serious misgivings about what he was going to do.

As they climbed to the top of the slide, Skye announced, "This is going to be fun! It's easy! Just watch me!" The agile girl climbed into the tunnel at the top, smiling at Morgan the whole time. "Just cross your arms and let go. I expect to see you down there, Mr. Morgan. I'm going to get a picture of you." With that, she let go, disappearing down the slide, screaming the entire way."

Morgan stood motionless looking at the young woman who was helping everyone into the tunnel. "Why was she screaming?" he asked, taking a step back.

"Because it's so much fun! I think you'd better go, Sir. Skye is expecting you down there, and if you don't go, she'll come looking for you."

Embarrassed, he shook his head, unsure why he let a nine-year-old talk him into such a thing. "You really think she'll have time to take a picture of me?"

"Knowing her, she probably has all of the ship's photographers waiting at the bottom with their cameras ready."

"Oh, great! She'll probably plaster it all over the Internet."

"Just lay back, hold your nose with one hand, and let go. Gravity will do the rest. You'll be okay. I've seen a ninety-three year old woman do this."

He groaned. "Maybe I should wait until I'm ninety-three."

The helper smiled, stepping back. Morgan saw that he was not going to get any sympathy from her, so he closed his eyes, grabbed his nose, and let go.

Screaming all the way, he reached the bottom, and went flying into the pool. When he finally surfaced, he saw Skye standing by Tammy. Next to them, a ship's photographer stood laughing.

When he climbed out of the pool, a sober-faced Tammy handed him a towel.

He overheard Skye saying, "I want a copy of that. It's a classic picture for my album. I may start with that picture."

"No extra copies. I want the original, so I can burn it," Morgan said, drying his face.

The photographer smiled, playing along. "Sorry, Sir, but Skye hired me to take the picture. You'll have to talk to her about it."

"Whatever she paid you, I'll double it."

The photographer walked away, grinning.

Morgan sprinted to catch up to the girls. "I get no pity from any of you."

"I understand why Skye screamed coming down. That's what girls do. But Honey, you sounded like a banshee." Tammy poked him in the ribs.

"Yes, I thought one of the ship's engines had blown," Skye said, grabbing Tammy around the waist as both of them broke out laughing.

"Go ahead; make fun of me. I thought you were supposed to scream." He pointed to the girl. "*She* did!"

Tammy groaned, rolling her eyes.

Between the hot sun and Skye's unlimited energy, Morgan was exhausted. It was almost four when he and Tammy returned Skye to her suite.

Skye's parents were still busy entertaining guests at the convention.

Maya, their housekeeper, was laying out their clothes for the evening.

"Hi, Maya!" Skye greeted the maid in her typical friendly way.

"Why, hello, Sweet Stuff. Did you have a good day?"

"It was great! Tammy and Morgan took me to the big pool, Splash Mountain, and we even took a king of the world picture at the bow of the ship."

"Did you? I thought that area was off limits," she glanced at the girl over her glasses.

"Evidently, not if you know the captain of the ship," Morgan murmured.

Turning back to the child, Maya added, "Oh, that's right, you know him well. I'm glad you had a fun day. Now, young lady, it's time for you to take a shower and a thirty-minute nap. Don't forget, tonight is the special dinner with the Gossets. After which, you will be going to bed. It's going to be early tonight. You've had a busy day, and tomorrow is dolphin kissing day. You need your rest."

"Okay, Maya." Skye faced Morgan, extending her hand. "Thank you for being with me today. I had a wonderful time."

Morgan shook her hand. "I had a great time, too."

"That's a lot better. Your handshake, I mean." She grabbed Morgan, and then Tammy around the waist, giving them each a giant hug.

She ran into her room, and closed the door.

Tammy sighed. "I sure wish I had some of her energy."

Maya smiled, and continued folding the clothes. "Skye is only nine, but she seems much older."

"Is she *always* that polite?" Tammy asked.

"Always! She never argues about anything. She... Well to put it bluntly, she's too good to be true. I sometimes wonder if one day she'll rebel.

However, I don't think she will. She's the real deal. I've never heard or seen her do anything wrong. She lives to help people and make them happy."

The happy girl could be heard singing in the shower.

"Her parents must have done something right," Tammy added.

"I believe it's more than the way she's being raised," Maya said with certainty.

"What do you mean?" Tammy asked.

"I don't know. I hesitate to say this. It sounds far-fetched, but I believe she's divinely gifted."

Morgan raised his brow. "What do you mean? In what way?"

"Sir, I can't really say. She just... Well, she's exceptional. She knows what to say, and when to say it. She hardly ever walks past someone without paying them a compliment, or finding something positive to say to them."

"If only we could all be like that," Tammy interjected.

"She has a good voice, too," Morgan said, listening to her serenade in the shower.

"Yes, she does. She sings all the time," Maya replied.

They paused, listening.

"Well, we'd better be on our way. We're worn out. Maybe we can still get a nap before dinner." Morgan grabbed his wife's hand.

"Goodbye. Thank you for taking care of her today."

Walking to the door, Morgan answered, "It was our pleasure. I look forward to tomorrow."

Morgan and Tammy strolled to their room, not saying a word, each pondering the events of the day, and their conversation with Maya.

"Wow! What a day!" Morgan said, collapsing onto the bed.

"I had a wonderful time. How about you?" Tammy asked.

"It was great. That little girl is full of energy. You never told me what you and Dr. Leontiou did at the conference."

As Tammy crawled into bed, she relayed the events of the day to her husband. "The convention today was mainly introductions. There are some big name scientists and physicians on this ship. I feel sort of out of place. You know, by reading Dr. Leontiou's books, I sense that he's far ahead of everyone else in the field. I'm honored."

Morgan grinned. "His daughter is amazing, also."

"She's so sweet," Tammy said before drifting to sleep.

After a short nap, somewhat revived, the couple got ready for a quiet, uneventful dinner and show.

They retired early, knowing daylight would be there before they were ready for it.

Chapter Eight

The knocking startled them.

Tammy stumbled out of bed, making her way to the door. Opening it a crack, she noticed Skye waiting, dressed in her swimsuit and cover-up, and carrying a tote half her size. A bottle of water dangling at the top of the bag looked as though it could fall out anytime.

"I'm here! Is Dad ready?" Her eyes twinkled with excitement.

"Dad?" Tammy blinked, still trying to wake up.

"Yes, my father said Morgan would have to be my dad today."

Skye leaned closer and her voice fell to a whisper. "He said something about parents having to be with me when I swim with the dolphins. I think it was some legal mumbo-jumbo."

Tammy nodded sleepily. "Oh, well in that case, your dad just got in the shower."

"Tell him to hurry! We don't want to be late. This is an important day. I'll run to get a couple of towels for us. You're going to eat with us this morning, aren't you?"

Tammy angled her head. "As a matter-of-fact, I'm having breakfast with your mother this morning, but I'll see you both off."

"Great! Tell Dad to meet me at the buffet, by the lighthouse man."

"Lighthouse man?"

"Dad will know what I'm talking about. Gotta go!" she squealed and was gone before Tammy could ask any further questions.

Part of the way down the hall, Skye turned around. "Oh yeah, make sure Dad brings a bottle of water and plenty of sunscreen. It's going to be a scorcher. Bye!"

Tammy shook her head, staring at the youngster sprinting down the long, narrow hallway, and almost running into a couple coming out of their stateroom. "Excuse me!" she yelled, without breaking stride.

Tammy couldn't help but chuckle watching the little girl dragging her giant tote down the hall.

Tammy pounded on the bathroom door. "Hey Dad, your date was here."

He opened the door. "Date? What date? You mean Skye was here?"

"Yes, and she's calling you 'Dad.' Did you know you were her dad for the day?"

"I *am*?" He laughed. "Why is that?"

"Guess a parent or guardian has to be with a child when they swim with the dolphins."

"Hmmm... Well, this should be an interesting day," he said, combing his hair.

"To say the least. By the way, Skye went to get towels for both of you. She told you to remember water and sunscreen. It's going to be hot day."

Tammy leaned close to her husband. "Also, she said to meet her by the lighthouse man. Do you know what she means?"

"Lighthouse man? Oh, right." He laughed. "My, she sure is well-prepared. I'm the one who's supposed to make sure she brings water and sunscreen. That little pill doesn't miss a thing, does she?"

"Prepared isn't the word. That little girl is a whiz. Did you know she speaks five languages?"

Morgan smeared shaving lotion on his face. "That's interesting. I guess with parents like hers, and the places she has visited, she would need to communicate in different languages."

"I wonder what nationality she is," Tammy said. "I mean, where was she born?"

"I don't know."

"I'm going to have breakfast with her mother this morning, so I'm sure I'll get a lot of information."

"What is the topic this morning at the conference?" Morgan asked.

"Batten disease."

"Batten? That's extremely rare."

"I know. They're discussing some of the rarest childhood diseases, and how we can raise awareness in our society."

"Interesting topic," Morgan said.

"Yes, it is. I do know that Dr. Leontiou is passionate about Batten. He wrote a couple books on it."

"What time do you speak?"

"I believe right after lunch." Tammy replied, gathering her belongings for her shower.

"I may get back in time to hear you."

Tammy smiled. "That would be nice. I'd love to have you there for support."

Morgan continued, "There is something I'm curious about. I wonder why today's meeting is so important that her father would miss spending the day with his daughter. Obviously, he adores her. I'm surprised that anything could keep him away from spending time with that girl. She means the world to him. I can see that."

"Unfortunately, that's a doctor's life. You and I both know it comes with the territory. That's one reason why divorce rates are so high among doctors. Their job keeps them away from their family."

"What are the statistics for doctor couples who work together long hours every day, like us?" Morgan asked, almost like a joke.

"The statistics don't say anything about that."

Her smile faded. "Honey, don't get too attached to that little girl. In less than two weeks we leave her, and will probably never see her again."

"Too late for that," Morgan said. "She's already captured my heart. She gets to you, too. Admit it."

"She *does* have a way with people, but we need to be careful."

Morgan finished shaving, his eyes indicating concern.

An ache settled in Tammy's heart. "I know how much you love children. I'm sorry I can't give you what you want."

He swallowed, noticing the room had grown quiet. "Honey, don't ever say that. This isn't your fault. Things just happen. We'll work it out. We love each other, and that's all that matters."

With that, the serious conversation ended, and small talk resumed as they dressed for the day.

Morgan asked, "What is your big speech going to be on?"

She picked up her laptop. "I don't know if you can call it a big speech. I'm just talking about what American doctors are doing to help with these dreaded childhood diseases. What more can I do?"

"What more can any of us do?" Morgan's thoughts flashed to his conversation with Skye's father the night before. Prayer came to his mind, but the thought quickly faded. There was a time when he and Tammy would pray for others, as well as their own needs. But their prayers seemed to never be heard; there was only silence from God. At least, that's what they felt. If God wasn't listening, if He didn't care, why bother praying?

Tammy interrupted his thoughts. "We'd better head to the lighthouse man. Your date is waiting."

Morgan smiled, reaching for his wife's hand.

As the couple stepped out of the elevator, Morgan caught a glimpse of Skye standing by the lighthouse man. She was chatting playfully with one of the waiters. As they neared her, they noticed that she was speaking in a different language.

Morgan greeted them. "Good morning." He noticed that the waiter's tag read, "Nicolai—Russia." It dawned on him that the girl was conversing in Russian.

"Well, good morning, young lady." Morgan asked, "Are you ready for our big day?"

"It's about time you got here, Dad." She grabbed Tammy and Morgan's hands and tugged on them. "Let's eat. I'm starving."

Morgan smiled at his wife.

Malinda Leontiou stepped behind Tammy. "That young one has a way of taking charge, doesn't she?"

"Yes, she does." Tammy nodded.

"She doesn't get that from me."

"Funny. Morgan told me your husband said the same thing."

They broke out laughing.

"I hope your husband is ready for a busy day. When Skye's feeling good, nothing holds her back."

"When she's feeling good? What do you mean by that?"

"You know, when a girl's happy and excited, nothing holds her back."

They watched as Morgan and Skye joined the buffet line.

"They look like quite the pair," Malinda smiled. "Dr. Hamilton?"

"Please, call me Tammy."

"Tammy, are you ready for a nutritious breakfast downstairs in the dining room?"

"Yes. I'm ready to be pampered."

"Well, good. Then let's go have some juicy girl talk."

The women sat at a small table overlooking the pier.

For a moment, they watched as the crew on the pier prepared for the passengers to disembark. Dozens of buses and taxies were lined up, waiting for their customers for the day.

Malinda sipped her hot beverage.

Tammy broke the silence. "How long have you been practicing medicine?"

"Almost twenty years. And you?"

"Seven years. I met Morgan in medical school. He was more interested in the administrative part than the medical aspect. Me? I wanted to save the world."

"I ran a computer search on you, and noticed that you were tops in your class. In fact, tops in the country. Layland was impressed. He told me that we could use someone of your caliber at our clinic. I agree. I could really use you. Keep it in mind; the door is always open for you and Morgan to join our team."

"Well, thank you. I'm honored. What is your history? I mean—"

Malinda smiled. "You mean, why am I so much younger than Layland?"

"Well, I wasn't really alluding to that, but since you said we would talk girl talk, where were you born?"

"My mother and father were from Canada, both well-known doctors. They traveled quite a bit. I was actually born in Sweden during a convention on the disease everyone was talking about at the time. Cancer."

Tammy sighed. "Cancer seems to be everywhere, but thankfully the medical field has made great strides in the last forty years. Is that the field your parents worked in?"

"Yes. You may have heard of them—Oscar and Dorothy Wright."

Tammy's eyes widened. "They were your parents?"

"Yes."

"Well, I'm impressed. They discovered several breakthroughs in cancer treatment. I actually heard your father speak twice. Once in medical school, and the last time was right before... before their plane crashed." Tammy reached for Malinda's hand as she recalled the accident, which three years before had tragically claimed the lives of her parents and six other distinguished doctors.

Malinda gave a sad shrug. "It's okay. They died trying to help others. They were delivering supplies to war-torn Africa when their plane was shot down by rebels." She hesitated. "It was rather ironic that they were killed by the same people they were trying to help." Her eyes grew distant.

Tammy hesitated, giving Malinda a moment. Finally, she spoke. "How long have you been married?"

"Oh, that's a hard one. I married a fellow doctor right out of medical school. We were married for two years when I found out he was unfaithful, so I dumped him like a can of beans."

"Good for you."

"I stayed single for years after that, dedicating every second to my lab work. I joined my parents in some of their experiments."

"You sure had good teachers. I bet that was exciting!"

"Oh, it was. Then I met Layland in Sweden. My father, mother, and I were all speaking at a convention, and dad introduced me to this handsome doctor. I'd seen him on numerous occasions, because he was a big contributor to my parent's causes. He was a gentle man, but strong. He had to be strong in the world of business. The next weekend, he flew me to Paris for lunch. We were back in time for my speech that night at the convention. We married three months later. I had Skye two years after we were married."

"How romantic, lunch in Paris," Tammy sighed.

"I'm sure you have picked up on how protective Layland is with Skye. He gives her a lot of freedom, but at the same time he's pretty strict. He absolutely adores her."

Tammy nodded her head, emptying a packet of sugar into her coffee.

"It grieves her father not to be able to spend these couple days with her, especially today. He really wanted to share the dolphin experience with her."

Malinda stirred her coffee. "Skye lives every day to the fullest. She's an extremely organized, happy-go-lucky girl, who never thinks of herself. She's always busy, always learning, and always excited."

"It's strange," Malinda said, "but she never has shown an interest in video games, like most of today's kids. She does things that help other people. And she's definitely gifted."

Tammy gave the older woman a curious look. "What do you mean by gifted?"

"Skye has tested extremely high academically, genius level. She's also a talented concert pianist and an amazing artist. Most parents push their gifted children too hard, but Layland and I believe it's more important to let her be a child and live life to its fullest."

"She seems to be doing that."

"She is. I love that little girl with every ounce of my being. We had to weigh the choices, and have agonized over them."

"What choices?"

Malinda sat rigid in her chair. "I mean, our lives with her. We're dedicated to our lab work, sometimes to the point that it interferes with her life. We've made major strides in finding cures for certain diseases. We do what we can, and let our money do the rest."

"How did you get involved with 'Cruise for a Cure'?"

"Layland came up with the idea about three years ago. He thought it would provide a much-needed vacation for doctors and their families. At the same time, they could share information about their research with other doctors."

"It's brilliant the way he turned it into a fundraiser."

"Yes, it's a great time to collect donations. The last two cruises we received almost ten million dollars. Every penny of that money goes toward our cause. Did you know that less than one-tenth of one percent of worldwide donations actually goes to the ten rarest diseases? This is a way we can help, and maybe in time, people will take notice. Layland invites the best doctors, scientists, chemists, and professional people in the world, those who have dedicated their lives to working with children suffering from rare childhood diseases. We not only share experiences, but also take the time to encourage each other. He believes if they could pool all of their information, put different pieces of the puzzle together, maybe, just maybe, they could cure at least one disease. We pay for these cruises, but always end up with donations a hundred times more than the cost."

Tammy inched closer. "What about your own studies and lab work? Have you made any progress?"

"We've been working on a few experiments that have shown promise, but we're not ready to go public. There are more tests we must perform first. Within the next six months, we hope to release our findings. Layland would like to keep it quiet until then."

Tammy looked stunned. "But if you're that close to a cure, why keep it quiet? Why not let the world know about it?"

"We have to be certain. We don't want to give hope to families who are already suffering, and then find out we were wrong."

Tammy placed her napkin on her lap. "Maybe that's not a bad thing. A little hope is better than no hope at all. Hope is what these families need."

"I understand what you're saying," Skye's mother responded quietly.

The topic ended when the waiter brought their eggs benedict.

As they ate, they chatted about their personal lives.

Morgan held Skye's hand tightly as she led him through the food line. He had never really babysat before, at least not by himself. Maybe babysitting was not the right word. He'd been entrusted with someone's child for a day.

Suddenly, a wave of panic swept over him. *Calm down,* he thought. *Yes, I will protect her at all costs. After all, I would expect nothing less if I had a child in someone's care.*

"Get your plate here, and don't forget your silverware and napkin," Skye reminded him, jarring him from his thoughts.

"Good morning, Skye. How are you?" A tall Jamaican man asked, putting sizzling bacon into the serving tray.

"I'm doing fine, thank you. Did you call Sasha?" Skye asked, helping herself to eight pieces of bacon.

"Yes, I did."

"When is the baby due?"

"Two weeks. I hope that we're in port the day he's born. I sure want to be there."

"You will be. I've been praying that you could be there. He always answers my prayers." Skye's eyes were clear and intense.

Morgan was surprised by her statement. After all, he and Tammy had been praying for a child for years, and their prayers were never answered. Why? Maybe this little girl had more faith than he had. There were many questions, yet the cold hard facts were all he could see at the moment.

"Will you be able to see Sasha today?" Skye continued the conversation with the worker.

"Yes, and I'm looking forward to it. I'll only be with her for about two hours because I have to serve lunch."

"Tell her I said 'hi,' and I'm praying for her."

"I will, Little One."

Morgan and Skye sat down to eat and the girl continued talking. "So, how long have you been a doctor?"

"Well, actually I'm an administrator. I haven't done a whole lot of doctoring. I studied to be one, but my gift is in administration. My wife's the doctor."

Skye clasped her hands and lowered her head, silently praying for breakfast. Morgan noticed her lips moving.

When she was finished, she immediately started chattering. "I know. My father has good things to say about Tammy. I think he wants her on his staff at the clinic."

"The clinic? Where's that?"

"It's on a small island off the coast of Greece. It's called Kardia. Isn't that a beautiful name? My father named it. It's located in the Aegean Sea. Have you ever heard of the Aegean Sea?"

Not waiting for a response, she continued. "Well, it's by the Mediterranean Sea. That's where I live most of the time." Her eyes widened. "It's close to where Atlantis was located."

Morgan stared at her, not wanting to ask the question, but knowing that he had to.

He took a bite of his omelet, then asked, "Atlantis? The one talked about in... um... *history*?" He wanted to say myths or fables, but Skye seemed to think it was real.

"That's the one," Skye said. "The folk singer, Donovan, sang about it back in the sixties."

Morgan watched the little girl pile five pieces of bacon, a sausage patty, and scrambled eggs between two pieces of toast, and take a bite. He toyed with the handle of his coffee cup, smiling at her creation.

"Um... this is good, but not quite as good as McDonalds."

Morgan asked again, "I thought that was just a myth."

"McDonalds?"

"No, Atlantis."

Skye laughed. "I know. I was just pulling your leg."

Morgan smiled, pressing on. "So, Atlantis is not a myth?"

"Nope. It's true! Plato talked about it. He never talked about anything but the truth."

Intrigued, Morgan laid his fork down.

Suddenly, Skye broke out singing Donovan's old song, *"Way down below the ocean is where I will be... Way down below the ocean..."*

Then, to Morgan's surprise, Skye stopped singing and began talking about the history of the lost city of Atlantis.

"It was destroyed by a tsunami," she said. "Or, maybe it was a meteorite. Some say it could've been a volcanic eruption. No one really knows. All we can be sure of is that Atlantis was completely wiped out. Nothing left, but historical hints and clues."

Her gaze grew distant for several seconds, as though she was searching the universe for the long-hidden location of the lost city. Then, her eyes snapped back into focus, and she seemed to shift mental gears.

"I wonder what this sandwich would taste like with catsup," she said. She motioned for a nearby waiter. "Eli, can you please bring me some catsup?"

"Of course," the waiter said. "I'll be right back, Skye."

Morgan was amazed at the girl's ability to learn, to remember. She obviously was brilliant. *How does Skye know everybody's name?*

The waiter returned with the catsup.

"Did you call your four sons, like we discussed, Eli?" Skye looked up with her big blue eyes, waiting for his response.

Morgan felt like he was interrupting a private conversation.

The waiter shook his head. "No. I've been busy and... well, really... too ashamed."

Skye loaded her sandwich with catsup. "Trust me on this," she said. "You need to call them."

Morgan's eyes widened as he watched the red condiment run freely down both sides of the girl's sandwich.

"It's not going to get any easier," Skye said. "The sooner you call them, the better you'll feel. And the better *they'll* feel too."

Eli nodded. "I promise. I'll call them when I get to the next port."

Skye gave the waiter a fist bump. "You'll be glad you did," she said. "And so will they."

Eli smiled, gave Skye a nod, and departed to tend other tables.

Morgan decided to steer things back to their previous conversation. "So, you live on an island?"

"Yup."

"Wow! That sounds like fun."

"Yes, it is. I have a lot of friends my age to play with. You have to come and visit us some time."

"Are there many beaches?"

"No. Only one. That's where my house is. Some believe the island at one time was part of Atlantis." She looked at her watch. "Oh no, look at the time! We have to go. I'm so excited! I've been looking forward to kissing a dolphin forever." She jumped up, grabbing her tote as Morgan tried to finish his orange juice.

"Let's go, slow poke. We don't want to miss the boat." She giggled. "I made a pun. Miss the boat. Get it?"

Morgan grabbed his bag, trying to keep up with Skye as she hustled to the elevator.

Neither of them noticed Layland standing by a pole in the cafeteria, deliberately out of sight, watching his daughter and Morgan disappear into the elevator. A tear came to his eye. He wanted to spend the day with his little girl, but he realized the significance of the conference today. *I know that she'll be safe with Morgan. He'll take care of my baby.*

Morgan and Skye rushed down the gangway and onto the pier, but not before stopping to get pictures taken by the cruise photographers.

A young woman at the pier welcomed Skye to the dock. "Good morning, Skye. How are you?"

Morgan just shook his head. *Is there anyone this little girl doesn't know?*

"I'm fine, thank you. This is my dad, Morgan."

"Hi, Dad," she said, winking her eye. "Welcome to Jamaica. Is Skye taking care of you today?"

"That's what it seems. Have I gotten in over my head?"

"I tend to think so. You're in for an entertaining and exhausting day." She grinned. "Do you have water?"

Morgan held up his bottle.

"It's going to be hot. Make sure you both drink plenty."

"Well, there they go." Tammy said, looking out the window, watching her husband and Skye on the pier below.

Skye must have sensed her mother watching her. She looked up, smiling, and waving.

Malinda and Tammy waved back sending the little girl a huge smile.

"You wish you could go with her, don't you?" Tammy said, feeling comfortable enough to ask her new friend a personal question.

"Yes, but at the same time, I'm happy. She was really looking forward to spending the day with your husband. I just hope she's easy on the poor guy."

They both laughed.

The two continued in conversation, sharing their medical victories, as well as defeats.

Chapter Nine

Skye and Morgan climbed aboard the large van.

She immediately started a conversation. "Good morning, Carlos. I didn't know you were going to take us today. How's the ankle?" she asked the driver.

"I do a little bit of everything for the cruise line. Me being from Jamaica, I already know the island. Thanks for asking about the foot. It's almost healed," the driver shot back in his strong Jamaican accent.

She moved close to his face. "I keep telling you, you're too old to be sliding in to home plate. You need to find something else to do. Have you ever thought about chess?"

Morgan tried not to laugh.

"Chess?" the driver asked.

"Yes, I can beat my father seven out of ten times."

"Chess?" he repeated, looking in the rear view mirror to make sure people were finding their seats.

"Right! Or checkers. Just no more baseball or rugby. You're going to kill yourself."

"I think you may be right," he said, giving the girl a hug. "Chess it is, from now on."

As they looked for their seat, Skye continued to be the center of attention. She introduced herself to everyone.

A lady in the front seat caught Morgan's attention. A wheelchair was folded up next to her.

"Mrs. Scott. I didn't expect to see you here. Are you going to swim with the dolphins?" Skye asked, bending over to give the elderly lady a hug.

"Oh, my!" she laughed. "No, Child. I just want to see them up close and personal. You know I hate water, but Roger loved it. He really wanted to go on this excursion."

"It's going to be a wonderful day, Mrs. Scott." Skye gave her another quick hug.

As they sat down, Skye whispered, "That's Mrs. Scott. Her husband just died. He died of a heart attack. Just finished eating supper, told her that it was the best meal he'd ever had. He went and sat in his easy chair and turned on the TV to watch *Andy Griffith*, his favorite show. When she finished cleaning the kitchen, she came in and saw that he'd gone to be with Jesus. It was very peaceful. He had a smile on his face. Mrs. Scott thought he must have been laughing at something Barney had said."

Skye held back tears. "She's taking this cruise in his memory. They were married forty-seven years, and they always wanted to go on one together, but they never got around to it. Mrs. Scott booked a room in both of their names. She sits at a table set for two, and even has his dinner served."

"I don't mean to sound insensitive, but doesn't that seem odd to you?"

Skye shook her head. "No, not at all. I think she loved him a lot. And she still does."

Morgan continued to listen to the tale the little girl shared about the elderly woman. He did not know if he should smile or be sad. He glanced at Mrs. Scott. *She seems happy enough. Maybe she's content that her missing mate is here in spirit.*

At Dunn's River Falls, the guide instructed the large group of tourists to hold hands with each other while they hiked up the rocky, slippery falls.

Morgan tried to keep an eye on Skye, but it ended up being the other way around. "Dad, please stop slipping. You're pulling everyone down when you do that. You're really embarrassing me," she joked.

One time he slipped, pulling Skye into the cool water with him. She was laughing so hard, she couldn't stand. "I wish I could've gotten a picture of that for my scrapbook. I bet it looked funny."

Finally, they reached the top.

Morgan was happy because the ordeal was over.

Skye was happy because of what was coming up next—the dolphin exhibit.

The ride to the dolphin exhibit was informative. Carlos, the driver, did his best to explain the history of Jamaica. Occasionally, Skye threw in a tidbit of information.

Along the way, they stopped so everyone on the bus could stretch and visit the booths set up by the locals. Eager Jamaicans were selling products they made, adding a little income to improve their simple lives.

Morgan stayed close to Skye as she looked at handmade trinkets and tried on hats. He laughed when she wore a colorful dreadlock hat. Morgan snapped over a dozen pictures while she posed playfully. When Morgan tried the hat on, Skye bent over laughing so hard that tears streamed down her cheeks.

Before they left, Skye pulled out her little change purse and bought a huge hat to wear in the sun. "Father gave me some money to buy a few things," she said. "How does this look?"

"On you, young lady, it looks fantastic." Morgan snapped another picture.

On the way back to the van, Skye noticed a few children on the side of the road with outstretched arms, selling novelties, whatever they had or made. They were dressed in old, dirty clothes. Skye sauntered over, looking at their wares. Nothing was worth buying. Morgan watched closely as the young girl took a few dollars out of her purse and purchased a woven, handmade wristband. She smiled, waving goodbye to the three children.

Morgan could see the sadness in Skye's eyes for the children who had so little. Skye returned to the van silently.

When they reached the dolphin exhibit, most passengers hurried off the vehicle, rushing to the exhibit to be first in line. Skye stood by the door, waiting.

Morgan was confused by her unusual behavior. *Why is she standing there?*

Finally, Carlos helped Mrs. Scott off the bus and into her waiting wheelchair. Skye immediately grabbed the handles. "I'll get it from here, Carlos. Thanks. See you in a couple hours."

"Little miss, you have a great day. Give the dolphins a kiss for me." Carlos waved.

"Righto," Skye quipped.

"Child, you need to get in line. Don't wait for me," Mrs. Scott cautioned.

"Oh, we have plenty of time. I'll have my turn. I want you to see this, so I'm going to push you to the bridge before the rest of the crowd gets there. Can I call you Grandma?"

The elderly woman looked at Morgan, smiling. "Thank you, Child. I'd love for you to call me Grandma. You're such a blessing, Dear."

After Skye pushed Mrs. Scott to a safe, comfortable place overlooking the dolphins, she locked the wheels, threw her arms around the woman, and held her tightly for a moment. "There," she said. "That's from Roger. Everything is all right now."

Morgan noticed tears dripping from the woman's eyes. He was moved by the love and warmth the little girl demonstrated for someone she barely knew.

Skye removed the camera from around her neck and handed it to the woman. "Do you know how to take pictures?"

The woman nodded. "Yes. Actually, I have a camera just like this at home, it was Roger's. He was an avid photographer, but I saw no reason to bring it."

Skye's face lit up. It was hard to tell who was more excited at the moment. "Grandma, you have the best seat in the house. Take as many pictures as you want. Its digital, so the pictures are free. Even has that big zoomy-thingy. Take pictures of everyone with the dolphins, in case their pictures don't turn out."

Morgan's eyes were fixed on the scene. He was amazed by what he'd just witnessed. Rarely had he seen such an act of selflessness in his life.

Skye grabbed Morgan's hand. "Let's go, Dad."

She dragged him all the way to the ticket gate. Morgan was glad to see that the line had shortened.

The man at the ticket booth asked, "One or two tickets?"

"Just one for the little girl here," Morgan replied readily.

"Dad, you're coming, too."

He smiled at the man. "I'm Dad," he offered with a guilty look.

"I see that. I think you'd better go. She seems sort of demanding."

"That she is." Morgan lifted his chin in agreement, sighing.

"Here, sign these forms, and then I'll put these bands on your wrists"

When they finished checking in, they walked quickly to the end of the dock where they spotted three dolphins showing off for the audience.

"Good Morning." A young man in the water spoke. My name is Simon, and this is Kami. We're going to teach you about these incredible dolphins, and show you some commands we use to control them." For the next several minutes, they were taught how to handle the dolphins safely. They were also told what various hand commands meant.

The woman guide explained how dolphins communicate through a high-pitched squeak, a unique sound that other dolphins recognized. "Many people believe that dolphins are almost as intelligent as people."

Morgan and Skye listened carefully and then were each assigned their own dolphin. Skye's dolphin was Jessie; Morgan's was named Priscilla.

The duo interacted with the creatures for several minutes, giving hand signals, and watching the intelligent dolphins obey their commands. After the dolphins got their belly rubs, they leapt through the air, splashing the small group. Skye screamed with delight.

Simon instructed, "Skye, I want you to take a hold of Jessie's flippers. She'll swim around the lagoon on her back. So grab hold, and enjoy the ride." Without hesitation, the little girl followed orders. Before she knew it, she was speeding through the warm, salty water. A bubble of laughter came from her.

"It's time, it's time!" Skye shrieked. Finally, the moment she felt like she'd waited for her whole life had arrived! Her blue eyes twinkled with merriment. On Simon's cue, Jessie jumped up and kissed the nine-year-old. Skye hugged the slippery bottlenose dolphin and planted a kiss on its nose. The girl grinned from ear-to-ear as Morgan watched with delight.

Skye glanced up at a smiling Mrs. Scott. Her friend gave her the thumbs up sign, and continued snapping pictures, one right after another.

The trainer announced that their time was up and almost as if Jessie understood, she rose out of the water and kissed Skye again.

Skye and Morgan climbed out of water and dried off. As they began walking away an agitated Jessie followed Skye to the end of the enclosure. The dolphin began to make a sound, apparently trying to get their attention. At first it was a clicking noise. Then the dolphin raised herself out of the water, making a loud, barking-like sound that grew louder and louder.

At the end of the lagoon, a crowd began gathering—all wondering what message the dolphin was trying to convey.

The commotion caught the attention of Simon and Kami.

Kami exclaimed, "Simon, I've never seen a dolphin get that upset! She seems to be trying to communicate with that girl."

Two other handlers ran over to investigate the disturbance.

Meanwhile, Skye had stopped walking and stood quietly, looking at Jessie. Then suddenly, Jessie began speeding around the lagoon until she propelled herself high out of the water, landing on her side with a huge splash. The trainer had already explained that was a process called 'breaching.'

There was no denying the fact—the dolphin was desperately trying to get Skye's attention.

Skye and Morgan walked to the edge of the enclosure. Jessie was swimming as close to the side as possible, continuing to chatter loudly.

Skye reached down, patting the dolphin on her head. "Oh, Jessie, I'm going to miss you too, but you're going to be okay. Maybe someday I can come visit you again."

The handlers joined them, apologizing for Jessie's odd behavior. "Weirdest thing I've ever seen," one of them remarked.

"Young lady, you're not a mermaid are you," Simon asked.

"No. My father says I swim like a fish, but I assure you, I'm just a girl. I'll be ten next week."

"Well, Jessie has sure taken a liking to you. A very special liking."

Morgan stood speechless. *Who is this child? Is there anything normal about her? She remembers everyone's name and all about them. She attracts people like a magnet wherever she goes. I mean, even to the point that a dolphin would exhibit extreme behavior after spending time with her because it didn't want her to leave.* Bewildered, he scratched his head.

Skye interrupted his thoughts. "Come on, Dad. Let's go." She ran to the bridge where Mrs. Scott was still snapping photos.

"Did you get the pictures, Mrs. Scott?"

The woman lowered the camera slowly, staring at the girl. By the look on her face, she too, was dazed by what she had witnessed—the interaction of the girl and the dolphin. "Yes, Child. I got some really good ones." She wiped away a tear.

Skye grabbed the handles of the wheelchair and began pushing the sweet lady back to the van. "I can't wait to see the pictures. I hope they're good."

"That's putting it mildly." The woman scanned the last dozen pictures, which clearly showed the dolphin breaching. She shook her head in disbelief.

Morgan's eyes demonstrated to the woman that he agreed with her. No words needed to be spoken.

As they climbed aboard the van, everyone took their seats.

Morgan realized how exhausted he was. As he closed his eyes and laid his head on the back of the seat, he relived the dolphin experience. Anyone who witnessed the event would probably have it permanently etched in their mind. He knew it was something he would never forget.

"That was fun! Did you have fun, Dad?" Skye jarred his thoughts.

Morgan gave her a weak smile.

"What can I do to get you to smile, really smile, Dad?"

"You seem to be able to smile enough for both of us."

"Dad, I'm worried about you." She shot him a concerned look.

"Why are you worried?" He raised his head from the seat.

"Well, look at you. The whole world is ours to explore and enjoy! There is no time to be sad."

"My Dear, when you get older you'll understand."

"I don't think age has anything to do with being happy and living life to its fullest." Her comment sounded wise beyond her years.

Morgan looked straight ahead, almost wanting to ignore the conversation. "Things happen in peoples' lives that cause them to be sad. Nothing can be done about that. Nothing!"

Everyone in the van had quieted. There were no distractions around them. Skye looked directly into the hurting man's eyes. "Believe me, Dad, there is nothing in life that Jesus can't fix."

Her words caught Morgan by surprise. *A nine-year-old child is talking to me about Jesus? It should be the other way around.* "I'm sorry, Skye. I shouldn't be talking to you about this. It's a... an adult thing. There's no way you can possibly understand."

Her answer was quick and to the point, but more importantly, it was sincere. "Jesus is not an adult thing."

"I wasn't talking about Jesus. I was talking about why I'm sad." He shifted in his seat, uncomfortable with the direction the conversation was taking.

"It seems to me that you lack faith." Skye reached over, brushing Morgan's forehead. "Sorry, but you had sand in your hair."

Morgan could hear the edge in his own voice. "Faith? What's that got to do with how I feel?"

"I may be young," Skye said, "but I'm not dumb. My father calls me a spider web. I catch everything that comes my way. I know you and Mom can't have babies. Remember what Jesus said about that?"

Morgan felt a heaviness in his chest. "No, I don't. What did Jesus say about it?"

"He talked about living each day by faith," Skye said. "You know, becoming like a child."

She gave Morgan a sadly knowing little smile. "It can be tough for you older folks to find your faith. You worry too much. You don't know how to believe, and accept what happens to you."

Skye flicked a few more grains of sand out of Morgan's hair. "Jesus has a plan," she said. "I want to be part of that plan. Do you want to be part of that plan, Dad? I sure want you to be."

Morgan couldn't find the words to respond, and fortunately didn't have to. At that moment, they passed the roadside stands they'd visited that morning.

Skye pressed her nose to the window and waved to the children she'd met earlier. "Carlos, stop," she shouted, startling Morgan and the other passengers.

The driver glanced in the rearview mirror at Skye, and without hesitation, pulled over. The girl grabbed her tote, which had her shoes, change of clothes, and towels in it. She looked to see how much money she had. She hurried off the van and ran to the children.

"What's that little girl doing?" one of the passengers asked.

Skye handed one of the children her bag, and another all of the money she had. She even gave them the big towels from the ship.

Everyone on the van watched and wondered.

"It looks like she's giving those poor kids something," one of the passengers said.

"Not just *something*," Mrs. Scott said. "She's giving them everything she has." The old woman smiled. "That's my little Skye!"

The Jamaican children each hugged the girl. She waved as she returned to the vehicle dressed only in her swimsuit, big hat, and the flimsy wristband she'd bought earlier.

Skye promptly walked back to her seat as everyone stared in disbelief.

The children looked in the bag to see what the kind girl had given them. Their mouths dropped when they realized she'd given them everything she had, including her money. They ran alongside the van, waving goodbye, jumping up and down as it drove away.

Everyone saw this kind, caring act. Many shed a tear, including Morgan. An act of kindness by a little nine-year-old girl to the less fortunate humbled those who were blessed enough to see it.

Skye cuddled up next to Morgan and closed her eyes.

He looked down at the child, and whispered, "How old did you say you were?" There was no reply. Skye had fallen asleep.

Morgan brushed the hair from her face, smiling, as he watched her sleep peacefully. He thought about her words, and the kindness she'd demonstrated. *If only there were more people like this in the world, it would be a better place.*

Chapter Ten

"Welcome back, ladies and gentlemen to our third annual Cruise for a Cure," Dr. Leontiou announced. "I want to first thank those who generously donated, not just money, but their time to our worthy cause. Time is probably the most important investment because with many of these diseases, *time* is what our patients don't have."

"As for donations, I'm proud to announce that almost three million dollars in pledges and gifts have been raised so far on this cruise, and it's just the third day. Thank you."

The crowd applauded, many standing in appreciation.

When they quieted, the doctor continued. "I was going to speak on Batten disease today, but we had an unexpected guest from the United States, who by coincidence, came on board the cruise just for leisure. I managed to talk her into speaking today about her clinic in Saint Paul, Minnesota. Many of you may recall the article she wrote, *Why We Are Concerned About Rare Childhood Diseases.* Ladies and gentlemen, please welcome, Dr. Tammy Hamilton."

Smiling broadly, Tammy gathered her papers. As she neared the podium, she shook hands with Dr. Leontiou.

She was at ease. "Good morning. If you'd asked me last week what I would be doing on the third day of this cruise, I certainly would not have predicted that I'd be speaking to a hundred of the greatest medical minds in the world. I'm humbled as I look at this distinguished gathering. It's like a Who's Who in the top echelon of the medical profession."

A few chuckled at the comment.

"It's an honor to be with you. Thank you, Dr. Leontiou, and colleagues. Even though we come from different parts of the world, we're all here today for a common cause. Each of us wants to find a cure for the horrible childhood diseases that plague the most helpless victims—our children. Dr. Leontiou asked me to speak on Batten disease and what we're doing at our clinic."

She took a sip of water from a bottle she'd previously placed on the side of the podium. "Let me begin by telling you my story. I became interested in this disease several years ago when Tony, a seven-year-old patient, was brought to my clinic. At first, I was at a loss of what was wrong with the child, until my husband said he'd read an article in a medical journal about Batten disease. Come to find out, Dr. Leontiou wrote the article, and I'm sure you're all familiar with it. That is when I became familiar with his studies, and that dreadful disease. Although I quickly diagnosed Tony with Batten disease, less than three months later, he was dead. It was devastating to me and my staff. It was the only case we had ever encountered in our practice, and I have not had one since, but I began researching it."

She cleared her throat. "This morning, we touched on the scientific facts about Batten disease, otherwise known as Neuronal Ceroid Lipofuscinosis, or NCL. I'll do a quick review. Batten is a terminal illness, an inherited disorder of the nervous system, which usually begins in childhood. Batten disease is the result of defective genes from the parents. One parent can carry the bad gene and not be affected. The problem comes when the other parent has the bad gene, also. Basically, what happens is the affected child can't produce the enzyme which is responsible for eliminating the waste that builds up in the brain. Early symptoms of the disease most often appear between the ages of two and five, when parents or physicians may notice a previously normal child has begun to develop vision problems, or seizures. In some cases, the early signs are subtle, taking the form of personality and behavior changes, slow learning, clumsiness, or stumbling. Over time, affected children suffer mental impairment, worsening seizures, and progressive loss of sight and motor skills. Eventually, children with Batten disease become blind, bedridden, and—perhaps the most disheartening—they descend into dementia. Batten disease is often fatal before children reach the age of ten or eleven."

"Since Tony died, my staff and I have been doing lab experiments trying to find out how to combat this horrible disease. Although we've made great strides, we still have a long way to go. Our biggest problem is the same as most labs who are working on a cure for Batten or other rare diseases. Money. Even if we donate our time, we still need funding. Almost no federal help is available."

A hand quickly rose. "I'm Doctor Everest from the Clavin Medical Clinic in Great Britain. I'm really at a loss for words. Why is this disease so important? Why not put our efforts toward more common childhood diseases like Leukemia, Multiple Sclerosis, or Muscular Dystrophy? We could save more lives."

"I hear what you're saying. Every life is sacred. Yes, not as many lives are affected, but the fact remains, this is someone's child. A daughter. A son. A precious life. These families are hurting! They love their children. They deserve the same care as the victim who has, for example, cancer. I would suspect Dr. Everest, that if this were your child you would be doing everything in your power to find a cure, or pushing your government to put more money towards that cause."

The doctor nodded humbly.

"Are there any other questions?"

A different doctor spoke up. "Dr. Hamilton, where do you see yourself in a year from now, or five years from now?"

She paused, pondering the question. She certainly did not see herself as a mother—that much she knew. "I see myself still doing what I do today. The only difference would be that I would have new patients. The thing I'd love to change is the *reason* I have new patients. Now, it's usually because the disease has won the battle. I'd like to be able to defeat the disease, so the children can live happy adult lives."

The silence was noticeable on the ride back to the ship. Occasionally, a head would turn, someone wondering what had happened to the little girl who directed much of the trip on the way to the dolphin encounter. It was obvious her chatter and playfulness were missed.

Morgan took the uninterrupted time to think about what Skye had said about faith. He realized she was right. He not only lacked faith, but had given up hope. After all, he was a doctor and he knew his wife's medical history. He understood the physical reason she couldn't carry a baby full-term. He also knew he had to come to grips with the reality of the situation. That's where he was stuck. He knew that faith really had nothing to do with Tammy and him wanting a baby. Faith had to do with the fact that God was in control of the situation, He had a purpose in it, and he and Tammy had to accept the truth. That's where the problem was. How could they accept it? No answers would come, they never did. Once again, he put it in the back of his mind.

When the van arrived at the ship, Morgan awakened Skye. "Hey, sleepyhead, it's time to board the ship."

She woke with a smile and outstretched arms. "This has been the funnest time I ever had. I'm glad I shared it with you." She threw her arms around Morgan's neck and squeezed tight, almost smothering him.

A genuine smile encompassed his entire face. He hugged the little bundle of energy who was tugging at his heartstrings.

After the passengers unloaded the van, they stood around waiting for the captivating child. It seemed the girl unknowingly was in charge.

"I'll be right there," Skye announced to the others.

She was not going anywhere until Carlos helped Mrs. Scott off the van. The elderly woman sat back in her wheelchair and Skye took over. "I have it from here."

She waved goodbye to the driver. "Remember Carlos, no more baseball, it's got to be chess from now on."

"Righto, Little One," he said with a smile, waving vigorously.

Skye began pushing the wheelchair back to the ship. Morgan followed behind her, trailed by the rest of the group. It was obvious that the nine-year-old commanded the lead, and everyone else followed.

Morgan noticed people expressing kindness to each other, more than usual. *I think the little girl's magic seems to be rubbing off on everyone she meets.* He shook his head wondering what would be next.

While they were walking, Skye announced that she was going to the computer room later to print copies of the pictures Mrs. Scott took. "Don't worry. I'll see that everyone gets their pictures." The tourists all smiled, playing along, but most didn't believe it would happen. After all, it was a child talking.

When it came time to separate on the ship, Mrs. Scott took the girl's hand, brought it to her face, and kissed it." Thank you, Child. You gave me some very special memories."

Skye hugged her.

The convention session was still going when Skye and Morgan arrived at the conference room. They slipped in and sat in the back, listening to the question and answer time led by Dr. Leontiou. Most questions were directed to Tammy.

Skye's father saw his little girl and decided to bring the meeting to a close. "One last question. Please, from Rio de Janeiro, Dr. Gosset."

"Dr. Hamilton, what's the most challenging problem you face at your clinic?"

The female doctor thought for a moment before replying. "The most challenging. At first thought, I would say the difficulty of holding everything together. You know, making the process run as smooth as possible: the check in, diagnosis, treatment."

She paused, trying to frame her words. "But when you get right down to it, the most challenging problem for us, as doctors, is not just treating the patients, but also dealing with the families. How do you break the news to parents that their child only has a short time to live? How do you tell a devoted mother and father that their child's days of playing, living, and breathing are numbered? Yes, while the diagnosis and treatment are challenging, the most important thing we must remember is that we're dealing with fragile human lives. No life is less important than another, especially to family members. The people, the patients, the families, are most important! If we all remember that, our jobs will not be easier, but they will definitely be more fulfilling."

Tammy hesitated, her mind drifting. *For too long I have focused on my own situation. Perhaps it's time that I concentrate more on the children, the families, and their pain.* "Yes, fulfilled is the right answer. In our profession, we see many defeats. With each, we must hold tight to the belief that we can and will make a difference. One day, that cure for Leukemia will be found, that cure for Multiple Sclerosis will be found, yes, even that cure for Batten disease will be found. Until then, we doctors, scientists, and chemists must continue the daily, grueling task of searching for that cure. Thank you for having me this morning. You've been a delightful audience."

The crowd applauded enthusiastically.

Tammy turned to Dr. Leontiou. "Thank you, Sir, for allowing me the privilege of speaking today."

"The pleasure was all mine," he replied, shaking her hand warmly.

While the crowd thinned, Dr. Layland Leontiou stayed in the front of the meeting room. His wife took her place beside him.

Skye bounded up to them. As the doctor picked up his much-loved daughter, she eagerly recounted her day. "Father, Father, you should've seen it! Jessie didn't want us to leave. She kissed me! And I rode her around the pool! And she jumped up right next to us, splashing us real big. It was the most amazing thing ever! We have pictures of everything. Mrs. Scott took over two hundred pictures. Good ones too!"

Morgan reached for Tammy's hand. "Good job," he said, "I'm proud of you."

"Thank you," she replied. What about you? Did you have a good time? I know someone else sure did." She winked at Skye.

"We had a great time!"

Tammy noticed his colossal smile.

Just then, Dr. Gosset stepped up. "Dr. Hamilton," he said, extending his hand to Tammy. "What you said touched my heart. I'd never thought of it like that, and when I get back from this holiday, I'll be implementing new orders to my staff. We'll be putting more emphasis on the people."

"Thank you for your kind words, Dr. Gosset."

He continued. "I'm on the board of the Leontiou Medical Research Foundation. Every year we give a substantial donation to clinics around the world to assist in their research. So far this year we've donated nearly a million dollars to worthy clinics. We have almost $280,000 left. On behalf of the LMRF, I'd like to make a donation in that amount to your clinic in Saint Paul. Would you accept that?"

Tammy's mouth dropped. "Well, I'm only a doctor there, I can't make that decision, but this is the administrator, and he can." She pulled Morgan in front of her.

"Great. Mister..."

"Hamilton. Doctor Morgan Hamilton."

"Hamilton?"

"Yes. I'm better known as the *other* Dr. Hamilton." Morgan smiled at his wife.

"Name is Gosset. Will you accept that gift?"

Morgan glanced over at the Leontious who were smiling broadly. "I would be honored to accept the donation. Thank You. Thank You," he said, shaking the man's hand vigorously.

"Layland, you need to get these two involved in your clinic in Costa Rica. Better yet, Kardia," Dr. Gosset advised.

"I'm working on it."

Morgan and Tammy stared at each other, still in shock from the generous gift they'd just received.

Chapter Eleven

The Hamiltons retreated to their suite where they spent the rest of the afternoon resting. The warm breeze and the fresh smell of the ocean were refreshing, just what they needed to relax. The sound of the splashing waves could be heard as the ship pushed its way through the Gulf.

Tammy finally fell asleep.

Morgan began reading. Suddenly, he was interrupted by a noise that sounded like footsteps, which appeared to stop at their door. There was an indistinguishable sound. Watching the door, he wondered what was happening in the hall. He heard a shuffling sound and noticed an envelope under the door. Then he heard some mumbling, which sounded like, "Oops." He remained still, listening intently to the person or persons outside his door. *What's going on?* At first, he thought it might be the ship's steward or Via dropping off the evening's itinerary. But then he spotted another envelope inching under the door, wiggling back and forth.

His curiosity got the best of him. Morgan slipped over to the door, all the while wondering about the strange happenings. The soft mumbling continued outside the door. Finally, he opened the door!

Sprawled on her stomach in the hall was a little body with a stack of envelopes next to her. It was Skye!

She looked up, her face showing her surprise. "Hi, Dad! Sorry. I put the wrong envelope under your door."

Morgan bent over, picking up the envelope. Opening it, he pulled out a dozen pictures of one of the passengers interacting with the dolphins earlier in the day. After studying the pictures briefly, he asked, "Are these the pictures Mrs. Scott took with your camera?"

"Yes. Came out pretty good, huh? She's a good photographer."

"Yes, they came out very good. They've been cropped. Did you do this?"

"Yes. I spent a long time getting them just right."

Morgan looked down at the pile of envelopes on the floor. "Are you telling me that you spent the rest of the afternoon cropping and printing the pictures Mrs. Scott took, and now you're distributing them?"

"Yes. It sure was fun. I want to get them to everyone before dinner."

Skye stood up, picked up her stack, and handed Morgan one with the word, "Dad" on it. "This one is yours. Mom will want to see them for sure."

He reached for it with a smile of gratitude. After reviewing the contents, Morgan's eyes widened, and his face showed astonishment. "You did this by yourself?"

"Yes. Came out pretty good, if I do say so myself." Her body bounced.

"Pretty good isn't the word. They're *perfect*."

He slowly skimmed though the twenty or more pictures and came across one that caught his attention. It was a picture of Skye planting a kiss on Jessie. Cross-faded into that image was Morgan with his dolphin.

"Wow! Pretty ingenious how you blended these two pictures into one. It looks great. They need to be entered in a contest."

"You think so? I can't take credit for taking them. Mrs. Scott gets credit for that."

"Well, it was your camera, and you cropped and printed them. Really, I don't think Mrs. Scott would care. Besides, you know what the law says."

Skye looked at Morgan so seriously that it almost made him laugh. "No. What does it say?"

"'Possession is nine-tenths of the law.' It was your camera. I think it's safe to assume these pictures are yours. And like I said, I'm absolutely sure that Mrs. Scott wouldn't have it any other way."

Morgan glanced down at the envelopes in her hands. "You printed off everyone's pictures?"

"Yes. Everyone on the dolphin excursion. It saves them a little money. Some of them couldn't afford to buy the pictures taken at the dolphin place."

"You truly have a kind heart, Little Girl. Don't lose that. It's a rare quality."

"I better get going. I still have to get all these pictures delivered and get ready for dinner tonight. It's dress-up night, you know."

"Skye?"

"Yes, Dad."

"Can I give you a hug for a thank you?" Morgan asked bending down.

She didn't say anything, she didn't need to. Instead she wrapped her arms around him tightly.

"Thank you," his voice cracked.

With that, she was gone. Skipping down the hall, she dropped one of the envelopes. She bent down, picked it up, and then continued on her mission. He watched the girl who captured people's hearts everywhere she went until she was out of sight.

He stepped back into his stateroom and thumbed through the pictures she gave him.

Tammy came out of the bedroom. "What's going on? I thought I heard voices."

Morgan grinned. "Oh yes, Honey. Skye was just here. You wouldn't believe what that girl did." He handed Tammy the pictures. "Skye spent hours, cropping and printing pictures for everyone who was on the dolphin tour today."

"You're kidding!" Tammy said, looking through the photos. "Wow! She sure did a good job."

Tammy stopped skimming though them when she saw the picture of the two of them. "Oh, my gosh! She did this? It looks like a professional photo. People would pay a lot of money for a picture of this quality."

Morgan laughed. "Mrs. Scott actually took the photos. She was snapping up a storm. It was rather cute. Skye calls her Grandma."

"That child is something else," Tammy said.

"That she is."

Tammy handed the photos back to Morgan. She sighed, "I need to get ready. You know, it's tux night."

"Yes," Morgan said. "Tux night." His mind was noticeably elsewhere.

Within an hour, strolling arm-in-arm into the dining room, the Hamiltons greeted the maître d. "Table for two, please."

He escorted the couple to an intimate table next to a window. A few scattered, low clouds made for a radiant sunset. As the orange ball of light descended, a quiet calm settled on them. It was a perfect end to a sublime day.

They watched the sunset in silence. Morgan reached for his wife's hand. It was a tender, wordless moment.

Suddenly, the quiet was shattered. "There you are," a little voice erupted as a child leaped in front of their table.

Tammy jumped. "Skye, you startled me!"

"Why didn't you come to our table? I had a seat saved for you guys. Can I sit with you?"

Tammy ignored the question. "You look beautiful tonight, Skye. What a pretty dress!"

"Thanks, Mom." Skye twirled around, showing off her burgundy dress. "Do you like what Maya did with my hair? She put big curls in it. Sometime this week she's going to braid it, maybe even with beads."

She walked over to a nearby table. "Hi! Excuse me, but can I borrow this chair?"

The woman responded with a smile. "Sure."

"Thank you." Skye pulled the chair over, adding a third place to the table for two. Before they knew it, she plopped herself down, looking quite content.

"Hey, Mom, Dad sure has a way with dolphins. He can't swim very well though. I thought I was going to have to save him from drowning a couple times."

Morgan made a deliberate, pouting face. "What do you mean I can't swim? I thought I did pretty well, considering how deep the water was."

"Dad, it was waist deep, and you never let go of that life jacket."

"Well, it fit too loose, I was afraid I might lose it."

"Excuses, excuses! I've told you for years that you need to learn how to swim better," Tammy joshed.

Skye laughed. "I was just kidding. Dad did very well. I don't think he's a very good kisser, though. I think Priscilla was really embarrassed about the whole thing."

His eyebrows rose. "What do you mean? I'm an *excellent* kisser!"

He nudged his wife. "Tell her, Honey. Tell her!"

A couple at another table overheard his comments and stifled their laughter.

"Wait a minute," Tammy said. "*Who* is this Priscilla?"

"You're evading the question," Morgan said with mock exasperation. "Am I, or am I *not* a good kisser?"

"Who is this Priscilla?" Tammy asked again.

"She was his dolphin," Skye sputtered, laughing so hard tears were running down her cheeks.

Morgan shrugged. "Well, I don't know how to kiss a dolphin. I mean they have such big... I guess you can call them *lips*."

Tammy started to laugh.

"I don't think it's funny." Morgan said, rolling his eyes." But, I can see you two are ganging up on me again."

Just then, the waiter interrupted the lighthearted chatter. "Hi, Skye! Can I get you anything?"

"Hi, Neut! Can you bring me a shrimp cocktail, please?"

"Sure. Coming right up!"

"And can I get a salad?"

"Do you want anything on it?"

"No, thank you, but please bring some catsup. I've been thinking of trying something different."

He took Morgan and Tammy's order and was gone.

"Dad, I was wondering. Will you and Mom take me line dancing in Costa Rica?"

"Line dancing?" Tammy asked.

"Yes. Father has to visit one of his clinics there. He's scared of heights. And Mother is all of the p's." Skye broke off a corner of a dinner roll and plopped it in her mouth.

Tammy looked baffled. "All of the p's? I'm almost afraid to ask. What does that mean?"

"You know," Skye said, "prude, prim, and proper."

"Oh, *those* p's. I almost forgot about them." Tammy made eye contact with Morgan, both of them trying not to laugh.

"Let's get back to the line dancing thing," Morgan said, trying to keep a serious face. "I thought that was some kind of country dance."

Skye wove her fingers through her curls. "No, silly. I mean zip-line dancing."

"Oh, zip-line! Why do you call it line dancing?" Tammy asked.

Skye leaned closer to Tammy, as if sharing a huge secret. "My father said I can go if you guys take me. I'm really too small to zip-line, but my father knows the man who runs the place. Problem is my weight." She held her arms out wide. "Sixty pounds of pure skin and bones."

The antics and vocabulary of the nine-year-old girl tickled the couple.

She didn't realize it, but Skye had attracted the attention of some nearby diners. Her unusual gestures had them staring and smiling, most wondering about the vivacious child.

"Father says that I weigh so little that when I start down the run, I will end up bouncing around like I'm line dancing through the jungle. He said all of the monkeys will fall out of the trees laughing. He even thinks that the laughing hyena will literally die of laughter."

Realizing they were being observed by people around them, Morgan decided he'd better get the situation under control. "What you're saying is that you want us to be your mom and dad for the day, so you can zip-lining, right?"

"Right. It's next Saturday. The day before we head home. Tomorrow is Stingray City, at Grand Cayman."

Tammy took a tissue out of her small purse and tried to clean away the smudges of mascara that her tears had caused.

Morgan made eye contact with his wife. "What do you think, Honey? Should we take this little girl line dancing?"

"I... I," she was trying not to start laughing again. "I would not miss it for the world."

Morgan glanced at Skye. "No water, right?"

"No water. Just trees."

The waiter arrived with their appetizers, allowing a welcome break in the conversation.

"This is my favoritest food in the whole world," Skye said, popping a juicy shrimp into her mouth and savoring the taste.

Morgan and Tammy watched the little girl devour her shrimp cocktail.

A couple minutes later, the waiter returned with their salads. "Hey Dad, will you please pass me the catsup? I want to see what it tastes like on my salad."

Morgan passed her the bottle, reluctantly. He watched her design a smiley face on her salad with the catsup using what seemed like half the bottle. Satisfied, she finally took a bite. "Yummy! It's good!"

Morgan eyed Tammy, who was reapplying her lipstick.

"You look so pretty in that color," Tammy said to Skye, in an effort to get their minds off the strange salad.

"Well, thank you," Skye said. "My dress would look better if I had my bumps."

Tammy raised an eyebrow. "Excuse me?"

"Bumps," Skye said. "You know..." She cupped her hands and held them out in front of her chest, simulating the curves of breasts.

Morgan changed the subject hurriedly. "Skye, did you see the sunset tonight?"

Tammy broke into an uncontrolled bout of laughter, and Skye continued eating her catsup salad.

A photographer came to their table. "May I get your picture?" she asked.

"I don't think so," Tammy said in a teasing voice. "My makeup is all smeared, thanks to Skye."

"Nonsense. It looks natural. It will add a little true-to-life substance."

Tammy didn't have a clue what the photographer meant, but she glanced at Morgan and Skye. "Oh, why not?"

Skye crowded between the table and window, standing between Morgan and Tammy with her arms around their shoulders, smiling. The woman snapped a number of photographs.

After the photographer left for another table, Skye jumped back. "I gotta go. Will you come with us tomorrow to swim with the stingrays? It will be fun. I hear it tickles when they touch you."

"Stingrays?" Tammy asked. "Won't they kill you with their stingers?"

"Not true," Skye insisted "They get a bum rap. They're really gentle, loving creatures. Come on, you'll love it. Please. You can get a good luck kiss from one of them or a back rub. I hear those are great."

"Back rub?" Tammy asked. "I could go for that."

"If you want, I guess we'll come." Morgan angled his head.

"Great!' Skye spun around and skipped away almost hitting a waiter. Suddenly, she remembered something. Peering at Tammy and Morgan, she called, "Oh yes, meet me at—"

"We know, the lighthouse man at seven." Morgan winked at her.

Skye shook her finger at him. "Right! And don't be late!"

"We'll be there on time," he assured her.

They watched as she disappeared out of the dining room going to who-knows-where.

"That little girl is a pistol. She steals the whole show!" Morgan crossed his arms.

"Where does she come up with those words and actions?"

"I wish I knew," Morgan shook his head.

While they ate their entree, the couple's conversation turned to business.

Morgan asked, "Did Dr. Leontiou offer you a job at his clinic, Honey?"

"He has alluded to it, but never has come out and asked. I've heard rumors that he and Malinda are on the threshold of some great discovery. Why do you ask?"

"Something Skye said about her father wanting you on staff." Morgan took a sip of water. "Maybe we should consider it. If they're on the brink of something big... Well, it would be nice to be on the ground level of something new."

"I don't think I could ever leave Saint Paul. That clinic is my life. What would happen to it if we left?"

Morgan squeezed Tammy's hand. "I'm just saying that I think we should keep an open mind. It might be an opportunity of a lifetime for you."

She smiled, but didn't respond.

The couple decided to miss the show that night and go to bed early. It had been a busy day and tomorrow would be another exhausting one.

It was almost one in the morning when they were jolted out of bed by a loud banging on the door. Morgan hurried to see what the racket was.

Skye was standing in the hallway, dressed in her night clothes. "Dad, you and Mom have got to see this. It's the coolest thing ever. Hurry! Come with me!"

"Skye, it's one in the morning." Morgan rubbed his eyes, still half-asleep.

"I know, but it's the best time to see it. We have to hurry before the clouds come. Meet me on the top deck by the kids' pool. They turned the lights off, so it's real dark. See ya there!" She disappeared before he could comment on her unusual request.

Morgan closed the door as Tammy rushed out of the bedroom.

"Was that Skye?"

"Yes."

"Why is she up at this hour?"

"She wants us to go to the top deck and see something."

"What has that little girl cooked up now?"

"I don't know, but she said we had to hurry before the clouds come."

Tammy slipped her robe on. "Then we better get going."

Still groggy, Tammy handed Morgan his robe as she walked out the door.

Morgan grabbed his key card and caught up to his wife.

Within minutes, they arrived at the children's pool area. Just as Skye said, the lights were off, but he could make out a group of people gazing into the sky.

Morgan noticed Dr. Leontiou and his wife, so they joined them.

"Looks like she woke you too," Malinda said.

"Yes, what are we looking for?" Morgan inquired, yawning.

Skye's father added, "It seems that our young lady has found her own comet. She named it Isaura. Tonight is a once-in-a-lifetime event. Evidently, it will be at its brightest tonight before it begins to travel out of our solar system."

He noticed a group of people viewing the sky through a large telescope. "She found a comet? How did she do that?"

Layland grinned. "You'll have to ask her. I'm just her father."

"Where is Skye?"

"She said she was going to get you. I thought she'd be with you," Layland looked around.

"No. She woke us up, rattled off something about being here before the clouds came, and then she was gone."

"She probably stopped by the bridge, to have the captain stop the ship," Layland said. "Or turn it around."

Morgan shot him a puzzled look.

"That was a joke," Layland said. "At least, I *hope* it was."

Just then Skye appeared, pushing Mrs. Scott in her wheelchair. A dozen other people, many who'd been on the dolphin adventure, trailed them.

"I guess I should've known," Layland remarked, watching the procession.

Skye pushed Mrs. Scott close to the telescope. Everyone else stepped aside thoughtfully.

"Now, Grandma, try not to touch the scope," Skye said. "It's set perfectly. Just look down into this screen and you'll see my comet."

Mrs. Scott peered into a six-inch screen attached to the telescope. It was zoomed in on a bright comet.

The elderly lady eyed Skye in the soft moonlight. "Land sakes, Child. How did you ever find a comet? And where did you get this fancy telescope?"

"Father bought it for me on my ninth birthday. It has all the extras— large screen, built-in camera, even an automatic finder, and a time thingy that lets me know when a certain star is coming into view, or leaving the solar system. Everything! Father built a small room off the balcony of my bedroom, so I could use my telescope."

More people gathered around her as the youngster told the story.

"One night, I was just scanning the sky when I noticed something strange. I didn't think much about it until a week later when my computer told me it had moved. So I studied some more, and found that the thing I saw was not on my computer's list of stars. So I called the man at the observatory the next day and asked him about it. His name is Mr. Risto. He said he'd check it out. He told me that it was probably just a faint star and my star finder was misaligned. He'd seen that happen before. Mr. Risto called two days later, and he was all excited. It was a comet! And no one had ever reported it before. He calculated the trajectory, and estimated that tonight would be the brightest time to see it. After tonight, the comet will start heading away from us. He said since I found it, I could name it. He suggested Isaura, so I said okay."

"Like our ship," Mrs. Scott interjected.

"Yes, like the ship." Skye confirmed. "The last time we'll ever see it will be Christmas Eve of next year. Isaura will leave our solar system, and never return."

Mrs. Scott studied Skye. "What are your dreams, young lady? Are you going to be an astronomer when you grow up?"

Everyone was quiet as Skye pondered the question; Morgan and Tammy listened with interest.

"I don't think so, but that's a hard question to ask someone my age. I do have dreams, and I have lots of prayers. My dreams are only dreams. My prayers are different, because I know they'll be answered. I've been asking Jesus for a miracle!"

Skye glanced at her mother and father who were standing quietly, and then her gaze shifted to Morgan and Tammy.

She reached her arms upward. "If you want your dreams to come true, you have to reach for the sky!"

Everyone watched as the young girl twirled around, hands extended skyward.

"Come on," Skye said. "Everybody, think of a dream! Say a prayer! Reach toward the sky! Everything will turn out all right."

Before long, nearly everyone was reaching heavenward. Even Morgan.

Tammy scanned the crowd, and noticed she was the only one without her arms up. She raised her hands, slowly, uncertainly. As a physician, she knew that her dream would never come true; her prayer could never be answered.

One-by-one, everyone looked into the telescope watching the amazing event.

Then, as quickly as they'd come, the people began to leave. There was still enough time to get a little sleep.

Chapter Twelve

Early the next morning, the weary Hamiltons met Skye and her parents by the lighthouse man. They found a large table and indulged in a protein-filled breakfast.

Following their meal, they boarded a bus that would transport them to the boat ride to Stingray City.

On the boat, Tammy waved to the honeymooning couple, Billie and Billy Hill, who were clinging to each other. It was the first time she'd seen them since the airport.

As they neared the site, the first glimpse of the large, dark creatures swimming close to the surface was breathtaking.

Skye's smile showed her excitement as the boat was anchored. She could hardly believe she was actually going to swim with the stingrays!

Her mother and father secured her life jacket, and together the family slowly entered the cool water.

Tammy and Morgan were fascinated by the antics of the sea creatures and the child. Skye pet the stingrays while the guide held them safely. Skye giggled when one of the staff put a stingray on her back.

Morgan enjoyed the encounter more than he anticipated. He laughed hysterically when the stingrays gave Tammy a backrub.

Skye moved closer to Tammy to have some pictures taken with a large stingray held above their heads, looking like a sombrero. It looked like all three of them were smiling—Tammy, Skye, and the stingray.

After the stingray excursion, Dr. Leontiou and his wife needed to return to the ship for the convention.

Tammy and Morgan spent the rest of the day with Skye.

Although they were exhausted after Stingray City, the three were looking forward to their last stop—the butterfly farm. They were greeted by a friendly guide, a woman people referred to as, "The Butterfly Lady."

They strolled along paths lined with flowering shrubs. Occasionally, the guide would raise her hand and a butterfly would land on her outstretched arm, as if on cue.

A large, dark-blue butterfly landed on Skye's shoulder. Tammy snapped a few pictures of the beautiful insect. When it flew away, Skye bounded after it.

Tammy noticed Morgan looking into a window and joined him.

"What is it?" she asked.

"It's a black light exhibit. The butterflies change colors under the light." Fascinated, they watched in silence.

"It's beautiful. Skye will love this." Tammy smiled.

Suddenly, they heard a commotion. The couple noticed a group of people gathering nearby.

Morgan frowned. "I wonder what's going on over there."

"I don't know, but The Butterfly Lady sure looks confused. Something must have happened!"

Morgan and Tammy rushed over to the growing crowd.

Skye stood with outstretched arms, giggling.

Captivated tourists surrounded her, cameras clicking, as dozens of butterflies clustered around the child. In an unexplainable way, the fascinating insects were drawn to her.

Shocked, Morgan and Tammy watched and wondered.

"It's the most amazing thing I've ever seen. I'm stunned," The Butterfly Lady admitted to the onlookers. "Maybe the butterflies are attracted to something she's wearing—a color, or a scent. That's the only way I can explain it."

Skye raised her arms upward. More butterflies, of all varieties, landed on her hands, arms, and head. She glimpsed at the Hamiltons. "Hey, Mom! Dad! Look, I think they like me."

Tammy snapped a few pictures and whispered, "Morgan, who *is* this child?"

Morgan couldn't speak, partially because he had no reply, partially because his emotions had gotten the best of him. There was no answer. Neither of them had ever met anyone like Skye. The girl seemed to cast an enchanting spell on everyone she met, even the butterflies and dolphins.

The couple would never forget the mystical events of that day.

The next few days were more relaxing. When Skye's parents were at the convention, the Hamiltons occupied their daughter, playing checkers, shuffle board, miniature golf, and even some basketball.

On leisure days at sea, Tammy and Skye spent hours exploring the shops. They laughed as they tried on various clothing and accessories.

One afternoon, an outfit in a window of a boutique caught Skye's attention. "Isn't that cute? I wonder if they have it in blue, my favoritest color."

"Let's find out," Tammy said entering the shop.

She pointed to the short set, and asked the clerk, "Do you have this in blue?"

After searching, the clerk reported she only had one box left, other than the display, and it was green."

Skye politely thanked her. Taking Tammy's hand, she commented, "Oh well, it's okay. Let's shop some more."

The Hamilton's balcony provided them the best possible view as the *Isaura* entered the Panama Canal. As the large ship crept through the famous locks, Skye explained its history, offering tidbits of information that astounded them.

On the tenth night, after the ship left the canal and reached the Pacific Ocean, Morgan, and Tammy planned to sit with Skye at the evening show. When she didn't show up, they were both concerned. Worried, they scanned the audience, but could not locate her.

Tammy whispered, "Perhaps she's sitting with her parents tonight."

Morgan saw the Leontious sitting in the front row, without their daughter. "She's not with them. Maybe she's not feeling well."

The lights dimmed before he could ask them about her.

The ship's cruise director strode on stage to announce the entertainment. "Good evening, ladies, and gentlemen. You're in for a special treat. Tonight is the night we allow our passengers to entertain us. Sometimes it's good. Sometimes it's... ah... not so good. But it's always a lot of fun. All I ask is that you respect the performers, no matter what. Now, let's get started."

Morgan and Tammy enjoyed the acts, some of them were people they recognized, passengers who sang, played an instrument, or presented a comedy routine. The Hamiltons were amazed at the talent onboard, but also amazed that some of their fellow travelers thought they could sing, but couldn't hold a tune.

Briefly, the couple forgot their concerns about the missing girl.

Finally, the cruise director introduced the last act. "Our last musician is known by almost everyone on this ship. How can you not know her? She's always first to say hello, or assist an elderly person. I heard rumors that she was talented, so I asked her to perform her favorite song tonight. She said she would, but she'd like to have our ship's string quartet accompany her." The cruise director chuckled. "Ladies and gentleman our next guest is celebrating her tenth birthday tonight. She'll be playing her favorite song on the piano, Pachelbel's Canon in D. Please welcome Skye Leontiou."

Morgan and Tammy jumped to their feet, applauding wildly. They were not embarrassed, even though they were the only ones on their feet.

The curtain parted.

The audience stilled.

The ship's string quartet was seated near a pearly-white grand piano.

Skye sauntered across the stage. She looked adorable with her curly locks and bright-blue, frilly dress. Like a trained entertainer, she sat on the piano bench, straightening her dress.

Tammy realized they were still on their feet. She sat, pulling Morgan down next to her. He sat upright at the edge of his seat, trying to get the best view. Anxiously, the couple observed a side of Skye they'd never seen.

Morgan had never cared much for classical music, but the song was captivating. He was visibly moved. With tears filling his eyes, he clasped his hands and brought them to his face. He lost himself in the beauty of the music, listening to the girl who in the last week and a half had captured his heart.

Tammy had tears stinging her eyes and her face was beaming with pride. At that moment, she knew Skye had made a lasting impact in her life. And this would be the highlight of the cruise.

The strings and the piano played harmoniously, and then suddenly the rhythm picked up. Self-assured, she presented the selection in a way that everyone in the room took notice. The piano's sweet melody burst into a fast paced, modern rendition of the classical piece.

When her performance was over, Skye curtsied. The audience erupted in applause. Clapping, she turned to the string quartet, and motioned toward them. They stood and bowed.

The Hamiltons jumped to their feet enthusiastically, right after Skye's parents stood.

"Wow!" the cruise director boomed, walking on stage. "That was beautiful!" He held the microphone to her mouth.

"Thank you." She smiled. "That was dedicated to my mother and father."

"You love them very much, don't you?"

"Oh, yes. I do." Skye waved to her parents.

"Have you had a fun cruise?"

"Oh, yes. I've met some wonderful people. Kim, Zack, Mrs. Scott, and I can't forget Morgan and Tammy. They're really special to me."

She looked out into the auditorium and shouted, "Mom, Dad, I love you, too!"

"Morgan grabbed Tammy's hand, squeezing it tight. For both of them, the words were bittersweet. Those were the words they longed to hear from their own child. At the same time, they were grateful they had been a part of this remarkable young girl's life, even if only for two short weeks.

The Hamiltons tried to find Skye after the show, but she had disappeared. They would have to wait until morning to congratulate her on her amazing performance.

Chapter Thirteen

The next morning, Morgan and Tammy were awake and ready to go zip-lining with Skye. They waited for the familiar knock on the door, announcing the start of another fun-filled, adventurous day. But the knock didn't come.

After about thirty minutes, Morgan decided to look for Skye. *It's not like her to be late.*

He knocked on the door of Leontiou's penthouse suite.

Maya, the maid, answered. It was obvious that she was upset, distracted.

"Good morning, Maya. Is Skye here? We're taking her zip-lining today," Morgan chuckled.

"I'm sorry, Dr. Hamilton. They're already gone. Dr. Leontiou had some very important business to take care of."

"Gone? What do you mean *gone*?"

"They left for the airport as soon as the ship docked."

Morgan glanced into the room, noticing the luggage and Skye's telescope still there.

Sounding doubtful, he questioned her further. "What about their luggage? Something must have come up fast for them to leave without it."

"I'm packing for them. Their belongings will be sent to them shortly," Maya said curtly.

"Sent to them?" He repeated her words. "Will we be able to see them again?" He realized he sounded desperate.

"I don't know, Dr. Hamilton. Did you ever receive one of Dr. Leontiou's business cards?"

"Yes. I guess I'll have to give them a call, when I get back to the states. Tammy and I were sure looking forward to zip-lining with Skye today."

"I'm sorry, Dr. Hamilton. I'm sure you can get a refund. Now if you'll excuse me, I still have a lot of packing to do." The maid closed the door.

Morgan stood in the hall, wondering what had happened. *That's strange! What's going on? Why would the Leontious leave without saying goodbye?*

The couple felt empty the last days of the cruise. They walked the decks, stopping at the back of the ship, silently watching the trail of ocean water churning white from the turning propellers. Everywhere they went, there were memories of the times they spent with Skye—there was no escaping them.

Spending so much time with the girl further showed the couple how badly they wanted a child of their own. Their yearning for a baby only deepened.

Walking by the boutique where she had shopped with Skye, Tammy looked into the window and spotted the same outfit that had caught Skye's attention. The woman in the store rushed out to them. "If you're still interested in this outfit in blue, we have it! You won't believe this, but it was inside the box marked green. Go figure!" She smiled.

Tammy thought for a second. *Will we ever see Skye again*? Tammy wasn't sure, but decided to buy the outfit anyway. *Maybe we can send it to her.*

The clerk gift-wrapped the box and handed it to Tammy.

The last day of the convention was merely closing formalities and goodbyes. Nothing was mentioned about the Leontious sudden departure.

Morgan kept mulling over the turn of events. *Layland is an important man. Business must have taken him away, but I can't imagine what was so urgent that they couldn't at least say goodbye.*

The Hamiltons were invited to return and speak at the conference next year. The officials suggested Morgan could speak about the administrative part of his clinic, but he felt it was too early to make that decision.

Finally, the ship docked in San Diego, and everyone disembarked. There were many goodbyes between the Hamiltons and the people they'd met, but there was no doubt, something, someone was missing. Without Skye's bubbly personality, things were dull, different. Sadness hung in the air.

Morgan waved to Mrs. Scott as one of the ship's attendants wheeled her down the gangway. *I wonder what her life will be like when she returns home. With the cruise over, and her husband gone, does she have anything to look forward to?* He recalled what Skye told everyone about their dreams and prayers—about reaching for the sky. *What were Mrs. Scott's dreams now? What were her prayers?*

Emptiness overwhelmed Morgan. Much of the past two weeks had been filled with a little girl who'd showed him what it would be like to have his own daughter. More importantly, she had showed him how to have simple faith, like a child.

Tammy was quiet—too quiet. She felt like the cruise hadn't accomplished what they had hoped for. Yet, for a short time—thanks to Skye—she had experienced what it would be like to be a mom. A shattered dream!

The same raw pain that she had when she boarded the ship returned. *Could God really be so cruel? I mean, we couldn't even say goodbye to the girl we grew to love.*

The return trip to Saint Paul was disheartening. The hole in their hearts was magnified by the loss of not only their own child, but also of Skye.

Chapter Fourteen

The Hamiltons immersed themselves in work when they arrived back home. They were different people when they returned. They operated the clinic with more compassion, and sympathy. Skye's influence had rubbed off on them. But that was at work.

Unfortunately, at home things were dismal. Tammy grew more distant, and there was nothing her husband could do to reach her. She was sinking into a pit of despair, a deep depression. He felt more helpless every day.

As a result, their marriage problems deepened—each blaming the other for their unhappiness. Seeking a solution, they started seeing a marriage counselor, but nothing the therapist suggested made a difference.

Morgan and Tammy simply co-existed, some days hardly speaking to each other. They were growing further and further apart.

From time to time, Morgan brought up the possibility of adopting a baby or an older child. Friends and relatives shared phone numbers of people or agencies they knew that dealt with adoption.

Tammy showed no interest. When adoption was mentioned, her body would quiver as she seemed to retreat inward, and then a glazed look would come to her face. Then, nothing! It was as if she couldn't hear Morgan's attempts to help her.

Occasionally, one of them would bring up the possibility of accepting Dr. Leontiou's job offer, but both of them let the idea slide. There was too much uncertainty in their lives to even think of a drastic change like that. At their clinic, they were established and could at least get lost in their careers. They loved their work and it gave life some normalcy.

They received a thank you note from Leontiou's clinic, handwritten by Layland, saying that the offer to come to the clinic still stood. Skye was not mentioned.

Some evenings, Morgan and Tammy sat on the sofa, silently scanning their cruise scrapbook. Their photos were the only tangible proof that Skye ever existed. Their memories of those times were fading.

Six weeks after they returned from the cruise there was a startling turn of events.

Morgan was at the clinic catching up on some computer work. Suddenly, a strange message, in bold letters, appeared on his screen. "Hey, Dad! What ya doing?"

Morgan typed a message quickly, "Skye, is that you?"

"Yes. Are you busy?"

"Just catching up on paperwork. How did you know how to contact me?"

"Hello? It's called a computer! You know website... WWW... dot... your clinic name, and there you are, big as day. Hold on a minute."

Morgan drummed his feet nervously against the floor, waiting.

A graphic of a red, shaking phone appeared on his screen, ringing.

Morgan clicked on the phone to accept the call.

A new window opened on the screen, and there was Skye with her radiant smile. "Hi, Dad!" she exclaimed, waving enthusiastically.

"Skye, we've been worried about you. We never heard what happened, or why you left the ship. And we never got to congratulate you on the concert, or say goodbye. Are you all right?"

"I'm great," Skye said. "How are you and Mom doing?"

"We're keeping busy. *Very* busy!"

"Hey, Dad, remember when Jessie didn't want me to leave? Wasn't that funny?"

"Yes, that was kind of strange. I bet she misses you. What do you think?"

"I read that a dolphin's brain is almost the same size as a human's. Maybe she *does* miss me. I miss her. And I miss you and Mom."

"We miss you, too." Morgan peered at the door, wishing Tammy would come join the conversation. "How are your parents?"

She sighed audibly. "Mother and Father are in the lab working. They have been there day and night since we got back from our cruise."

He'd almost forgotten how cute, how bubbly, her voice was. "When they're in the lab, what do you do to keep yourself busy?"

"Oh, I have plenty of things to do. There are a lot of children my age to play with. And I play my piano, paint, and do most anything I want. I just wish we had a nicer playground—where all my friends could play safely without getting hurt. One of these days, I'm going to get one built."

"Sounds like you have a plan."

"I have..." Skye was interrupted by a muffled sound, which seemed to shake the camera, and then a siren. She turned her head. "Oh-oh, something's going on. I better go check it out. Maybe we can do this again sometime."

"I'd like that. Skye..." Her image disappeared. The only words on the otherwise blank screen were, "Lost Connection."

"That was bizarre," Morgan said.

"What's that?" Tammy asked, walking in as he spoke.

"I just got a call from Skye."

"Really?"

"Yes, she called me on my computer. I saw her, talked with her for a few minutes, and then something strange happened—it seemed almost like an explosion or an earthquake. I heard a siren in the background. She said she had to go, and the connection went dead."

"Can you call her back?"

"I guess I could try." He remembered Layland's business card was on his desk, so he reached for it and dialed the number. "It's busy."

"Think she'll call back?"

"I hope so," Morgan said. He studied his wife's face. "How are *you* doing?"

"Compared to what?"

"I don't know. It's just that every time I talk to Skye, she gets me excited about life again. I think we should seriously consider adopting."

Tammy's demeanor changed instantly. "Let's not get on that subject again. I'm not ready, and I may never be. Maybe God wants me to dedicate my life to the children here in Saint Paul."

"Or, maybe he wants you to dedicate your life to the children in Leontiou's clinic."

Tammy stiffened. "You know I can't leave here. I have too much invested in my clinic... my time... my life." Her mouth grew tight.

"But—"

Before Morgan could say anything else, Tammy turned and stalked out of the room.

Chapter Fifteen

Nearly two months had passed since they'd heard from Skye.

Morgan tried a few times to contact Dr. Leontiou, but only received a recording. He left messages, but never heard back. He finally gave up.

He felt they'd made a mistake by not checking out Layland's proposal. *I think he has given up on us. Who could blame him?*

Morgan realized he needed to get his life back on track, and work on saving his marriage. The stress since the miscarriage had mounted, and so had the problems.

Each day, the couple toiled at the clinic twelve to fourteen hours. At the end of their long work day, they came home exhausted. There was little energy left at the end of the day to even talk to each other.

Knowing they could never bring their own baby into the world was more than Tammy could bear. She blamed herself. Every night she cried herself to sleep.

Morgan would turn over in bed, his heart breaking. He didn't even hold her anymore. It didn't seem to help. Nothing did!

Many times, Morgan suggested getting involved in church again, but that topic always ended in an argument.

Neither liked the downward spiral of their marriage.

Even the staff at the clinic was sensing the turmoil between the two.

The turning point came one rainy afternoon when a stranger appeared at the clinic. A well-dressed young man in his early thirties spoke with a slight accent. "I'm looking for a Dr. Morgan Hamilton."

"That would be me. May I help you?"

The man stepped closer to Morgan's wife. "Would you perhaps be Dr. Tammy Hamilton?"

"Yes, I am."

"Perfect! Two birds with one stone. My name is Lance Laskari. I have a personal letter for each of you. I represent Dr. Layland Leontiou. You are hereby requested to be at the law office of Barrows and Sons in Athens, Greece, Monday morning at nine."

"Athens, Greece! You're joking, right?" Morgan scoffed, as he scanned the paper the mysterious stranger handed to him.

"No, Sir, I'm not." If his words weren't enough, the intense look on his face would have told anyone how serious he was.

Brow tight, he handed each of them an envelope. "Inside these envelopes are first-class round trip plane tickets to Athens. Included is a check for each of you in the amount of five thousand dollars, for personal expenses."

Morgan's expression softened. "Lance Laskari? I recall a famous tennis player by that name. Would that be you?"

"At one time, yes. Tennis players should never ski. I broke my knee skiing in Germany, and my tennis days were over in an instant." The man gave a hint of a smile.

"If I remember correctly, you won a silver medal at the Olympics for Greece, right?"

"That's correct. One of the proudest moments in my life was winning that medal for my country. Do you play tennis?"

"Yes. It's my favorite sport."

"Well, don't ski," Laskari warned.

Getting back to business, Morgan waved his envelope in the air. "What's this all about?"

"You do know a Dr. Leontiou, don't you?"

"Yes. We met him on a cruise about three, maybe four months ago."

"I'm sorry, Dr. Hamilton, but I'm not at liberty to divulge any more information to you."

The couple looked at each other blankly.

"Excuse me. You're expecting us to leave our jobs, our lives, with no explanation?" Tammy asked with a hint of sarcasm.

"You're being compensated very well for your time. Plus, if memory serves me correctly, several hundred thousand dollars have been donated to your clinic, from the Leontiou Medical Research Foundation. Is that not correct?"

"Well, yes, but—" Tammy stammered.

Laskari's voice sounded definite. "Nothing more need be said. Please have the common courtesy to do what the doctor has asked. I assure you, it's of the utmost importance."

Tammy persisted. "Can you give us any idea what this is about?"

"No, but I'll say this—it involves your future, and Skye's."

"Skye? What's she got to do with this?" Tammy and Morgan asked simultaneously.

"Everything! I'm sorry, but that's all the information I can give you. I've already said more than I should. The tickets are in the envelopes. We can't force you to come, but if you want to know more, please be at the law office Monday morning at nine. As I said, in the envelopes are first-class tickets to Greece for Sunday. You will be picked up at the airport and delivered to your hotel. The following morning we'll transport you to the law firm of Barrows and Sons. After that, you will be flown to the island."

"Island? What island?" Tammy eyes widened.

Morgan stepped in. "I remember that Skye told me she lived on an island. I don't recall the name."

"Kardia," Lance replied.

"Yes! That's it. Kardia!"

"That's all I can tell you. Thank you and good day." With that, he was gone.

Morgan and Tammy stood stunned, speechless, each of them holding their own information.

Inquisitively, Morgan opened his envelope and pulled out the contents: a round trip ticket to Greece, a check for five thousand dollars, and a hotel voucher.

Tammy was looking through her envelope, which had similar contents.

Morgan rubbed his forehead. "What do you think this is all about?"

"You have Leontiou's card. Give him a call." Tammy barked, more like an order than a suggestion.

Morgan opened his desk drawer, and sorted through a stack of business cards. He stopped when he found the one he was searching for—Dr. Layland Leontiou.

Before he could talk himself out of it, he called the number on the card. "This is Dr. Layland Leontiou. You've reached my private number. I'm unable to answer right now. Please leave a message, and I'll get back with you."

"It's a recording," he mouthed to Tammy.

"Leave a message," she whispered. "We have to find out what's going on."

"Yes. Dr. Leontiou, this is Morgan Hamilton. We met on a cruise a few months ago. I'm confused. We received a visit from a Lance Laskari wanting us to come to Greece and meet with a Mr. Barrows. What's this all about? Please give me a call back. We need more information. Thank you."

Morgan hung up, studying Tammy's face for a sign that she may know what to do next.

Within minutes, the phone rang. "Dr. Hamilton, this is Victoria, Dr. Leontiou's secretary. I'm unable to give you any more information over the phone. Please, just be here Monday morning at nine. Everything has been taken care of, and you will be well cared for. Thank you." There was a click, followed by silence.

"Ah, wait, Ma'am, just a minute."

"What happened?" Tammy asked, obviously bewildered.

"She hung up on me."

"Who hung up on you?"

"Dr. Leontiou's secretary."

"Call her back."

Morgan immediately pushed redial, only to get a different recording. "I'm sorry. The number you dialed is no longer in service. If you feel this message is in error, please check the number and try again."

"What?" Tammy asked softly.

"It says the number is disconnected." Morgan sighed.

"Disconnected? How? You just called it. Call again. Hurry!"

"No, it's the right number. This whole thing is strange. *Very* strange."

"Morgan, we can't just up and leave, we have jobs to do. Our clinic needs us!"

"Something isn't right," Morgan said. "We *have* to go. Something may have happened to Skye. We haven't heard from her since her call."

"You think she may have been hurt?"

"I don't know. When she called that day, I thought it was weird that she left so suddenly. And I was surprised that she never called back. I checked the internet for bad weather or earthquakes in Greece, but nothing was mentioned."

Morgan shoved his phone into his pocket. "Why would a lawyer want to talk with us?"

"Okay," Tammy said. "I guess we have no choice. I'll get someone to cover me for a week. Maybe I can give Skye the outfit I bought her. Can you get away?"

"Yes. I'll work it out."

"Morgan, I'm worried." Tammy put both hands on her hips, waiting for a word from her husband—a look, a touch, anything to calm her. That was something he'd always done. He had an amazing ability to soothe her fears and doubts in the midst of a storm. Until recently, at least.

Morgan gave his wife a smile that contained more comfort than he actually felt. "Everything will be all right," he said. "Everything will be fine."

He picked up his check and ticket, examining them closely. "Who would send a couple two first-class round trip tickets to Greece, along with two checks for five thousand dollars? And *why*?"

Chapter Sixteen

The Hamiltons reached Athens on Sunday afternoon.

During the lengthy flight, the couple made small-talk about what they thought might be viable possibilities, but the conversation never led anywhere. There were no real answers to the mystery, only questions. Both of them were on edge, unsure what to expect when they deplaned. Eventually, their conversation fell to an uncomfortable silence, both consumed by their individual doubts and fears.

Fortunately, a few of their questions were answered quickly when two skycaps picked up their luggage and took it to a waiting limo, then ushered them to the same vehicle.

The driver smiled, welcoming them. "Good afternoon, Mr. and Mrs. Hamilton. Welcome to Athens. I hope you had an enjoyable flight."

"It was very nice, thank you," Morgan answered politely. "Where are we going?"

"I'll be taking you to a local hotel for the night." The driver took a few bills out of his pocket, and handed the tip to the baggage handlers.

"Then what?" Tammy persisted.

"I'm sorry, Ma'am. I'm just a driver. I'm sure you'll be contacted soon. They know you're here."

"Who are *they*?" Morgan asked. His voice indicated he was getting agitated with the vague answers.

The man gave a slight grin. "Again, I'm just a driver. I can say nothing more."

"We may as well make the most of the situation," Morgan mumbled softly enough that the driver couldn't hear.

Tammy responded with a heavy sigh.

The Hamiltons leaned back in the comfy vehicle, watching out the windows at the historic sites they passed. It was the first time either of them had been to Greece. It wasn't long before they noticed a number of fire trucks and other emergency vehicles in a charred neighborhood. Some buildings and cars were still smoldering.

"What happened here?" Morgan asked.

The driver spoke in a strong Greek accent. "My country is on the edge of financial collapse. The government spends more money than it takes in. They can't raise taxes without the people screaming, so they have to cut back on government programs, which results in ugly protests." He pointed in the direction of the devastated ruins. "This is what happens."

"Our country has problems, too," Tammy responded with a combination of bitterness and sarcasm.

"I suspect the entire world is on edge. All of us are going to have to sacrifice a little here and there to work this out. Trouble is most people don't want to give up their things or wants. They feel they're entitled to them." The driver glanced into the rearview mirror as he spoke.

With that, the conversation ended.

When they arrived at the new five-star hotel, a couple bellhops quickly opened the door and proceeded to get their luggage. "Please, follow me."

Morgan asked again what was going on, but still no one would comment. Either they were not allowed to say, or they knew nothing themselves, Morgan wasn't sure. *I guess time will tell.*

As they entered the lobby, they immediately noticed the hi-tech features. It was obvious that the fancy hotel catered to fast-paced, business patrons.

There were flat screen monitors strategically placed around the lobby. A couple of screens displayed the ticker tapes of the world's financial markets—Wall Street, Tokyo, and London stock exchanges, as well as many smaller ones. Financial news played continuously on other screens.

The lobby was bustling with men and women dressed smartly. Others were involved in deep discussions in the upscale coffee shop.

"Wow!" Tammy said. "I've never seen anything like this. I feel out of place."

"So do I!" Morgan dramatically rolled his eyes. "I see millions of dollars passing by us."

The American couple tried to look inconspicuous, hopefully lost in the craziness of the crowd.

"Remind me, how did we get into this mess?" Tammy mumbled.

Just then, something caught Morgan's attention. He nudged Tammy's arm and nodded in the direction of the bar off the lobby. "Isn't that Todd Spencer?"

The well-known Hollywood actor was having a drink with a beautiful woman. Next to them were two huge men, obviously his bodyguards. They glared at Morgan and Tammy as they walked by, their eyes never leaving them. It made the doctors feel more uncomfortable.

"I feel like a fish out of water," Morgan grumbled as they reached the elevator.

When the door opened an unknown man darted between them as he exited. "Excuse me." The young man had a strong accent. He looked directly at Tammy, smiling, and spoke in Italian, *Buongiorno*.

She returned a weak smile, trying not to let her nervousness show.

They stepped into the elevator. As soon as the door closed, Tammy asked her husband, "What did that guy say?"

One of the bellhops pushed the button for the twelfth floor, and replied, "He said, good morning."

"He seemed to be very happy," Morgan replied.

"He should be! That was Giovanni Bonucci, the Italian soccer star. He just signed a one hundred million dollar contract to play soccer.

"You're kidding! One hundred million dollars to play a game!" Tammy shook her head in disbelief.

The bellhop nodded in agreement without further comment.

"This sure is a ritzy establishment. Are you sure we're in the right place?" Morgan inquired.

"Yes, Sir. If you are Doctors Morgan and Tammy Hamilton, from Saint Paul, Minnesota, you're in the right place. A little overwhelming, isn't it?"

"To say the least," Tammy agreed.

"Put yourself in our shoes. We put up with this every day." The man chuckled cynically.

"Don't we have to check in?" Morgan eyed the bellhop.

"All arrangements have been taken care of."

"So, do the rich and famous leave big tips?" Tammy asked.

"Some do. Bonucci did. He seems to be a good man. I hope success doesn't destroy him. We had C.J. Terry here a couple weeks ago."

"The American rap star?" Morgan raised a questioning brow.

"Yes, he was in town for a concert. He and his entourage had the entire twelfth floor. He didn't tip well."

The elevator door opened.

They walked a short distance and one of the men unlocked the door to a large suite. "This is your suite, the same one C.J. was in. Many famous people have walked through this door."

"Wow! Are you sure this is our room?" Morgan asked, glancing around.

"Yes, Sir. Enjoy your stay. Anything you need, just call the front desk." They placed the luggage on its stand and turned to leave.

Tammy cleared her throat to get Morgan's attention.

Understanding her signal, he reached into his pocket and grabbed some bills. "Can you take American money?"

One of the bellhops replied, smiling. "We can, but we've already been tipped extremely well."

They stepped into the hallway. "Like I said, anything you need, call the front desk. Ask for Antonio or John. Have a great stay."

The door closed and the Hamiltons toured their magnificent suite.

"This is nicer than our home," Tammy said.

"This is nicer than *anyone's* home," Morgan joked.

The ringing of the phone jarred them.

Morgan answered. "Hello."

"Dr. Hamilton, this is the front desk. Will you be using room service, or will you be dining out?"

"I think we'll probably eat out. Any suggestions?"

"Only one. The revolving restaurant on top of the hotel is the best in town."

"Did you say revolving?"

"Yes, Sir. And the food is outstanding."

"Then upstairs it is. How about six?"

"That's perfect, right before sunset. The Sacred Rock is beautiful that time of evening."

"Sacred Rock? What's that?" Morgan asked.

"It's one of the most famous landmarks in the world, better known as Acropolis Hill. Built in honor of the Greek goddess Athena. At sunset, the lights are on. It's a sight you have to see to believe. You must visit it during your stay."

"We'll try. You certainly piqued my curiosity," Morgan responded truthfully.

"Have a good day, Sir."

Morgan hung up the phone, staring at Tammy.

"What's the matter?" she asked.

"I don't know. This is all overwhelming. What's this all about?"

"I don't know either, but I do know I'm hungry. You can only eat so much airplane food. I'm ready for a real meal." She patted her stomach.

"That's probably the reason the airlines give you so little to eat," Morgan said trying to get Tammy to loosen up.

She smiled slightly.

"Let's go have an enjoyable meal," he said, grabbing his key card.

The dining room was on the twenty-first floor, overlooking the city. As night fell, the couple was mesmerized by the sparkling lights silhouetting the ancient Greek buildings in the distance.

When the couple read the menu, their expressions told the story. "Morgan, did you see the prices of these meals?"

"I did. This is definitely a swank place."

"Maybe we should look for a less expensive restaurant," Tammy said.

"Remember, we were given ten thousand dollars to get here. So far, we haven't spent a dime."

"I was thinking that was more for compensation for missing work. I don't want to be here. I was making progress in the lab." Tammy realized how self-centered she sounded, but didn't change her tone.

"Maybe that's why we're here. Leontiou may have heard about your lab work, and wants to know more about it."

"How could he know?"

Before Morgan could answer, the waiter appeared at their table. "Mr. and Mrs. Hamilton, welcome to my country. Anything on the menu is yours. It's been paid in full."

"You're kidding! Did Dr. Leontiou pay for it?" Morgan leaned forward, clasping his hands together.

"Yes, Sir, I would assume so. After all, he owns this hotel, so he can do most anything he wants."

Morgan raised an eyebrow. "He *owns* this hotel? I thought he was a doctor."

"He is, Sir, among many other things. And he controls a large empire, employing thousands of people."

Tammy stared at the waiter. "Empire? What do you mean by *empire*?"

Before the waiter could answer, the conversation was interrupted by Lance Laskari, the young man who brought the mysterious packets of information to their clinic only days before.

"So glad you made it." He nodded for the waiter to leave, and spoke to him in Greek.

"Your waiter will return in a minute for your order. I'm sorry about all of the secrecy around this trip. My employer—"

"Dr. Leontiou," Tammy interrupted.

"Yes, Dr. Leontiou, is a very important man. He's also a fair and honest man. He needs your help. He's putting a lot of trust in you."

"Why are we here?" Tammy demanded.

"Tomorrow morning, I'll pick you up in a limo and take you to the airport. From there, we'll travel by helicopter to his island, where you'll get your answers. Until then, please enjoy your stay. If you ask at the front desk, a driver will take you to the Acropolis. The beauty and history there are beyond your wildest imagination."

Tammy eyed her husband to see his reaction, but couldn't read him.

Lance continued, "Everything you do here is paid in full, but please don't ask questions. All of these people are employed by Dr. Leontiou, but none of them knows what's going on. Furthermore, if the press finds out, there's no telling what will happen. Please just enjoy your meal and the hospitality of my country. You'll have your answers tomorrow."

"I thought we were going to talk to a lawyer?" Morgan interjected.

"We are, but we've changed the plan. Barrows will be meeting with you on the island. It's a safer location."

Morgan didn't like the sound of that. "Safer? What do you mean safer?"

"Please, Dr. Hamilton. I know you're curious, but you'll get answers soon enough. I'm only the liaison between you and the Leontiou's lawyers."

Morgan nodded his head, agreeing, but not understanding. One thing was certain—they weren't going to get any more information until they met with the attorneys.

"Oh, there's something else." Lance bent over, whispering, "I'm blocking your view, but there is a couple in the corner by the mirror. Don't look at them if you can help it. They're reporters. If they should venture over, please don't reveal anything about your trip. They're bad news, if you'll pardon the pun. Understand?"

The couple nodded halfheartedly, still too confused to know what they were agreeing to.

"Good. They may come over and talk to you. Just tell them you are on... how do you say it? Vacation, I believe. I will meet you at nine in the morning, in the lobby."

Laskari took a couple steps, and then had an afterthought. "Oh, one more thing, Dr. Hamilton. During your stay, would you like to play a set of tennis?"

Morgan's eyes gleamed. "With the great Laskari? I would *love* to."

"I don't think you can call me great, but I do enjoy the sport. The sound, the feel of the ball hitting the racquet, you never get out of your blood." For a minute, the former tennis great was consumed in thought, perhaps of what once was, or maybe by what could have been.

"Mr. Laskari?" Morgan interrupted his thoughts. "That ball was out!"

"Excuse me?"

"The judge's call was wrong, when you lost that second set in the Olympics. I watched that game, and the ball was clearly out. That should have been your set point!"

He smiled. "Well, that's water under the bridge now. I believe it cost me the match, but looking back, it was just a game. In some ways, it seemed like a lifetime ago."

"I hear you. See you in the morning. Oh, and Mr. Laskari—"

"Please, call me Lance."

"Lance. Will we be able to see Skye?"

Laskari grinned. "She's looking forward to that more than anything. She has told me about her adventures with you. She's very fond of both of you. Now, enjoy your dinner. Oh, another thing, Skye's right."

"What's that?"

"Doctors are not hunks," he chuckled.

"Oh, great! I'll never live that down."

During the meal, Morgan eyed the couple that Lance had warned them about. It was obvious he and Tammy were being watched. He hoped he had not aroused suspicion. The whole situation made him queasy.

Tammy seemed uninterested in the couple. Her thoughts were still at her clinic in Saint Paul.

After they finished the main course, the waiter left to get their dessert and coffee.

The couple who'd been watching them saw it as their opportunity. They sauntered over to the Hamiltons.

They appeared to be around thirty. Dressed in business attire, they seemed to fit in well with the clientele of the establishment.

With a stern face, and not even a hint of a smile, the young man began what seemed to be a well-rehearsed speech. "Dr. Hamilton, my name is Markus Klitou. This is Anna Klitou. We're free-lance reporters and have written major stories in top newspapers throughout the world. We know who you are, but we don't know why you're here. Could you shed some light on the subject?"

Morgan shook the man's hand, uncertain how to respond. Even *he* didn't know why he was there.

"I notice you both have the same last name," he said. "Are you husband and wife?"

"Very good, Dr. Hamilton. I can see you're observant, I also can tell you're trying to change the subject."

Morgan fixed him with a glare. "Right."

He took a sip of water, trying to appear calm. "I'm sorry, I don't want to seem rude, but I'm not interested in talking to a reporter. Furthermore, I see no reason to tell you anything about my private life. So, if you would excuse me, I'd like to finish dinner with my wife."

Not budging, the arrogant reporter pushed further. "I understand your position, Dr. Hamilton, but I don't think you know the gravity of the situation. It's rumored that the Leontious and their daughter were killed in an accident several weeks ago. However, nobody can substantiate this rumor. I believe we have a major cover-up."

Tammy gasped.

The reporter noticed their stunned faces. "I see. It's obvious that you've been left in the dark as well. May we join you for coffee?"

"Mr. Klitou, again, I don't want to be rude. But we're here in this nice restaurant enjoying a fine meal. The *last* thing I want to do is talk to a reporter about something I know nothing about."

"I understand, Dr. Hamilton, but as reporters it's our job to get the facts. We already are aware of some things. I know that Laskari, the former tennis pro, is Layland Leontiou's right-hand man. Leontiou has not been heard from or seen in almost three months. He seems to have locked himself on that island of his, which no one can get on or off without permission. Something is wrong and it's my job... *our* job..." he glanced at his wife, "...to find out what's going on. Leontiou is a powerful man in my country. If anything were to happen to him and his wife, this country could collapse. He owns many properties, including this hotel. If he's dead, the world needs to know. The stockholders need to know. *You* need to know."

All was quiet when the waiter returned.

"I can't give you information that I don't have," Morgan said. "But, I'm curious about something. If what you say is true, and this country of yours will collapse if Leontiou is dead, why would you want to break such news to the world?"

Klitou's eyes were coldly intense. "My job is to report the news, not to *create* it."

"I disagree with you," Morgan said. "I don't deal in politics, but I believe the problems of every country are politically motivated. Most newspapers are biased. They either lean toward the left, or the right. They're not interested in the true news. They are interested in 'their' news. In other words, only the news that fits their beliefs, or supports their agenda. My wife and I are interested in one thing. Saving lives. Now, Mr. Klitou, if you would excuse us, we'd like to have our dessert."

Markus glanced at the German chocolate cake and ice cream. "Very well."

He handed a business card to Morgan. "When you find out what's going on, please give me a call. I only want the truth. Enjoy your dessert."

Morgan reached for the card reluctantly and watched the couple leave.

"Wow!" Tammy exclaimed. "I thought you were going to knock him for a loop."

"I'm sorry, but he irritated me. He was obnoxious! What person in his right mind would chase after a story that could collapse the economy of his country, or turn it into a possible war zone?"

"Okay," Tammy blurted. "You've got my interest. What in the world is going on?"

Morgan stared at the card. "I don't know, but I do know one thing."

"What's that?"

"They said they believed Skye was dead, yet Lance said she couldn't wait to see us. Somebody is not telling the truth!"

It was quiet as they ate their dessert. Each was wondering about the future. About Skye.

"Okay." Morgan stated, wiping his mouth with his napkin. "I'm going to bed right now, so I can get up in the morning and see what this is all about. Are you with me?"

She looked at the last bite of cake on her plate and then at Morgan. She stood, placing her napkin on the table. "Yes. Let's get to bed. I'm tired after that long trip. Tomorrow will come quicker if we get some shut-eye."

Chapter Seventeen

Just like clockwork, Lance Laskari met the couple in the lobby the next morning. "Good morning, doctors. I trust you slept well?"

"Most comfortable room I've ever had." Morgan responded honestly.

"Yes, Layland did everything first class."

"Is he dead?" Morgan crossed his arms, his lips in a straight line, waiting for a response.

Lance rubbed behind his ear, avoiding the question.

Morgan wasn't going to back down. "Is Dr. Leontiou dead? You used past tense when you mentioned him."

The young man was startled by Morgan's boldness, but wasn't deterred. "I understand your frustration. All of your questions will be answered in about an hour. Now, please come with me. The limo is waiting to take us to the airport where a helicopter will deliver us to the island."

Laskari headed to the front door of the hotel.

Morgan looked at Tammy who was holding Skye's gift. She shot him a questioning look, and then looped her arm through his. Together, they followed the man they knew little about, to a situation they knew nothing about.

As they walked, a barrage of questions flooded their minds. *Where on earth are we going? Could Dr. Leontiou really be dead? Will we see Skye? What have we gotten ourselves into? And, most importantly, why have they chosen us?*

Morgan noticed the reporters who'd confronted them the night before, standing by a window, watching them. He shot them a piercing glare.

The three climbed into the limo.

Morgan watched the reporters sprint to a car and jump in. Sure enough, the vehicle spun around and followed them.

Laskari sat directly across from the Hamiltons in the limo. Noticing how jittery they were, he attempted to put their minds at ease. "Yes, I know they're following us. They're persistent, sort of like cockroaches. Don't worry, they can't get on the island. It's well protected. Only people

106

who live and work there are permitted on the island, unless they have my permission."

"Your permission?"

"Yes, that's a significant part of my job."

Morgan didn't hesitate. "What exactly is your job, Mr. Laskari?"

"Dr. Hamilton, I hear frustration in your voice."

"Go figure!" Morgan glanced out the back window. The Klitous were following close behind. "I understand that you're Dr. Leontiou's right-hand man."

Lance uttered a short laugh. "I see you've been talking to Markus."

Morgan scowled. "He came to our table last night, and told us some interesting things."

Laskari rolled his eyes. "I'll bet he did. He and his wife are very good reporters. Sometimes *too* good. Unfortunately, they're on the wrong side, politically. They're extremely liberal. They don't know how capitalism works, and they have no understanding of the chaos that will ensue if they wreck the free market economy."

"Is what they said true?"

Laskari shrugged. "I don't know. What did they tell you?"

"They said the Leontious were killed in an accident, and everything is a big cover-up. They also said Skye was killed. Is any of that true?"

"Sounds like you got an earful from Markus and his wife after I left. As head of security for Leontiou Enterprises, I guess I should have had them kicked out. They only ordered water." He chuckled sarcastically.

Morgan's tone turned more hostile. "Oh, come on. Just answer the question."

"You seem to be really angry today."

Morgan's voice grew louder. "Now, why *wouldn't* I be? The last couple months, I tried to contact Leontiou a number of times and never got a response. Suddenly, a strange man showed up in my office with two first-class round trip tickets to Athens, Greece, and ten thousand dollars. We arrive here and are given the royal treatment in an upscale hotel. Then we're questioned by two reporters who apparently have an agenda of bringing this country down. Put that together with all the other secrets, it's like something out of a spy novel, and Tammy and I are the main characters."

Laskari shook his head. "There may be some truth to that, but I assure you both, you'll be safe here."

Tammy put her hand on her husband's arm in an attempt to calm him.

He took a deep breath and leaned back in the seat. It was obvious he was not going to get answers, not here, not now.

Arriving at the airport, a guard allowed them passage through a private gate.

Morgan glanced over his shoulder in time to see Markus slam his fist into the steering wheel in a fit of rage when the gate closed.

They quickly boarded a helicopter, which bore the emblem of Leontiou Enterprises.

Within minutes, the chopper lifted.

Morgan noticed the Klitous below, standing by their vehicle watching the chopper disappear from view.

Tammy spoke first. "Mr. Laskari?"

"Let's not be so formal. Please call me Lance."

"Okay, Lance, skiing ended your career as a tennis player?"

"Yes. Only three months after the summer Olympics, I went skiing with my wife. The first day, I misjudged a sharp turn and hit a tree. I was unconscious for two days. When I woke up, besides a serious concussion, I'd dislocated my shoulder, and shattered my leg. After four surgeries, I finally walk without a limp. I can even play a limited amount of tennis, but I still have to be careful of twists and turns."

"You can never play professionally again?"

"No. Those days are over." He hung his head, the disappointment of the injury still evident in his demeanor.

"What happened after your surgery?" Morgan added.

"You mean with my life?"

"Yes. I had read about the accident, but then I heard nothing afterward."

"I took a job as a television tennis broadcaster, which lasted only six months. That's when Layland Leontiou stopped by, and offered me a job. I had never met the man, but I'd heard about him. Who hadn't? Many thought he would be the leader of Greece one day."

"Is he dead?" Tammy asked boldly.

"You sure are insistent! You know I can't answer that. You'll find out what's going on quick enough. If you look out the window you'll see 'Kardia'—Dr. Leontiou's island."

The young couple turned their gaze to the lush green island in the distance.

The helicopter made a deliberate circle of the entire island for the Hamiltons to get a clear view of the beautiful landscape.

"Wow, look at those cliffs!" Tammy gasped.

"Almost the entire island is surrounded by cliffs." Lance pointed to a large structure. "That big complex in the center is the clinic."

"Looks like a prison." Tammy swallowed hard.

"Actually, at one time it was. Part of that building was built by the Romans two thousand years ago. It was used to exile Caesar's political prisoners. The main section was built in the seventeenth century and used by Greece until the 1930s. That's when the Nazi's took over, using it for captured English and American soldiers, and political enemies. It's really almost impossible for anyone unauthorized to get on or off the island, much like your Alcatraz. It's rumored that John was kept here while he was imprisoned."

"John?" Morgan and Tammy asked simultaneously.

"Yeah, John from the Bible, but there's no way it can be substantiated."

"Wow!" Tammy felt her heart rate pick up.

"How many people live on the island?" Morgan asked.

"There are about four hundred and fifty. That includes staff and their families, as well as patients and their family members. We have everything—shops and restaurants. There is even a movie theater, school, and bowling alley. Only a few vehicles are permitted on the island. Most people drive bicycles, motor scooters, or golf carts. The residents have all the conveniences of home. For all practical purposes, it *is* their home."

"That's incredible!" Morgan took a deep, calming breath.

"It became too costly for Greece to run as a prison, so Leontiou bought the island thirty years ago. He was going to tear down the prison, but his plans changed. About eight years ago, he remodeled the old building, and turned it into a medical clinic. That's when he moved his family to the island."

The Hamiltons were fascinated with the history, but their faces displayed concern over what would happen when they got off the chopper.

"There!" Laskari pointed to a large house overlooking the south side of the island, facing a beach cove. "At the end of the island, you can see his mansion."

"Nice place, but not what I would expect for a man with his kind of money. Does he own other homes around the world?" Morgan inquired.

"Layland? Oh no! He was a down to earth individual, never putting himself above anyone else."

"There you go again, saying his name in the past tense."

"Sorry. Just the way I talk."

Tammy chimed in, "How did the doctor make his fortune?"

"Computer software, inventions, shipping, oil, pharmaceuticals, even the fishing industry."

Morgan continued to scan the island. "It looks like the only way to get on the island is that area where his house is located."

"Yes. It's the only way to get on the island by boat. Most people come by helicopter. I guess you could always scale the cliffs." He snickered. "Layland built the home for his wife and daughter. That's why they have the large sandy beach."

"Where do you get your drinking water?"

"We have our own distillation plant that turns the salt water into fresh water. Leontiou created the system for the island and ended up selling hundreds of the treatment plants to other countries. Many military and cruise ships also had them installed."

"Impressive! Sounds like the man is a genius." Morgan sat back in the seat, putting his arm around Tammy.

"What do you know about Skye?" Tammy asked.

"Know about her? What do you mean?"

"Is she okay?"

"Dr. Hamilton, Skye is excited and waiting to see you. She has done nothing but talk about both of you. You know Skye. Once she gets going, nothing will stop her! She's one exceptional young lady."

Tammy and Morgan breathed a sigh of relief. After all, that was the most important thing. Skye was okay!

The helicopter began its descent into a courtyard and set down next to another chopper.

They climbed out of the large chopper and were escorted by two armed guards into the building.

Morgan immediately noticed the scent of freshly mown grass. The building was surrounded by wide walkways, and colorful, fragrant gardens. Flowering shrubs accented the thick plush lawns, and huge trees dotted the landscape.

Glancing around, he stated, "Beautiful place, but what's with the armed guards? I thought nobody could get on or off this island."

"We've always had some security here. Reporters are always trying to get on the island, to see what's happening. The tabloids refer to this island as, 'The Island of Dr. Moreau.'"

"The old sci-fi story about the mad scientist who does weird experiments?" Morgan asked.

"Right. The press knows about all the medical equipment the doctor has brought over through the years. They want to know what it's for."

Walking up the sidewalk to the clinic entrance, they continued their conversation.

"Why would they question medical equipment for a clinic? That's a normal thing," Tammy queried.

"It's the type of medical equipment."

"Like?"

"In time, doctor. In time."

They were escorted into a spacious office with a large, mahogany table in the center.

Lance motioned for them to be seated at the table. "Good morning, Victoria." He greeted a woman warmly.

"Good morning, Sir. Everything is ready."

"Great! Thank you. This is Victoria, Dr. Leontiou's private secretary."

The Hamiltons stood to shake hands with the attractive woman who appeared to be in her fifties.

"She was Layland's first employee," Lance added.

"Would you like some coffee or tea? We also have sweet rolls if you'd like." Victoria turned toward them and a smile tipped her lips.

"I'll take some coffee, and my wife loves tea."

"I'll get it right away. I'll tell Mr. Barrows that you're here."

"Thank you," Lance said, sitting next to Morgan.

Morgan glanced around the room, studying the décor. It was nothing elaborate; in fact, it almost looked like a school office. There were a dozen or so paintings of children on the wall. Morgan began reading the captions. Some had a girl's name, or a place. Others had numbers printed on them, which appeared to be dates.

Two men and an older woman entered the room. "Good morning, everyone. You must be the Hamiltons. I'm glad you could make it."

The older man extended his hand to Morgan, then Tammy. "My name is Alton Barrows. This is my son Arlen, and my secretary, Leah."

After a brief nod, Leah sat down and opened the lawyer's briefcase. She separated a number of folders and stacked them neatly on the table while Arlen shook hands with the Hamiltons.

Alton got straight to the point. "I know you're wondering what's going on, so let's get started."

He apparently didn't like idle chit-chat, which pleased the Hamiltons who only wanted answers, and quick.

Victoria stepped in with coffee, tea, and pastries arranged tastefully on a silver platter.

As she poured the beverages, Alton began his story. "Let me begin by telling you that I've been with Layland Leontiou since the beginning of his career. I have always been his personal lawyer, and friend. When I heard the news, I was shocked and deeply saddened."

"Sir, please just tell us what this is all about." Morgan was ready for the mystery to be solved. After all, they knew nothing more than they did the day Lance mysteriously arrived at their clinic. They'd certainly been patient.

"On October third of this year, Doctors Layland and Malinda Leontiou were killed in a fire here at the hospital."

Morgan's face clouded over with concern. "Killed? A fire? We haven't heard anything about it. Why wasn't it in the newspapers or on TV?"

"Security! Dr. Hamilton, my country is in major turmoil. If it was released that one of the richest, most powerful men in Greece was dead, it would turn my country upside down. It could even crash the economy. You'll learn soon exactly who Layland was. Eight years ago, and even still today, he was considered by many to be the future leader of Greece. But unknown circumstances occurred, which changed his perspective on life. The fact is only the people in this room and a handful of outsiders know the reason."

"Will you please get on with it? We want to know why we're here. And we want to know if Skye is all right." Tammy said sharply.

"Skye is fine," Barrows said. "I talked with her this morning. She's looking forward to seeing you."

"Was she hurt in the accident?" Morgan asked.

"In a way, yes. You'll learn all about that when the time comes. Please let me finish. Leah, go ahead and pass out the notebooks."

The woman placed a large, black binder in front of each person at the table.

"Would you like more coffee or tea?" Lance asked.

"No, thank you. We don't want to appear rude, but please tell us what we want to know," Morgan stated emphatically, annoyed by the interruption.

Arlen gave Lance a frustrated glance, but the former tennis star gave no acknowledgment.

"Go ahead and open the notebook," Barrows instructed.

On the front page were the words in English—"Last Will and Testament of Layland Leontiou."

Morgan and Tammy stilled, letting the truth settle.

Barrows added sugar to his coffee and took a sip. "Normally in a will everything would be left to the spouse. Mrs. Leontiou was also killed, which means that everything Layland owned would go to his children. In this case, they only have one daughter—Skye."

He continued, "We've managed to keep his death hush-hush until we could meet with you. When the rest of his family learns that he's dead, there will be court battles throughout the world. To further complicate things, Layland was previously married to an Italian model. There were no children from that union. She and her family would like to do nothing more than try to take everything he has, or should I say *had*. That would tie everything up in the courts for years."

The attorney looked directly into Morgan's eyes. "Skye's future depends on what you decide."

Tammy stood. "Where is she? I want to see her."

Morgan grabbed her arm, trying to calm her down. "Tammy," he pleaded. "Please sit down and listen to what Mr. Barrows has to say."

Reluctantly, she did what he asked.

"As I was saying, his ex-wife, as well as his brothers and sisters, will go after Leontiou's empire and try to dismantle it. Layland cautioned me about that. He said it was essential that does not happen."

Morgan didn't hesitate. "You said they died October third. That was the day I was talking to Skye on the computer."

Barrows looked at Lance, confused. Obviously, he hadn't heard about Skye contacting Morgan.

"Yes, it was," Lance agreed.

"I noticed the date of death is blank on the will. Why?" Morgan persisted.

"Dr. Hamilton, for all purposes, Layland Leontiou is still alive. On paper, at least. If it's leaked that he's dead before we have everything in place, the courts will take over."

Morgan felt his anger rising. "You're joking! Isn't that against the law?"

"We are walking a thin line," Lance replied. "Much is at stake."

Morgan jabbed a finger toward Barrows. "Don't give me that. It's against the law. You're a lawyer; you should know that more than anyone."

"Dr. Hamilton, please listen to me," Lance said. "There's a reason for doing what we've done. Many lives are in jeopardy. Even Skye's."

"Just cut to the chase," Morgan said. "What do you want from us?"

Lance nodded for Barrows to proceed.

"I have all the documents for you, Morgan and Tammy, to adopt Skye, and care for her for the rest of her life. I understand that you can't have children of your own. This is your opportunity to adopt Skye Leontiou, making her your daughter. At the same time, you would protect the Leontious' dream, using their money in the medical world to find cures and keep this island, this clinic, forging ahead."

Barrows glanced at the Hamiltons. "Frankly, when Layland's family learns of his death, they'll shut this island down, and this clinic will cease to exist. All the work he and his wife have done will be lost, and the hope for the children here will end."

Tammy sat up straighter, crossed her arms, unable to respond.

Morgan inhaled, taking a deep, calming breath.

Tammy jumped up. "How dare you bring our personal life into this! Morgan I want to leave now." Her tone was sharp.

Morgan stood, and gently put his arm around her. "Honey, let's see what they have to say. We can do that much. After all, we've come this far."

Tammy sat back down, trying to focus on what the attorney was offering. Her heart was beating loud and fast.

"Okay. Mr. Barrows, you have our interest. What's this all about?" Morgan sounded calmer, more rational.

Barrows continued, "If you agree to the terms, you'll be in charge of the Leontiou estate."

"You're joking, right?" Tammy shot back.

The lawyer didn't respond to her comment. "There is one major requirement."

Morgan's tone was cynical. "We're all ears."

"Layland has entrusted you not only with his prized possession, his daughter, but also with this clinic that he loved. He wants the two of you to take over the clinic, and run it as you see fit. Everything he owns will be at your disposal. If something were to happen to Skye, you would have to agree to stay on to continue Layland's chief goal in life—keeping this clinic running and searching for a cure."

Tammy looked at Morgan and then back at the lawyer. "I don't understand."

Lance stepped in, looking concerned. "Morgan, Tammy, Mr. Barrows is telling you the legal side. Let me tell you the human side. This room that we're sitting in is the conference room for Leontiou's clinic. This complex has the newest medical technology money can buy. We have the most brilliant minds in the world working here. They're tied in with clinics all over the world. This clinic's sole purpose is to find a cure for Batten disease. Nothing more! Girls from all over the world come here with the hope of finding a cure for the debilitating disease. Perhaps other cures will come from our clinic. Last year Malinda and her staff discovered a cure for a rare virus, which literally saved an entire village in Africa. There have been many other great discoveries that you've never heard of."

Morgan's head was spinning.

"This island houses the patient's entire family. Many family members even have jobs here. Layland employed all of them, so they could spend as much time with their child as possible. You see, they know they only have a limited time until the inevitable happens, and their child dies."

Tammy felt her stomach tighten.

Lance searched for a way to sum it up. "Tammy, I was not at the convention on the ship, but I heard about your speech. You said that one of the most important aspects in a doctor's treatment is dealing with the child's parents. They're hurting, suffering terribly. Dr. Leontiou took that extra step. There are twenty-three girls here, all suffering from Batten. All knowing they have a couple years, maybe only months, or days, to live. Here they have the best care in the world, and their parents can be by their side twenty-four hours a day. They work, sleep, eat, and live life to the fullest on this island. All thanks to the generosity of Dr. Leontiou!"

Morgan tapped his fingers on the table. "You're saying this is totally funded by Dr. Leontiou? Everything here? This entire island?"

Lance responded with a nod.

Morgan reached for his wife's hand. "You're also telling me, if we don't adopt Skye and take over this facility, Leontiou's family will shut it all down, and send every one of these patients packing?"

"That's it in a nut-shell, doctor. It not only can happen, but *will* happen. Everything he has accomplished will be wasted. He has entrusted, and I don't use that word lightly, entrusted both of you to continue his work that he was so passionate about. He had that much faith in you." Lance paused, giving the couple time to absorb what he was asking of them.

Morgan put his arm around Tammy who was weeping softly.

"I'm sure you're wondering why you were chosen. Layland and Skye had an open, mature relationship. He asked her who she would want to be her parents in the event something happened to him and Malinda. Skye chose you two, with no hesitation whatsoever. In addition, Tammy, you're the most qualified person to continue Malinda's work. You two women are a lot alike."

Morgan continued to hold his wife as she cried. It had been a long time since he'd seen her display so much emotion. She'd turned off her emotions, becoming complacent, lost in her work. Her sorrow from not having her own child had turned into disappointment, then bitterness. Her heart had turned cold, distant.

After a few minutes, Morgan spoke. "What do you want from us?"

Lance put his elbows on the table, looking directly into Morgan's eyes. His sternness left no doubt about the enormity of the decision. "Once you sign these papers, you have adopted Skye. You will take over the responsibilities here at the clinic. You will live and work here on the island. Everything you want will be at your disposal for as long as you live."

Barrows reinforced, "Your jobs for the rest of your lives will be to take care of Skye and run this clinic. Mr. Laskari will take care of the business end of things."

Morgan couldn't believe what he was hearing. "What about our clinic in the United States?"

Without hesitation, Lance answered, "You can run your clinic in Saint Paul from here. Make the staff part of your medical team. With today's technology you can talk face-to-face with your teams in the United States, or anywhere else in the world. Layland's dream was to link every reliable laboratory and clinic in the world to one major network, so all breakthroughs would be available immediately. The quicker a cure is found, the more lives can be saved. It will no longer be a money thing, but it will be an answer for the suffering children."

"Why can't we operate this place from Saint Paul?" Morgan asked.

"That's an option, but Skye's home is here. This is what she knows. What she loves."

Barrows sounded confused. "Frankly, I'm surprised that you're hesitating. Most people in your position would jump at this opportunity."

Morgan gave him a reproving glance. "We haven't had a chance to process any of this. It's all happening too fast. We need time to think about it."

The lawyer's voice dropped. "You can think about it, but as I said, not too long. This will become worldwide news soon, and then we won't have any control over it. As it is, we may not be able to prevent this from getting tied up in the courts. Understand this, if the court gets involved, Skye could end up in a state home, and the Leontiou estate tied up in the legal system for years. This clinic would no longer have the assets to operate. And yes, everyone here could end up in prison. Yet all we're trying to do is save the lives of children. We didn't ask for this either. We're only doing what we think is necessary to keep the clinic going. It costs about fifty million dollars a year to operate Kardia."

"Fifty million a year?" Morgan drew a deep breath.

Lance asserted, "Layland employs the entire family of each child here. The doctors, medical equipment, and experiments, cost tens of millions of dollars. This island has its own power and water supply. These things are not cheap. The doctor has spared no expense. At the same time, he continued his ambitious interests in the business world."

Morgan glanced at Tammy, who was finally gaining her composure. "May we see Skye now?" Her eyes lit up.

"By all means, she's waiting for you," Lance answered swiftly.

Lance and the attorney shook hands. "Alton, thank you for your time."

"Don't wait too long! The piranhas are biting at our feet. We can't hold out much longer. They'll find out the truth. We're already getting phone calls from Layland's family, wondering where he is, why they haven't heard from him."

"I know. Let the Hamiltons visit with Skye, and I'll show them around the clinic—that may pique their interest."

"I'll be back next Monday. At that time plan B will go in effect, or we may spend the next fifty years in a Greek prison."

"May I ask what plan B is?" Morgan wove his fingers through his hair.

"Plan B is that my wife and I would adopt Skye," Lance answered calmly.

"Why will that not work?" Morgan cast the former tennis star a questioning look.

"The whole point is to give Skye what she wants, and to keep this clinic going. I don't have the expertise to operate a clinic. We need a good scientific doctor, and an excellent administrator. It sounds like you two would be perfect! You may not know it, but Layland considered you the best in the world. Will you please spend a few days, a week here, and see how things go? If need be, we can make changes. This can be your baby."

Morgan thought for a second. "A week? Well, our plane doesn't leave until next Tuesday. That should give us ample time to decide."

"We can live with that. I need to tell you that only a select number of people on the island know the truth, so please don't mention his death to anyone." Lance was adamant.

He turned to his wife who still didn't know what to make of the latest developments. "Is that okay, Honey?"

Dabbing her eyes with a tissue, she forced a nod. She was unable to speak, overwhelmed by all she'd heard.

Chapter Eighteen

Lance escorted the Hamiltons down the halls of the clinic, introducing them to several members of the staff.

"Everyone sure is friendly," Tammy whispered to Morgan. "And they seem to work so well together! I don't sense any strife. Matter of fact, it sort of seems like they're one big, happy family."

Morgan understood, because he felt it too. There was no obvious tension among the staff.

Tammy loved the way the clinic was designed around a spacious courtyard. "Where does this corridor lead?"

"It brings you right back here," Lance replied readily. "Basically, it's a giant square. Around the inside of the square are the patients' rooms. Most of the rooms on the outside are offices, as well as the medical facilities and dining room. As you can see, the courtyard is right dab in the middle." He gestured down the hall. "At least, you can never get lost in it."

"It's so clean and modern." Tammy was obviously impressed with the facilities. "And the children seem content, even happy. Are all these girls suffering from Batten?"

"Yes, and many of their parents work here in the clinic. Others work elsewhere on the island. We have one couple who has two daughters with Batten."

"How sad! Do the children live here, or with their parents?"

"A little of both. Some of the children live in their own homes on the island. Others, especially when they're bedridden, live in special rooms here at the clinic. The rooms have separate bedrooms and bathrooms for the parents, siblings, and patient. They're near the medical facilities, and a doctor is here at all times. That way, family will be with them when the end comes."

"That's great," Morgan added.

"Yes. As a doctor, you know how important it is for both the parents and the child. Just knowing their parents are close means a lot."

Stopping at a room with a closed door, Lance looked in briefly. Then he stepped back, so Morgan and Tammy could peek through the window.

They noticed an elderly woman in a wheelchair. Skye was sitting on the edge of the bed chatting with her.

"Skye! Can we see her?" Tammy asked excitedly.

Lance held his hand, palm out, to quiet her. "I believe she had her check-up this morning. Skye has had the flu, so we've been keeping a close eye on her. Usually, by this time of the day, she's trekked all over this island. I'll be right back."

He opened the door and said something to the young girl. Skye looked at the window and a huge smile encompassed her face. Adorable, in a bright-pink short outfit, she looked as cute as they remembered. Seeing her instantly lifted their spirits. She jumped off the bed and ran to Morgan and Tammy.

Morgan thought it strange that the elderly woman never looked up as Lance wheeled her out another door.

Skye bounded into Tammy's arms. "I've missed you so much," she shrieked.

Morgan continued watching Lance push the wheelchair to a room at the end of the hallway. The elderly woman opened the door and wheeled herself in. As the door closed, Morgan couldn't help but wonder what the disabled woman's story was.

Lance joined the Hamilton's reunion with the child.

Skye hugged Morgan. He knelt to her eye-level. "How are you feeling?"

"Oh, I'm getting better. Dr. Rozak said it was the influenza. I never got my Swine Flu vaccine. Oink, oink! Now that you're here, I'm sooooo excited. Dad, 'member when Jessie kept jumping up trying to get our attention," she replied in her perky voice.

"How could I ever forget that?"

"What was she thinking?" Skye cocked her head.

"I think she knew she was going to miss you."

"Yeah, she did, didn't she? You think she misses me now?"

"I'm sure she does. Remember, dolphins have brains similar to humans. I think she has emotions. I do know they're always smiling."

"Yes, they do always smile. I wish people would do that," Skye added honestly, but not critically.

Tammy took a step back and brushed the hair off the girl's face. "Honey, how are you holding up? I know you must miss your parents very much."

There was sadness in the child's eyes as her gaze tracked towards the floor. "I... I have a lot of friends here. They help keep my mind off that."

"Yes, but they can't take the place of your parents," Morgan interjected.

"No, but now it's better because you're here. I consider you my parents, too. You're my mom and dad."

Tammy's heart skipped a beat.

Morgan took another look at the girl. Sadness consumed him as he tried to comprehend what the ten-year-old had gone through. *How can she still seem so contented, so happy?*

Suddenly, Skye grabbed a hand from Tammy and the other from Morgan. "Come on! Let me show you around the place, and then I'll take you to my real home."

"Your real home?" Tammy raised an eyebrow.

The young girl released her grip and walked over to Laskari. Batting her thick lashes at him, she asked, "Can I show them my home, Mr. Lance?"

He lowered himself to one knee and held her hands in his. He looked directly into the girl's eyes. "You know the rules. You can do whatever you want within those limits. Understand?"

"Yes, Sir, I do." She saluted, and it took everything in their power for the Hamiltons not to laugh.

Lance snickered. "Skye knows this clinic and this island better than anyone, so she'd love to be your guide today."

Skye grabbed Tammy and Morgan's hands. "Come on, I'm going to show you the entire island."

"The entire island?" Tammy asked as the little girl began pulling them down the long corridor.

"Yes, come on! I'll take you around the clinic, and then I'll show you my home on the beach. It's really nice. It has a pool and tennis court." Skye babbled, never giving anyone else a chance to get a word in edgewise. "Do you play tennis? I beat Lance once. Don't tell him, but I think he let me win! He used to be the champion of the world."

Tammy stopped walking. "Oh wait! I almost forgot something. Here, I brought you a gift." She handed the package that she was still carrying to Skye.

Her eyes doubled in size as she looked at the package and then back at Tammy, not saying a word. She tore the wrapping off and opened the box. "It's the outfit in the window on the ship. You got it in blue? How? Where did you find it?"

"It seems the one in the box marked green was actually blue."

"Thank you! I love it!" She wrapped her arms around Tammy.

The woman doctor felt her eyes begin to fill, but quickly wiped the tears away. Unwilling to have another display of emotion, she challenged, "Let's get going, sounds like we have lots to see."

As they walked, Skye pointed out certain rooms, some which Lance had already showed them, but they politely let her think it was the first time they saw them.

Skye knew everyone who walked by, so the introductions never seemed to end.

When the girl noticed one of the doctors, she ran over and hugged him. Skye came closer to Tammy and whispered, "Shhh!" She put her index finger to her lips. "Don't let any of the other doctors know because I wouldn't want to hurt their feelings, but this is my favoritest doctor... Doctor Rozak."

Dr. Rozak extended his hand, smiling.

Morgan shook it. "I'm Dr. Morgan Hamilton, and this is my wife, Dr. Tammy Hamilton."

"The privilege is mine. I've heard a lot about you, and I've read what you've written in the medical journals. Are you going to join our staff? I certainly could use some help from professionals of your caliber."

"That's something my wife and I need to discuss in great detail," Morgan responded courteously.

"If I can be of any help to persuade you, just call me." Rozak smiled. "I'm about to make my rounds. Would you like to join me?"

"Skye is showing us around. Could we take a rain check?" Morgan countered.

"She'll do a good job. She knows this island like the back of her hand. But as far as the medical rounds, how about tomorrow morning?"

"I'm not sure we'll be here tomorrow morning." Tammy spoke without thinking.

Skye's face saddened. "You can't leave. You have to give it a chance! Give me a chance! I don't want you to leave." A tear came to the little girl's eyes—something the couple had never seen.

Tammy knelt down and held her arms out. Within seconds, Skye melted into them.

Dr. Rozak motioned with his head for Morgan to join him, so they could talk privately. "Doctor, we must be very careful. This child has been through a lot and is about to go through even more. We have to be delicate with her. I know you have a life in the United States, but this clinic badly needs you and your wife. We had a major setback a couple months ago, but we're beginning to recover. The loss of Skye's parents created a huge void. I've heard that you're one of the top administrators in the medical world. I know your wife's expertise can prove beneficial, not only for this clinic, but especially for this little girl. Keep that in mind when you discuss your future plans. Just give me a few days to show you around, and above all, give Skye a chance. Her future and her life depend on your decision."

Morgan glanced at Tammy who was still hugging Skye, and then back to the doctor. "Our return flight is not scheduled until next Tuesday. I gave my word that we'd spend a week here, so that's what we'll do. After that, we'll see."

Rozak understood the doctor's concerns. It would be a difficult decision, one that needed much consideration. "I understand, but please keep an open mind."

The men shook hands. Rozak disappeared down the hall.

Tammy and Morgan watched him walk away.

Skye broke the silence. "Let's get a move on!"

The Hamiltons were amazed by the girl's resilience and her ability to bounce back after tragedy, heartache.

"Why would anything she does surprise us?" Tammy whispered to Morgan.

They began walking and Skye began talking, always using her animated gestures, and sounding much older than her age.

With open arms, she explained, "This used to be a prison. The worst criminals in the world were kept here, because it's almost impossible to get on or off the island without being noticed, or hurt really bad. The cliffs are very dangerous."

Her eyes grew large. "The Apostle John was kept here by the Romans for a while."

"Oh, really," Tammy grinned.

Skye smiled. "Well, maybe. That's what they say."

"My father bought the whole island," she said. "Because of the prison, it was called Thanatos, which means death. My father didn't like that name, so he changed it to Kardia. That means heart. It's not a large island, but it sure is nice. There are several homes on it, and a school, too. We have a shopping center, which has a movie theater, bowling alley, grocery store, barber shop, and some other small stores. I'll take you down there later. It's fun! Our residents can spend an entire day shopping, or going to the movies. This is a great place to live. I hope someday you'll live here with me!"

Chapter Nineteen

Eventually, they made it to the large home on the southern tip of the island.

Skye sprinted ahead and opened the front door. "Maya, I'm home!"

She called back to Morgan and Tammy, "Come on, slow pokes!"

The couple picked up their pace, following the youngster into her house.

"We have a guest house in the back overlooking the sea. It's furnished and has a nice library. My father has a million books." She glanced around. "Maya must still be gone. Come on! I want to show you my room."

Tammy and Morgan were having a hard time keeping up with the enthusiastic girl.

Skye ran up the stairs. Waiting for them at the top, she grabbed a hand of both Morgan and Tammy, dragging them into her spacious room. The lower walls were pink and faded into orange, much like a sunset. The eye-catching upper walls were cheerful with a rainbow that stretched the full length of the room. The sky-blue ceiling was adorned with clouds, sun, and moon.

"Teddy!" she shouted, running up to the cat that was sleeping on her pillow. The cat in return, stretched, purring.

"This is my room." She grinned, her blue eyes beaming with glee.

She climbed on the bed and started jumping. "I don't get to spend much time here anymore, but it's still my very own room," she squealed.

Tammy looked around the nicely decorated room. Everything seemed to be in its place, almost like a show home. *The housekeeper here does a great job.*

"Where do you spend most of your time now?" Tammy asked.

"At the clinic." She stopped bouncing. "When we got back from the cruise, Mother and Father worked there day and night. They wanted to spend as much time with me as they could, so we lived there, but on weekends we'd come home."

Skye sat on the edge of the bed and picked up Teddy. "The past couple months, I've been staying at the clinic. I haven't been here very much, but that's okay. Dr. Rozak, Ty, and Nurse Penni take real good care of me." Sadness filled her eyes as the realization of her life hit her.

"Where do you go to school?" Tammy inquired.

"Sometimes I go to the school here with the girls at the clinic. My mother and father taught me most of the time. And when they were not available, I had Maya. She's a whiz in algebra."

She laid the cat back on her pillow. "It's lunch time. My father said that I make the best PB & J in the whole world. Can I make you one?"

"Sure. We'd love to have one of your famous PB & J sandwiches," Tammy chuckled.

Skye led them downstairs to the kitchen and asked them to sit at the table. She opened the refrigerator and took out a gallon of iced tea. She thoughtfully placed it in front of Tammy and took three glasses out of the cupboard. "Can you pour the tea, please?" she asked, handing the glasses to her.

"Sure." Tammy began pouring.

"Just pour me a little bit." Skye said spreading her fingers open a little.

"Okie dokie," Tammy responded.

Remembering her strange eating habits from the cruise, Morgan was suspicious that Skye might try to put catsup on the sandwiches. He watched her lay out the bread neatly in a row on the counter. She evenly spread a thick layer of peanut butter on both slices of bread and then spread jelly on both.

He thought it was cute the way she was concentrating so hard that her tongue stuck out of the corner of her mouth. It took everything he had not to break out laughing, especially when she licked off the knife before placing it in the dishwasher.

Skye grabbed the plates and placed the sandwiches on them. Proudly, the child handed the meal to her guests. She joined them at the table.

As the couple picked up their scrumptious sandwiches, Skye folded her arms across her midsection. "Wait! We can't eat until we pray."

"Sorry," Tammy and Morgan both murmured at the same time.

Skye extended her hands, one to Tammy, the other to Morgan. Before anyone could close their eyes or bow their heads, she began. *Jesus, we thank You for this food. Please bless it to our bodies. And Jesus, one more thing, please help my Mom and Dad stay here. I need them so much. And don't forget that miracle I asked for. Thank you. I love You! Amen.*

She released their hands and began shoveling her sandwich into her mouth.

Tammy and Morgan sat motionless, stunned by the girl's prayer. She spoke to God with such honesty and passion.

"Better get eating," Skye ordered.

Still staring at the little girl in front of them, they picked up their sandwiches slowly.

Of course, Skye broke the silence. "This sure is good. I think it may be the best PB & J I've ever made."

Morgan took a bite, but there was so much peanut butter on it, he found it hard to swallow. He tried to tell her how good it was, but with a mouthful of peanut butter, the words came out wrong. "Theth is the beth thanwich I have ether hath."

"Thank you," Skye said, somehow understanding every word he said.

Tammy gave him a strange look.

Morgan responded to Tammy's gaze, "Watha madder?"

They finished eating in near-record time. Skye put the dishes in the dishwasher.

Before long, they continued on their tour of the house, and island, finally winding up back at the clinic. It was almost five, and much of the day staff was heading home.

In the dining room, dinner was being served.

Skye asked Tammy and Morgan to eat with her and the rest of the girls, and they agreed readily. She demonstrated how to get a tray, plate, and silverware and how to proceed through the line. "Every time I go through this line, it reminds me of the buffet on the ship—except no lighthouse man." Skye giggled.

Morgan smiled, remembering the times he met up with Skye on the ship and followed her on her exploits.

Most of the children could help themselves to their food, but some had to be aided by a staff member. A few times, Skye excused herself to assist some of her playmates who were having difficulties.

Tammy was impressed with the workers. They appeared to be gentle and patient. She noticed they did not hurry the girls to finish their dinner. She could tell that part of the program was to let each child do what she could do.

Morgan and Tammy were introduced to each of Skye's friends. Before dinner was finished, they had met every child in the dining room.

"Sammy, Dana, and Tiffany are very sick. They can no longer make it down here. Tomorrow morning, I want to introduce you to them. They're the sweetest girls you will ever meet. Sammy's mother was a beauty queen from South Africa. Her schedule doesn't allow her to get here often, but she came here for two weeks last year. She's beautiful. Sammy sure misses her. Well, her real name is Samantha, but we all call her Sammy. She likes that better."

Morgan and Tammy did not interrupt Skye's chatter.

"I've been trying to talk my father into turning the entire courtyard into a playground for the girls. With pathways, flowers, and a big fish pond in the middle. I think my friends would love to watch the fish. I know I would. Maybe even put in a swimming pool that all the girls can use. I think I almost have Father convinced." Suddenly her demeanor changed, her face looked pained.

Poor girl, she was so close to her father. She must miss her parents a lot! Tammy wrapped her arms around Skye. As she held the girl she'd grown to love, she could feel the youngster's heart pounding. Tammy ached for her.

Trying to redirect Skye's thoughts, Tammy suggested, "Maybe you could show Morgan, I mean Dad, your plans for the playground. Get his opinion."

A smile lit up Skye's face. "Good thinking, Mom. Can I show you sometime, Dad?"

Morgan smiled. "I'd love to hear your plan."

Just then, Dr. Rozak broke in with an announcement. "Everyone, I have good news. Tonight we're having a special showing of a new Disney movie. Popcorn and soft drinks will be served. I'm sure you will enjoy the evening."

Rozak turned his attention to the visiting couple and continued, "Girls, if you have not been introduced to the Hamilton's, then allow me do it now. This is Dr. Morgan Hamilton and his wife, Dr. Tammy Hamilton. Please make them feel welcome. Now, finish your supper, and head to the auditorium where the movie is ready to go."

Rozak walked over to the couple. "Did you get a nice tour of the island?"

"Yes, we did. Very thorough!" Morgan laughed. "Skye is a great tour guide. Wish I had her energy!"

"Did you tour the Leontiou mansion?"

"Yes, it's beautiful."

"That's where you'll stay while you're here. I think Skye would like to sleep in her own bed."

"Oh can I, Dr. Roz?" Her big, blue eyes searched his face.

"If you want to. That will give you some time to spend with Tammy and Morgan."

Skye peered down the hall, a sad smile played on her lips. She seemed a bit reluctant, but agreed. "I think that will be all right, at least, for tonight."

Morgan noticed her sadness and was confused by it. *I wonder what that's about.*

Everyone enjoyed the movie; it was comical, and entertaining.

Afterward, the visitors mingled with the children.

When it was time for them to leave, Skye led them to a golf cart. "I'll drive," she announced, taking her place behind the steering wheel.

"Is that safe?" Tammy asked.

"Yes, I drive everywhere."

Morgan cast a worried look at Tammy as he took a seat in the back. "Okay, chauffeur. Take us home."

"Hold on," Skye giggled, taking off at a fast pace down the nicely lit road that led directly to the mansion.

"Do you have a license?" Morgan kidded.

"You don't need a license here, silly."

Morgan smiled. *Of course. Why should she have a license? Her father owns the island.* He thought it was interesting that though her parents owned the island and were extremely wealthy, Skye never talked about it, never bragged, and never brought it up. She mingled with children and adults alike, and even took her place at the end of the line, waiting like everyone else.

When they arrived at the mansion a light was on.

Skye skipped to the door and opened it. "Maya's back," she shouted. Leaning her head in the door, she hollered, "Maya, we have company."

Morgan and Tammy followed Skye into the entryway.

A familiar-looking woman came from the kitchen with a cleaning cloth in her hand.

Skye ran up and hugged her. "I'm glad you're back. It has been so lonely without you."

"Land sakes, Child, I was only gone three days to visit my family."

Maya smiled at the Hamiltons. "Hello, again!"

"I thought you worked on the cruise ship," Morgan noted.

"No, I'm the Leontiou's housekeeper. Have you eaten yet?"

"Yes, we had a great dinner and watched a movie."

"We're going to spend the night here," Skye reported excitedly, clapping her hands.

"That's wonderful. It gets lonesome in this big house, and I'm happy to have some company." Maya meant every word; she was thrilled to know she had visitors spending the night. "Well, Child, show your guests to their room—the blue bedroom at the top of the stairs."

"The blue room! I thought they would have to stay in the guest house." Skye tipped her head, waiting for a response.

"That's being painted now. It will be closed for at least a week."

Skye's face brightened. "Goody! You get to stay in the room next to mine."

"Young lady, you know it's past your bedtime. You'd better get to it."

"Okay, Miss Maya."

"Do you want me to tuck you in?" Maya asked.

Skye bunched her eye brows together, sticking out her lower lip. "I hope Mom and Dad will."

"We'd be happy to," Tammy replied.

There was no way the couple could refuse that sad puppy-dog look, and they were fairly certain Skye had already figured that out.

"Run up and get into bed, Little One." Maya bent over, planting a kiss on her forehead. "Have a good night's rest, Sweetheart."

Skye glanced at Morgan and Tammy. "Don't forget to tuck me in."

"I'll go with you. I'm awfully tired, too." The long, exhausting day was catching up to Tammy.

Skye reached for her hand. "Come on, Mom! Let me show you where everything is."

Morgan watched them as they headed up the stairs.

Skye stumbled on one of the steps, but Tammy caught her from falling. They giggled like a couple of schoolgirls.

Chuckling, Maya turned to her remaining guest. "Would you like a cup of coffee, Dr. Hamilton?"

"Yes, that sounds great."

Morgan followed the housekeeper into the living room. A small painting of Malinda Leontiou hanging over the fireplace caught his immediate attention. *Nice picture, but too small to be hanging over such a large fireplace. It didn't seem to go with the more elaborate décor.*

Upon entering the kitchen, he sat at the small table.

Maya poured two cups of coffee, grabbed the cream and sugar, and joined him at the table. "I always drink coffee before I go to bed. Sounds strange to some people. They claim it keeps them awake, but seems to soothe me."

"I know how you feel. I'm the same way." Morgan glanced around the kitchen. "You sure keep the house looking good, especially Skye's room."

"Oh, mercy me, Skye does that. That's her room, and I never touch it. That's just the way she is, everything of hers has a rightful place. She even painted it herself, the rainbow, everything. Wait till you see what she did with the ceiling."

"You mean the sun and clouds?"

"Oh, no—I mean at nighttime! Well, you'll just have to see it."

"You don't say. The more things we find out about her, the more astonished we are."

"You'll find out even more! She's truly a godsend."

Morgan tilted his head, hoping for more information, but Maya quieted for a short time. Neither knew what to say, yet both of them wanted to continue their talk.

Maya finally broke the awkward moment. "I'm so glad you're here. Skye has done nothing but talk about you and your wife since the cruise."

"Really?"

"Yes. She won't stop talking about the dolphins and butterflies."

Morgan grinned. "Yes, that was amazing. It was surely a memorable experience!"

Again, there was silence.

Morgan finally spoke. "Maya, what's going on? The pieces are not adding up?"

The woman looked at Morgan. "Dr. Hamilton, I'd like to tell you everything I know, but it's not my place. I'm employed by Dr. Leontiou and he has faith in me. He's been very good to me."

"How did you meet him?"

She slowly stirred her coffee, lost in the past. "Where do I begin? I guess it was a little more than eight years ago. My daughter, Missy, had been diagnosed with Batten disease. Once my husband found out that our daughter only had a few years to live, he left us. The medical bills were mounting. Eventually, I lost everything—my husband, my job, my home. Everything! I was finally told that there was no hope for her. All help was cut off—financial, as well as medical. I was left to fight the battle by myself."

Morgan sipped his coffee. "Is that when you met the Leontious?"

"Yes, I'd heard about a hospital in Germany, and decided to investigate. They were there. I first met with Malinda, and she told me about their clinic on the island. I was excited, but I told them I couldn't afford anything like that. She told me there would be no charge. In fact, she offered me a job taking care of their home, and teaching their daughter. I've been with them ever since. Furthermore, she told me their foundation would pay Missy's outstanding medical bills. Needless to say, I was shocked."

"How is Missy doing?"

Maya blinked back some tears. "She died a couple years after we arrived here."

"I'm sorry."

"I am too, but she had the best care imaginable. I was able to spend all the time I wanted with her, all because of the Leontious. I miss her, but I will always cherish the time I had with her. She was in so much pain near the end, that I began to pray for God to take her."

There was a hush as they sipped their coffee.

Finally, he spoke, "Do you know what happened to them? Can you tell me about it?"

"I do know the entire story, but at this time, I can't talk about it."

"What will happen to you now?"

"I don't know." She stared at Morgan, trying to read him. "I hope I can stay on here. I pray that you and your wife will take over the clinic so I can keep my job." She studied Morgan's expression, hoping to get an answer, or at least a hint of one.

"That may not happen."

"I pray you keep an open mind, Dr. Hamilton."

"We will, but something miraculous would have to happen."

"Well, Sir, I will pray for that miracle. Both of the Leontious spoke highly of you and your wife."

"Dad," a small voice called from the top of the stairs. "Please, come tuck me in bed."

Morgan smiled at Maya. "I would like to continue this conversation."

"Go ahead. Tuck her in and come back. I will make some fresh coffee."

Morgan bounded up the stairs and into Skye's room. Classical music was playing softly in the background. The ceiling was alive with stars illuminated by a constellation light on her dresser.

Tammy was sitting on the side of the bed.

Skye was lying with her cat snuggled next to her—the more she pet him, the louder he purred.

"Aw! Looks like Teddy really missed you," Morgan whispered.

"Yes, he does when I'm gone for more than a day. He won't leave my side."

"I like your ceiling." Morgan pointed to the stars.

"I do, too. I lay in bed watching them for hours. Sometimes I make a bed on the balcony where I can spend all night watching the real thing." Without a pause, she continued, her voice bubbly, as usual. "See that strange cluster of stars." She pointed directly above her.

"Yes."

"That's really a double cluster. It's called NGC1850, and it's located in the Magellanic cloud. I think that's where heaven is."

"Wow! I'm impressed. You really know your stuff." Morgan felt like he was listening to an astronomer, not a young child. *Why should I be surprised?*

Skye interrupted his thoughts. "You can't see it, but my comet is right below it. It will disappear into the Magellanic cloud next year."

Tammy was enjoying watching the two interact, but knew it was getting late. "What do we do when we tuck you in? We've never done this before."

"Well, you read or tell me a story, and then we pray! Mother would sometimes sing to me. She was a famous singer. Did you know that?"

"No, I didn't." Tammy brushed a finger across Skye's brow.

"Yes, she was an opera singer. Once she sang with the great Ben Heppner."

"Really!" Tammy tried to hide the fact she had no idea who Ben Heppner was.

"Yes, and she also starred on Broadway."

"Broadway? Wow!"

"One morning she woke up, and she couldn't hit many of the opera notes anymore. She had studied to be a chemist, and so she returned to her quest for scientific achievement. That's how she met Father. If it weren't for losing her opera voice, she never would have met him, and I would never have been born. She told me that losing her singing voice was the best thing that ever happened to her."

"Does she still sing to you?" As soon as Morgan said the words, he wished he could have taken them back.

Skye continued as if it never happened. "Yes, she sang me to sleep many times. Usually songs from Phantom of the Opera. That's my favoritest opera ever. I got to see it last year in Paris. It was divine."

He thought it was funny when she used grown up words like divine. "What kind of music do you like?"

"I love Trans-Siberian Orchestra." She drew out the word 'love.' "I wish I could play one song with them, just one song. Wouldn't that be cool?"

"That's my favorite rock band, too." Tammy asked, "Which song would you play?"

"Christmas Canon. I know how to play it just like TSO!"

"Pachelbel's Canon, that's the song you played on the ship." Tammy would never forget that experience.

"Yup," Skye said.

"We never got to congratulate you. You did such a wonderful job." Tammy and Morgan told her together, almost word-for-word.

"When I die, I want that song played at my funeral."

Tammy straightened the cover. "Well, you won't have to worry about that for a long time. Let's talk about happy things."

Morgan bent over and kissed her forehead. "Good night, Sweet Girl."

Tammy gave her a kiss. "Goodnight, Hon." The couple turned to leave.

"You forgot something," a little voice called.

"What's that?" Tammy asked.

"You forgot to pray."

Tammy responded, "Oh, Sweetie. We're not really in the praying mood. We're sort of out of practice."

Morgan piped up, "Why don't *you* pray, Skye?"

"Sure." She propped up on her elbows in bed. "I love to pray. It's a special time, a time I can talk with Jesus face-to-face. Give me your hands, please." She sat up in bed and reached her hands to them.

Tammy and Morgan joined hands with her.

"Now, let's form a circle. You have to hold hands with each other, too. We can't let the circle be broken. Jesus is in the center of this conversation."

Morgan peeked over and saw Skye's eyes squeezed tightly shut, obviously concentrating. *Dear Jesus. Thank You for bringing my mom and dad back into my life. I pray that they will stay here on the island. I ask that You fulfill all their hopes and dreams. Also, God, be with Dr. Rozak as he makes important decisions regarding my friends' lives. Amen.*

She fell back on her pillow. "There, now we can all sleep better!"

Tammy smiled, pulling the blanket up to Skye's chin. "Good night," she whispered.

Morgan and Tammy headed to the door. They stopped when they heard a child's soft voice. "Mom, Dad, I love you."

The gentle words drifted through their minds like a sweet fragrance.

Tammy stilled, letting the truth settle. She looked back at Skye who was still snuggling with Teddy. "We love you too, baby. Good night."

They shut the door behind them, and stared at each other for a time. Without knowing what to say, feel, or do, Tammy sighed, "I'm going to bed."

"I'll say good night to Maya and be up soon."

The housekeeper was still sitting at the kitchen table.

The aroma of freshly brewed coffee smelled heavenly. He noticed the steam coming from his cup. He sat down, added some creamer, and raised it to his lips.

"You're confused, aren't you?" Maya asked.

"Yes, very."

"Dr. Hamilton, I don't know all the details of what's going on. I just do my job. But I do know this much: with the Leontious gone, that little girl's life is even more vulnerable. My job is to see that this household stays clean and organized. I do everything in my power to ensure a healthy, safe lifestyle for Skye. She doesn't ask for much. She never has."

Maya stood with misty eyes, her face stern. "I'll keep this short... Don't you dare hurt that child. Good night, Sir."

She turned and was gone before he could say a word.

Stunned, Morgan contemplated Maya's words. Although the message seemed harsh, he knew it was out of deep concern for Skye. He finished his coffee and put the empty cup in the sink.

He marched up the stairs past Skye's room. He stopped, and then backed up a few steps, and opened the door quietly. The light reflected on the little girl who looked like a sleeping angel. She had her arm wrapped around Teddy. The pet looked up at Morgan with that look only a cat gives, one of contentment, as it stretched its paws back and forth on the girl's side.

Morgan sat in the chair next to Skye, watching her sleep for a couple minutes. He bowed his head, and lifted a silent prayer to the God he hadn't spoken to for a while. The prayer seemed different than his past prayers. It didn't seem to hit the ceiling and bounce back down.

In fact, he was startled when he heard a voice reply, "Take care of them." The voice sounded so real he opened his eyes and looked around.

He gazed at the sleeping child, then back toward the ceiling. For a moment, he felt like he was outside looking at the stars in the galaxy making their trek across the universe.

"Take care of them? *Who*?" he whispered, still looking heavenward.

Nothing more was said.

He stood quietly, closed the door, and headed to bed.

Chapter Twenty

Tammy and Morgan slept so well that they didn't even notice what happened sometime during the night.

When Morgan awoke, he immediately knew they weren't alone.

He nudged Tammy who reluctantly opened her sleepy eyes.

Skye and Teddy were nestled next to her, both sleeping soundly.

A smile encompassed her face as she reached down to brush away the hair from the sleeping girl's forehead.

Tammy and Morgan lay motionless, each contemplating the recent developments. So many unanswered questions, so many major decisions that needed to be made—decisions that would alter their lives forever.

As they pondered what could be, Skye awoke, stretching her arms. "Mom? Dad? How did I get here?"

"Well, I'm certain that we didn't carry you." Morgan sighed.

"I must've walked in my sleep."

"You must have walked with Teddy." Morgan chuckled.

Tammy tickled Skye. The little girl rolled up into a ball, giggling.

Soon the room filled with the aroma of bacon.

Excitedly, Skye bounded out of bed. "Maya's cooking breakfast! You have not lived till you've had one of her breakfasts! Come on!"

"Hold on, Girl!" Tammy exclaimed. "Let me get cleaned up first. I'll be down in a few minutes."

"Okay, but hurry. Come on, Dad." Skye pulled Morgan out of bed, and down the stairs.

Skye greeted the housekeeper. "Good Morning, Maya. Breakfast smells absolutely heavenly!"

"Yes, it does. Same exact words I was going to say," Morgan joked.

A couple minutes later Tammy joined them in the kitchen. Her mint-green robe covered her nightgown. She'd brushed her hair. "Anything I can do to help?" Tammy asked, yawning.

"No, thank you. Skye and I have a routine," the maid answered.

Maya brought sizzling bacon, fried eggs, and sausage links to the table. She joined her guests.

Skye buttered the toast, poured orange juice for everyone, and a small glass of milk for herself. She sat at the table and held out her hands.

This time, Morgan and Tammy knew what the youngster was waiting for. They all joined hands, and Skye led them in prayer.

"Maya, Skye said your breakfasts were the best, and she's right. It's delicious," Morgan emphasized, eating his hearty meal.

"Skye, how do you like living on the island?" Tammy asked.

"I love it. I have plenty of friends to play with, and I can help where I'm needed." She reached for her glass of milk and grasped it wrong, knocking it over. "Oops," she said nonchalantly.

Maya jumped up and caught most of it with a dish cloth. "Land sakes, Child! Now I see why you never fill your glass to the top."

Skye took her napkin and helped soak up the spilled drink. "I'm sorry, Maya. I had my mind on something else."

The housekeeper stopped what she was doing, looking directly into Skye's eyes. Together they blurted out, "Don't cry over spilled milk." With that, they broke into uncontrollable laughter, tears streaming down their cheeks.

The Hamiltons couldn't help but join in the fun. They, too, began to laugh, something they hadn't done much in the past several months.

As the laughter wound down, Tammy realized how long it had been since she'd had a good belly-laugh. *That felt good. I have missed being cheerful, full of joy. It was especially great hearing Skye giggling—the laughter of a child is a wonderful sound.* Her leftover smile radiated her happiness.

When they finished the meal, Skye spoke up. "Mom, Dad, I want to show you the beach this morning."

"I would love that," Morgan replied instantly.

Maya sighed, folding her arms in front of her. "It will have to be later this morning. It's getting late, and Dr. Rozak called and told me to get Tammy to the clinic by nine. He wants to show her the entire building and introduce her to the patients."

"Do *you* have to go, Dad?"

"Well, I don't know." He toyed with the handle of his coffee cup.

Maya answered, "I think only Tammy needs to be there this morning. Mr. Laskari wants to spend time with Morgan, but he's on the mainland and may not be back till late morning. Go ahead, you and Skye head to the beach. Lance will catch up to you."

"How will he know how to find me?"

Maya shrugged her shoulders. "You'll be with Skye. That's how he'll find you."

"Goody," Skye cheered. "I have to brush my teeth. Meet me down here in ten minutes."

"Ten minutes? I need to shower," Morgan shouted to Skye as she dashed to the stairs.

She stopped a few steps up, looking at Morgan. "Okay. Make it fifteen, but not a minute later." She shook her finger at him.

As Morgan resumed sipping his coffee, Maya and Tammy stared at him.

"What?" he grumbled, returning their stares.

"She wasn't kidding. Skye likes to be on time, so now it's fourteen minutes," Maya said, gazing pointedly at the kitchen clock.

"Tick-tock, tick-tock," Maya droned, and Tammy joined in.

"Oh, for crying out loud!" Morgan snapped. "Can't a man enjoy his coffee in the morning?" He walked toward the stairs.

"Thirteen minutes," Maya joked, as Tammy continued with, "Tick-tock, tick-tock."

With a theatrically nasty look, Morgan darted up the stairs by twos.

When they heard the door slam, the women high-fived, laughing.

"That little girl will bug him if he's not ready in time," Maya said. "She's very precise."

"We've noticed that. Speaking of being precise, what time did you say the good doctor wants to start his rounds?"

"Nine sharp."

"I guess I'd better get a move on too."

"When you're ready, come on down," Maya said. "I'll drive you to the clinic. We'll let Skye show Morgan the beach area. I don't think they'll get into too much trouble."

"I hope not."

Morgan showered, and was shaving when he heard a loud knock on the door.

"Dad, come on! Time's a-wastin'. I want to show you my hideout before the tide comes in."

"I'm just about finished."

""I'll meet you downstairs."

Morgan finished and rushed down the stairs.

Skye stood tapping her toes, hands on hips, waiting at the base of the stairs. "Dad, I think I need to have a talk with you."

"About what?"

"About being late all the time."

"Late? How late am I?" He glanced at his watch.

"You're six minutes late. Now, if you were at a real job and you were six minutes late, you could get fired." Skye began shaking her finger at him. "If you were playing a tennis match at Wimbledon and you came six minutes late, you would have to forfeit the game. So let's be on time from now on. Got it?"

Morgan stared at the girl for the longest time. "You're pulling my leg, right?"

Studying him with a serious, stern look, she broke out laughing. "Let's go, Dad."

Skye grabbed a backpack and took off galloping out the back door.

Trying to keep up, Morgan shouted, "What are we doing? Is there anything I need to know about? Like swimming, or going down water slides?"

The girl stopped and turned around, walking backwards. "No silly, the water's too cold. Only rock climbing and cave exploring."

"Oh, great! I hate caves. Any snakes?" he shouted, but she was too far ahead to hear him.

When he finally caught up to her, he was out of breath. Skye was sitting on the beach throwing stones into the sea.

She looked at him and smiled. "Dad, can I ask you a question?"

"Sure, go ahead."

"Are you and mom going to get divorced?"

Morgan shook his head, as he plopped on the sand next to her. "No, silly, what makes you think that?"

"You just don't seem happy. I keep praying you will be happy. I know Jesus answers my prayers, but I'm worried about this one."

Morgan raised his face toward the sky, gazing at the fluffy clouds. "That's one prayer I can answer for you. No, Tammy and I are not getting divorced. We just have a few problems... well, one in particular, to work through. Unfortunately, that one thing is major."

He shifted his gaze to the chatterbox next to him. "No, Little One, you don't have to worry about that. We're solid. We work well together. We'll work things out!" As soon as he said the words, he had a sick feeling in the gut. *We'll work things out, won't we?*

"Good. I couldn't bear to see you two apart." She threw a rock into the waves.

Morgan picked up a small stone and tossed it.

"Is that one thing because you two can't have babies of your own?"

Morgan swallowed back a lump in his throat and tried not to look as surprised as he felt. *After all she's only a little girl; what business is it of hers? Then again, she's an extraordinary child.* He politely responded, "Yes, it is."

"Well, have you prayed about it?" It was a typical, straight-to-the-point, Skye-kind of question.

"Yes, we have."

"No, I mean really prayed about it?"

He sat silent for the longest time, unsure how to respond. He could see that the ten-year-old was dead serious.

A large, blue butterfly flew by. Skye raised her hand and the colorful insect landed on it, slowly fluttering its wings.

"You're right! We really aren't praying seriously about our problem."

"Well, you need to. God always answers prayers, if you pray from a believing heart."

She shifted her position and brought the insect closer to her face. Morgan smiled as the girl's eyes crossed while she studied the intricate details on the butterfly. She passed it from one hand to the other, never missing a beat in the conversation. "He always answers our prayers! Although, sometimes He says no, but when He does, He fills that emptiness in your heart with something else. " She raised her hand high into the air, releasing the butterfly.

Clasping her hands together over her heart, she continued, "Something even better!" The butterfly continued to flutter around her.

Morgan breathed in slowly, letting her words find a place in his heart. "I understand what you're saying." He threw another rock. He knew she was right. Wanting to change the subject, he took another deep breath.

Glancing around the beach, he queried, "Now, where is this cave you were talking about?"

Skye grabbed Morgan's arm. "Come on, I'll show you. It's so cool."

After following her across the beach and climbing behind a few rocks, they stopped. "There it is!" She pointed to a large cave opening at the bottom of the cliffs.

Morgan stepped across a few lava rocks, and peered into the dark cave. "How far back does it go?"

"A long ways. All the way to the clinic."

"Really?" Morgan asked.

"Yes. Part of the clinic was a prison once. It was used by the Nazis during World War II. At one time, there were over two hundred prisoners there. The POWs spent three years digging through the rocks and ended up right here. I understand that they started digging in a prison cell. They used kitchen tools to dig, you know, like spoons. Lucky for them, they hit a lava tube, large enough to walk through. Do you know what a lava tube is?"

He nodded. "Isn't that how lava travels to the ocean?"

"Good thinking, Dad! So, back to my story. They followed the giant tube all the way to the breakout point at the ocean. Unfortunately, the waves had collapsed the opening over time. They knew they must be close to freedom, so they dug the rest of the way out." She pointed to the cave. "It was only a small opening back then. Just wide enough for one person to slip through."

"You don't say. Did they manage to escape?"

"No, that's what was so sad."

"Why do you say that?"

"They drowned," she said, letting the story unfold. "The German guards came back unexpectedly. Many of the POWs were in the tube at the time. They thought they were heading to freedom. Those prisoners, who didn't make it into the tunnel, quickly covered the hole in the cell trying to protect their friends below. They had no idea what was happening in the escape tunnel."

Morgan was intrigued by the story.

Skye continued, "By the time the men in the tube realized the tide was coming in, it was too late. The current was too strong to swim against, especially in their weakened condition. They were pounded by the waves and tossed against the sharp rocks. The tube was lower than the sea, so their only way to escape was being flooded. Their only chance to survive was to return to the hole they dug in the cell, but they were out of luck because their own men had covered it. Those who were not killed by the sharp lava rocks, drowned. The POWs still inside the prison, heard screams coming from below. In an effort to save their fellow prisoners, they told the German guards about the escape tunnel, but it was too late. By then, almost all of the escapees were dead."

"That's awful!" Morgan's jaw dropped.

She looked at the cave, sadly. "Yes, over forty men died in this cave. The prisoners misjudged the depth of the cave, and the time the tide came in. They did not know that the tide changes as many as eight times a day here."

"Eight times a day? I thought it just changed twice."

"Not around here. There is a myth that Aristotle was studying the changes in the tide. He got frustrated because he didn't understand why it changed so much. So he threw himself into the sea and drowned. Legend says that he studies it to this day! I guess you could say, the tide comes and goes whenever."

"Interesting," Morgan commented as they both stared into the cave opening. He'd rarely seen Skye solemn. It was like she was feeling the struggle of the POWs plight.

"But, there's more. The current was too strong, and the water too cold, to swim out. The only men who had a chance of survival were the last ones in. They saw what was happening and quickly climbed back up, but the opening was closed! With water rising fast, they had to fight for air. In the end, only two survived. One committed suicide days later. I heard he left a note saying that he could not live with himself knowing he'd fought to stay on top, which resulted in the death of his fellow prisoners. Isn't that sad, Dad?"

"Sure is. What a story!"

Skye put her hands on her hips, drawing marks in the sand with her feet. "For almost eight years this was a Nazi prison camp. During that time, over a thousand prisoners were kept here. A couple years ago, there was a reunion for all of the POWs, but only eleven showed up. My father and I watched them put flowers on the graves of their friends. They were all old, and not a one of them had a smile on his face. I asked Father why so few came. He thought it was because it was too painful an ordeal for them to return. The ones that died during the prison escape are buried on the old church grounds. Would you believe that their headstones are the same stones they dug out of the tunnel when they tried to escape?"

Morgan was not only amazed by the story, but also by how Skye told the tale, sounding more like a tourist guide than a child. Her words were exact, she didn't vary in details!

Skye inhaled a deep breath. "Other prisoners, who have died since, have asked to be buried here, with their buddies. Father allowed it, if they were cremated."

She shifted her gaze to Morgan. "I guess when you think about it, they did escape the prison."

"Unbelievable story!" he replied. "What happened to the lone survivor of the escape attempt?"

A swarm of yellow butterflies fluttered around Skye before continuing on their way, but she wasn't deterred. "I heard he came back after the war. He walked around the island keeping it clean and caring for the graves of his fellow soldiers. The islanders said he was crazy, so no one bothered him. They found him dead in the cemetery one day, and that added to the strangeness of the story."

"What do you mean?" Morgan waited for her answer.

She didn't blink. "He died exactly forty years after the failed escape. Forty years to the *day*!"

"How did he die?"

"The ghost story is that one of the men who drowned grabbed his leg from the grave and tripped him. He hit his head on that man's tombstone."

Morgan studied the knowledgeable girl, and then faced the ocean. There was silence for a moment as he processed the story Skye had related.

His eyes narrowed, and then brightened with a daring glint. "How much time do we have before it fills up? You know, before the tide comes in?"

"Like I said, nobody knows for sure. I'd guess about two hours."

"Can I use your flashlight?"

"Sure." Morgan turned the light on, looking deeper into the cave. "The prisoners dug all this out?"

"I think the crashing waves made it bigger through the years."

"Amazing—a real escape tunnel!" Morgan was fascinated with the cave and its history.

Stepping through the opening, the light illuminated the jagged walls. He could see why the men would be cut. "I'm just going to go back a little ways."

"I'll wait here. Be careful, Dad. The sides get sharper the deeper you go."

Skye stayed at the entrance, watching Morgan and the light disappear into the blackness. She filled her lungs with the damp, salty air.

Suddenly, a noise on the beach caught her attention. Sneaking over to check it out, she came face-to-face with a man she'd never seen before. He was wet and bleeding. Skye could tell he was in pain, perhaps desperate.

She was frightened, but she didn't scream. "Who are you?"

The man stared blankly at Skye.

She studied him, backing up slowly toward the ocean. "You're not from here. What do you want?"

The man took a few steps closer to her, blocking her way to the cave and Morgan.

She stepped back even more, now ankle-deep in the salty water.

"You're Skye Leontiou, aren't you?" he asked, trying not to frighten the girl.

"I don't know you." She scrunched her face.

"I'm a friend of your father. I used to work with him. I need to talk with him. Is he around?"

Without missing a beat, Skye growled, "You don't know my father. I don't trust you." She scanned the area for a possible escape route, but realized she was trapped.

"Yes, I do know him. I suspect he's dead, isn't he? He was supposed to meet up with me two months ago, but never showed. Something bad must have happened!"

He took a few steps closer to her.

She continued to back up, now knee-high in the ocean.

"Your mother is dead too, right? You can trust me. I already know. I just don't know how it happened. Can you tell me?" He grabbed her arm.

Struggling to get away, she stepped deeper into the cold water, almost slipping on the rough rocks.

"Let go of me! Dad! Dad!" she screamed.

"Dad? What are you talking about, little girl?"

Before Skye could answer, the stranger collapsed into the shallow water, smashing his shoulder on a sharp rock. In pain, he groaned. Blinking, and trying to gather his bearings, his eyes finally focused. The first thing he saw was Morgan standing over him with a piece of driftwood, ready to hit him again, if need be.

Skye waded over to Morgan. Grabbing his leg, she peered around him. "Dad, who is he?"

Morgan recognized the intruder instantly. "How did you get on this island?"

"It wasn't easy," the trespasser admitted, standing up and grimacing in pain. "I almost drowned a couple of times. Cut myself up on the rocks." He clutched at his bruised shoulder.

"Who is he?" Skye repeated, holding tight to Morgan who still had the makeshift club raised in the air.

"He's a reporter."

"What does he want?"

"A story. A story about your family."

Unhindered by his injury, or the conversation, the reporter interrupted, "Why does she call you Dad, Dr. Hamilton? I see a front page story here." He held his hand in the air, pretending to write. "Billionaire Father is dead, but Dad is alive."

Noticing Morgan's scowl, the newshound stopped his charade. "Oh, come on, you might as well tell me. I'm going to print this story, no matter what."

"If you print anything, it will be from inside a jail cell, "a voice boomed from behind.

"Lance," Morgan called, "I'm sure glad to see you."

Laskari took a step closer. "We've been searching for him almost an hour. We knew he was on the island; we just didn't know where."

Lance motioned to the two armed guards who accompanied him. "Take Mr. Klitou to the clinic. Have Dr. Rozak check him out, and bandage his wounds. Then put him in the holding cell. We'll decide what to do with him in a couple days."

"You can't hold me. I'll sue you for everything you have."

"Trespassing is a crime," Lance argued.

"Trespassing? My boat capsized when I was sailing, and I was forced aground here."

"That—pardon the pun—will not hold water. Get him out of here!" Lance ordered.

He didn't have to tell the guards twice. Pointing the rifles at the prisoner, they headed down the road.

"What's going to happen to him?" Morgan asked.

"We'll hold him for a day or two, and then I'll take him to Athens and turn him over to the police. He'll be booked for trespassing, but his political friends will put up the bail to set him free."

"Political friends? I thought this was for a story."

"On the surface you would think so. Actually, it's all politics."

Morgan addressed Lance. "Can we talk about this privately?"

Lance looked at the young girl still clinging to Morgan. "Skye, run ahead for a moment. I need to talk to Morgan."

She looked up; her blue eyes showed the stress she was feeling.

"Go ahead," Morgan reassured her. "I'll be right along."

A curious look came over Skye. "I get it. You need to talk about grown-up stuff, right?"

"Right." Morgan smiled.

She ran ahead picking up rocks along the way, throwing them into the sea. Another swarm of butterflies encircled her.

Laskari crossed his arms, leveling his gaze at Morgan. "She knows what's going on. She's one brave girl."

"She has been through so much—losing her parents. Things like what just happened don't help."

"No, they don't. Dr. Hamilton, when the world finds out about Layland's death there will be a ripple effect which will have a tremendous impact on my country."

"Greece?"

"Yes. Greece is vulnerable at this time. Not only that, but if Greece falls, it would affect the entire European economy, and if that happens—"

"The U.S. and the world may follow," Morgan added.

"Right." Laskari gave a grim smile.

"Why would someone want to do such a devastating thing? It can't be only for a story. It would affect them too, right?"

"Yes, it would. Remember, they're not capitalists; they're Socialists. Communists."

"Markus is a communist?"

"I tend to think he's more of a pawn being used by them. Many newspapers are on the left and want nothing more than to see a global economy, a global nation."

"A one-world government."

Lance continued, "That's one way to put it. They don't realize what would happen if that occurred. What would happen to the freedoms they enjoy."

"Shades of Armageddon," Morgan nodded. "But, I don't understand why putting this news off will help. The truth's going to come out, it always does! And how can Tammy and I help? We've been put right smack in the middle of this complicated, very dangerous, situation."

"You have. Unwillingly and unknowingly you have. You see that little girl?"

They watched Skye play with the butterflies on the beach.

"Skye? What has she got to do with this?"

"Everything! She's the sole heir of the Leontiou Empire. She inherits everything. Billions of dollars."

Morgan's eyes widened. "That's a big responsibility for such a little girl."

"You don't know the half of it, Morgan."

"What else could there be?"

"I'm not at liberty to release that information."

Morgan exhaled, his frustration was evident. "If there's more I should know, then tell me."

Lance smiled. "Unfortunately, Sir, it's not my story to share."

"Then whose is it?"

Lance peered over at Skye.

"Skye? It's up to Skye to tell me? Tell me *what*?"

"In time, Sir. In time. Right now, let's get back to the clinic, and see how our prisoner is doing."

Chapter Twenty-One

Maya drove Tammy to the clinic. Along the way, she pointed out areas of interest.

At almost nine, they reached Dr. Rozak's office. He was busy studying data on his computer and did not hear them enter.

Tammy's attention was immediately drawn to three large monitors on the wall.

"Good Morning Dr. Rozak. We made it," Maya announced.

"Good Morning, Maya." Dr. Rozak pushed his chair a short distance away from the computer.

He faced Tammy, asking, "Did you have a good night's sleep?"

"Very good, thank you." Tammy was amazed by the technology around them. "What *is* all this?"

"I'm checking the updated medical information on my patients. They're monitored twenty-four hours a day, seven days a week. All results come into my office using our new computer system."

"You're kidding me." She filled her lungs, keeping her focus.

Dr. Rozak stood. "Let me show you." He walked over to the monitors.

"I can operate it from my desk or use the touch screen." He pointed to the first screen. "As you can see, all twenty-three patient's names and their pictures are on the screen. More information can be displayed about a patient by touching her picture or entering her name. We can also access it by using the personal identification number, which is usually her date of birth."

Rozak demonstrated by touching the picture of a beautiful redheaded girl. Instantly, a number showed on the red screen, followed by the girl's picture, and pertinent medical information.

"The number 071104 is her birthdate?" Tammy asked.

"Yes. July 11, 2004."

Tammy read the details on the girl. "Born 07-11-2004... South Bend, Indiana... NCL... 03-02-2008." Tammy backed away from the screen. "She's adorable. Look at that bright red hair." She cleared her throat.

"NCL... 03-02-2008. That would mean she was diagnosed with the disease on March 2, 2008, right?"

"That's correct. She probably could have been diagnosed with the disease at birth, but many doctors aren't familiar with Batten disease. The symptoms are silent, until one day the disease rears its ugly head and begins its dreadful task of destroying a beautiful child." He pointed to the screen, "Like this little girl."

Dr. Rozak stepped forward, his expression solemn. Concern showed on his countenance. He stared at the picture of the redheaded girl. "As you can see, this is Tiffany Kraft. Sweet little girl! The digital clock gives her age by year, month, day, hour, and minute. The monitor also displays where she was born. "

Rozak continued, "She and her parents wear security bracelets. The family can be alerted at any given time. Most of the parents live and work on this island."

Rozak directed her attention back to the monitor. "The system keeps track of the girl's whereabouts, as well as her vital signs and other indicators."

"How is Tiffany doing?"

Dr. Rozak touched the screen and it scrolled to more information.

Scanning the results, Tammy didn't have to ask any more questions. She could tell by her history that Tiffany's condition was declining at an alarming rate.

"May I?" Tammy asked, pointing to the screen.

"Sure, go ahead. You can touch the screen to find out more information. For example, say you want to find out the results of her blood tests. Simply touch, 'Blood tests.'"

Tammy touched the screen and a graph of the patient's blood tests appeared. "I assume the red screen shows the patient is in critical condition."

"Correct. The orange screen means she's in serious condition. The green screen signifies that they're in good or stable condition. "

"What are the other two monitors for?" she asked.

"The second monitor runs a continuous loop, displaying updated information on each patient, one-by one. Each patient is displayed for one minute, and then it goes to the next girl. If something abnormal appears, like a seizure, an alarm will sound, and the screen will freeze on the patient in question.

"You access the search engine on the third monitor. We're connected to ten other clinics, twenty-four hours a day, including Leontiou's Costa Rica lab. I can download any information I need at any time to help my patients.

Leontiou's dream was to eventually be connected to every major laboratory, clinic, and pharmaceutical company in the world."

He touched the newswire button. Scrolling down were hundreds of notes from doctors, chemists, and laboratory personnel. "All I have to do is put in the name of a certain disease. Let's type 'Batten' here. Instantly, every letter or resource with the word 'Batten' in it will be displayed."

"That's impressive! How long have you had this going?"

"We've had this new system a little more than a month."

"What happened to the old one?"

Rozak hesitated. "That's a story in itself, one which Lance will have to tell you."

"I heard there is a storm coming in later this week. Will it affect you getting information in or out?"

"No. We're hard-wired and programmed by satellite. We have our own power here—wind, solar, and petroleum. We're in the process of doing away with land line phones. Eventually we'll only have cell phones, but the tower won't be finished for another year. We even have our own satellite."

"Your own satellite? You're joking."

"No, I'm not. Our only worries are hackers."

"Have you had problems with hackers in the past?" Tammy searched his face.

He answered with a nod.

"Why would anyone want to hack a place like this?"

Dr. Rozak shrugged his shoulders. "I'll never figure that out. Come, let me introduce you to my patients."

For the next hour, Dr. Rozak introduced Tammy to the patients in the clinic, and many of the staff who were on duty.

Morgan, Lance, and Skye caught up with them, and continued on the tour.

Skye, of course, took over introducing the visitors to the children.

As they drew close to one of the rooms, Skye ran ahead and stopped at the bedside of a young girl. "Tiffany, how are you this morning? You look spiffy."

Tammy immediately recognized her as the same girl she'd seen on the monitor, although her once-full head of auburn hair was thin. Tammy could tell by her skin color that her blood was not circulating properly. Blindness had set in. She was incoherent.

Skye reached for her hand, and began to talk to her. In a typical Skye-manner, she began to encourage the deathly-ill child.

Morgan whispered to Dr. Rozak, "Does the girl understand what Skye is saying?"

"I pray that she does. Skye is wonderful to her, and all the other children. She's an inspiration to all of us, in more ways than we can count."

"How much time do you think she has?" Tammy asked, concern written on her face.

"Two months ago, she would have had more time," Dr. Rozak added.

"What happened two months ago?" Morgan raised his eyebrows.

Lance stepped in. "Computer problems."

"Like hacking?" Tammy inquired.

"You catch on pretty quick, Dr. Hamilton," Lance responded.

"My husband and I try to stay alert. It's our nature."

"I'll have to remember that when I play tennis with him."

Morgan laughed.

"Skye, we're leaving now," Dr. Rozak whispered.

"Okay, Dr. Rozak. I'd like to stay here and talk with Tiffany for a while. Is that all right?"

"Sure. You can catch up to us at lunch. We'll be down in the dining room about noon."

"Bye, Skye," Tammy called.

Skye looked up, still holding the girl's hand. "See you at lunch, Mom and Dad. I may be a little late." She began to chat with Tiffany again, as if they were best friends sharing stories, memories, and happy thoughts, except Skye did all the talking.

As soon as the doctors started down the corridor, Tammy spoke, "Skye is so good with her. It's hard to believe that Tiffany... I mean that Tiffany doesn't—" Tammy stopped, not knowing how to frame her words.

"You mean she doesn't know what's going on?" Rozak asked.

"Well, yes. My understanding is in the last stage of Batten, dementia sets in, and it's just a matter of time until her body shuts down."

Dr. Rozak nodded. "Dr. Hamilton, I didn't want to say this in front of Skye. Personally, I don't believe Tiffany knows what's going on, but prayerfully, I hope she does. Hearing is the last thing to go when one is near death. Skye is amazing with her, and all the other girls. She's been by the bedside of many of her friends in their last hours, singing and quoting Scripture to them."

"She knows much of the Bible by heart—even down to the chapter and verse," Lance added.

"That's true," Rozak agreed.

"She's been with them when they died?" Morgan asked. "Isn't that difficult for a ten-year-old girl? I mean, emotionally?"

"Dr. Hamilton, the more you get to know Skye, the more you'll see how exceptional she is. We don't question what she does, or how she does it. Her parents raised her in the world of... how should I say it? *Orderliness*. Everything has its place, and everything belongs in its place. Some would say she has 'Obsessive Compulsive Disorder,' but that's not the case. She just picks up after herself, plain and simple, and she expects others to do the same."

"I noticed her room," Morgan said. "I see what you mean."

"She's very intelligent. She has her mother's IQ, and her father's business savvy. No, Dr. Hamilton, to answer your question, we don't think Skye is too young to be seeing death. In fact, she believes that it's her responsibility to be with her friends when they meet their Maker."

"You mean Jesus?" Tammy blinked and sighed deeply, knowing the answer before she asked the question.

"That's correct," Rozak stated, without hesitation.

Tammy couldn't shake the cold feeling in her heart.

As the tour continued, they walked by the same doorway that the old woman had disappeared into the day before. His curiosity heightened. "What's in this room?" Morgan said, stopping at the closed door.

"That was Dr. Leontiou's private study. It hasn't been opened since his death," Lance answered.

"Who was the elderly lady you wheeled in there yesterday?" Even Morgan was surprised with his unusual boldness.

Laskari looked stunned, like he had been caught in a trap. "A friend of Skye's." His voice sounded nervous.

Dr. Rozak drew in a deep breath. "You know how Skye is with older people."

"Why was she taken into this room?" Morgan wiggled the door handle. "Is there a reason why it's locked?" He straightened, looking directly into Rozak's eyes.

Suddenly, a red emergency light began flashing at the end of the hallway, and Dr. Rozak's phone alert sounded. He checked his message, glanced at Lance, nodding his head. "I'm sorry. I'm needed in the ER."

"Anything I can do to help?" Tammy offered.

"No, I'm afraid not," he called over his shoulder as he hurried off.

"Dr. Hamilton, I appreciate your candid observations. But the fact is you will learn all you need to know when you make your decision about staying. Until then, that's all the information I can give you. Now, if you'll excuse me, I have to go. I'll meet up with you at lunch." Lance turned and was gone.

Tammy stared at her husband.

"Why are they giving us the barest of answers?" Morgan tossed his hands in the air, exasperated.

"I'm going to get some answers right now," Tammy blurted. Before Morgan could respond, she darted toward the emergency room.

She was stopped abruptly at the ER door by an armed guard. "I'm sorry, Ma'am; only authorized personnel are permitted to enter."

"I'm a doctor. I might be able to help."

"Sorry, Ma'am. I have my orders."

Just then two orderlies rushed by her. The guard admitted them, no questions asked.

That was Tammy's opportunity to peek into the busy room. Unfortunately, the people standing around the patient blocked most of her view. Frustrated, she stormed back to her husband.

"What did you see?" Morgan's mouth was tight with irritation.

"They won't let me in, but something big is happening. I saw Dr. Rozak and a half dozen other people working on a patient, and I don't think it was a child."

Morgan caught a glimpse of Lance and Skye sprinting down the hallway from the other direction. The guards opened the door for them, and they rushed in.

"Why would Skye need to go in there?" A shiver ran down Tammy's spine.

"Perhaps it was the old lady she befriended."

"Did you really buy that?"

"Not all of it." Morgan backed up to the mysterious room, trying the knob again.

Another guard appeared. "I'm sorry, Sir, but I need to escort you to the dining room. We have an emergency here, and outside guests are not allowed in the area. Please, follow me."

Not pressing the subject, the Hamiltons willingly followed the security officer.

Entering the dining room, the guard offered, "Please enjoy something to eat. This is not your run-of-the-mill cafeteria food. We have a professional chef who prepares the food, nothing but the best. Mr. Laskari will return shortly." The guard left.

Chapter Twenty-Two

Everything seemed normal in the dining room. Patients and staff were getting their lunches. Others had already finished, and were leaving, chatting amiably as they walked.

The Hamiltons opted for only an iced tea.

As soon as they were seated, a number of children hurried over to say hello.

Finally, the couple was alone, and could discuss the morning's bizarre events.

"I told you, something big is happening here." Tammy let out a huff of breath, her tension showing.

"I agree." Morgan nodded decisively.

"Do you think it's a coincidence that the locked room is next to the ER?" A frown accompanied the question.

"Kind of strange, isn't it?"

For a short time, they sat still, deep in thought.

"How was your morning?" Tammy asked.

"Interesting, but you go first. Did you see the entire clinic?"

"Yes. It's an impressive place. There are twenty-three patients here. I saw the brains of the operation—an intricate computer system controlled in Dr. Rozak's office. It's tied in to several other clinics around the world. They eventually want to connect to every lab in the world for up-to-date developments on all diseases and possible cures."

"Right, as if *that* will ever happen." Morgan put a packet of sugar in his tea. "The almighty dollar will prevent it. Many pharmaceutical companies are more interested in their pocketbooks than saving lives. We both know that. They need to make their stockholders happy."

"You think this is all about money?"

Morgan shrugged. "I thought Layland Leontiou was just a doctor. But since arriving here, I'm absolutely dumbfounded at the power the man has, or should I say *had*. Lance said he was worth billions, but if he can control every laboratory, clinic, and pharmaceutical firm in Europe, and the world, he could become an overnight multi-trillionaire, if that's even a word."

Tammy grinned, wiping the condensation from the side of her glass with a napkin. "Yes, but if he's dead, like they say, then who is running this whole operation? And why?"

Morgan glanced around the dining room. "I can't shake the feeling that the key to this mystery is behind that locked door."

"You think we need to see what's behind it?" Tammy's heart beat faster.

Morgan leaned forward. "Yes, I do. And if they're not going to tell us, we'll have to find out ourselves. After all, I think we have the right. We deserve answers!" He let out a huff of breath.

"I think we should ask first. After all, they do need us. I can see why they would want both of us."

"What do you mean?"

"There is no leadership. I mean, if what Lance says is true, they need someone with your administrative skills to make it all work." Tammy folded her arms.

Morgan finished her thought. "And someone with your talents as a physician to continue the experiments."

"Since you brought that up, Dr. Rozak showed me around the lab. It's certainly high-tech, and all new since the big fire. They're still waiting for more equipment to arrive. Dr. Leontiou obviously has spared no expense. Do you know he has his own satellite?"

"His own satellite? Interesting! But, where does Skye fit into all this?"

"What do you mean?"

"I don't know. Lance told me that she's the key. She seems to be the center of this entire puzzle."

Tammy said nothing, her mind still reeling from the recent events.

Morgan changed the subject. "Were you given a tour of the emergency room and the lab?"

"Yes. The emergency room and the operating room are attached. Very clean, large, with equipment I've never seen before."

"Did you ask about the equipment?"

"Yes. They seemed to be upfront. They have a machine that replaces the blood, and one that replaces bone marrow."

"That's expensive equipment for a clinic like this. Maybe Markus was right."

"About what?"

"Maybe this *is* the island of Dr. Moreau."

Tammy allowed a nervous laugh. "Not funny, Morgan. This is serious."

"I *am* being serious. You haven't heard about my day."

"Okay, what happened?"

"Skye took me to a cave. And, if what she says is true, there's an unbelievable amount of history connected to this island. However, it was what happened when I came out of the cave that shocked me most."

"You went into a cave?" Tammy looked at her husband with piercing eyes that seemed to look right through him.

"Okay, enough of the sarcasm. I can be brave when I want to be."

Tammy snickered.

"I saw Markus Klitou."

"The reporter? How did he get here?"

"He said his boat capsized, so he swam to shore."

"Do you believe him?"

"His boat probably did capsize. And the only way to get on this island is the heavily guarded beach area by the mansion. He was pretty beat up and sopping wet."

"That guy gives me the creeps. What was he doing here?"

"Looking for a story, I expect. I snuck up behind him because I heard Skye talking to him. Poor thing, she was scared to death. He tried to grab her, so I hit him from the back knocking him to the ground."

Tammy's concern was etched on her face. "That man being here is too much of a coincidence. I'm in suspense. Go on!"

"I only had a short time to talk with him. Lance and two guards showed up. He said they knew Markus was on the island and had been searching for him. That's when Lance told me that Skye is the key to this entire thing. He said that if they don't settle what happens to her life quickly, Greece will collapse, which could send a ripple effect throughout Europe, and possibly even the world."

"How can a ten-year-old have that much power?" She looked doubtful.

"I don't know... money, maybe. Leontiou is one of the richest men in Greece. From what I gather, he controls a lot of different things. I tend to think it's Leontiou's empire that's keeping Greece alive. Since he's dead, his empire will be torn apart by greedy relatives."

She could tell he'd been trying to work it all out in his mind.

Morgan blew out a long breath. "But Skye? How can she help? What possible power does she have? She's a remarkable young lady, but maybe it's not just her. Maybe it's us. Or *you*."

"Me? Why me?" Tammy took a breath, but it didn't seem to help.

"Perhaps it has something to do with your lab work."

Just then, Lance came in, interrupting their conversation. "Sorry about that. We had an emergency. One of the patients had major problems."

"Did she make it?" Tammy asked.

"No, she didn't. That's why Skye won't be joining us. She's very upset. She was especially close to this patient."

"Poor girl! Was it Tiffany?" Tammy's question was quick, direct.

"No, although Tiffany only has days left, if not hours."

Lance looked dejected. "We need someone desperately to take over the administration of this clinic and believe me, it's not an easy job. But more importantly, we need someone to take over the lab."

He made eye contact with Tammy. "Someone like *you*, Dr. Hamilton."

Tammy frowned. "What? Why me?"

"We have a few experts here, but none of your caliber. Dr. Leontiou was impressed with you. Your youth; your vigor; your experience. He had faith in you. That's good enough for us. He was an excellent judge of character, one of his many fine attributes."

"You really think that what we decide could determine the fate of the world?" Morgan felt the heat rising in his cheeks.

"For some people, yes."

"That's really a big burden you're putting on us!"

Lance's phone rang. "Yes. Okay, I'll be right there."

"More trouble?" Morgan asked, as Lance put his phone back in his pocket.

"Yes. It seems our newest guest is having a temper tantrum and is trashing the room."

"What are you going to do about it?"

"Well, Dr. Hamilton, remember, this was at one time a prison. There are rooms where we can put him and he'll never see the light of day. The dungeons below still exist." Lance winked.

Morgan and Tammy still didn't understand Lance's sense of humor; they hoped he was kidding.

Lance stood, eyeing the couple. "You're free to do whatever you want the rest of the afternoon. Walk around the island, or hang out at the clinic. But if I were you, I'd start praying hard about your decision. Frankly, if I was in your shoes, the choice would be simple—adopt Skye and take over the Leontiou Empire. You will never have a financial worry as long as you live. Plus, think of all the children you can help with all that money at your disposal. Be back at the mansion by six; Maya will have dinner ready for you." He turned and walked away, leaving them to ponder his words.

"He's right," Morgan said. "What are we thinking about?"

Tammy was slow to reply. "I don't want to give up what I have in Saint Paul."

"And what do you have? What would keep you there?"

With that, the conversation was over. Tammy didn't know how to respond. He certainly had given her food for thought.

Chapter Twenty-Three

The Hamiltons walked around the island the rest of the afternoon.

The islanders were friendly. Most were English-speaking, which made them feel at home. Many of them had children in the clinic, or at one time did. They came from all parts of the world—different races, different financial classes, and different religions. The common denominator was Batten disease. Every one of them spoke highly of the Leontious.

Tammy and Morgan discussed the possibilities of staying on the island. The financial backing would always be available for both clinics—that was a plus. But at the same time, the unstable country of Greece was something to consider.

"Let's go talk to Markus." Tammy's radiant eyes twinkled with mischief.

She didn't have to suggest it twice. Within seconds, they were headed to the intruder's cell.

As they arrived two guards stepped aside, allowing Tammy and Morgan access.

"That was easy," Morgan mumbled under his breath.

When they opened the door they realized it was not really a cell, but more like a hotel-room. They noticed things were in disarray—the table overturned, and the television smashed.

"What happened here?" Morgan asked one of the guards.

"He decided he didn't like the movie on the telly."

Morgan grinned. "Did it not occur to him that he could have turned it off?"

The guard chuckled. "Apparently not. If you need us, just holler, and we'll be right there."

As the couple stepped into the room, they saw Markus sitting on the floor under the barred, broken window. "Did you decide to come and hear my side of it?" The reporter glared at them.

"Why not sit on a chair or the sofa?" Morgan asked.

"Are you kidding? That would give Leontiou one up on me. I can't have that."

At first, Morgan thought the man was kidding, but then he realized he was dead serious. "You remember my wife, Tammy?"

"Yes, I do. I know all about the great Dr. Tammy Hamilton. I'm an investigative reporter, remember? I know all about both of you. What does Leontiou want with you? I have asked that question many times, and I'm totally baffled by it. But, there has got to be money in it." Markus mocked sarcastically.

"Why do you hate him so much?" Tammy asked.

"Oh, I don't hate him as much as I hate what he represents." Markus stood.

"Do you have any idea what this clinic is?" Tammy asked.

"Let me ask you a question. Do you believe what you've been told? If so, why all the secrets?"

The prisoner grabbed a couple of the overturned chairs and sat them upright. "Have a seat, if you're going to stay awhile."

"No, we just stopped by to see if they were treating you right."

"They better. The army will be here soon to rescue me. I told my wife if she did not hear from me by evening to send in the troops."

"I thought you said you were sailing."

The reporter didn't respond. "Just what is this place anyway? What sort of crazy experiments is, or should I say was, Dr. Moreau doing on this island."

"This is a clinic for children dying of a rare disease," Tammy said. "Layland Leontiou dedicated his life to find a cure."

"Oh, and you believe that? You two are just as crazy as everyone else on this island. I managed to get into their computer a while back and I found the strangest things."

"Like what?" Tammy and Morgan echoed in harmony.

"Like experiments being done on innocent children. Experiments that are not sanctioned by any government. The doctor is a mental case." Klitou raised his voice and pointed to his head. "He's crazy!"

"How did you get into the computer?" Tammy kept a calm voice, believing she was more apt to get answers if she remained unruffled.

"Not me. I'm not the computer man! My wife is. She dropped a virus. I sure hope the good doctor lost all his records."

A sudden anger consumed Tammy. "*You're* the hacker!"

The reporter smirked. "Forget that I said anything. I will deny everything."

"Morgan, I want to leave," Tammy demanded.

"I'm with you. Markus, from what I've seen, *you're* the crazy one. I do know there are secrets here, but from what I can tell, this clinic is legitimate. The people that work here want only the best for these children."

"So you say," Markus sneered.

"Morgan, lets go. I don't want to be around this man one more second." Tammy stormed off heading toward the door.

"Right," Markus yelled. "Go ahead, run, and turn your back on the biggest story of this century and probably the most hideous. There's a cover up. I guarantee it."

Fuming, Morgan forcibly stood Markus up by his shirt. "What's your problem, man? You're the one who's sick in the head."

"You're wrong! Leontiou and those like him are a menace to society. They all need to be locked up. They cause nothing but trouble. Hungry for money!"

The commotion caught the attention of the guards who stepped in to see Morgan and Markus nose-to-nose.

"Let me tell you about people like Layland Leontiou." Morgan pushed his finger hard on the journalist's chest. "Yes, they're rich, but almost every one of them started out at the bottom. They had an idea, a dream, and they worked hard to see it through, making it work. Men like Edison, Ford, Walton, Gates, and yes, Layland Leontiou. Yes, they were rich and powerful, but they were also *giving*. They created millions of jobs, and gave *billions* to charities. What have people like *you* done?"

Hamilton kept shoving Klitou until he was pinned against the wall.

Tammy watched cautiously from the door.

Morgan continued. "You protest in the streets, riot, and stop other hard working citizens from earning money to feed their families. Why? Because your kind wants what people like Leontiou have. But you want it at someone else's expense. You don't want to *work* for it! People like you don't have the smarts, the expertise, or the ambition to produce anything except anarchy, and a socialistic society built on destroying capitalism. No, Markus, *they* are not the problem. You, and people like you, are the *real* problem."

Lance heard the racket and rushed in. Pulling Morgan away from Markus, he ordered, "Let's go, doctor. He's too hard-headed. It will take more than that for you to get through his thick skull. It's impossible to defeat an ignorant man by arguing with him."

Realizing Laskari was right, people like Markus can't be reasoned with, Morgan headed to the door.

Not giving up, Markus continued shouting, "You're all talk, Hamilton. Believe me, there is something weird and illegal going on here. I'll get to the bottom of this," Klitou shouted, raising his fist in rage.

They hurriedly walked away, not wanting to hear another word.

"Do you hear me, Laskari?" The prisoner continued his rant.

Markus picked up a chair and threw it at the closing door.

"Wow! I never knew you had that much anger in you?" Tammy confessed.

"I'm sorry, Honey. I lost it."

"I'm not sorry," she claimed. "That man needs to be brought down to where he belongs, and I think you just did it."

"Sorry, Lance. I hope I didn't cause any more problems." Morgan exhaled.

"None that weren't already there." Lance shrugged his shoulder.

Laskari shoved his hands in his pockets. "Listen Morgan, I wanted to tell you that I will be busy the rest of the day. We have a very important meeting tonight among the staff and I need to get prepared. I'll see you in the morning. Maybe we can get that tennis match in."

"I would love that. Is there anything we can help with at the meeting?" Morgan offered.

"No, it's leadership roles. I'll see you in the morning. Goodnight." Lance hurried off.

Tammy watched Laskari walk away and she quickly turned to face her husband. "I didn't want to say this in front of Lance, but I think Klitou is totally responsible for destroying the files on Leontiou's computer."

"What?" His expression showed his confusion. "You've lost me. Destroyed *what* files in *whose* computer?"

"Morgan, everything is beginning to add up. I've been listening to Lance, Markus, and Dr. Rozak. And from what I can gather, Leontiou's computer was destroyed by a hacker. I think all the files on Batten were lost, including all the lab records. Everything! I believe that Markus... well, his sweet wife, is the guilty party."

"Whoa, Girl!" Morgan said. "You've been watching too many James Bond movies."

"No, I think I'm right." She peered back at the room where Klitou was being held. "In fact, I think Klitou may have had something to do with Leontiou's death. Maybe indirectly. He might not even know it."

Morgan stared at Tammy. He finally took a deep breath and grabbed her hand. "Let's head back to the mansion."

Skye was already home when the weary couple arrived. The second they opened the door, she rushed to them.

Tammy opened her arms to the sobbing child. "I'm sorry, Honey. Was she one of your friends?" She embraced the girl lovingly.

Through sobs, Skye mumbled, "She was... she was my best friend in the whole world."

Maya joined them, her face showing grave concern.

The three adults comforted the heartbroken child.

Finally, she calmed down enough to eat a few bites of dinner.

The Hamiltons were concerned because Skye was subdued the rest of the evening, not a side of the girl they'd seen before. They were surprised when she asked to go to bed early.

When Tammy and Morgan tucked her in, she didn't talk much, not a hint of a smile crossed her face.

Morgan and Tammy wondered if every child's death devastated her this much. Their hearts broke for the emotionally drained girl.

Tammy went to bed early.

Morgan went downstairs to have coffee with Maya. They talked about the housekeeper's life and what it was like working for the Leontious. She had the highest respect for both of them. Of course, she loved Skye.

When it was time for Morgan to retire for the evening, he walked by Skye's bedroom and heard muffled sobs.

He peeked in and saw Skye sitting on her balcony looking at the stars, weeping.

Morgan sat beside her, and handed her a tissue.

She looked up at him, wiping away her tears.

He did not know what to say or do; he just knew he wanted to be there for support.

After a short time, she jumped up, and grabbed him around the neck. "Are you and Mom going to stay?"

"I can't answer that now. There are many things we need to consider."

"But we *need* you. What will the girls do without you? Dad, you *have* to take care of them."

She leaned against his chest, quietly crying herself to sleep.

After tucking her in bed, he gazed at the sleeping beauty. *I'm sorry, Little Girl... I just can't make any promises.*

He lifted his head toward the ceiling and watched the stars continue their celestial journey. Recalling the voice from the night before, which certainly seemed audible to him, he suddenly realized what God was trying to tell him. It was the same message Skye told him minutes before—"Take care of them!" *God is using this child to get His message through to me. He wants us to care for the girls at the clinic!*

He retired to his room, but sleep wouldn't come. His mind kept replaying the events of the day. Everything always came back to the locked door at the clinic. *Exactly what is behind that door?*

After hours of tossing and turning, he finally drifted into a few hours of fitful sleep.

Chapter Twenty-Four

The next morning the silence of the island was shattered by the distinct roar of two approaching helicopters—one military, the other private.

Morgan dressed hurriedly.

"What's going on?" Tammy asked, struggling to wake up.

"I'm not sure. Stay here until I return."

"Be careful."

"You know me."

"After the way you confronted Klitou yesterday, I don't know what to expect from you." She smiled with approval.

He groaned. "Check on Skye. She was pretty upset last night."

"I'm on it."

Morgan bounded down the stairs, nearly bumping into Maya.

"I see trouble. One of the helicopters is military. Be careful," she warned Morgan as he dashed out the door.

Morgan rushed over to where the helicopters were setting down. He joined Lance and a few guards. "What's going on?"

"Looks like the left is coming out in force," Lance's eyes flashed anger, perhaps fear.

"What do you mean?"

"The green chopper is military; the black one belongs to the cable network Markus works for."

"If he was just sailing, why would they think he was here?" Morgan asked innocently.

"Exactly. What did he tell you when you talked to him yesterday afternoon?"

"He said everyone here was crazy, and you're doing weird experiments on the girls to make money."

Lance rolled his eyes. "Is that what he said?"

"Not in those exact words, but that was what he was implying. Well, now that I think about it, those *were* his exact words."

Lance chuckled nervously, shaking his head.

A team of military men jumped out of one of the choppers, weapons in hand.

"Morgan, you'd better take cover, this could get bloody," Lance ordered protectively.

Morgan watched Lance grab a pistol from his shoulder holster.

Five guards with AK-47s rushed over to stand beside them.

"You've got to be kidding," Morgan said. Are they that serious?"

"Deadly serious," Lance said, shifting his gaze to the top of the old prison, where other guards aimed rifles at the choppers.

Morgan drew a deep calming breath; it didn't help. "But that's the Greek army."

"Maybe," Lance said. "Or maybe not. One thing for sure; they're not on our side."

"How do you know?"

"This is a private island in international waters," Lance said. "That was one of the stipulations, when Layland bought the island. It' no longer considered part of Greece or Turkey."

Lance gave Morgan a quick glance. "Dr. Hamilton, you're standing on a self-governing island. An independent country, with its own laws, its own constitution, and its own leaders. Recognized by the United Nations. Legally, they're trespassing. Or, a more accurate term would be *invading*. It would be like a Russian helicopter landing in Washington D.C. with a small army. What would your government do?"

Morgan's answer came swiftly, confidently. "They couldn't do that. We would shoot them down."

"Precisely. Under international law, what they've just done could be considered an act of war."

Morgan's hands were sweaty, his pulse racing. "Are you actually going to fight? I mean, they're *real* military."

Lance's focus shifted back to the intruders. "So are my guards," he said. "It's a small force, but strong and well-trained. Many of them are former American military personnel."

Just then, the door of the black chopper opened. Three men and a woman stepped out.

"Well, looky there," Lance said in a deadpan voice. "Markus's wife came along. She's a scorpion; her sting is lethal. Stay here Dr. Hamilton, while I find out what their demands are."

"No way!" Morgan said. "If I'm going to be the administrator here, I want to know what's going on."

Lance nodded his head. "Good! Stay behind me, but let me do the talking."

Morgan followed Lance and the guards who held their weapons ready to fire. He couldn't believe this was happening, and he certainly couldn't believe that he was bold enough to participate in it! He felt like he was an actor in an action flick.

Anna Klitou stomped towards Lance. She was quick and to the point. "Where is my husband? I know you have him here."

"Why Mrs. Klitou, you seem to be a little upset," Lance said, in a sarcastic tone.

"Stop with the jokes. I want him freed—right now!" she hissed.

"Oh, was that your husband that we caught trespassing earlier?"

"He wasn't trespassing. He went fishing and his boat must've hit some bad weather."

Morgan gave her a look of feigned surprise. "*Fishing*? That's odd. He told me that he was *sailing*, when his boat capsized. As for bad weather, you work for a cable news network. You should know that the weather in this area has been clear as a bell for days."

The woman glared at Morgan. "You're in way over your head, Hamilton. I suggest you head back to America where you belong, and let us take care of our own problems."

A man in military uniform stepped forward. "I believe you're holding Markus Klitou. You will release him immediately!"

"Or *what*, Colonel?" Lance shot back. "I remind you, this is a private island, an independent country. You're trespassing. In fact, what you're doing could be considered an act of aggression."

"There are those who believe this island is still part of Greece," Anna snapped.

Lance and the colonel stared each other down.

"We've come for Markus Klitou," the colonel said in an iron-hard voice.

"I'm curious about why you think he's here," Lance said.

"Just bring him to us. *Now!*" Anna roared.

"Colonel, wouldn't it have been better to follow the proper procedures?" Lance asked. "A polite phone call to inform us that one of your citizens had run into a little misfortune, and might have had to seek refuge on our island. Perhaps a friendly advisory that you were going to send out a search and rescue team. Wouldn't that have been better? Or at least, more *legal*?"

"We're not interested in your legalities!" Anna said.

"Obviously," Lance said evenly. "You're clearly willing to throw the law out the window when it suits you. And, instead of abiding by the legal obligations of Greece, you deliberately violate the territorial sovereignty of an independent island that's recognized by the United Nations. And, to compound your list of transgressions, you *threaten* us."

"Just get Klitou," the colonel bellowed, "or I will order my men to—"

Lance cut him off. "Again, you threaten us."

For a half-dozen heartbeats, there was silence. Finally, Lance turned a cold eye to Anna. "Your husband is being brought here right now. He was treated well. We were going to send him back on our supply run tomorrow, but I figured you would come for him."

Two guards drove up in a golf cart. Markus Klitou, unharmed and unrestrained, rode in the rear seat.

When the cart rolled to a stop, Anna ran to her husband, and embraced him. "I was afraid I'd lost you. You need to come home with me. Sonya was taken to the hospital right after you left. She's very sick."

Markus Klitou's facial expression flashed instantly from triumph to concern. "My little girl? What happened?"

"We don't know," Anna said. "It might be a tumor. Let's get out of here!"

Lance raised an eyebrow. "Interesting... Apparently, there's a human side to you after all."

"Keep your opinions to yourself, Laskari," Markus growled. "You haven't heard the last of this. Something strange and illegal is going on here, and I'm going to find out what it is."

Morgan grabbed Markus's arm as he brushed past.

The reporter glanced down at the hand on his arm, and then glared at Morgan.

"I hope your daughter gets better," Morgan said. "If you need any medical advice, I'd be glad to help."

The news reporter pulled free of Morgan's hand. "Don't flatter yourself, Hamilton. You're part of the problem."

Before Morgan could respond, Klitou and his wife were hurrying toward the helicopters with the soldiers in tow.

Lance gave a cheerful wave, and shouted, "I'll be filing a formal complaint with your country, Colonel."

The officer climbed into the military chopper. "You can file anything you want, Laskari."

Lance stepped back as the two helicopters rose, heading to the mainland.

"I hope you run out of fuel," Lance murmured.

"What's going to happen now?" Morgan finally could breathe.

"Now, Markus, and his wife will go back to the office and write a news story stating that his boat capsized, and he ended up on this island. He'll report that he was beaten, kept in a damp cell, and only fed bread and water for three days."

"But, we caught him yesterday." Morgan's eyes widened.

Lance began walking. "Oh, that's right! Better make it *five* days!"

Morgan sprinted to catch up to him. All sorts of emotions played through his mind as he traipsed back to the house. *I have never seen such excitement in my life. What's the rest of our time on this island going to be like?*

Chapter Twenty-Five

The next few days the Hamiltons began to feel more comfortable in their new surroundings.

Tammy stayed busy working with Dr. Rozak at the clinic. She was actually enjoying herself, feeling whole again, challenged. The doctor was a master at making her feel important. She was impressed by his bedside manner with his patients. No doubt, he loved what he was doing.

The teamwork in the clinic captivated her, such a positive atmosphere.

Sometimes she worked in the lab helping install the new equipment arriving daily. Soon the facility would be fully functional.

Tammy discovered that Ty was not just an orderly, but a computer wizard. He'd come to the island five years before with his wife, Jane, and their twin daughters. Sadly, both of their young girls were suffering from Batten, and have since died. He stayed at the clinic, steadfastly fighting for the cause. His wife helped write the software for the computers.

While his wife was busy at the clinic, Morgan investigated the island thoroughly. He thought Skye must have introduced him to every islander.

Every day at noon, Morgan would meet Tammy for lunch, and Skye would leave to visit her friends.

On two occasions, Tammy caught a glimpse of the girl chatting with the old woman in the wheelchair, but was never able to catch up to the elderly lady. She always seemed to disappear before Tammy could reach her. When she asked Skye about her, she would reply, "She's just someone special."

It had been six days since the Hamiltons arrived on the island. Each night they would get together and talk about the day's events. It was quite a contrast from back home, where they barely spoke a word to each other at the end of the day.

Morgan was in favor of accepting the job offer, but Tammy was still undecided. She missed her clinic in Saint Paul. After all, it was her baby; she started it from scratch.

Late that evening after tucking Skye into bed, the two discussed the day's happenings.

"I've noticed something strange with the computers," Tammy stated.

"Like what?"

"Well, there are twenty-three girls being treated in the clinic. I know that the person who died this week was not one of them. I have no idea who it was, maybe someone from the island."

"Stranger still, since I've been working on the computer, I found three additional screens, making a total of twenty-six. Who are the extra three screens for? What's weird is that there are no pictures, no names, no birthdates, only medical information, and a number."

"What color are the screens?"

"One was red, with all indicators in the critical area. The second screen was green, but the vitals were declining on that patient, also. The third screen was completely black." She pushed her hair away from her face.

"Could those screens be the average of the twenty-three patients?"

"I thought of that possibility, but I don't think so. They were password protected, so I couldn't access them. Something isn't right, but I can't quite put my finger on the problem," Tammy reasoned.

"Do you think Dr. Rozak is lying to you, or holding something back?"

"I don't know. He seems pretty candid with me. When I ask a question, he's immediately on it. He doesn't stammer around. I think he's probably telling me the truth, but maybe not all of it."

"What about the mysterious room and the lady in the wheelchair?"

"I saw her and Skye together today, so I guess we can scratch her off the list of possible people who died at the beginning of the week."

"I guess so," Morgan readily agreed.

"I thought you were with Skye all day."

He nodded. "All except an hour at lunch. She said she was going to eat with her friends. She leaves for almost an hour every day. Today, Maya had made some chili for me, so I went back to the house and ate."

Not letting the subject drop, Tammy continued, "It's interesting to note that there is a door in the emergency room that goes nowhere. I asked what was in there and was told that it's the electrical room. It's locked tighter than a drum, I think it goes into the same room that the door in the hallway does."

"Have you tried to get in through the hall door lately?"

"Yes. Twice, and it was locked. It has a digital combination lock on it. You know what else is strange? Before I could turn around, a guard was standing behind me."

"That quick?"

"Yes, it's like the room is being monitored twenty-four hours a day. I noticed a camera facing the door. Of course, security cameras are everywhere on this island."

They looked at each other for a brief time.

Morgan inhaled, taking a slow, cleansing breath. "Now, on a different subject. I made an executive decision. This is what I think we should do. I'm going to spend time with Skye tomorrow. When she leaves at noon, I'll follow her and watch where she goes. Once I discover that, I'll meet you in the room across from the ER. Since I know she'll be gone the entire lunch hour, we'll have time to figure out how to get into that room. We're going to find out once and for all what's going on, if anything. I believe what's in that room holds the key, but time is running out. We have until morning to make up our minds about staying here. We deserve answers!"

That night, they went to bed early, the next day's plans fixed in their minds. As Morgan tried to get some needed rest, questions bombarded his mind. *Why did Skye cry so hard after the girl died at the beginning of the week? Why does she spend so much time with that nameless old woman? What's behind that door?*

Finally, his thoughts turned into dreams as he drifted to sleep.

Chapter Twenty-Six

The next morning, Tammy went to the clinic with Dr. Rozak.

Morgan and Skye traipsed along the beach searching for shells, as they did every morning before they headed to the clinic.

After that, they visited some of Skye's friends in the outside play area. She watched a few of them playing on the small climber. Commenting again about the need for a bigger playground, she stated, "I think we should build a playground here for all my friends."

"This is a playground," Morgan replied.

"Yes, but it's small, and not very safe. Many of my friends can't play here because they lose their balance easily. That's why most of them wear helmets and pads when they play. I read that you can use rubber mulch from old tires that have been chopped up into little pieces. It would make the playground bouncy. If someone falls, she won't be hurt. And all the equipment should have safety pads for the poles. We have enough room to make the playground a lot bigger. We could have walkways, flowers, and trees. Even a swimming pool, so children like Tiffany who can't walk, can enjoy the water. And we could have a big pond with a waterfall and fish. Not to eat, but to watch. Maybe we can get some frogs and listen to them croak. Wouldn't that be cool? I love the sounds of frogs at night. We should begin a crusade to get a new playground! What ya think, Dad?"

Morgan smiled. "That's a great idea."

Skye skipped over to the group of girls and began playing with them.

Ty joined Morgan. "I bet she's talking to you about her playground idea."

"I think she needs to be put in charge of this facility." Morgan chuckled.

"She comes up with some grand ideas, doesn't she?"

"Skye is one special young lady."

"No doubt about that!"

Just as Morgan expected, at lunchtime Skye ran up to him and said, "I'm going to eat with the kids again today. I need to see how everyone is doing. Is that okay, Dad?"

"If that's what you want. I'll see you after lunch."

He waved to her as she left.

"If you'll excuse me, Ty, I have to meet my wife for lunch."

"I need to do that, too. We're going to eat at 'The Cliffs.'"

"The Cliffs? Oh, that little restaurant overlooking the ocean. How's the food?"

"It's the best! They have the best seafood. The couple that operates it has a child here in the clinic. They were actually chefs in Spain before coming here."

"I'll have to take Tammy there before we leave the island."

"Consider me selfish, but I hope you don't leave. We need you here." Ty patted Morgan's arm.

"I understand what you're saying. You don't have to convince me." Morgan gave a glimmer of a smile.

"So I need to talk Tammy into staying, right?" Ty's voice dropped.

"Right. And good luck with that! She can be quite hardheaded." With that, Morgan bid a quick goodbye to Ty and was off to meet Tammy.

He followed Skye cautiously, trying not to be noticed. Of course, she carried on with her daily routine, totally focused on her friends. He felt certain he was safe from being seen.

He watched as she visited a few of her friends. Morgan saw a sparkle come to one little girl's face when she noticed her. Skye fluffed the girl's pillow, and chatted with her. Morgan wondered if her friend could understand her; the look on her face made him believe that she could.

Finally, she made her way to the locked room. She entered the combination without looking up and walked into the room, hastily closing the door behind her.

Morgan hustled to the door, trying the knob; it was no surprise that it was locked. Within seconds, a guard appeared behind him. "May I help you, Dr. Hamilton?"

"Oh, no, thank you. I was just looking for another way out. What's in here?"

"That was Dr. Leontiou's study." His answer came quick.

"I thought I saw Skye go in here, and I wanted to talk with her."

"I believe she did go in there. That's where she finds comfort. Poor girl has been through a lot," the guard's reply seemed rehearsed.

"I'm sorry. You're right. I guess she does need her privacy."

"Good afternoon, Dr. Hamilton."

Morgan nodded his head and began walking away.

The guard turned and strode the other direction, glancing back occasionally.

"Psst." Morgan turned to see Tammy hiding in a storage room across the hall.

Making sure the guard was out of sight, he darted into the room. "I thought we were supposed to meet in that other room. What are you doing here?" he whispered.

"A little covert action. I held the door open a crack and looked though this little lens. Guess what? I got the combination when Skye went in." She held up a small telescope.

"What's the combination?"

"8-16-1!"

"8-16-1?" Morgan repeated.

"Yes, and you know what?" Tammy's voice showed an excitement he hadn't heard for a long time.

"What?"

"That's the same number that I saw on the mysterious green screen."

Morgan's mind started racing. "The same number? Didn't you say that the numbers on the screen were the patient's birthdays?"

"Yes, that's what Dr. Rozak told me. Why do you ask?"

"8-16-1, August 16, 2001. Oh, my gosh! That's Skye's birthday!"

"Skye's birthday? Why would Skye's birthday... why would Skye even be...?"

There was sudden silence.

Tammy's eyes widened. "Oh, no! Are you thinking what I'm thinking?"

"Yes, but I don't want to." Morgan sounded as confused as he looked.

Tammy leaned forward, her expression solemn. "I'm afraid Skye has Batten disease."

"No!" Morgan snapped. "She doesn't have any of the symptoms."

"Think about it," Tammy said. "Remember the times on the cruise, when we were eating with her and she had a hard time grasping her drink? That one time she knocked it over?"

Morgan stared blankly into space. "So, she spilled her drink. All kids do that. *I* do that."

"She did it again that morning, in the mansion. Remember? Maya and Skye made a joke of it. And then there was the time she stumbled on the stairs. Those are symptoms of Batten disease."

"I'm not buying it," Morgan said. "Skye is ten-years-old. If she had Batten, the progress of the disease should be significantly more pronounced by now. Most of the other girls her age have more serious symptoms. Unless..."

"Unless *what*?" Tammy shot back.

Morgan paused, trying to form his thoughts. "Unless they found a way to control it. Slow it down. Or possibly even a cure."

Tammy shook her head. "If they found a cure, why wouldn't they release it to the medical world? Such a discovery could save many lives."

"There may have had a reason to keep it to themselves," Morgan said.

"A selfish reason," Tammy said. "Like they only had enough of the cure, or the treatment, for Skye."

Morgan and Tammy both knew how far-fetched that idea sounded, but everything about this situation was on the crazy side. Maybe the Leontious had a cure, or at least a treatment, and they were suppressing it. Maybe *that* was the big secret.

Morgan sighed. "I suppose that's possible, but I think it's more than that. You said that all the girls seemed to be okay until about six weeks ago?"

"Yes."

"That's a starting point," Morgan said. "What happened a little over six weeks ago?"

Tammy's brow knotted in concentration. "You tell me."

Morgan searched his thoughts. "Let's see," he said. "I was talking to Skye in my office a couple of months ago, when something happened... something that frightened Skye. There were sirens and alarms going off in the background."

"What are you getting at? Do you think that's when Klitou hacked the computer?"

Morgan felt breathless, on the verge of understanding something dreadful. "Right! What if the computer crashed during a precise step of an experiment? Lance told us that Skye's parents were killed by a laboratory accident. If the computer was hacked at the right time—or rather, the *wrong* time—it might have triggered a chain reaction..."

Tammy continued the train of logic. "...which not only destroyed the computer, but caused an explosion and fire that killed her parents. It possibly did more damage than we've been told about."

Morgan nodded slowly. "If we're right, something happened here that caused a major setback. I believe it was more than the death of Layland and Malinda."

Tammy swallowed hard. "Skye could very well be the patient on the green screen, but what about the other two unaccounted screens?"

"Were there any numbers on them?"

"Yes, but I don't remember what they were. I had to look really fast. I didn't want Dr. Rozak to get suspicious of me. Besides they have security everywhere, so I'm sure they have it on the computer. They know exactly what I'm doing every minute. They seem to know what *everyone* is doing on this island."

Tammy stopped talking. A sudden realization hit her! "The bracelet!" Tammy exclaimed.

"What?"

"The bracelet Skye wears," Tammy muttered stiffly.

"What about it?"

"All the girls are wearing one."

"Right, I understand it's a security device, so they know where the girls are at all times."

"It serves more than one purpose. All the girls' vital signs are monitored through the bracelets, twenty-four hours a day."

"That's too sci-fi," Morgan said skeptically.

"Actually, it's not. I've read about this kind of technology; now I've seen it. Did you notice that everyone here has a bracelet?"

"I know that all the children and their parents have one. They're used for contacting a person in an emergency."

Tammy nodded. "True, but Lance has one. Dr. Rozak even wears a bracelet. Their every movement is followed on this island."

Her brown eyes were wide with wonder. "Could one of the screens be the old lady? If so, who is she?"

"That's the million dollar question. I still think the answer is behind that door." Morgan nodded tersely.

"Do you think they know we're here now, in this room?" Tammy whispered, scanning the room for cameras.

Morgan hesitated, and his expression changed. "No. We don't have bracelets. That's why it took so long to find Klitou on the beach. Security finally discovered him by tracking Skye."

"You've probably got something there," Tammy said. "I've been wondering. Do you think they'll come clean with us if we tell them we're going home?"

Morgan shook his head. "Not if we refuse their offer. Why should they? At the same time, I don't want to do something that could get us into trouble. As much as I hate to say it, maybe Klitou is right. Maybe something illegal *is* going on here."

"Like what?" Tammy asked, peeking out the slightly opened door.

"I don't know, but at the same time, it's not the people here I'm afraid of. It's the Greek government, the Klitous, and the press. That's who I'm worried about!"

"What if nothing is behind that door over there? What if it's just an office, or electrical panels, like they say?" Tammy asked.

"Then we have a decision to make, right?"

"Shhh... Skye's leaving the room." Tammy put her finger to her lips, and closed the door further.

They watched as Skye closed the door of the secretive room and skipped down the hall.

"Okay, we have to act fast," Morgan said. "Once I step close to that door, security will know it. Let's get to the bottom of this, right now. The number is 8-16-1, right?"

"Right."

Morgan glanced around the room, and noticed a fly swatter hanging on the wall.

"What are you thinking?" Tammy's voice sounded nervous.

He picked it up, raising it in the air.

"What are you doing?"

"I've got an idea. I want you to take this flyswatter. Judging by the angle of that camera, there may be a blind spot against the wall. Walk close along the wall and hold the fly swatter up against the lens, I'll rush to the door and get in. When I'm safe inside, move the fly swatter to the side. Hopefully, they'll think it's a glitch in the system."

"Do you think it will work?"

"It will get me in at least. If they figure it out, the most that will happen is that they shoot me on sight." He gave his wife an uneasy grin.

"Not funny," Tammy said.

Morgan sighed. "I guess not." He took a deep breath. "Are you ready?"

Tammy took the fly swatter, and raised it above her head a few times practicing how to hold it correctly. "Can we do this?"

"Hey, we'll just pretend that it's 'Mission Impossible.'"

"Morgan, they *failed* in the last Mission Impossible movie."

They looked at each other for a split-second. Morgan leaned in and gave her a quick, but passionate kiss. His heartbeat was so loud, he wondered if Tammy could hear it.

Tammy's voice was a nervous whisper. "Let's do this!"

Chapter Twenty-Seven

Morgan opened the door slightly, looking both ways. The coast was clear, so he opened it the rest of the way and exited the storage room.

Tammy moved snug to the wall until she got under the camera. She lifted the flyswatter covering the camera's lens and hopefully protecting their covert mission.

Morgan rushed to the locked door and punched in the combination. He heard the lock click open. He turned the knob cautiously, stepped in, and closed the door behind him.

Tammy lowered the fly swatter, and hurried back into the storage room, hopefully undetected. She felt compelled to do something she had not done for a long time. She prayed. It was the only thing that made sense at the moment.

Morgan glanced around the room. It appeared to be what people said—an office. There was a large desk with book shelves behind it. On the desk was a computer, which caught Morgan's attention. He noticed it was on, so he walked around and peeked at the screen. The information on the screen showed the stats of the children slowly scrolling from one child to the next.

Suddenly, he heard a noise behind another door and inched closer. Reaching the door, he put his ear against it, listening. He slowly opened the door. His arms were quivering.

Peering in, he noticed a large sofa and some other living room furniture. *I've come this far, I can't turn back now.* He opened the door further.

The room was immaculate. There was a large flat screen television on the wall showing stock results throughout the world.

He heard another sound coming from an adjacent room. He wiped the perspiration from his face with his hand. He cautiously opened the door, and stepped into a large bedroom.

The first thing he noticed was a woman's wig on a nearby stand. Next to the bed was a wheelchair. He was tempted to pick up the wig, but was startled when the door behind him burst open.

He turned and was standing face-to-face with Dr. Layland Leontiou! For a brief moment they stood, staring at each other. Morgan looked like he'd seen a ghost. Shocked, he eyed the man who only a few months earlier had been so fit and debonair. Now, before him stood the merest shell of a man—bald, skin and bones.

"Dr. Leontiou, you're alive!" Morgan could barely make a sound, let alone form the right words to speak.

The billionaire shuffled past him slowly, making his way to the wheelchair. He lowered himself carefully into the seat.

Morgan was too stunned to offer a helping hand. He stood motionless, paralyzed by uncertainty.

Noticeably out-of-breath, Layland spoke slowly in a weakened, hoarse voice. "I told Lance you'd figure it out. But he said you could not know yet, in case you turned our offer down." His hands were trembling.

Morgan stared, his eyebrows bunched together, confused. "What happened? Why all the secrets? What's going on?"

"I'm protecting my family," Layland said. Even in his weakened voice, the anger came through loud and clear. "And perhaps the world as well."

"Protecting your family from *what*?"

"People like the Klitous, the government, politicians, pharmaceutical firms, even my own family. I've been fighting them, and I will continue to do so." His weakened fist clutched spasmodically.

He continued, but his mind seemed to drift. "You know, I began on the docks loading freight. I took night courses learning how to write computer software. I created a software program that kept track of ingoing and outgoing freight on the shipping dock. Before I knew it, I was making millions in the software business. I always enjoyed the sea, so I bought an oil freighter. Then I bought a whole fleet of them, shipping oil around the world. I spent my entire life building business after business, and I made billions. I created tens of thousands of jobs, and people like the Klitous and others want to take it from me. They think that people like me don't deserve to have it."

Morgan scowled. "You haven't answered my questions. Why all the secrets?"

"I'm sure you've figured it out already," Layland said. "You and Tammy are brilliant!"

In a subdued tone, Morgan let the words fall from his lips, partly a statement, partly a question. "You found a cure for Batten?"

"No, not a cure. We found a way to temporarily control it, to slow it down. Hopefully, slow it down enough to give us a chance to find that cure."

"Why haven't you told the world?"

"That's what we were trying to do."

Morgan could tell it was difficult for him to speak. Every word was an effort.

"You mean by networking with other labs around the world?"

He nodded. "We were so close. Malinda wanted it perfect, but at the same time, she was afraid the pharmaceutical companies would try to steal the information for their own gain. It never pays to underestimate the power of greed. I was also afraid that the government would step in. They'd done it before. I was not going to play that game."

"When you say 'government,' do you mean *your* government?"

"It doesn't matter which government. They're all the same. I knew this was too big for me, but it was also too big for them. More importantly, it didn't belong to them. It belonged to my patients. Their families. Those little girls, dying of that horrible disease."

"The green screen without a name is Skye, isn't it?" Morgan asked. He was afraid to hear the answer, but he needed to know. "She has Batten, doesn't she?"

The frail doctor lowered his head, sadness overwhelmed him. "Yes. She inherited our good genes, as well as the bad ones. We found out when she was just two. Malinda noticed Skye moving erratically. We first thought she was having vision problems. We took her to an ophthalmologist, who couldn't identify the problem. He referred us to a neurologist named Dr. Rozak. It took a while to diagnose, because Batten is so rare. She was finally diagnosed with Late Infantile NCL. Malinda immediately dedicated her life to finding a cure. I dedicated every penny I could, to help my daughter live."

Morgan's eyes moistened, but he blinked the wetness away. "Things are starting to add up. That's why she never filled her cup to the top; she was afraid she would spill it."

Layland's throat was dry, and he began coughing. He drank a sip of water, which helped.

Morgan waited for the coughing to subside and then asked, "She visits you every day over lunch, doesn't she?"

"Yes. It's the highlight of my day!" A weak smile brightened the ailing doctor's face.

Morgan noticed Layland wearing a bracelet like Skye's. "The bracelet the girls wear is more than a tracking device, isn't it?"

"Yes. It monitors their vital signs and indicators twenty-four hours a day. We know if their heart races or plummets, or if their blood pressure elevates or drops, and other medical information. The data is transferred immediately back to the main computer in the lab."

Morgan was entranced by what he was hearing.

Layland continued, "That's why we left the cruise so abruptly."

"Because something happened to Skye?"

"Yes. Her bracelet signaled that her indicators had changed. Also, Malinda noticed that Skye had been forgetting things, and moving unsteadily. We almost pulled her from the show that night, but it meant too much to her. She desperately wanted to perform that song for you and Tammy."

Layland's eyes grew distant. "We had to get back to the island. The injections were no longer working, and we had to make her dosage stronger."

"Injections?"

"Yes. She and the other girls have been on special injections in hopes of defeating Batten. Most of the girls were showing significant improvement. Almost as though the disease was in remission."

He lowered his head. "But that's all gone now."

Morgan leaned closer. "Why? What happened? According to my wife, all the girls are declining rapidly now."

Leontiou closed his eyes, repositioning himself in the wheelchair. He grimaced in pain. "In order to continue our success, we have to continue the shots. The shots. All gone now... all gone." His voice drifted off.

He seemed in another world as he recalled that fateful day almost two months before. "It was a sunny afternoon, a beautiful day. Malinda was experimenting with a new drug that had amazing potential. She'd found positive results by using stem cells from dolphins since their brain structure is so close to the human brain. Of course, it didn't hurt the dolphins. The stem cells were being harvested in our Costa Rica lab. Malinda began using the injections on Skye."

"Dolphins? You're joking."

Layland's tone lifted a little. "The weaker injections showed great promise. Remember that Skye was our—I hate to say it—our guinea pig. She received the experimental injections first. If they worked, we would use it on the other patients. We always had written permission from the parents, who knew the possibilities, as well as the risks. Skye's blood test results were perfect. All of her vital signs were strong. Her vision was normal. No seizures."

Morgan could see how hard Layland was fighting to keep his mind focused.

"All the girls receiving the injections were showing great improvement even though they were receiving a lower dose than Skye. Malinda believed this was it! We had found the cure! It was actually attacking and replacing the defective genes. Unfortunately, our enthusiasm was short-lived. The bad genes eventually won the battle. We had to make an even stronger strain, one that would reproduce good genes, and eradicate the bad ones, defeating them in the battle for the human brain. The experiment had to be precise. If anything went wrong, it could reverse the process and spread the defective genes at an alarming rate."

"What do you mean reverse the process?" Morgan took a step closer.

"If the replacement genes lost the battle, they could be subverted. Turned into allies of the disease, to help it grow and advance. If someone was exposed to the live virus, they would catch it, and it would spread rapidly."

Layland breathed in slowly through his nose, his face holding a cold stare. "It was a sudden and deliberate computer attack. Was it done for malice, or to bring my empire down? Was it for kicks? I don't know. What I *do* know is dozens of lives were affected immediately. Ultimately, thousands of lives will be affected."

Morgan couldn't speak.

Layland continued his compelling story. "My system was hacked and a worm-like computer virus shut down the entire system."

Morgan shook his head, unable to speak.

"At the moment of the hack, the chemicals were being compounded. It had to be precise or it could be catastrophic. That was why we had the computer combining the ingredients to the Planck constant. The computer was administering the exact dosage when it crashed, pouring all the ingredients into one vial."

The doctor paused, trying to muster the strength to finish his story. "I watched through the window, safe from exposure, as the event took place. I saw Dr. Whitman, a top researcher in the field of nuclear physics, throw himself in front of the door—using his body to shield the others. Miller and Bowers pushed Malinda into the decontamination room. The air hit the vial and the enclosure exploded. The lab burst into flames. Whitman was killed instantly. In a way, he was the lucky one."

"Malinda and her fellow scientists were all exposed to the virus. It was a live strain. Me? Well, I didn't use common sense! All I could think of was Malinda. I had to get her to safety. I rushed into the chamber to help my wife who had collapsed on the floor. I never realized that some of the virus had escaped into the room. I was exposed too, but not to the extent of the others."

Morgan didn't blink. "Why would anyone want to destroy what you're doing? You were trying to help children..."

"You can't get into the position I'm in without making enemies." He hesitated. "I don't know why. I guess it's a game to them, but in this case that sick game wiped out everything we had worked for. Eight years of work destroyed! It cost almost five hundred million dollars to get to that point. All gone!"

"Didn't you have backups?"

"Of course," Layland said. "We had *multiple* backups. One was on Malinda's laptop, which was destroyed in the fire. Everything happened too fast. At first, we thought it was a computer error. We didn't know until afterward that it was a hacker. Hours later, Ty had rebooted the system. It was then we realized we had been hacked, and a virus had been planted inside the system. The virus found its way into the main processor. Unfortunately, it was propagating faster than Ty could correct it. The entire system was wiped clean."

The love Layland had for his wife was evident when he talked about her. "Malinda's mind was failing rapidly. She recognized us, but that was about all, so we couldn't get any information from her that would help us. I knew very little about the lab work." He shook his head. "I lost everything of value to me that day, everything except my little girl." He shifted his gaze to the floor."

"Your wife was the one who passed away earlier this week, wasn't she?"

"Yes." Layland wiped away a single tear. "She was the last one to die. The other two scientists died a couple weeks after the accident."

"That was why Skye was so upset," Morgan mumbled. "Things are finally starting to make sense."

"Yes. My little girl has had a lot to deal with."

No one had to convince Morgan how amazing Skye was. He'd never seen anyone who impacted as many lives as that young girl. She was beyond amazing.

Morgan exhaled, his confusion was noticeable. "What about the injections? Would they work on you? Did you try them?"

"No. Dr. Rozak said he could try to save me, but there was no guarantee they would work. Besides, it would have left Skye and the other girls with no hope. As much as I wanted to live to see Skye grow up, I was not willing to use injections that could help her and the other girls. She's what I live for. And she's what I will die for."

That statement was almost more than Morgan could bear. "You created this place for Skye?"

After a short time, Leontiou found the strength to continue.

"Yes. It was just a vacation home to begin with. When Skye was first diagnosed with Batten, eight years ago, Malinda put every effort into finding a cure. But from the beginning, we knew it might be futile. We knew the odds were against us. The disease receives very little money from the government or big business. They've got their eyes on the larger prizes: cancer, AIDS, MS. But this was our little girl. We agreed that we would put all of our time and resources into finding a cure, so we turned this old prison into a clinic."

The doctor continued his painful story. "Skye knows about all the experiments. Everything! We've kept no secrets from her."

Morgan said nothing in response.

"Malinda and I went around the world looking for patients. Of course, we always took Skye with us. We had to set some sort of criteria. We decided that they must be girls between the ages of four and twelve, who were diagnosed with Late Infantile Batten Disease. As you can tell, we found our patients."

Chapter Twenty-Eight

Morgan's gaze shifted to another room. The door was slightly ajar.

He caught a glimpse of a nicely framed picture adorning a shelf—it was an oil painting of him kissing the dolphin.

Without asking, he walked slowly over to the door.

Layland continued talking, but Morgan was no longer listening to the feeble man. His focus was on the painting. He pushed the door the rest of the way open and noticed paintings on all the walls.

He glanced around the room. Under the window, a small neatly made bed was covered with decorative pillows. A child-sized desk held a computer. Next to the computer were dozens of photographs. Close by stood a painter's easel.

Morgan was drawn like a magnet to the paintings on the wall—pictures of himself, Tammy, and Mrs. Scott. All painted from photos that Skye had taken with her camera. As he studied the paintings, he recognized other people from the ship—workers and cruisers.

Then his gaze shifted to another wall. Walking closer, he noticed all the pictures on that wall were of the same person—Jesus Christ.

Layland wheeled himself into the room to join him.

Morgan spun around. "Did Skye paint these pictures?"

"Yes. All of the paintings in this clinic were done by Skye. She has painted since she was seven. She painted a picture of her mother with watercolors—we were amazed. It's on the wall above the fireplace at the house." The father, even in his sickened condition, beamed with pride.

"I noticed that picture! Skye was seven when she painted it?"

"Yes! I treasure that picture, now more than ever with her mother gone." Layland's voice cracked with emotion.

"These paintings are magnificent."

"If you examine them closely, you'll discover Skye's initials somewhere on every one."

Morgan studied one large painting of Christ. "I can't find her initials on this one."

"You know, since the accident, I've had plenty of time in here. I guess I kind of made it a game to find her initials. That was the most difficult one. I studied it for days before I found them. Look carefully in the right eye of Christ."

Morgan stepped forward. "Well, I'll be." He grinned.

"I asked Skye about it one day. She said it signified that God had His eye on her all the time. Now, look at the left eye."

Morgan looked closer. "His pupil is the earth?"

"Yes, it is. She told me that it signifies that He has His eye on each of us."

Morgan could see that the failing man was tiring.

For a space of a few minutes, the room was quiet. Layland was resting, but Morgan was deep in thought.

Finally, Dr. Hamilton broke the silence. "I understand many of these pictures, but why are there so many of Jesus?" His voice sounded as uncertain as he felt.

"That was my biggest question, too. When I asked her about it, she always responded the same. Nonchalantly, she'd say, 'Oh, because He walks with me and talks with me.'"

"I recall an old hymn with those words," Morgan smiled.

"It made a believer out of me."

Morgan stared at the hurting doctor, grinning. "When you say believer, do you mean a Christian?"

Layland nodded his head confidently.

Morgan's voice sounded more upbeat. "I recall our conversation on the ship. You were an agnostic at that time."

"Much has occurred since then. I never really thought about religion, or really cared, for that matter. It just wasn't important to me. One day I sat down with Skye, and came right out and asked her about it. Can you believe that an adult asked a ten-old-girl why she believes the way she does? Anyhow, she just said, 'Father, I wish you could understand. I see a train coming down the track towards millions of people—how can I not warn them that it's headed directly toward them?'" Unashamedly, tears fell from Skye's father's eyes. "Yes, I'm a believer. Skye was thrilled when we prayed together."

"Because of Skye's love, commitment, and obedience to God, there is probably not a person on this island who has not heard about His love. She's not judgmental, or pushy. Just loving."

Morgan's eyes began to well up. "Doctor, how much time do you think you have?"

There was silence for a few seconds. He slowly responded. "Days... Maybe only hours."

Morgan stared at the brilliant doctor. A man who only months ago commanded an audience of thousands. A man worth billions of dollars. A man admired and praised by multitudes in the business and medical world. Now, near the end of his life, he was a shell of a human being. Morgan couldn't speak—he knew his emotions would overtake him.

"Dr. Hamilton, Skye is dying too! Once that occurs, who knows what will happen? We're simply buying time."

"Buying time for *what*?" Morgan barely could get the words out.

"To find that cure. But at the same time, trying to protect my clinic and country. We had hoped the injections Skye had been receiving were helping, but just today Dr. Rozak informed me that all of her tests for Batten have come back positive."

"Meaning *what*?"

"Meaning that we're losing the battle. The damaged genes are winning, and they'll continue to win if we don't find a cure. We are back to square one. I had hoped to extend my daughter's life, and at the same time, save my country."

Morgan continued gazing at the pictures Skye had painted. "Your country could collapse economically anyway."

"True, but at least we will have tried."

"Sad! Does Skye realize the role she has to play in all this?"

"That's the hardest thing about it. Yes, she does. If you haven't noticed, my little girl does not miss a thing. She has a photographic memory. Everything she hears, sees, and feels, she remembers. She can repeat word-for-word a conversation that took place at dinner three weeks ago. She remembers names, dates, places." He paused. "Yes, Dr. Hamilton, she knows! She knows exactly what's going on."

"That's a big responsibility for a ten-year-old."

"Especially for a ten-year-old who knows she may only have a few more months to live. She's certainly no ordinary child."

Morgan scratched his head. "It's like she's chasing after life."

A voice from behind startled them. "Or running from death." It was Tammy!

A guard rushed in behind her, apologizing. "Sir, I'm sorry. They tricked me."

"It's all right, Benton. I should have told them from the beginning. You may leave us." Layland's tone was calm.

Tammy stood next to her husband, and took hold of his hand.

Morgan noticed her trembling.

The shock of finding Dr. Leontiou alive was written on Tammy's face, but she said nothing.

Layland took an unsteady breath and continued. "Skye's not afraid of death! She's enjoying life to its fullest. And she believes the way to do that is by helping others. Just imagine if everyone on earth had her ambition and love for each other."

Morgan added. "Yes, I hear you. If everyone lived like Skye, the world would be a much better place. I remember how she helped the elderly Mrs. Scott and made her feel important."

Tammy joined in. "Or the way she literally gave the shirt off her back to the poor children in Jamaica."

Morgan put his arm around Tammy's shoulder in a display of support.

Tammy added, "And the way she prayed with Tiffany on her deathbed."

Tightening his hold on his wife, Morgan agreed. "You're right, Layland. She's not afraid of death. She is enjoying life, and helping to encourage everyone she encounters, including us."

Morgan blew out a breath of sadness that had lumped in the deepest part of his soul. "Skye has been a trooper. She has not mentioned this at all. Is keeping this inside good for her?"

Layland's tone lifted. "Skye is free to do and say what she wants. I know she loves me. She knows what's about to happen to me, and to her. You have to understand that her attitude is one of total conviction. There is no doubt in her mind where she'll be when she dies. She puts everything, every effort, all of her being, into living. Living and setting the example of being a servant like Jesus. Yes, she knows that only days are left here on earth with me. She also knows that her time is very limited. Yet, she takes one day at a time, and lives every moment—helping people, lifting them up, loving them, praying for them, and telling them about the train that's coming."

A tear came to Morgan's eyes. "If we could all be more like her."

"Exactly. As I said before, she did not get that from me or her mother. She got that from God. The painting shows that."

Morgan frowned. "Painting?"

Leontiou wheeled himself over to a large painting covered by a sheet. "What I'm about to show you is astonishing." He removed the covering.

Tammy and Morgan gasped.

The large, lifelike painting displayed Jesus walking up to a pearly gate, hand-in-hand with Skye. Standing inside the gate, smiling, with open arms, were a man and a woman. The resemblance was striking—it was her mother and father, Layland and Malinda.

They stood awed, studying the intricate details in the masterpiece.

Finally, Layland spoke, "That picture was painted before we went on the cruise. Notice, my wife, and I are inside the gate. Skye is walking up to the gate holding the hand of Jesus. I did not piece it all together until after her mother died, and you brought her that special gift. Notice she's wearing the outfit you bought for her on the cruise and gave her when you arrived here. Also notice that she has not aged. Think about the time frame. The painting was finished before she ever went on the cruise."

He paused. "I only have days left on this earth, and I know that she'll soon follow, probably before the end of the year."

Fresh tears stung Tammy's eyes and she clutched Morgan's hand tightly.

Morgan stepped closer to the wheelchair-bound man. "Skye has been a godsend to us. She has showed us that there are more important things in life than our problems. True, we may not be able to have a baby, but these children may not even have tomorrow. I believe that what you've done here is give these children a special gift—hope for a miracle." His expression held a resolve that he'd made up his mind. "I believe it would be selfish on our part to pass this opportunity up."

He tenderly raised Tammy's head, so she was directly looking into his teary eyes. Not saying another word, he waited for her response.

"You're right," Tammy cried. "I have twenty-three—"

She swallowed hard. "No, counting Skye, I have twenty-*four* children to care for. God has blessed us abundantly."

For a short time, Tammy and Morgan looked deeply into each other's eyes, grateful there were no more secrets! There were finally of one mind.

Layland spoke in a barely audible voice. "Dr. Rozak is doing a great job, but his time and emotions have reached their limit. We need your help urgently. I would personally like to ask you, will you raise my daughter for the rest of her life? Will you commit to putting everything you have into operating this clinic and caring for our little girls? Will you continue to fight for a cure for Batten disease?"

With resolve, Morgan stated, "Doctor, you can depend on us staying as long as Skye fights. We'll be in her corner, but after her battle is over. Well, we'll have to wait and see."

"It's not just her battle that concerns me. It's also the other girls, and those who will follow. We must be open to helping these families, no matter who they are. Give them hope, no matter how faint it is." Layland leaned forward, folding his hands on his lap.

"That's something the two of us will have to decide when the time is right. If either one of us says no, then the answer is no! What I see now is how emotionally difficult it would be to stay here after she's gone."

"How are you leaning now?" Dr. Leontiou was never one to give up easily.

Morgan didn't blink. "I'm still at a loss knowing why you think we're properly qualified for this. You're able to obtain the greatest minds in the world to work for you."

"You can add much more than anyone else, because you will add *heart*."

Morgan shot a questioning look at the doctor he admired. "Heart? I don't understand."

"You may not now. But you will. Skye sees it, and that's why she loves you and Tammy. She talks about the two of you all the time. She's a great judge of character. She sees your kardia. Your heart." Dr. Leontiou patted his hand over his heart.

Layland added, "Tammy, you said that better than anyone when you spoke at the conference on the cruise."

"I'm sorry," Tammy said. "But heart is something we're lacking these days. We're mad at life, and at God, for not allowing us to have a baby."

"You don't know His plan," Layland said.

"No," Tammy said. "I guess we don't. But God could have given us a baby, somehow. If he wanted to."

Layland lowered his gaze, sadness overwhelmed him. "And He could take one away, too. He'll take my precious Skye from me one day, very soon, I think. Should I be angry at Him because of that?"

There was silence.

Dr. Leontiou continued, "Let me ask you this, Tammy. You've spent a lot of time with Skye. Has she ever told you that she's sick or dying?"

Tammy pondered the question, but really didn't have to because she knew the answer immediately. "No. She's never mentioned it. She only talks about life."

Layland replied, "She believes with all her heart in where she stands as a Christian. She accepts the possibility that she may not be cured, but she trusts God."

Morgan nodded in agreement.

The dying man continued, "So don't blame God. We don't know His plan. All we can do is follow Skye's example. Help those who are less fortunate, or can't help themselves, and believe me, there are more than enough people like that to go around."

"Sounds like Skye's rubbing off on you."

Layland reached over with trembling hands, and gripped Morgan's hand. "If I may be so bold, I love Skye with all my heart, and I may be her father, but you're her *dad*. I gratefully accept that. You see, there's more than enough of her to go around. The fact is, she loves the two of you very much." He grimaced in pain as his body reacted to the disease.

Suddenly a familiar voice rang out, "Father, are you all right?" Skye bounded to her father.

Lance watched from the doorway, hands folded. "What now, Sir?"

Layland engulfed Skye in his arms and tears flooded his eyes. "I'm not sure, now that this charade is finally out in the open."

"How many people know about this... this fake death of yours?" Morgan inquired.

"In addition to Skye, most of my staff knows and of course my lawyers and guards. Everyone on the island knew about the accident, we couldn't hide that. We began circulating a rumor that we were away on business. That's why I dressed like the old woman. We couldn't allow the truth to leak out prematurely. Just a hint that I was incapacitated would have sent my ex-wife and members of my family to their lawyers. They would like nothing better than to shut this place down, and get their hands on my money."

Layland's breathing was growing shallower and more labored. "Lance, I'd just like to spend some time with Skye. In fact, I need to say—"

Layland could tell his time on earth was slipping by. His energy level was depleting rapidly. He believed he only had hours left and needed to say the one thing he did not want to say to his little girl... "Goodbye."

A warm smile covered Leontiou's face. "Lance, let's open the dining room tonight to the entire staff, children, and their families. I'd like to thank everyone, and introduce my successors. Could you get a turkey meal together by six?

"Turkey!" Skye squealed. "I *love* turkey!"

Layland perked up. "I know you do. That's why I chose turkey. Lance, let's have a feast! A celebration!"

"Consider it done, Sir."

Morgan held Tammy in his arms, as they watched the demonstration of love by this extraordinary father and daughter.

"Dr. Hamilton... Morgan, Tammy, will you join us for our celebration?" Lance asked.

Morgan grinned. "Yes, let's get that turkey dinner together. We're looking forward to it!"

He addressed Layland, "Dr. Leontiou, we'll be honored to carry on your work. We share your vision, and we will fully commit ourselves to such a worthy cause. We're ready to sign the papers."

He reached down to shake hands with the failing man.

Morgan knew that those left in the Leontiou family needed time alone. Now that everything was public, they no longer had to meet in hiding.

If all goes well, the next morning the papers will be signed, and Skye will be officially adopted by the Hamiltons. Everything Layland owns will be transferred to Skye and her new mom and dad.

Chapter Twenty-Nine

It took a joint effort to prepare the turkey and trimmings for over a hundred people in less than five hours. But they pulled it off, and dinner was ready, as promised.

Nobody knew it then, but it would be a goodbye ceremony for Uncle Leon—that's what the children lovingly called Dr. Leontiou.

The Hamiltons had no idea what Skye and her father did during their time together, but when they came to the dining room, they were all smiles. Perhaps he beat her in a game of checkers.

When Dr. Leontiou entered, anyone that could stand rose in thunderous ovation.

Skye's face beamed with pride as she pushed her father's wheelchair to his place at the head of the table, right where he belonged.

Morgan could see how deeply admired, respected, Layland was. *I wonder what the Klitous would think if they saw this?*

Moved by the loving show of support, the honored guest, Dr. Layland Leontiou, spoke to the diners. "I've missed being with you the last couple months. With a heavy heart, I have an announcement to make. Due to a freak accident, my wife Malinda passed away earlier this week. I will soon follow, but it's all right. Thanks to Skye, I know where I'm going. You all mean so much to me!"

He faced his trusted doctor. "Dr. Rozak, you've given many selfless hours to this clinic in my absence, I pray that you continue the good fight when I'm gone."

"Lance Laskari, my dependable right hand man, I've entrusted you with my life, my work, my vision. I know you will continue to operate Leontiou Enterprises with integrity."

Facing his computer expert, he added, "Ty, I want to thank you and Jane for everything you've done. Your computer skills have proved beneficial more times than I can count."

"Maya, what can I say to you? You've been instrumental in helping us raise our daughter. You have kept our house in order when we were away. Thank you!"

Facing Penni, the nurse who appeared to be all business, he commented, "Nurse Penni, you come across hard-nosed at times, but I know that you're the finest, most caring nurse in the world. Believe it or not, kids, she loves you more than anything."

A noticeable tear ran down Nurse Penni's face, a display of emotion none of them had seen before.

"Victoria, my first employee... You've been with me on this ride since the beginning. You are more than a secretary. Without your efficiency, your faithful assistance, this business would not be what it is today. Thank you."

The respect Victoria felt for her boss could not be expressed with words. She couldn't fathom what life would be like without him, but she would deal with that later. Right now, she would remain strong. She mouthed the words, "Thank you."

The doctor's face brightened as he spoke to his patients. "To all my little girls, you're very special to me! Keep the faith, and keep praying that we'll find the cure that will give you an extra day, an extra month, maybe even a full life."

Some of the girls were sniffling, others nodding in agreement.

"I know I've missed mentioning some of you, but I also know that you're hungry! A special thanks to each of you in this room. You've all made a difference in my life."

Applause erupted for the great doctor, but also in support of the clinic employees.

Skye was clapping more enthusiastically than anyone.

Layland, in his weak voice, continued, "Before we indulge in our feast, I am honored to introduce the clinic's new administrator and lab director. They come highly qualified. Beginning immediately, they will be in charge." He motioned for the Hamiltons to join him.

"Everyone knows them by now. They've been here a week. Ladies and gentlemen, children, let's all welcome Dr. Morgan and Dr. Tammy Hamilton."

Morgan and Tammy smiled as everyone acknowledged them with applause.

When the dining room finally settled, Layland added, "Tonight, let's celebrate! I'd like to ask my daughter, Skye, to pray for God's blessing on the food."

Skye stood and bowed her head, ready to pray. As she pursed her lips, she was interrupted by the sound of helicopters in the distance.

As the sound grew louder, a guard rushed through the door making his way to Lance. He whispered, "Three military helicopters are landing in the courtyard. Armed!"

Lance flashed a look of concern. Speaking only to the guard, he muttered, "Gather all the men! Meet at the helicopter pad."

"It's already done, Sir. The men are waiting."

Overhearing what was said, Morgan glanced at Tammy. His eyes were filled with fear.

Lance whispered the urgent message to Layland.

The frail man nodded his head before he spoke to the crowd. "Please, everyone stay seated. We have a slight delay." He was trying not to alarm anyone, especially the children.

Worried, Skye grabbed her father's arm.

Lance looked at the children, all anxious to eat. He didn't want anything to ruin their last meal with Uncle Leon. However, he knew their parents were concerned by the developing activity outside—their faces showed it.

"If you'll excuse me, I have something to take care of," Lance said, loud enough for all to hear. He left the dining room and headed to the landing site.

Morgan jumped up to join Lance; Tammy grabbed his arm. "Honey, be careful." She tried to sound upbeat, keeping her composure.

He lowered his eyebrows. "When was the last time you talked with Senator Talbert?"

Tammy nodded, understanding what he was asking.

He hurried outside to catch up to Lance.

Morgan noticed Laskari had put on a bullet-proof vest, and a guard was handing him a weapon.

Hamilton stepped forward. "I need one of those, too."

"You know how to use one of these?" Lance inquired.

"I've fired guns before. I used to hunt with my father."

"This isn't a gun," Lance warned. "It's a weapon." Facing the guard, he issued an order. "Give Dr. Hamilton your vest and weapon. Then, run and get another."

"Yes, Sir," the guard replied, removing his vest and handing it to the doctor.

Lance dished out quick instructions. "Keep the barrel pointed up unless you intend to use it. The lever on the left is your safety. Push down on it to release it. The trigger is very temperamental. One light squeeze, and it will fire a burst of three rounds."

Morgan nodded confidently, grasping what Lance was telling him, but unsure of what was developing.

"Let's move!" Lance ordered.

Morgan followed close behind, joining the other guards. By the time they arrived at the landing site, the military helicopter's engines were shutting down.

Over thirty armed men jumped from the helicopters, settling into a defensive position with weapons pointed at Lance and his small army.

Three additional men stepped out of a chopper.

Morgan immediately recognized the colonel who had paid them an unwelcomed visit at the beginning of the week. "I recognize the one on the left, who are the other two?" he asked quietly.

Lance was quick to reply. "The one in the center is Dimitri Petrou. He's a high political figure in the Greek government. The other one is a judge who serves on the high court."

Next, Klitou and his wife bounded from the chopper. Behind them was a cameraman with camera rolling.

"Well, look what we have here. I should have known the press would be close behind," Laskari murmured loud enough that only Morgan could hear.

Lance stepped forward to greet them, his weapon ready. In a confident voice of authority, he shouted, "I'm placing everyone here under arrest, and I'll be confiscating these three choppers. I demand you drop your weapons, now!"

Without budging, Petrou hollered, "Laskari, you're in no position to order anything!"

"I'm afraid I am. You see, you're in direct violation of the treaty signed by the Greek government. The Leontiou-Greece Treaty, which gave all rights of this island to Dr. Layland Leontiou."

Petrou shouted, "That treaty will never hold water in the new Greek government, and you know that. Besides, if I recall correctly, that treaty was in effect only while Leontiou was alive. We believe he's dead, and you're covering for him. That's illegal, no matter how you try to justify it. There's no doubt that the World Court will rule in our favor. I don't have to remind you how much the World Court hated Leontiou. He stepped on a lot of toes. Once the world finds out about his death, the Greek government will fall. Then my party will take control, at which time the new Greek government—with me as its new leader—will step in, and if need be, with force, remove everyone here, including Leontiou's precious little heir to the throne."

"This is a clinic for children dying of a rare disease," Morgan said. "Are you going to leave them in the streets?"

"So you say. I think illegal experiments are being done here, which gives me another opening to the World Court. It will take me only a few days to shut you down. Drop your weapons, and allow us to do the inevitable! You can't win this!"

"First, you'll have to leave this island alive." Lance raised his hand, and dozens of people appeared on the rooftops surrounding the intruders.

"Well, well, well. Where did you get the army, Laskari?"

"The islanders—this is their home, these are their children. They'll fight if they have to, and die if it's necessary. Because everything they have that's worth defending is right here, right now."

Klitou and his wife were carefully monitoring every word. At the same time, his cameraman was filming the unfolding scene.

Morgan yelled to the reporter, "I'm curious Markus... If the Greek army, or should I say *Petrou's* army, opens fire on civilians, how will you explain your video to the world?"

"This island is made up of conspirators and criminals," Petrou shouted. "Plotting against the Greek government."

Ignoring the politician, Morgan yelled, "Markus, is that what the press is going to tell the world?"

The reporter didn't respond.

Petrou replied for him. "Yes. And we'll get away with it."

"Did you hear that, Mr. Klitou?" Morgan asked. "Your friends are willing to massacre innocent people, just to get their hands on this island. They're not interested in the truth. They only care about what they can take! What they can steal, at the point of a gun! Is *that* what you want to be a part of?"

Petrou turned and motioned to his pilot. "Enough of this talk! Your tiny army has no chance against us. You will see now that we mean business."

Within seconds, four jet fighters thundered low over the island.

The colonel leered. "I don't suppose you have any anti-aircraft weapons to shoot them down, do you?"

Lance and Morgan looked upward and watched the jet fighters as they continued to circle the island.

Lance responded, screaming over the noise, "The Greek government... the *real* Greek government, would not do this."

"I will sweep those fools away with a wave of my hand!" Petrou bellowed. "When the world discovers that Leontiou is dead, the Athens Stock Exchange will crash, and the government will collapse. When that happens, my party will take power."

The last word seemed to hang on the air like an echo.

"My patience is at an end," Petrou shouted. "Put down your arms, or die."

Lance's shout was equally loud. "You're bluffing! You won't harm innocent civilians."

With that, the colonel raised his hand, signaling the helicopter pilot to relay a message to the fighter jets.

Breaking formation, one of the jets roared straight overhead and fired two missiles at the water tower on the end of the island. The tower disintegrated into an expanding cloud of fragments and water vapor.

Petrou roared, "You are all under arrest for conspiracy. Concealing the death of Leontiou—one of Greek's most influential leaders—for your own gain, will be seen as treason. I will be a hero, and the next leader of Greece."

"Somehow, I don't think so," said a voice.

Lance spun around to see a small crowd of people standing a few yards away. Tammy, Dr. Rozak, Skye, and all of the guests who had gathered for dinner. At their head was Dr. Layland Leontiou!

The rest of the island's population was converging on the spot. Men, women, and children coming together around Morgan and Lance, in an unmistakable display of unity.

The Klitous' faces were masks of pure shock.

Petrou's chest seemed to deflate. "Dr. Leontiou... I thought you were dead."

"And I thought you were *smart*," Leontiou said. Then, he sighed and shook his head. "No, I suppose that's not really true. I always *knew* that you were an idiotic socialist with dreams of grandeur. But I never expected you to stoop this far, willing to murder innocent children for power."

"It's not like that," Petrou said quickly.

Layland spoke with power and authority. "Of *course* it's like that," he said. "We've all heard and seen everything you've been saying, and it's *exactly* like that. But the question is, what are you going to do *now*? I'm clearly alive, and these fine people are obviously not concealing my death. So, what are you going to do? Are you planning to gun us all down, and falsify the video?"

Before the politician could answer, Leontiou turned toward Klitou. "What about you, Markus? What do *you* think of this?"

The ailing doctor made a sweeping gesture with his hand, taking in all the children gathered around. His voice became louder and steadier. "Do you see these children? Look at them!"

Morgan couldn't believe Leontiou's forcefulness. *Is this the same man who only minutes ago could hardly stand? Where did his strength come from?*

"They're dying," Layland said. "They have Batten disease, a degenerative disorder that steals their muscle coordination, eyesight, and mental faculties. I've dedicated the last eight years of my life to searching for a cure."

The doctor's eyes were blazing now. "You see these people standing around the children? They're the parents. They live and work here, so they can be with their precious children, and remain close to them in their final moments. You always claim to be searching for the truth, Markus. Well, the truth is standing right in front of you! What are you going to do with it?"

"Stop talking to that ignorant reporter, as though his opinion matters!" Petrou screamed. "It's over! This ends *now!*"

As the word left his mouth, there was another deafening roar in the sky.

Every head in the crowd jerked upward, as every pair of eyes searched for the source of the noise.

Six American Super Hornets were streaking across the island, in hot pursuit of the Greek planes. Out numbered, outgunned, and outclassed, the Greek jets wasted no time in beating a hasty retreat.

The rotors of the helicopters began to revolve, and the soldiers retreated to their choppers. Evidently, the order had been given to return to Greece.

In a surprisingly short time, the helicopters were airborne, and then disappearing into the distance.

Petrou, the colonel, and the judge stood mute—still baffled by the sudden turn of events. Anna and Markus Klitou, and their cameraman, looked equally bewildered.

Although Lance was delighted by the rapid change of fortune, the expression on his face showed no less surprise.

Morgan directed his words to Petrou. "Did you know that NATO is holding war games just a few miles from here?"

The politician said nothing.

Morgan grinned at him. "You might also be interested to learn that Tammy once saved the life of a United States Senator's son. Senator Talbert serves on the Senate Armed Services Committee, and he'd like nothing better than to repay that debt. Tammy phoned him when we heard your merry little band of cutthroats landing on the island. After that, I figure the chain of command was followed. Senator Talbert called the President of the United States, who called NATO command. You see, the island of Kardia falls under the protection of NATO, a fact of which your government has just been reminded."

Morgan's grin grew wider. "The government of Greece doesn't want to be accused of violating international treaties, and it certainly doesn't want to find itself on the wrong side of its NATO allies. That means that somebody has to go down in flames for this little debacle. If I were a betting man, Mr. Petrou, I'd wager that you're not going to be having a good day, probably for the rest of your life."

The politician's eyes were vacant, as if he couldn't understand how his plan could have gone so wrong, so quickly.

"You're on your own," Morgan said. "I strongly suspect that you'll be arrested about five seconds after you set foot on Greek soil. But that's not really my problem, is it?"

Morgan squared his shoulders and raised his voice. "Gentlemen, and I do use that term loosely, as the administrator of this clinic and this property, I am ordering you to leave this island immediately. You're interrupting our turkey dinner."

Tammy watched in disbelief. She'd never heard such confident tones of command in her husband's voice. But suddenly, it was imminently clear to all that Dr. Morgan Hamilton was assuming the mantle of leadership. Tammy felt a surge of pride. She now had no doubt that Morgan was up to the challenges facing him as the clinic administrator. She also had no doubt how much she loved him.

Without saying another word, the three power-hungry socialists returned to their helicopter, knowing that their fates would be decided when they returned to Athens. The Greek authorities would be waiting for them.

Markus and his wife stared at Layland Leontiou. They couldn't believe that he was alive. They were also still astonished by Dr. Hamilton's confident handling of the tense situation.

The reporter blew out a breath; raw emotions flickered across his face. Without another sound, he and his wife stomped off to board the remaining helicopter, joined by his cameraman.

The American jets streaked over the island again. The islanders waved and cheered as the U.S. warplanes tipped their wings in acknowledgement.

Tammy joined her husband and reached for his hand.

Emotionally numb, Morgan stared at his wife, until he finally felt himself relax.

He turned to the crowd. "I believe we have a turkey dinner waiting for us."

As the crowd filed back to the dining room, Morgan faced Lance, scratching his head. "They blew up our water tower."

Lance laughed. "It's okay. That was the old one. It's only for cleaning the streets, watering gardens, and fire protection. The distillation plant wasn't damaged, so our real water supply is safe."

They returned to the dining room and everyone made their way back to their seats.

Skye stood to pray. She folded her hands, and squeezed her eyes tight. *Dear God, thank You for protecting us. Help those people that we were just with, to find You, so they can stop making bad choices and start making good choices. Most of all, thank You for my father, and the influence he's had in my life. You'll be meeting him in person soon. Tell Mother to get her best dress on to welcome him home, okay? I'm glad my father and mother love You. I do too! Oh yeah, thanks for this food and bless all the workers who prepared it. We're going to celebrate Father's life now, so I'll talk to You later. Amen*

The Hamiltons were overwhelmed by Skye's prayer. She talked to God like she was chatting with her best friend. Again they thought, *if only we could be more like Skye.*

While Morgan ate, his mind was still reeling with the recent events. What had given Dr. Leontiou the strength to do what he'd done? Or, rather, *who* had given him the strength? Morgan had never seen anything like it!

Layland knew he no longer had to worry about the Greek government trying to take over. What happened today was newsworthy, even Markus knew that. No doubt, it would be broadcast throughout the world.

When dinner was finished, Uncle Leon said his goodbyes to the gathered crowd. He appeared to be growing weaker by the minute. He'd put every ounce of his energy into confronting Petrou and his cohorts. The island people had won their victory, but Layland had paid a price.

Lance wheeled him to his room where he would spend a peaceful night under the watchful care of his daughter, Skye.

They talked about small things—the time she learned to ride a bike, their deep-sea fishing adventure, and their trip to Disneyland. She fell asleep in his once-strong arms. He watched her for the longest time, and then gave her a kiss on the cheek. Even though he did not want to miss these last moments, he drifted into a deep sleep.

Late that night, while Dr. Rozak was reviewing data on his computer, a red screen popped up on the monitor. The rhythmic beep leveled off to a steady hum. It was the all-too familiar sound. The heart of the champion, Dr. Layland Leontiou, had stopped.

Rozak slipped into Layland's room. With the help of Lance, they picked up the sleeping child from the late Dr. Leontiou's arms, placing her in her own bed.

Morgan and Tammy were immediately notified. They rushed over to be with Skye when she awakened.

The sun shone brightly. The birds sang their cheerful melody, while the cool ocean breeze blew through the open window.

Skye opened her eyes, noticing Morgan and Tammy sitting next to her bed. She stretched her arms, smiling, "Good morning," she said in her usual, chipper way.

"Good morning." Heavy-hearted, they didn't know what else to say.

Her eyes quickly shifted to the open door of her father's room. Noticing his empty bed, she darted into his room with the quickness of a gazelle.

The bed had been changed; it looked like it had never been slept in.

The sweet little girl looked at Morgan and Tammy blankly. Her eyes filled with tears.

Tammy dropped to her knees, opening her arms to the hurting child.

Racing to her, Skye allowed herself to be lost in her warm embrace.

Morgan knelt, wrapping his arms around both of them. Not a word was said as Skye's weeping grew louder, her sobs more pronounced, releasing the tears that she'd held for many months.

After a short time, her quavering voice uttered. "My father is in heaven with my mother. I know I will see them again, but it's still hard."

"I know, Honey. I know it's hard." Tammy took a tissue and wiped some of Skye's tears.

The three of them shared stories about the little girl's father. They cried and laughed, mingling tears with memories.

Soon the familiar sound of a helicopter was heard—Leontiou's attorneys had arrived.

Lance greeted them at the chopper site and told them about the death of their employer.

Barrows felt great sadness, but knew the mourning of the great leader would have to be put off long enough for them to transfer power.

Sitting around the large table in the meeting room, Barrows explained what happened when Petrou and his associates returned to Athens. "They, along with fifty other government officials, were arrested. The socialists on the left had been working quietly trying to bring the Leontiou Empire down, and overthrow Greece. Fortunately, their efforts were thwarted by Lance and Morgan."

As the attorney started separating papers, he continued, "The news footage of what happened here was shown all over the world. As far as the world knows, Dr. Leontiou is alive and well. Little do they know that the giant of a man passed away during the night. As a result, there will be no challenge to the transfer of power of the Leontiou Empire to Skye and the Hamiltons. This clinic and the island are safe from outside intervention."

He shifted his focus to Laskari. "Is there anything you would like to add, Lance?"

He nodded and directed his comments to the Hamiltons. "I want you to know that the orders were to tell you the entire truth if you decided to stay. Layland did not want to deceive you, but he had to know that you were staying for the right reasons—Skye and the children, not for his money and power."

Morgan and Tammy nodded, finally understanding the reason for the secrecy.

Lance added, "After what you did yesterday, he had no doubt that your hearts were in the right place. He knew that you loved Skye and would take care of her, but what would happen when she was no longer here? Would you stay? At the end of his life, he knew that you would!"

The Hamiltons were touched by his kind, affirming words.

"One more thing, I'd like to say," Lance continued. "Dr. Rozak has informed me that he'll stay until the end... either the day he dies, or the day the cure is found. You can depend on him! The rest of the staff will remain, also. And the same goes for me!"

Lance leaned forward, cupping his hands together. "Are you ready to sign? Are you ready to become one of the wealthiest couples in the world?"

Morgan reached for Tammy's hand, squeezing it gently. "Lance, we're already the wealthiest couple in the world, but not because of Leontiou's money or power, but because we have a little girl we love very much, and many great friends. Now, could we please sign these papers? There's a ten-year-old girl who needs our attention right now."

Tammy added, "And I have a lot of work to do. I intend to work fast and furious to find that cure."

Dr. Rozak assured her, "You can count on me!"

Tammy smiled. "Let's get this show on the road."

Barrows responded, "All right! I've just finished writing in the date of Layland's death. Today, Skye becomes your responsibility. Everything is in her name, and will be run by The Leontiou Board of Trustees: Lance Laskari, Dr. Rozak, Arlen Barrows, Tammy and Morgan Hamilton, and me. Business decisions will be made by that board. The clinic's decisions will be made by the Hamiltons exclusively."

"Wow! He put a lot of trust in us. I hope, no—I pray—that we can live up to his expectations." Morgan sighed.

Dr. Rozak stated, "As a doctor, I understand the struggles you'll have. You will experience more defeats than victories, and each victory will be small compared to the defeat, but it will still be a victory. We all know that we're asking the impossible; but it's the impossible that we *must* and *will* achieve."

Chapter Thirty

Carrying a bouquet of hand-picked flowers in one hand, and holding Tammy's hand with the other, Skye led the procession to the small church. Almost everyone on the island followed, each of them somehow touched by Layland's kindness and generosity.

Many had to stand outside the over-crowded church.

It was a simple service, the way Layland wanted it.

Skye sat on the first row between Tammy and Morgan, her new parents.

Lance gave the eulogy; he'd known the man best.

Dr. Layland Leontiou was buried next to his wife on the cliffs, overlooking the magnificent ocean.

After the ceremony, under the watchful eyes of Morgan, Skye walked over to the edge of the cliff and threw her bouquet into the ocean below. She watched it land and waited for the tide to swallow it.

Sadness filled her eyes, but when she looked at her new mom and dad, she smiled. "Father is with Jesus now. Mother is so happy. He wouldn't want me to stay sad for too long."

Hand-in-hand the three of them walked along the beach to the mansion.

Maya had freshly brewed tea waiting for them. The housekeeper joined them on the back patio where they reminisced for hours.

When nightfall came, they tucked Skye in.

Sitting on the edge of her bed, Tammy asked, "How are you really doing, Sweetie."

"I'm not sure. I will miss Father, but at the same time, I know how much he was suffering. I also know he's very happy now because he's with Mother. They're probably going to the park; they loved the park. I will join them someday."

Tammy felt her eyes grow misty. "Someday all of us will join them. Right now, let's just enjoy being together."

Morgan reached for Skye's hand. Trying desperately to relieve some of her pain, her grief, he asked, "What can we do to make you happy? Do you want to go anywhere... do anything?"

"Right now, I think I want to pray and then go to sleep."

"Would you like me to tell you a story?" Tammy asked.

"No, thank you... not tonight. I just want to sleep."

Tammy and Morgan listened to her prayer and kissed her goodnight. The stars on her ceiling began their nightly travel across the universe.

Quietly closing the door, Tammy asked her husband, "Are you coming to bed now?"

"No, I think I'll have a cup of coffee with Maya. I need to find out how she's doing, and what her plans are."

"Right. I think I'll head back to Saint Paul this week, and put things in order."

"Maybe I should do that, since I'm the administrator."

"No, I need to have closure on that part of my life. I know my future is here with you and our daughter, Skye."

"Our daughter. Can you believe we have a child?" Morgan's eyes locked on his wife's.

"No, it hasn't hit me yet. That's a big responsibility."

"I know. And living in this mansion is going to really take some getting used to."

"Not for me... did you see the size of the closets?" Tammy smiled.

Morgan returned the smile, but could not get an image of Layland and Malinda out of his head. *Those are big shoes to fill. How will we ever manage to fill them?*

Chapter Thirty-One

The next morning, Morgan and Tammy were awakened by Skye's bouncing on their bed. "Hey Dad, wake up! We have to take our morning walk along the beach. Do you want to go all the way back in the cave? It's scary!" Skye pretended to shudder with fear.

Morgan, half-awake, peered at Skye, yawning. "Have you ever done that?"

"Only once... Ty took me. It was creepy because we didn't know if the tide would come in. He figured that since it had just gone back out, we'd have enough time to really explore. He's a smart guy."

"How far did you get?" Tammy asked, snuggling up to Skye. Her new mom was glad the girl's mind was on something other than the events of the last few days.

"We made it all the way. We actually could stand up straight and walk the entire way. The sides were sharp, so we had to be very careful," Skye's tone changed. "But it was sad."

"Why was it sad, Honey?" Tammy asked.

Skye's gaze fixed on the ceiling, remembering the day she explored the cave with Ty. "It was sad because there were scratch marks everywhere. Ty said they were fingernail scratches caused by the soldiers trapped in the cave, fighting to survive when the water rose. They tried so hard to live."

Her mind drifted as she reflected on the struggles the POWs must have had as they fought for freedom and ultimately for survival. Sorrow gripped her.

Morgan noticed her mood change and changed the subject. "We won't have time for exploring today, because I have a big tennis match with Lance. How would you like to be our ball girl?" He nudged her shoulder.

Her expression changed to joy. "Oh goody, can I?"

"You sure can! Now, let's go get a hearty breakfast and go on that walk."

As they strolled along the beach, Morgan's heart burst with gratitude. Each moment he spent with Skye was a blessing, and he couldn't help but smile.

Later that day, Lance and Morgan played their highly anticipated tennis match. Skye was thrilled to chase the balls hit out of bounds, mostly by Morgan. It seemed the great Lance Laskari still had it! Although he couldn't move with the quickness he'd once been famous for, he still had the accuracy of his hits and the power of his serves. Morgan put up a good fight and managed to even win a couple games.

Morgan's spiritual faith had begun to be restored. He enjoyed taking Tammy and Skye to the little church overlooking the ocean. Skye usually played the piano for the service, making it even more enjoyable.

Work quickly consumed Morgan and Tammy, but they were committed to spend every moment they could with their new daughter. As busy as they were, Skye was their first priority, but finding that cure for Batten disease was a close second. Not just for Skye, but for all the children.

Although Tammy and Morgan didn't talk about it often, Skye's limited future with them was always in the back of their minds. An ominous cloud hovered over them causing them to wonder when their happiness would come crashing down. When they thought about it, their heart would grow heavy, knowing that whenever it would be, it would be far too soon.

Dr. Rozak left for two weeks on the annual Cruise for a Cure. Morgan felt it was essential that he and Tammy stay on the island until the lab was up and running at full capacity.

Clinics from around the world were being added every day to Leontiou's network.

For Skye's eleventh birthday, Tammy successfully pulled off a surprise party. Everyone on the island was invited, and almost everyone came. A big barbeque in front of the clinic with balloons, streamers, and cake was just the kind of party Skye had always dreamed of. To her, it was perfect!

Morgan suggested Skye enter some of her quality photographs in a contest. They spent the better part of a day editing and printing the best ones. Anxiously, they sent the photos to *Today's Photography,* a new magazine, which was offering a ten thousand dollar first prize. Now all they could do was wait to hear from the publisher of the magazine.

Morgan and Tammy usually were awakened to the tantalizing aroma of fresh coffee brewing, and bacon sizzling. That was not the case one particular morning when they were jolted out of slumber into the real world.

"Mom... Dad... I was hot last night, so I got up and opened the door to the balcony... just a little." She spread her fingers slightly open to illustrate the distance.

She faced Morgan, blue eyes filled with wonder. "Did you know we had black squirrels?"

Morgan smiled slightly, wanting to go back to sleep. "Oh, that's nice." He turned over and groaned. Seconds later, when the reality of her words set in, he sat straight up in bed. "Squirrels? Where?"

Skye chattered faster. "There are two of them and they... well, I guess they came into my room in the night. This morning when I opened my door, they scampered down the stairs. Those silly guys!"

At that moment, Maya let out a blood-curdling scream. "Skye, did you let those varmints into the house?"

Skye's eyes twinkled with mischief as she began to giggle. "Maya called them varmints." She laughed so hard she rolled up in a ball, a sight that her new mom and dad loved to see.

Finally, she stretched out and looked straight at the ceiling, speaking in a low, cowboy-like voice. "I guess I better go and help Maya round up them... thar ... varmints."

Still laughing hysterically, she ran to the door, then stopped and faced her parents. Placing her hands on her hips, she drawled, "I'm going down to the saloon and get myself a sarsaparilla. Are you comin', pilgrim?" She turned toward the door, shoved her hands in her pockets, and pretended to spit.

"Who are you talking to?" Morgan asked, trying to suppress his laughter.

"I'm talking to both of you pilgrims." Skye glared at them for a second. "Oh come on, don't you know John Wayne?"

When they realized, their daughter was trying to imitate John Wayne, they could not contain their laughter any longer. They laughed so hard their sides hurt.

Skye and Maya spent the next two hours trying to get the squirrels out of the house, finally succeeding using a fishing net and laundry basket.

For the next two months, Morgan and Tammy found life interesting and challenging.

Relationships with the staff, children, and islanders began to take root.

Morgan put together a team of world renowned men and women to continue the work that the Leontious began. With all the new equipment in place, they began a race against the clock to find a cure for Batten. Partnering with over two dozen clinics around the world, information was shared at a fast pace, but they were still a long way from where the Leontious were when the virus attacked the computer system.

Every day the Hamiltons relationship with Skye deepened. It was painful to see the child suffer, but she never complained.

Tammy was frustrated, because she had no idea if the treatments Skye had received the past few months had helped or hindered her progress. Her worst fear was the possibility that the treatments had accelerated the disease. She clung to hope that the treatment had slowed, or even stopped the progression of Batten.

One Sunday morning, her questions were answered.

Skye was always the first one up on Sunday mornings. "Time for church," she would bellow at the top of her lungs, jumping on her parents' bed.

She loved singing in the choir and playing the piano. She always added a spark of life to the church. Standing at the front door, she would greet everyone that entered, and she rarely failed to ask about all their family members by name.

But this morning was different. There was no jumping on the bed. No coaxing her parents to get ready for church.

During the night, a major storm blew in, knocking the power out, including the phone lines.

In bed, Morgan wrapped his arms around Tammy and whispered, "Looks like somebody overslept."

Tammy glanced at her watch. "It's getting late. You better wake her up. I'll hit the shower."

Groggily, Morgan opened the door to Skye's room. "Hey, Little One, it's time to get up," he called.

With eyes still half-closed, Morgan sat on the side of her bed. He gently shook Skye, but she didn't respond. "You sure are sleepy today!" He reached over to brush the hair out of her face. She was clammy and limp.

His smile faded and his eyes grew wide with fear. "Tammy!" he shouted in a panic-stricken voice. "Tammy!" He immediately picked up his daughter, trying to rouse her from her unresponsive state.

Still in her robe, Tammy ran to Skye's bedside. One look and she ordered, "Get her to the clinic immediately. I'll call ahead!"

Hearing the commotion, Maya rushed in. "The ambulance is here. What's wrong?"

Ty and Penni raced into the room right behind her.

Quickly assessing the situation, Ty shouted, "Lay her on the bed."

"Her alarm went off about ten minutes ago," Nurse Penni reported as she helped Ty hook up an IV. "We got here as quickly as we could."

Ty explained the situation as he tried to stabilize the girl. "This couldn't have happened at a worse time. The phone lines were down! A power surge caused a number of the girls' alarms to sound, but they were all false alarms. By the time I fixed the problem, Skye's went off. It took me a few minutes to realize that hers was real. I would have called, but of course, no phones were working. We rushed here and I sent someone to Dr. Rozak's home to contact him. He should be on his way to the emergency room, as we speak."

Penni gave the girl an injection.

"Are we in time?" Morgan asked, his voice cracking with emotion.

Ty answered truthfully, "We won't know until we get her to the ER. Let's hurry and load her in the ambulance." He gently picked her up and carried her down the stairs, followed by Penni holding the IV bag.

Close behind, Tammy shouted, "This came on too fast... way too fast! It might be something else."

"Pray that it is," Ty replied.

They loaded the unconscious child into the ambulance. They knew every second counted.

"Any idea what happened?" Morgan asked his wife.

"We won't know for sure until they do further tests." Tammy answered, trying her best to sound in control. "Go with her. I'll be there as soon as I change." Tammy said, rushing to her room.

Tammy slipped on a pair of jeans and a T-shirt. She was not far behind the ambulance. She joined the staff in the buzzing emergency room, moments before Dr. Rozak hurried in.

All Maya and Morgan could do now was wait, and pray.

They hurried to the small chapel in the hospital. Since word had already spread about Skye, the prayer room was quickly filling. Many people of all ages were on their knees, asking for God's mercy on the young girl who had touched their lives in one way or another.

When Morgan and Maya were finished pouring out their hearts to God, they went back to the waiting room where there was standing room only. Many children were anxiously waiting to hear news about their friend.

Finally, the wait was over.

It was hard to read Tammy's expression when she entered the hushed waiting room, but there was no doubt that it registered concern. "Skye had a seizure. Her body shut down to combat it. It could have been more serious, but thank God, we got to her in time."

A smile came to Tammy's face. "She's responsive now, and asking for chocolate."

Morgan looked heavenward and whispered, "Thank you, God!"

"The bad news is that the downward process has begun, and unless we reproduce the drug that Malinda was giving her, or create a new one, she'll fail quickly."

"Is the disease accelerating?"

Dr. Rozak shook his head. "No, it's just catching up. Usually kids her age with Batten are blind, and bedridden. Dementia has often begun. The treatment she has been receiving has been fighting off the disease. I've called the team in and we're going to work today. In fact, we're going to work around the clock until we get as far or farther than the Leontiou's were."

"How close are you?"

"We're not." Tammy answered, frowning.

Urgently, Morgan spoke directly to Dr. Rozak. "You were there while they were working. Surely you know what was going on."

"No. I'm afraid not. I was seldom in the lab. My job was to administer the injections and other procedures. I took care of the children's health and reported the findings to the research team. That was it!"

"Do you still have the old hard drives? Maybe we can send them off, and have them—"

Dr. Rozak put his hand on Morgan's arm in an effort to calm him. "Ty is one of the best computer men in the business. There was nothing left. Not only were the hard drives fried, but they were wiped clean. The intent was not to gather information. The intent was to destroy. And that's exactly what happened."

"I feel so helpless."

"No more than the rest of us," Dr. Rozak replied, his tone grim.

There was a brief silence. Morgan's eyes filled. In a shaky voice, he asked the question he didn't want to ask. "How much time does Skye have? What will happen?"

Tammy studied Dr. Rozak, knowing the answer before he replied.

"A year tops, perhaps only months. As I said, the treatments she received helped prolong the inevitable. The problem is that it's now catching-up time for the disease. There's a possibility that she won't get all the symptoms. What I mean is that it may not take her sight, and I pray that it will bypass robbing her mind. That's usually the hardest thing for loved ones to take."

Morgan closed his eyes tight, trying to wish away what was happening. *We haven't had her long enough. This can't be real. God, please help our sweet little girl.*

The doctor continued, "Hopefully, she'll respond to the limited amount of treatments we have left."

With fresh optimism Morgan began to speak, starting in a whisper, but growing louder with each phrase. "She'll get better! I know she will. We're going to beat this! Skye is going to beat this! Everyone get to work. We have a job to do. Lives to save!"

Morgan rushed out of the room to Skye's side.

Nurse Penni was placing warm blankets on her, the IV still attached.

Skye immediately noticed Morgan. "Dad, I missed church! I was supposed to play the piano this morning."

He held her hand. "I know baby, but that's all right. The important thing is for you to get better."

"Do you want to know what I saw?" Her face radiated excitement.

"What did you see?"

"I saw how frightened everyone was. I saw Ty and Penni come rushing in. It was strange seeing me laying there. I sure looked still and white. Really weird!"

"You saw that," he said with an arched brow.

"Yes, and it was crazy. Sort of like I was a bird looking down. But, I was sad."

"Why were you sad?"

"Because I saw how concerned you and mom were. You care about me so much!"

Tears came to Morgan's eyes as he hugged her.

"Don't cry, Dad. I'm still here! Besides remember what Jesus said: *Proverbs 3:4—Trust in the Lord with all your heart and lean not on your own understanding.*"

Skye could not see her dad's expression, or hear his concern. *That's true, God, I really don't understand!*

Chapter Thirty-Two

Morgan and Skye sat at the edge of the cliff overlooking the ocean, sunrays beaming on their faces. The ocean stretched as far as they could see, almost making it impossible to find the boundary where the sea ended, and the sky began. The brilliant blue was the perfect backdrop for the bright red kite dancing in the wind.

"Dad, how high do you think heaven is? I mean, do you think we could reach it with this kite?"

Morgan smiled, watching the kite tugging hard at the string, almost as if it were trying to break its hold and fly free.

""No, I don't think the kite can reach heaven."

"But we can. How do we do that? I mean, I've seen heaven before."

Morgan glanced at Skye, trying not to let her notice his skepticism. "You've seen heaven?"

"Oh, yes. Jesus showed me once. He took me by the hand, and walked right up to the pearly gates."

"Pearly gates? What does Jesus look like?"

Skye grinned. "You know what he looks like, you silly goose!"

"Right." Morgan stared at the kite. "Skye, you know that painting in your room at the clinic."

"The one with me and Jesus?"

Morgan nodded. "Yes. Could you explain it to me? When did you paint it?"

"Right before we went on the cruise," Skye said. "It was a dream I had. Well, not actually a dream. It really happened. At least, it *seemed* like it happened. It was so real, Dad."

Her demeanor changed. She glanced up at Morgan, squinting from the sun's brightness. "I should have brought my sunglasses. Can we talk about something else?"

Morgan noticed pain in her eyes. "Okay," he said.

The two of them watched the kite again.

"Isn't the wind strange? It comes and goes, but nobody really knows where it comes from or goes to. I mean, where does it start? And when does it end? How does it start, and how does it end? Maybe it's always there. It's like that old saying, 'If a tree falls in a forest when nobody is around, does anyone see it?' Right, Dad?"

Morgan couldn't suppress his laughter. He never quite knew what the eleven-year-old might come up with next. After he caught his breath, he said, "I think it goes like this, 'If a tree falls in the forest and nobody is around to hear it, does it make a sound?'"

"I knew that," Skye said. "I was just pulling your leg."

They burst into another bout of laughter.

"Words are funny sometimes." Skye said, shifting her gaze to the crashing waves.

"Yes, they are. You seem to have a way with words. Did you learn that from your parents?"

"No. I just picked it up. My father once told me, 'Your words are like gold... treat them as such.' I tend to think that words are like windows to your heart. The words you use show what your heart is really like. If they're kind, your heart is kind. If they're harsh, your heart is harsh. If your words are rude or bad, well, so is your heart. And how you act depends on your heart."

As Skye focused on the kite again, Morgan watched the young girl who was filled with an abundance of wisdom. He thought about what she said, and realized she was right.

Skye broke the quiet. "A couple years ago Mother and Father went to Costa Rica to visit his clinic, and then we went to America. They took me to Disneyland and to the Grand Canyon. We watched an eagle soar gracefully over the canyon. It was so beautiful." Skye handed the kite string to Morgan. She jumped to her feet and began slowly twirling around with outstretched arms.

Still spinning slowly, she closed her eyes and quoted a Bible verse. *The Lord is the everlasting God, the Creator of all the earth. He never grows weak or weary. No one can measure the depths of His understanding.*

Skye extended her arms toward heaven. A swarm of butterflies surrounded her, but she wasn't fazed by them. *He gives power to the weak and strength to the powerless. Even youths will become weak and tired, and young men will fall in exhaustion. But those who trust in the Lord will find new strength. They will soar high on wings like eagles. They will run and not grow weary. They will walk and not faint.*

She stopped twirling and looked seriously at her dad. "Isaiah 40:28-31, that's my favoritest Bible verse in the whole world."

She spun one last time and then looked toward the sky. Pointing, she said, "Look at that cloud... it looks like a frog. Ribbit... ribbit."

Morgan looked where she was pointing. "It does look like a frog."

She lay on her back next to her dad. He returned the kite string to her, and joined her cloud gazing venture.

"That one over there looks like Nurse Penni riding a broom," Skye said loudly, pointing to another cloud. She was so tickled with the sight that she got into one of her laughing spells.

They continued to laugh as they pointed out other funny cloud formations.

Finally, Morgan asked a question. "If you had one wish, what would it be?"

Skye thought for a second. "What I'm doing now, hanging out with someone I love."

Morgan grinned. "No, really, one wish... anything."

"I wish... I wish I could play piano with the Trans-Siberian Orchestra."

Morgan studied her. "Really?"

"Yeah. Or play Christina in The Phantom of the Opera." She started giggling again. "With Justin Bieber as the phantom."

Morgan loved the sound of her laughter.

Just then, Tammy walked up behind them. She watched from the background as her husband interacted with his little girl; it warmed her heart. "What are you two silly guys laughing about this time?"

"Come watch the clouds with us, Mom. We're guessing what they look like."

Tammy joined them, on the other side of Skye. "How are you feeling?" she asked Skye.

"Oh, Dr. Tammy... will you please stop being a doctor for a while and be a mom?" Skye shot back, smiling.

"I'm sorry, baby. I'm just concerned about you. That's what moms do."

"I know you're worried, but there's nothing you can do to change it. I'm doing fine." She pumped her arm, showing her muscles. "See? I'm strong! I just want to enjoy being with my mom and dad."

When she grabbed for her mom's hand, the kite string she was holding broke loose. As the kite took flight, Morgan tried to grab the line, but missed. He began to get up to chase the runaway kite, but Skye quickly grabbed his hand. "Dad, it needs to be free... let it go. Stay with me... please!"

The truth in her words hit him like a ton of bricks. He fought back the tears and lay back down. He realized there would be a day when he would need to let go of his daughter, and he was afraid that time was drawing near.

In silence, the three of them watched the kite fly free, rising over the ocean until it disappeared from sight.

Suddenly, a thought came to Morgan. *Before that day arrives, there is something I must do.*

Chapter Thirty-Three

Morgan woke up early. The aroma of the fresh coffee seemed stronger than usual, but there was not even a whiff of sizzling bacon as he headed downstairs.

Maya was pouring her first cup of coffee when Morgan entered the kitchen. "You're early," she said calmly, handing him her cup of coffee.

He took a quick sip. "There's something I need to do."

"Do you have time for breakfast?"

"No, thank you. I'm going to Athens in a few minutes."

"What should I tell your wife when she gets up?"

"Tell her... tell her I need to fulfill a dream."

"A dream... umm, that sounds exciting. Can I be part of it?"

"I'm counting on it. I'll be back this afternoon." He handed the cup back to her, and shot out the door.

The chopper was waiting for him. Soon Morgan was on the way.

While he was gone, Skye joined Tammy on her usual rounds to a few of the girl's rooms.

In Becca's room, Skye was chatting non-stop with her friend. Suddenly she stopped talking and turned to Tammy, "Mom, I feel funny." Skye collapsed.

Tammy called for assistance. A nearby orderly helped rush the unconscious girl to the emergency room.

Morgan was notified and flew back immediately.

When he returned, Penni gave him the dreaded news. "Skye has taken a turn for the worse. Her body is losing its battle with the disease. The shots are no longer strong enough to combat the bad genes."

On the way to Skye's room, Dr. Rozak stopped Morgan. "She's resting comfortably. She had a seizure and is unconscious, but breathing on her own. I'm concerned that when she awakes, she'll no longer have her sight. Morgan, I hate to tell you this, but it's possible that dementia will have set in. She's going to have to stay at the clinic for a while, maybe permanently."

Morgan couldn't speak. He quietly stepped into the room to see his little girl.

His worried wife sat at Skye's bedside.

When he entered, nothing was said, nothing needed to be. On the verge of tears, Tammy stood and enveloped her husband in her arms.

He walked over to Skye and kissed her forehead.

Tammy went to her office to get some needed rest, while Morgan spent the entire night in a chair next to Skye, waiting.

It was early morning when the birds began their exquisite harmony, their song piercing the tranquil air.

Morgan did something he hadn't done in years. He lowered himself to his knees next to Skye's bed, and began to pray softly. *Lord, I know it's been a long time since I have talked to You. Truthfully, I've been angry at You. Why is it that good people get hurt so much in this world? Tammy and I have only wanted to help people. We work hard doing the right thing. All we asked in return was to have a child of our own, a baby to love. We have accepted the fact that will never happen. Yes, Lord, You have given us Skye, but look at her. She has never hurt anyone, and has spent her life helping people. Her whole life... that's only eleven short years. Lord, I plead with You, please let her live a while longer. I have a dream to fulfill, a promise to keep.*

Tammy walked in quietly. As she listened to her husband pleading with God, tears streamed down her face.

Morgan finished his prayer. *Please, Lord... please!*

He was holding his little girl's hand when Tammy knelt beside him, sobbing. Morgan released Skye's hand to comfort his wife. They wept in each other's arms until it felt like there were no more tears left.

Morgan gently moved Tammy's face toward him. "Honey, I just figured out why we can't have children." His voice was strong, decisive.

"What possible explanation can you give me for why I can't have a baby? Tell me," Tammy replied with a touch of sarcasm.

"Think about it." Morgan wiped some tears from Tammy's face.

"If we hadn't had that last miscarriage, we never would have gone on that cruise, and we never would have met Dr. Leontiou."

"I would have given up meeting him, if just one of my three babies could have survived."

Morgan nodded. "Yes, but what about Skye? What about the other girls? If our heartbreak hadn't occurred, we wouldn't be here. We would not be helping the countless children in the world who are depending on us to find a cure for the disease. They *need* us!"

"I understand that," Tammy sniffed. "But look what it's doing to us emotionally. I don't think I can take any more of this... death... sadness."

Morgan's eyes shone a little brighter. "Maybe we're looking at it the wrong way."

"How's that?"

"Maybe instead of looking at it as death, we need to look at it as life."

"Life? What do you mean?"

"I mean that with every step we make toward a cure, we give one more day to these children. If people like us and Dr. Rozak were not doing what we're doing, these children might have died weeks, months, maybe even years, before. These families would not have had the extra time to love and hold their children."

Tammy's face was stained by tears. "But I don't think I can take any more, emotionally."

A small voice interrupted them. "What are you two doing down there on the floor?"

Morgan and Tammy looked up slowly. Their little girl was staring down at them.

"Skye?" Morgan was astounded.

They jumped up, hovering over her.

"Skye, how do you feel?" Tammy asked.

"Well, I would love to have some chocolate."

Morgan's arm's engulfed the young child, her arms squeezing his neck. The very grateful dad looked up to heaven and smiled.

After Tammy embraced her daughter, she stood and gently touched Morgan's shoulder. She whispered in his ear, "You're right. It's not about death... it's about life. It's about another day in the life of a child."

Tammy pushed the intercom button. "Dr. Rozak."

Seconds later came the reply. "Yes, Tammy."

She took a deep breath. "Dr. Rozak, you'd better get down to Skye's room... and please bring some chocolate."

"You're kidding." His tone changed. "She's conscious?"

"Conscious and talking."

"That's great news. I'll be right there."

Tammy added, "And Dr. Rozak, have Victoria call the team together. We have work to do. We have lives to save!"

"I'll see to that."

Tammy walked toward the door, and then turned around and gazed at Morgan chatting with Skye. She smiled and headed to the lab.

"Dad, Jesus wants me to tell you that He heard your prayer and not to worry because He has a plan."

Morgan's eyes grew wide. "Oh, He did, did He?"

"While I was sleeping, I saw you praying over me. Jesus was holding me in His arms, listening to your prayer."

"You heard my prayer?"

"I didn't hear all of it, but Jesus did. He also said that He loves you, and He only wants the best for you. He said He has a plan for you and Mom."

"Did He say anything... about you?"

"No, He just held me and smiled. He said I was his little angel."

"That you are, Little One. That you are."

Dr. Rozak and Penni rushed in, anxious to see the babbling patient.

"I'd better go and let Dr. Rozak take care of you. It looks like he has your chocolate," Morgan grinned.

Smacking her lips, she sighed, "Yum, yum."

Three days later, Skye had regained much of her energy. She was walking around the clinic encouraging the patients, and helping wherever she could. She was still weak, but never let on, never complained.

Morgan entered the doctor's office. "Dr. Rozak, can Skye fly? I mean, could she go on a long trip for a few nights?"

"I don't see why she couldn't do that. Why do you ask?"

"I've been making a few calls. I want her to be able to do a few things before... before—"

"You mean like a bucket list?"

"Well, I didn't want to say that."

"Morgan, we can't escape the inevitable. It's going to happen one of these days. Hopefully, later than sooner, but it *will* happen. Death will rear its ugly head. That's true with all of us."

"It's just so hard to say that five-letter word about somebody you love."

"Imagine how Skye feels. It has hit her on both ends. She saw it with her parents, and now she's living it herself. Morgan, I'm not the kind of doctor who would ever stop a dying child from doing something she really wants to do. Quality of life is as important as quantity."

Morgan stared at Dr. Rozak for a long minute. "Thank you for your support, as always."

"Because of the treatment she has been receiving, I can't tell what will happen, or when. Her symptoms are not the same as a usual Batten patient because of the injections. She could test tomorrow and be completely cured, or the disease could be put into advance mode. We just don't know." The doctor shook his head sadly.

Rozak continued, "What are your plans? I would like to be part of it, or would you like them to remain a secret?"

Morgan smiled. "Let's go get a cup of coffee."

Chapter Thirty-Four

The mist had settled over the island before dawn. A foghorn from an oil barge sounded in the distance.

Dr. Rozak was making his rounds earlier than usual. "Good morning, Skye. Rise and shine."

"Good morning, Dr. Rozak. I was awake anyhow, I was just dreaming." She stretched her arms.

"What were you dreaming about?"

"Nothing special, just how much I love living on this island. Why are we getting up so early, Doc?"

Rozak took the stethoscope from around his neck and listened to her heart. "Well, Little One, your mom and dad have a special treat for you."

Just then, Tammy walked in. "Let's go, Girl. We have some traveling to do, if the good doctor gives the okay."

"I think she'll be fine. You'll be with her, so she'll be in good hands."

Skye gasped. "We're going somewhere? Where are we going?"

"It's a surprise, so don't ask any questions. Take your shower and get dressed. We're going on a long trip."

"Oh, goody! I really could use a vacation." Skye jumped out of bed, hustling to the bathroom to get ready.

Tammy studied Dr. Rozak. "You're sure she's strong enough to travel?"

"Yes. She's fine, very good, as a matter-of-fact. Her blood test results are good. She's one tough cookie."

Skye was ready in record time.

Tammy sat across from her in the dining room, and the two exchanged small talk. Of course, Skye kept trying to get any information she could from Tammy about the surprise, but her mom remained tightlipped.

Morgan stopped to visit with a few of the other children on his way to his two girls. When he arrived, he obviously was in a good mood.

When Skye noticed him, she jumped up. "Where are we going, Dad?" she asked, still trying to solve the mystery.

He picked her up and swung her around. "We... are going to brush our teeth."

"And then where?" She asked, batting her lashes at him.

"Then we're going on an airplane ride."

"Where, Dad?"

"Florida."

"Do we get to swim?"

"We might be able to swim a little, but that's not the surprise."

"Can you tell me, pretty please?" She raised her eyebrows in his direction, teasing him.

"No, I can't. If I did, it would no longer be a surprise, right?" Morgan said giving her the same look back.

"Right, so let's get a move on, so I can find out," Skye said excitedly.

Moments later, the Hamiltons were on a helicopter heading to the airport in Athens.

In Greece, they boarded Leontiou's private jet. Skye of course knew everyone on board, and asked how each was doing. Then she did what she always did when she flew, she ran up to the cockpit and sat with the pilot when they lifted off.

When they were at cruising altitude, she came back and nestled between Tammy and Morgan.

"I'm sooooo excited," she exclaimed. "I can't wait to find out what my surprise is."

To pass time, Morgan and Skye played their favorite game, checkers. He tried a number of times, but still could not beat her.

Tammy teased Morgan for losing to an eleven-year-old girl.

"You think that's bad. Even when she was nine-years-old, I couldn't beat her."

"It won't get any easier the older she gets. It'll only get harder." With that remark, Tammy grew sad for a few seconds, but then shook it off. *Nothing will ruin this special trip... I won't let it!*

Skye slept much of the way.

Within minutes after landing at the Orlando Airport, they were picked up by a hotel shuttle and whisked away.

Morgan hated to leave the privacy of the island because usually the paparazzi harassed them, trying to get a picture, especially of Skye. But, he was not worried about the reporters this time because he felt they were far enough ahead of the newshounds.

Early the next morning, they headed to the beach where they played for a couple hours. Morgan and Skye tried to body surf in the salty, cool water, but neither was good at it. They just laughed at each other.

Tammy smiled as she thought about the close bond the two had formed. She was concerned about Morgan. *How will he take it when the end comes?* She shook the thought away. *Think of today, Tammy. Right now... that's all that matters.*

The last couple weeks, they'd both noticed Skye growing weaker. Her motor skills were becoming more erratic. Even her fun smile was losing its radiance. Her eyes didn't sparkle the way they once did.

"We need to get her out of the sun," Tammy knew she sounded like a physician, but couldn't help it. Her concern for the child was intensifying.

"Right," Morgan agreed. "We have to leave soon to make the noon show. They'll be expecting us."

As they watched Skye make a sand angel, Morgan pulled Tammy close. "I can't wait to see her face," he said, eagerly.

"I'm really amazed that you managed to put this all together."

""Well, it's not finished yet. Let's go to the second part of the plan. Sea World, here we come!"

"Skye, let's go. Your surprise is waiting," Morgan announced.

"She ran over to Morgan, tripping on the way. She stood up, brushing the sand off. "I'm such a klutz!" She didn't linger on it. "Another surprise? What is it?"

He looked at her with a pretend stern face.

She responded in perfect sync with Tammy. "If you told me, it wouldn't be a surprise."

"Right. Now run over to the shower with Mom and get the sand off. We're going to visit an old friend."

Skye had no idea who he was talking about, but she was thrilled.

In less than an hour, they were delivered by limo to the front gate of Sea World.

"Wow!" Skye exclaimed, "I've never been to Sea World. Mom, Dad can we go see the dolphins?"

"That's where we're headed right now," Tammy replied. She was excited, too.

An attendant picked them up at the gate in a dolphin-shaped cart. He delivered them to the entrance of the well-known whale and dolphin show. Another aide showed the excited family to their seats.

Skye was ecstatic watching the acrobatics of the dolphins. Her dolphin encounter with Jessie was never far from her thoughts.

At the time in the show when the trainers normally ask for a volunteer from the audience, they waived their usual routine. A trainer came to the stands and stopped next to the Hamiltons. "Skye," she said smiling. "Would you like to come meet the dolphins?"

The look on the girl's face was priceless. Grinning from ear-to-ear, she took the hand of the female trainer, who helped her down the steps. When they arrived at the front of the stage, she was introduced to the audience. "Tell everyone your name, beautiful."

"Skye."

"And where are you from, Skye?"

"I live on an island near Greece."

"Greece. You mean the country Greece, in Europe?"

"Yes."

"Wow! You're a long way from home. Would you like to touch one of the dolphins?"

"Yes, I'd love to."

"Well, let's see if we can find one." Excitement filled the air as everyone watched and waited.

With that, the gate rose. Three dolphins burst into the giant pool, and circled it.

The trainer raised her hand, and the intelligent mammals did a series of jumps in perfect synchronization.

People in the arena were touched by the way the girl's face shone with delight watching the dolphins perform.

Skye took a deep, cleansing breath, trying to soak in the moment.

Unexpectedly, one of the dolphins broke away from the others, swimming straight toward the trainer and Skye. The lone dolphin jumped up onto the platform and stopped directly in front of them.

Skye's breath caught in her throat, and she took a step back. A sudden realization swept over her. "Jessie," she shouted shrilly. Bending down, she gave the dolphin a hug as the mammal made whistle sounds in an attempt to communicate with her.

A man's voice boomed through the loud speakers. "Dolphins are extremely intelligent. They also have a long memory." He walked closer to Skye. "Jessie met Skye a year ago in Jamaica and for some reason the two bonded, unlike anything I'd ever seen."

He smiled at Skye. "Do you remember me?"

"Yes, you're Simon. You were the guy in the water with Jessie and me."

"Right... I'm Jessie's trainer. About three months ago, Jessie and I moved here to Sea World. A couple weeks ago, your dad called and told me he wanted you to be able to see your favorite dolphin again. I wasn't sure how Jessie would respond, but I agreed to give it a try."

The other trainer pushed the dolphin back into the water. The mammal took several quick laps around the big pool, each time stopping in front of Skye and speaking "dolphin-talk."

Simon reacquainted the youngster with a few hand commands, and allowed her time to direct the dolphins in flips, jumps, and spins. Between each trick, the dolphins would chatter until Skye fed them some small fish from a nearby bucket.

Finally, Simon asked Skye to give the goodbye command to the dolphins. The dolphins waved their flippers to the audience.

The crowd roared with approval.

No one was happier than Morgan and Tammy who were standing, snapping pictures, and cheering for their girl.

It was time for Skye to say goodbye to her dolphin friend. Jessie swam to the side of the pool. Skye bent over and kissed her on the nose. "Bye, Jessie. I love you." She patted her on the head before Jessie swam away to join the other dolphins.

A thunderous applause engulfed the stadium.

All eyes centered on the adorable child who just stole the show. Skye ran back to Morgan and Tammy, embracing both of them with all her might. "Thank You," she giggled.

As the stadium began to empty, Skye glanced at the pool one more time. Jessie was still swimming around the edge. The youngster waved one last time from the top of the walkway and then turned and disappeared from the dolphin's view.

As a river of tears cascaded from Skye's big, blue eyes, Tammy's thoughts went wild. *Were her tears an expression of joy or sorrow? Joy over seeing Jessie again, or sorrow because she would never see her again?*

Despite the tears, Skye sprinted ahead of them to the nearby gift shop. She stared at the stuffed dolphins through the window.

Tammy noticed she was pale. "We need to get her back to the condo. She needs her rest if we're going to be able to pull this off tonight."

"Do you have any more shots left?"

"Just two... that's all. We're at the end of the line. We need to wait as long as we can before we give it to her."

"I know." A shudder of terror ran through him.

"I keep thinking I should've stayed back at the lab, and kept working."

"There was nothing more you can do. You left the lab in good hands."

They drifted their attention to their daughter—their little girl who was so full of life. It amazed them that she never complained about her bleak circumstances. And she still prayed with her whole heart for that miracle.

Skye interrupted their thoughts. Holding up a stuffed dolphin, she exclaimed, "Mom... Dad, this looks just like Jessie."

"It sure does." Happy to purchase it, Morgan walked over to the cashier, and handed her some cash. He proudly presented the souvenir to the child.

She squeezed it tight. "Thank you! I'm going to call her Jessie. She'll always be with me."

In the afternoon, they headed back to the hotel to rest.

Tammy injected Skye with a much-needed shot. She was soon asleep.

Morgan and Tammy sat at the foot of the bed watching her snuggle with the dolphin. The time was wordless; once in a while a stray tear would roll down their faces.

Eventually, they slipped out of the room. Grabbing a bottle of water, they made their way to the balcony.

"What are you thinking about?" Tammy asked.

Morgan took a sip of water, staring almost trance-like at the still swimming pool below. "I would give literally anything if we could find a cure for Skye."

For a moment everything was still, not even the palm trees were swaying.

Gazing at the horizon, Tammy finally spoke. "Well, I believe we'll find a cure for Skye's disease... but unfortunately, not in time to save her."

Reaching for her husband's hand, she continued, "I now realize we made the right decision in staying. For her, and for children like her in the future, we must find that cure. We must, and we *will*." There was no dismissing her pure determination.

"What about children for us?" Morgan asked.

"Children? I have a clinic full of children waiting for me at home right now. I believe that's what God has prepared me for." She glimpsed back into Skye's room.

Morgan's mouth barely lifted as he attempted to smile. The more her words sunk in, the more peace he felt.

The couple embraced, but this time was different. They were in complete unity.

Tammy took a deep, calming breath. "I finally understand what this life is about. It's not about what I want, but what He wants." She pointed heavenward. "God wants us to help those who can't help themselves. Our children at the clinic can't help themselves... it's up to us to help them!"

Morgan nodded gratefully. This was the moment that he had been waiting for. It took a while before he could speak. "I now understand what Lance meant when he said that Skye held the answer to the future of the world. It was not only the seriousness of the political situation at the time, but more the amazement of the young girl's attitude, her zeal for life, her unconditional love, and encouragement. All qualities she demonstrated in every aspect of her life—she set the example. Now it's time for us to lead. To lead by following her example."

Turning his chair to face his wife he held both of her hands. "We can't count the days that remain with Skye, but we can make the days that do remain count." Tammy looked deep into her husband's eyes and nodded, understanding how right he was.

They bowed their heads and shared their innermost thoughts with their creator. It was an offering of thankfulness, a request for forgiveness, and a petition for guidance.

And it was a moment neither of them would ever forget.

Chapter Thirty-Five

Tammy awakened Skye, to get ready for the evening festivities. "Hey, sleepy head, are you feeling better?"

"Yes, Mom, I am." She rubbed her sleepy eyes. "What are we going to do next?"

"Well, *you*, young lady, are going to take a shower. After that, I'm going to take you downstairs to get your hair and fingernails done."

Tammy removed a small makeup kit from her bag and waved it in front of Skye's face. "And then, we're going to put some makeup on you."

Skye's eyes grew wide. "Makeup," she jumped up and grabbed Tammy around the neck. "I've never had makeup on before. Does that mean I may get my bumps soon?"

Tammy looked a little embarrassed. "No, it means you're going to a special place with us tonight and you need to look your best. I even bought you a gown."

Walking over to her closet, Tammy removed a dress. She held it up, waiting for Skye's approval.

A huge smile came to her face. "It's a Christmas dress! I can't wait to show Dad!"

"Neither can I, mine is identical."

"Yay!" Skye clapped. "What's Dad going to wear?"

"He's wearing a tux. He may be a little overdressed for where we're going, but he said he didn't care, only the best for our little girl." Once again, Tammy fought to keep her emotions under control.

Skye looked at Tammy lovingly. "I love you, Mom, and I can't wait to see my surprise."

"I love you too, baby. Now hurry, go take that shower! Meet me back here in fifteen minutes, and we'll walk down to the beauty parlor and begin the butterfly transformation, if you catch my drift." Tammy nudged her kiddingly.

"Dad will never recognize us, will he?"

"No, he won't. Let's go! Hustle!"

The girls spent the next couple hours getting their hair and nails done. It was hard telling who was having more fun, the stylists, or the Hamiltons.

Tammy and Skye were making funny faces at each other in the mirror while they were getting their hair done. The stylists were tickled by their cute antics.

After the beautician finished, the pedicurist, and manicurist had their turns.

Skye had Christmas trees painted on her toenails, Tammy chose wreaths.

When they were finished with their girl-time, they continued to giggle all the way back to their room.

While Morgan was getting ready, Tammy dressed in Skye's room, helping her prepare for their big night.

"Girls, we've got to go." Morgan announced, glancing at his watch. "The limo is waiting."

Tammy replied, "Morgan, have you seen Skye's camera?"

"Yes. It's right here on the counter."

"You'd better get it ready for the unveiling."

"Got it!"

"Are you ready?

"Ready to shoot."

Tammy stepped into the room first. Morgan couldn't snap a picture, he stood motionless, staring.

"Take a picture, silly," she said in a flirty tone.

"You're... you're beautiful. Honey, you look as gorgeous as you did on our wedding day."

Caught up in the moment, Morgan was about to put the camera down and passionately kiss his wife.

Tammy playfully put her hand on his chest. "Hold it right there, cowboy. Get that camera ready as I introduce the one and only Skye Leontiou Hamilton."

Tammy stepped aside and with outstretched arms presented her daughter.

Skye strode into the room. Wearing a sparkly, bright, red dress, she looked gorgeous. Her red shoes shimmered. Her curls flowed perfectly down her back. Tammy had applied just the right amount of makeup.

Morgan stood gasping. "Skye, you look absolutely stunning. You're beautiful!"

She twirled around. "Right, I have everything except the bumps."

The couple broke out laughing.

Morgan snapped pictures of the two of them, in different poses—some serious, some funny.

When he was finished, he held his hands out and both girls reached for them. "Shall we go? I have a date with the two most beautiful girls in the world. I don't want to miss a moment."

Their waiting limousine delivered them to an elegant restaurant.

As they were enjoying their entrees, two men approached them. Looking directly at Skye, one of them asked, "Excuse me, but aren't you Skye Leontiou, the eleven-year-old girl who inherited over a billion dollars?"

The other man started snapping pictures.

Before Morgan could stand, the maître' d of the restaurant came over with two security guards and spoke to the unwelcomed guests. "This is a private party, and you don't have reservations."

One of the guards quickly knocked the camera out of the man's hand and it crashed to the floor.

"Oh, I'm sorry. How clumsy of me," the guard said in his low voice. He bent down and picked up the camera. After removing the video card, he handed the camera back to the stunned photographer.

"Get them out of here! And don't be nice about it!" the maître d ordered.

"You can't do this," one protested. "This is a free country."

"But this restaurant is a private establishment. I can and will protect my patrons from harassment. Now leave quietly, or I'll have you arrested."

The security guards pushed the men all the way out the door.

The maître d turned to Morgan. "I'm sorry, Sir. I saw them come in, but I couldn't get to them in time."

"No problem. Thank you for helping us out." Morgan stood and shook his hand.

With a serious look, Skye asked, "Was that my surprise?"

Tammy, Skye, and Morgan looked at each other and broke out laughing. Nothing or no one could spoil their special evening.

They enjoyed their leisurely dinner. While eating, they discussed funny things that happened on the cruise and reminisced about more recent events.

Morgan kept looking at his watch; everything had to be timed perfectly.

When dinner was over, they hastened to the waiting limo.

As the vehicle departed, Morgan pulled a black blindfold out of his pocket. "You have to wear this."

"My... you really do want to surprise me," Skye responded.

He carefully put the mask on her, trying not to disturb her hair.

"It sure is dark. I can't see a thing." All Skye could hear was the sound of traffic, horns honking, and the quiet hum of the motor.

The vehicle came to a halt in front of the mysterious location.

Skye heard the limo door open and a cheerful woman's voice, "Hello Sir, everything is ready."

"Thank you." Morgan responded, his voice sounding nervous.

Morgan reached for his blindfolded daughter's hand. "Okay. Mom and I are going to take your hands, so relax, and let us lead you."

"You're not going to bump me into anything, are you?" she snickered.

"You don't have to worry about that. This is your night... your very special present. Think of it as an early Christmas gift," Tammy's voice cracked.

Skye could hear music in the background being overshadowed by people talking. The noise grew louder with each step.

When they reached their seats, Morgan placed his hands on her shoulders and gently turned her around. "Okay, sit down and remove your blindfold."

Skye sat down between her parents, and carefully removed the covering from her eyes. She had no idea what to expect!

To her surprise, only darkness filled the room. The confused girl could hear people murmuring, but could see nothing... only black. "Where are we?" she whispered."

Her parents watched and waited, but didn't answer.

She sighed and took a deep breath.

The room hushed.

Suddenly, a guitar broke the silence. Then another instrument joined in.

The lights flickered.

Skye's jaw dropped when she realized that she was sitting in the front row at the Trans-Siberian Orchestra concert—her all-time favorite group!

Too overwhelmed to speak, she jumped to her feet and threw her arms around her mom and dad. Tears flooded their eyes.

Enthralled, she sat at the edge of her seat as the concert began. Her smile said it all, but still she mouthed the words, "Thank you."

Morgan watched his captivated daughter as she took in the sights and sounds of the progressive rock band, which the young girl had followed most of her life.

Tammy shifted her gaze to Morgan. As their eyes met, she realized how much she loved her husband. She also recognized the extent of love they felt for their newly adopted daughter—their precious Skye. She didn't think it was possible to feel any happier than she was at this moment.

For the next couple hours, they listened to and watched the dazzling array of sights and sounds. The high energy performers never disappointed their fans.

Near the end of the concert, an announcement came from the darkened stage. "Christmas is a season of miracles. It's a time for children to believe that dreams really do come true."

Skye's eyes sparkled with excitement.

"Tonight we have a special treat. A children's choir from the city of Orlando is here. In addition, there is a special young lady in the audience who we hope will join us at the piano."

The spotlight highlighted a white, grand piano.

The voice continued, "She has come from a long distance to be here. Skye Leontiou Hamilton, will you please come and play, *The Christmas Canon?*" The dark figure's hand pointed to the spectacular piano.

Two children dressed in white, flowing gowns, walked to Skye, and helped her to her feet.

Skye stood motionless for a second, and then looked back at her mom and dad who were smiling from ear-to-ear. The look on her face couldn't be described in words.

All eyes in the auditorium were on Skye. Not a word was said as the children helped her up the stairs and across the stage to the piano.

Skye glanced around the dark room. Only one light shone and it was directly on her.

Suddenly, another light revealed a guitarist. He watched her with a warm smile.

Like a little lady, Skye moved in front of the piano bench, straightened her flowing dress, and sat down. She cracked her knuckles and moved her fingers quickly across the keys without touching them.

She glanced up at the guitarist, and he nodded his head. He began the silent countdown, motioning each beat slightly with his head.

Skye had played the song many times, and her anxious parents knew she had it memorized. They prayed that she wouldn't forget the notes. More importantly, that she was well enough to perform the entire number.

She began to play the familiar melody. Soon the children's choir joined Skye, singing a beautiful rendition of *The Christmas Canon.*

For the next five minutes, Skye was where she deserved to be, and doing what she loved. Her hands moved with precision, and her head moved slowly back and forth as though she was conducting.

The melody seemed to evoke various emotions—hope, joy, and faith. The audience was silent as the symphonic rock band continued its most celebrated Christmas song.

Morgan and Tammy clasped each other's hands, watching their daughter play with accuracy and grace. She swayed to the music, obviously lost in the magic of the moment.

Too soon, it was over. There was silence for a few seconds as Skye sat reflecting.

When she finally looked up, the house lights came on, and although thousands in the audience jumped to their feet in thunderous applause, she only noticed two people—her new mom and dad.

The children's choir gathered around her, applauding.

The entire band stood in ovation.

Tears cascaded from her eyes as she moved to the front of the piano and bowed to the audience like a professional entertainer.

The same two escorts helped her back to her seat.

Her mom and dad wrapped her with hugs. All three of them had tears flowing freely, but so did most of the audience. The scene was powerful, dramatic.

Tammy put her arm around the happy child.

Morgan watched as the two women in his life embraced. *Thank You God for this special time. Thank You for giving our little girl this opportunity. And thank You that we could share it with her!*

The audience did not know the story behind Skye's appearance. They could only see her passion for music, and the love she shared with her mom and dad.

When the concert was over, Skye was escorted backstage to meet the children's choir, and the singers and musicians of the Trans-Siberian Orchestra.

Most of the band members knew her story. They knew the sweet girl's life was slowly slipping away, and this may be her last Christmas. The musicians were as thrilled to meet Skye as she was to meet them.

Too quickly, the evening was over.

Back at the hotel, Skye was so wound up she couldn't stop talking about her big night. It was past midnight, before she finally calmed down.

Her parents prayed with her and gently kissed her on the forehead. They turned off the light and began to leave the room.

"Mom... Dad," she whispered. "Thank you for the most wonderful day of my life. I will always remember this... always!"

Within minutes, she was asleep. Morgan knew his lovely daughter would have sweet dreams tonight—not visions of sugarplums, but dreams of playing the piano with the Trans-Siberian Orchestra. He also knew that the music she'd played tonight would continue playing in her mind.

He, too, could still hear, *The Christmas Canon. On this night... all is right... on this Merry Christmas night. This night... we pray... our lives... will show... this dream... she had ...*

Morgan smiled. *This dream... his little girl had... had been met... tonight.*

Chapter Thirty-Six

A couple of days later, they returned to the clinic. Skye had an amazing story to tell the other children and staff. All of them were delighted for her.

Lance Laskari stopped by Morgan's office to greet him upon his return.

Morgan told him his idea. "Lance, I want to set up a new trust fund. Every child here deserves to have a dream come true, like Skye did. My idea is to take each child on their dream trip."

Lance nodded. "Something like the Make-A-Wish Foundation?"

"Right. So, if I'm in charge here that's one of the conditions. I want to see their dream fulfilled.

"I think it's a great idea. I know of many who will donate to that cause."

When they were finishing their conversation, Morgan's cell phone rang. He looked at the number. "Excuse me while I take this call."

Tammy entered the office while he was talking. She could tell he'd something else up his sleeve.

Morgan placed his cell phone on his desk. A wide smile spread across his face.

Tammy put her hands on her hips, staring him down. "Okay... are you going to tell me what the secret is?"

"It's not a secret, it's a promise. And I think it's time to show everyone. You and Lance had better go change. What we're about to do requires casual clothes."

Morgan rushed out of the room to see Dr. Rozak. They sat down in his office, a few doors away.

"Doctor, I need to take Skye out for the afternoon."

Dr. Rozak eyed Morgan with skepticism. "Skye is pretty weak, but I think it will be all right. Do I need to be concerned with what you have planned?"

"Well, do you remember what we talked about a few weeks ago?" Morgan asked.

Rozak grinned. "Oh, yes. Is it ready?"

"It sure is."

"Only Skye?"

"No! This is for all the children. I want Skye to share this experience with all her friends!"

Just then, Skye pushed one of her friends in a wheelchair into Dr. Rozak's office. Noticeably out-of-breath, she announced, "Becca wants to go outside. You know if we had that playground—" She stared at the men, challenging them with hands on her hips.

Morgan wheeled Becca out to the hallway, Skye followed.

He knelt in front of his daughter. "Guess what? I have a surprise for you, Becca, and all the other girls."

"Another surprise? What is it?" she tried to jump up and down, but didn't have the energy. Still, her face lit up.

"I'm keeping a promise."

Skye blew a wisp of hair. "A promise. What promise?"

A familiar voice sounded in the background. "Are we interrupting an important conversation?"

Skye turned to see who was speaking. "Zack! Kim!" she shouted, somehow finding enough strength to jump into Zack's arms. Kim joined them for a bear hug.

"What are you guys doing here? Did they let you off the ship? Who's running the exercise room?" Skye jabbered, still held by the visitor.

"Your dad asked us to come. We actually have been here for three days," Zack replied.

"Three days, and you haven't come by to visit. Why?" She frowned deliberately.

"We have been busy building something special, for you and your friends."

"Building something? *What?*"

"We have vans outside waiting to take you, your friends, and their caregivers."

"Where are we going?"

"To the hilltop."

"What for?"

"That's the surprise. If I told you, it wouldn't be a surprise."

Skye rolled her eyes dramatically. "I've heard that a billion times!"

Kim looked around. "Morgan, are we ready to go?"

Morgan made eye contact with Dr. Rozak. "Doctor, can we shut the clinic down for a while?"

"Dr. Hamilton, you're the one in charge of this place."

"Well, I want your backing on this," Morgan replied.

"I'm all for anything to help the children feel normal."

"Okay. Let's get on our way!" Kim shouted.

Dr. Rozak announced over the intercom, "All patients, and personnel, outside immediately. We're going on a field trip."

"Tell them to wear old clothes," Morgan added.

"And wear play clothes."

"What about lunch?" Tammy inquired.

Morgan stepped in. "Ah, if you notice, you can't smell any food cooking. We're going on a picnic."

Tammy peered at her husband. "You thought of everything, didn't you?"

"I certainly hope so." He smiled cunningly.

It took about forty minutes to get all the children to the vans and harnessed in. During their ride to the destination, the kids tried to guess the surprise. *What would Zack and Kim work on for three days?*

When Skye saw how futile their guessing was, she started singing. The other kids in her van joined in song as they traveled the streets of the town waving at everyone they saw.

When they arrived at the forested part of the island, the vans came to a stop. There were several large tents, each filled with tables and chairs.

"Look! The cooks are here!" one girl yelled, pointing to the kitchen staff.

Lunch was ready to be served.

The wheelchair-bound children were pushed through the serving line first. There were plenty of hotdogs and burgers with all the side dishes. And of course, there was an abundance of soft drinks and chocolate. A special treat for Skye, but enjoyed by all.

When lunch was over, Morgan stepped to a microphone. "Did everyone get enough to eat?"

There was a hefty, "Yes!"

"Great. Is everyone having a fun time?"

"Yes!"

"Okay. While we let our food settle, I'd like to say a few things. I know everyone is wondering what we're doing here. I realize you girls don't get out much and that's something I hope to change in the future." He winked at Skye.

"Right now, I'm fulfilling a promise."

His wife gave him an affirmation nod, but it was Skye's big thumbs-up that almost sent him over the edge.

He'd seen a big change in her the last few days. She continued to be her happy self, but she had slowed down considerably. No longer was she a constant chatterbox. Her motor skills were declining rapidly. He knew time was not on her side. Of course, it really never was.

"When I decided to put this secret project in motion, one name jumped out at me. It needed to be done safely. I recalled a conversation I had with Zack on a cruise almost eighteen months ago, and I knew he was the perfect man for the job."

He glanced at the friendly faces before him. Some of the children were weakening fast, others still appeared healthy. He looked at their parents' faces—they were desperately still clinging to hope for their daughters.

"Zack, why don't you and Kim come up and explain what's about to happen. This involves everyone."

Zack and Kim joined him. "Thank you, Morgan. Thank you for including us in this secret project. The last few days have been challenging, but well worth it. Let me first say that it's completely safe, so don't be afraid. I bet you'd like to know what I'm talking about. Well, Morgan called me and asked me to come here and build a zip-line for the children." He waited for his revelation to sink in.

Skye's jaw dropped. Without waiting, she hurried as fast as her legs could still take her, to give her dad a giant hug of appreciation.

Morgan knelt down in front of her.

Even though her body was failing, her attitude remained upbeat. "Now, I remember. You did promise to take me 'line dancing,' but I got sick and never got to go. I never expected you to do this, and you didn't need to."

"Yes, I did, Little One. God placed it on my heart. It was something I had to do, not only for you, but for all your friends."

Zack continued, "Now everybody, listen up. This is what's going to happen. There are three zip-lines starting at the top of the boulders. From there, you'll travel over the treetops. One run takes you over the ocean from one cliff to the next. If you're afraid of heights... um, I suggest you don't look down." He snickered.

"The children can each go with an adult if they want. It's easy, it's fun, and it's safe. Everything is handicap accessible."

"I've made a special harness that will hold two people. I will demonstrate what you need to do to enjoy zipping through our vast jungle." Zack emphasized 'vast jungle.' He knew there were only small trees, but the kids would enjoy it as much as if it were an enormous forest.

He continued. "Now, each of you must find a partner. Children, you may want to pair off with one of your parents." It took several minutes, but with the help of the staff, everyone found a buddy.

The excitement on the children's faces was as real as the worry some parents showed. Many parents didn't want to be suspended in the air over the ocean, but realized they needed to support their daughters. Most of all, they were excited because for a short time, their child could feel normal.

Zack and Kim would secure all the harnesses at the first line. They made sure everyone wore a safety helmet and gloves.

Morgan and Skye led the way, while Tammy took pictures of everyone. The excited father-daughter team traipsed to the end of the ramp that Zack and his team had built. Their hearts were beating fast. Without hesitation, they were off, gliding over the treetops and ocean.

Skye shouted, "Hey Dad, I'm soaring like an eagle."

Morgan smiled. Seeing the excitement on his little girl's face caused his uneasiness to disappear.

It was everything Skye had ever imagined and more.

Ty zip-lined with Becca. The sweet, wheelchair bound girl laughed with glee.

Even Nurse Penni took one of the girls. The children giggled because the rough and tough nurse screamed most of the way.

At the end of the ride, there was ice cream for everyone.

That evening Kim and Zack met the Hamilton family for an exotic meal at The Cliffs.

"I'm so glad you two came." Skye put her elbows on the table, resting her chin in her hands, and looked directly at them. "When do you have to return? Are you going to stay on my ship, the *Isaura*?"

"We have to head back Sunday, but there is something we need to take care of first."

"What?"

"We need your help," Zack announced.

"My help? Doing what?" She angled her head.

Kim stepped in. "We were talking to your dad before we came here, and told him that we wanted you to do something for us. He said that you couldn't come to us, so we decided to come to you."

"Come to me for what?" She looked as confused as she felt.

Kim pointed to a man walking down the road toward them.

"That looks like Captain D! It *is* Captain D! What's he doing here?" Skye shouted.

Zack took Skye's hand. "I asked Kim to marry me over a year ago. But, we wanted to be better prepared financially, so we delayed the wedding.

We decided now is the perfect time, and what better place than the little church on this beautiful island. Captain Dimitriou has come to perform the ceremony Sunday afternoon. He was home in Greece for vacation, so he agreed."

"You're getting married... this Sunday... here?" Her eyes were wide, her smile so big.

As the captain approached the table, Skye ran unsteadily to hug him. "Oh, I've missed you so much. I'm sorry I didn't make it on the cruise this year."

The sea captain hugged her tight. "I missed you, too. It was not the same without my little co-pilot to steer the ship. I wanted to come and visit you, and this seemed like the perfect time."

Everyone greeted the captain warmly.

Skye announced, "I'm so excited about the wedding!"

"So are we, but we've got a problem," Kim said.

"What's that?"

"We don't have a flower girl. Do you know of any eleven-year-old on this island who would volunteer to do that?"

Skye thought for a second, and a big smile came to her face. She threw her arms around Kim realizing what they were asking. "I know of many little girls who would love to do that, but can I please be your flower girl? I've never been in a wedding before."

Kim smiled. "It would be our privilege."

Skye replied, "Uh oh! I don't have a dress. What are we going to do about that?"

Zack picked up a bag and handed it to Skye. She opened it and her eyes grew big. She held up a blue silk gown.

"That's beautiful," Tammy chimed in. "You're going to look gorgeous in that dress. We're going to have to fight the boys off with a stick."

Skye blushed as she held it up in front of her, sizing it up.

The couple wanted a small, intimate ceremony.

Guests attending included Zack's family, a few people from the ship, Lance and his family, and of course, the Hamiltons.

The church was tastefully decorated, thanks to Tammy and Skye.

Skye appeared as nervous as the bride on the day of the wedding,

As the processional began, the groom and best man took their places at the altar of the church. Zack's brother was honored to be the best man.

Zack's sister who was Kim's maid of honor, walked down the aisle, and joined them.

It was time for the eager flower girl to make her entrance! Even though Skye had been losing weight, she looked stunning. She walked slowly, holding a colorful bouquet of island flowers.

To everyone's surprise, except Kim and Zack, Skye took her place at the piano and began playing her favorite classical melody—*Pachelbel's Canon*.

The small crowd stood as the beautiful bride made her way down the center aisle of the church.

Zack's eyes grew misty when he first saw Kim in her wedding dress, the woman he would pledge to spend the rest of his life with.

Since Kim's parents were deceased, it seemed appropriate for Zack's father to give her away.

Skye was too weak to stand for the entire wedding, so she sat between her parents. She smiled broadly as her buddy, Captain D, performed the simple ceremony.

The reception was held at The Cliffs.

Afterwards, the newlyweds said their goodbyes and boarded a helicopter. They honeymooned in Venice.

Captain Dimitriou also needed to return to his family in Greece, but not before he told a little girl goodbye. He knew it was the last time he would see Skye alive. He was heavy hearted.

That night when Tammy tucked Skye in, she shared, "Mom?"

"Yes, baby."

"I'm the most blessed girl on this planet."

"Why do you say that?"

"Because I have the awesomest friends in the world, like Kim, Zack, and Captain D, and all my friends on the island. But even more than that, because I have the bestest mom and dad in the whole universe." She opened her arms wide.

She grabbed hold of her mom's neck, closing her eyes, unwilling to let go.

Tammy knew that her daughter was coming to grips with what was happening to her.

Tammy held Skye until she was sound asleep. The busy day had caught up to the little girl.

Morgan watched the tender scene.

The hurting couple locked eyes. It was evident from their expressions they would need each other desperately in the coming days.

Chapter Thirty-Seven

Skye no longer had the strength to get out of bed. She was slowly slipping away, but still mentally alert and smiling.

Morgan held Skye, so that the three of them could decorate a Christmas tree in her room. She enjoyed putting candy canes on the tree.

The lab was up and running at full capacity, in the continuing effort to find the cure for Batten disease.

Tammy worked relentlessly with the other doctors. At the same time, she tried to be near Skye. She was in the lab when the word of Skye's relapse reached her.

Morgan was making his rounds, when he saw the doctors rush by.

At that moment, an announcement came over the intercom, "Dr. Morgan Hamilton, emergency room... stat!"

He felt a wave of panic and voiced aloud, "Oh no, Skye!" He rushed to the emergency room.

Tammy was already there, assisting the doctors who were frantically working on the unconscious girl. When she was stabilized, there was a collective sigh of relief.

Dr. Rozak stared at Tammy blankly, and lowered his head. He gently touched the woman's hand; nothing needed to be said. She realized the end of her little girl's life was near.

Morgan slipped his arm around his wife. Watching their helpless daughter as she fought for her life, they each prayed silently.

Later that night, Tammy finally yielded to a few minutes of sleep in the recliner.

Morgan continued to hold his daughter's hand.

When they'd almost given up hope, a hoarse, small voice cracked, "Dad, can I have some water?"

Morgan jumped up. "Yes, baby, let me get you some."

He tapped his wife on the leg. Her eyes immediately sprang open. Jumping to her feet, she bent over the child looking into her sick, blue eyes.

In a frail voice, Skye mumbled, "Hi, Mom, sorry I woke you."

Tammy grabbed her hand. "No, Sweetie. I was just waiting for you to wake up."

She lifted the girl's head slightly, while Morgan held a straw to her mouth.

Skye took a few sips of water and licked her dry lips. "That tastes yummy." She laid her head back on the pillow.

Morgan asked, "Would you like some more?"

"No, thank you. I need to tell you something really important. I was just talking to Jesus, and He asked me if there was anything in the world I wanted. I told him there was only one thing."

"What was that, Honey?" Tammy held a cool, damp washcloth on the girl's forehead.

"I don't think I can tell you yet. It's a secret between Jesus and me. But it's a big surprise."

Morgan and Tammy looked at each other sadly, believing her high doses of painkillers were making her hallucinate, a normal side effect.

The family spent the rest of the day together, reading books and reminiscing.

Once in a while, Skye would say something about her mother and father. She mentioned repeatedly that she'd been talking with them. "Father said there is a large beautiful park where they walk. A river runs through the park. And all kinds of flowers. He told me he has my red kite, and he can't wait to fly it with me. They're waiting for me to come and live with them, but they told me not to hurry because we would be together forever."

The hurting couple tried to smile, but couldn't. The heartbreak was emotional torture.

Early in the afternoon, Skye asked her mom to brush her hair and put a little makeup on her. "I want to look pretty like the night we went to TSO."

Tammy put some color on her face, and a little foundation. She applied some lip gloss to her dried, cracked lips. Her mom brushed her hair, while Morgan read her favorite book to her.

Dr. Rozak leaned against the door frame. "Are you guys still here? You need to get something to eat. Go! I will stay with Skye."

Neither wanted to leave, but they knew they should freshen up, and get some needed nourishment.

"I promise I'll call you if anything develops. We'll be okay. Right, Skye?"

"Oh, yes, we'll be just fine. Dr. Rozak, will you tell me the story about when you rescued those earthquake people? That was so amazing."

He sat down on the side of her bed. "Sure. Let me see. It was about eight years ago that my family and I were on vacation in South America, in a country called Chile."

Skye listened attentively.

Morgan took Tammy's hand, backing out the door, not wanting to lose sight of their little girl.

They made their way to the dining room. It was busy, but not a chipper place, as it usually was. Everyone walked around like something or someone was missing. The smiles were forced. It was obvious that everyone was worried about their friend, Skye.

The doctor continued his story, but Skye interrupted, "Dr. Rozak, will you sit me up and hand me my video camera? I have something I need to say to my mom and dad."

Dr. Rozak braced her against a couple pillows. "Okay, what do you want to say?"

"It's really a secret. I'm not supposed to tell anyone. Can you come back in a few minutes?"

"Skye, I'm not supposed to leave you."

"You can just stand outside and watch. I'll tell you when I'm done."

"I guess that will be all right."

"Do you have a big envelope?"

"How big?"

"One of those big ones that important papers come in."

"Sure. In my office. I'll have Nurse Penni get one for you. Now, I'll be right outside. If you need me, wave."

"Okay, Dr. Rozak."

The doctor stepped outside and asked Nurse Penni to fetch the envelope. He watched through the window as the young girl spoke into the video camera. He had no idea what she was saying, but she had a smile on her face, and was speaking with her hands, a gesture she was known for. At the end, she threw a kiss toward the camera, and waved to Dr. Rozak.

Seeing him enter, she asked, "Can you hand me that paper and pencil, Dr. Rozak?"

Gently, he placed them on her lap.

She wrote for a few minutes and then asked for the envelope. She put the paper and mini camcorder in it, licked the envelope, and handed it to the waiting doctor. "I have a big job for you. You can open this after I die."

"Skye, you're not going to die. We're going to do everything in our power—"

She frowned. "Dr. Rozak, I may only be eleven-years-old, but I know what's going on. It's okay. I'm not worried or scared. Jesus will be with me. So, please just listen to me."

Dr. Rozak realized that he'd just been scolded. "Yes, Ma'am!"

"Don't open the envelope until you're supposed to. Then, you can read the letter."

"Skye, how will I know when to open it?" His expression showed his confusion.

"You'll know. Something extraordinary will happen. Now, don't forget. We are looking for miracles here... that's very important."

She looked at him, shaking her finger. "Not until the miracle happens, right?"

Dr. Rozak assumed that she was talking about being healed, so he readily nodded his head.

Just then, Tammy and Morgan opened the door.

"Right?" she demanded as she kissed her fingers and held her hand up.

"Right," Dr. Rozak confirmed, kissing his fingers and gently touching hers.

"There, now our deal is sealed with a kiss." Skye smiled.

Skye pulled her hand across her lips like a zipper.

Rozak did the same. Without another word, he took the envelope and left.

Occasionally, when Tammy came by Skye's room, the girl was conversing with someone, but no one was in the room with her.

Finally, Tammy asked, "Who do you talk to when nobody is around?"

"Jesus."

"What does He say?"

"He says He loves you and me. He says He looks forward to talking with you again."

"Why does He want to talk to me?" Tammy raised a questioning brow.

"Because He loves you. You like talking to me, don't you, Mom?"

"Of course I do. I love talking to you."

"Then why should it be any different with Jesus. He wants you to talk with Him. Remember the song that says, *He walks with me and He talks with me*."

"Yes, I remember that old hymn."

"Well, it's true, Mom. Jesus loves you, but you haven't made room for Him in your life lately. It's time that you did."

Tammy held Skye's hand as she listened. The child's wisdom never ceased to amaze her. Skye was right. It had been too long since she'd prayed.

Skye slipped back to sleep.

Morgan came in to check her.

"Honey, will you stay with her for a few minutes. There is something I need to do," Tammy insisted.

"I intend to stay here the rest of the day. Go, I'll let you know if her condition changes."

Tammy kissed Morgan on the cheek. She walked down the hall to the chapel. She entered the room quietly, focusing on the large cross on the wall up front. She walked slowly up to the altar and knelt. Tears burst forth. It took her a while to be able to say anything, but she finally began to pour out her heart to God. She had no idea how much time had elapsed, but when she was done the tears had subsided, and there was an inner peace. *Skye was right. Talking with Jesus helped.*

It was almost three in the morning on Christmas Eve when Morgan was awakened. He'd fallen asleep in his office, a normal routine.

"Morgan?" Dr. Rozak said, shaking his shoulder. "Skye's vital signs are down. You'd better come. She's asking for you. Tammy is already there."

Morgan jumped to his feet and ran full speed to Skye's room.

Tammy was standing next to her and had been joined by a number of staff and patients.

When they saw Morgan, everyone left quietly; a few of them touched Morgan in a show of support.

Only Tammy and Morgan remained. They sat on the edge of their chairs, one on each side of the bed, holding her hands. Her speech was soft, but unlike most in her condition, her brain was still active.

Skye noticed the tears in Tammy's eyes and wiped one of them away. "What am I going to do with you two? Am I going to have to get a hairdryer to dry those tears?"

A slight smile came to their faces.

"Do not be afraid. In my Father's house are many mansions. He showed me my mansion. You know, there is a big piano there, and I can't wait to play it!"

"What else has Jesus told you," Morgan asked in a shaky voice.

"He told me to tell you both that He loves you... even more than I do... and that's lots. He said that He will always be with you. Just believe!"

"Baby, we do believe. You've showed us how to do that," Morgan answered.

Tammy nodded in agreement.

"I'm so happy about that. Just don't be sad. I'm going to heaven with Jesus, and my Mother and Father. Did I ever tell you that Mother and Father accepted Jesus, so I know I will see them soon?"

Morgan replied, "Yes, your father told me!"

"Dad?"

"Yes, Baby."

"I'm worried about one thing."

"What's that, Baby?"

"Please take care of Teddy. He's going to be *so* lonely."

Morgan felt a lump in his throat so large that he couldn't swallow.

"Don't worry about Teddy. He and I get along great. He loves you very much."

"I love him, too. I hope there are cats in heaven. I know there are horses."

"Have you seen them?" Tammy asked.

"No. I haven't really seen any, but the Bible says that Jesus returns on a white horse. So there have to be horses in heaven. If there are horses, I'm sure there are cats and dogs, but I don't know about spiders and rats." She scrunched her nose.

Tammy smiled. "I never thought of it that way, but I bet you're right." She bent over and gave her a kiss on the forehead.

Morgan was about to lose it when Skye squeezed his hand tighter. "Dad, please don't cry. You know I will always be with you... in your heart. Don't forget to walk the beach every morning and skip rocks into the ocean. When you do, remember me, and know that I'm with you."

Tammy had to look away as tears cascaded down her face like a waterfall. She wiped them with tissues.

"You'll be staying here at the clinic like Father wanted, won't you? All of these children need you. I might be your daughter, but these other girls are all your children. They need your love and help."

"You can count on that. This is where God wants us. This is where we'll stay," Morgan said decisively.

Tammy drew nearer to her daughter, gently touching her cheek. "Like you said, these are our children. There is nothing more I need. I understand that now." Her upper lip trembled. "And you, young lady, will always be our very special little girl."

"I'm so happy! I knew you would stay. Father will be delighted."

"Mom... Dad... you know that I love you guys with my heart whole heart, and I've been told my heart is very big. Thank you for coming into my life."

Tammy's voice quivered. "Thank you for coming into our lives and demonstrating real love."

"Just remember if you ever need me, all you have to do is reach for the sky."

Skye held tight to one of each of their hands and reached as high as she could, pulling their arms with hers. "Just reach for the sky."

Suddenly her eyes opened wide. Speaking loud and clear, she stated, "Mother... Father... Is it time to go to the park? Oh goody, you have my red kite."

Her eyes closed and her body went limp, as the heart monitor leveled off.

She was gone.

Morgan and Tammy collapsed on the body of the little girl who touched the life of everyone she met.

Dr. Rozak sat at his desk, staring at the screen. When he saw the flat line on 081601, he covered his face with his hands and wept.

Within moments, patients and staff lined up at the door waiting to tell their good friend, Skye, goodbye.

Chapter Thirty-Eight

That night, Morgan walked quietly into Skye's room at the mansion. Why he was being quiet, he didn't know. Maybe he thought for a split-second that she was asleep, or perhaps his silence was an unconscious gesture of respect.

He sat down on the edge of Skye's bed.

Teddy crawled on his lap, purring.

"Well, my furry little friend, what about you? You've lost your best buddy. I guess I'll have to take over." Morgan stroked the feline a few times.

He noticed a scrapbook on the nightstand. He read the title, *My Favoritest Cruise*.

"Favoritest." He smiled. "I can't even say it like she did."

On the front cover was the picture of him with Skye on his shoulders at the bow of the cruise ship. He recalled that moment and whispered, "We're the king of the world."

Scanning through the pictures, he laughed when he came to the one of him flying through the air at Splash Mountain, obviously screaming. Of course, the dolphin pictures were there. Then he came to the photo of Tammy, Skye, and himself—the night she surprised them at their table. Tammy's makeup was smeared from her laughter.

He was lost in the memories, when he heard a faint beep. Then another, and another.

He put Teddy down on the bed, and followed the mysterious sound coming from the balcony. He noticed that Skye's telescope had turned on and was making the strange beeping sound. He looked into the monitor on the base of the telescope, careful not to disturb the coordinate settings. He spotted a faint, white dot. Remembering that Skye wrote down everything she did with the telescope, he opened her notebook to the last entry. She had written in bold letters, "Isaura will last be seen on Christmas Eve."

How strange, he thought. Gazing back into the scope, he realized that the faint light was Isaura, the comet Skye discovered. Organized, she had the exact coordinates set, as well as the timer, so she could see her comet at the precise time.

Folded neatly in the book was a letter from the observatory.

Dear Skye,

My latest calculations on your comet, Isaura, have revealed that the final time it will be seen with your telescope will be on December 24th at the coordinates listed below. Lock them into your computer, and don't miss that special night. Isaura will disappear into the Magellanic Cloud. Thank you for your find in the heavens. It has been a fun experience searching the 'sky' with you.

Risto Rodino

National Observatory

Morgan massaged his temples. This is December 24th, the last time to see Skye's comet. There's no way I'm going to miss this moment.

While he was staring at the screen, Isaura disappeared into the heavens, exactly as the letter said it would, just like his precious Skye.

"Maybe she was right. Perhaps that's where heaven is."

Morgan slowly moved his gaze from the monitor. He took a deep breath, and reached for the shutoff switch turning off the telescope. The monitor turned black.

The funeral visitation was held in the small church. Almost everyone on the island showed up to say goodbye to Skye.

Before the visitation for the public began, Morgan and Tammy walked into the empty church. The small casket sat on a golden stand in the front.

The couple sat on a back church pew, trying to find the strength to do what they needed to do.

The church was tastefully decorated for Christmas. A giant tree, glimmering with clear lights was a reminder of the special holiday.

Tammy studied the tree. She recalled how only weeks before, her husband lifted Skye so she could place the angel on the tree. Morgan was on his tiptoes, and Skye shouted, "Dad, hold still! I can't put the angel on... you're making me giggle."

Morgan closed his eyes, remembering how Skye used to say, "Christmas is my favoritest day of the year... Jesus' birthday!"

It was time! Hand-in-hand Morgan and Tammy walked down the aisle to see their little girl one final time.

A slight smile could be seen on Skye. Her cute blonde curls, framed her perfect face. She had on the sparkly dress she wore to the Trans-Siberian Orchestra concert, complete with her red shoes.

Morgan fought back the tears as he placed Jessie, the stuffed dolphin that he bought her at Sea World, under her arm. He bent over and gave her one last kiss on the forehead, whispering, "Goodbye, Little One. I'm going to miss our morning walks and that cute voice of yours."

Tammy quietly whispered, "I love you, Sweet Baby. You've taught me so much! You'll always be my little girl."

For a long time, the couple wept in each other's arms.

Scores of people streamed by the small white casket to pay their last respects.

Pachelbel's Canon, and Beethoven's Ode to Joy, played in the background—Skye's two favorite songs. "The greatest music ever written," she said on more than one occasion. Perhaps she was right. After all, she was right on everything else.

Except the miracle... it never occurred.

After the visitation, Morgan and Tammy joined the large crowd that had gathered outside.

Her small casket was moved to the foot of the church steps.

Due to limited seating, the funeral was held in the beautiful park-like setting outside.

At her service, many people spoke a sentence or two, sharing a memory, and expressing how Skye touched their lives.

Captain Dimitriou shared a few tidbits. He told how she came to the ship's bridge to chat with him. "She used to sit in my captain's chair steering the ship, and comparing the *Isaura* to the other ships that passed by." He paused. "I'm sure going to miss her sweet smile!"

When Morgan delivered the eulogy; his wife stood by him for support. He knew it would be difficult, but something he must do. Even with the sound of the ocean in the background, every word was heard.

"Today we say goodbye to someone who touched each of our lives and our hearts in a way none of us can adequately express. How many times did this little girl uplift a shattered heart, fulfill a broken promise, or help someone less fortunate than herself?"

His palms were sweating. "I was only privileged to know Skye for a brief moment in time. Oh, how I wish I could have known her longer!"

"I will never forget her smile, her bubbly, jubilant voice. The way she giggled so hard that she rolled up in a ball. The way she talked with her hands, really her whole body. Her wit and even her spontaneous, dry humor, which surfaced when you least expected it."

He paused when a large dark-blue butterfly landed on her casket. He almost lost his composure, but somehow found the strength to keep going.

"And I was never able to beat her at checkers."

He swallowed hard and Tammy squeezed his hand for support.

"She never said an unkind word about anyone. No, Skye was always positive, even up to the end. She lived up to this islands name, Kardia—heart. And while this island is small, Skye's heart was large. Some of her last words to her mom and me were, 'Don't be sad, I'm going to heaven to be with Jesus.'" He paused, trying to compose himself. "And if we ever need her, or want to talk with her—" Morgan's voice quivered, "Just reach toward the sky, because that's where she'll be."

Trembling, Morgan released Tammy's hand, and extended his arms toward the sky. Tammy followed, and then Zack and Kim. Within seconds, almost all hands on that island were raised in honor of the very special girl who loved everyone she met.

As the funeral procession began four men picked up the casket, it really only would have taken two, but honor was given where honor was due—Zack, Ty, Dr. Rozak, and Lance were the honored pallbearers.

As the pallbearers began their march down the path to the small gravesite, the islanders stepped aside allowing the casket of Skye to pass.

Skye was buried at sunset on Christmas day, next to her Mother and Father. Her final resting place overlooked the ocean.

Skye would have wanted everyone to be happy, after all, she was in a better place. People knew that, but they were sad because they would miss that bundle of energy immensely.

Two days after the funeral, Morgan received a special delivery envelope. Inside was the latest edition of Today's Photography. Morgan gasped when he saw the cover—it was the picture of Skye and him kissing the dolphins. He opened the popular magazine to a three-page spread of Skye's pictures. Under the dolphin kissing photo was the inscription, "Photograph of the year, by Skye Leontiou Hamilton." Enclosed was a check for ten thousand dollars.

Aloud, Morgan stated, "First place prize photo. I sure wish Skye could have known this... I wish she could have seen how famous her pictures are."

It had only been six months since the death of Skye.

The Hamiltons were in charge of the Fifth Annual Cruise for a Cure. They were on the *Isaura*, the same ship where it had all begun. Everywhere they turned, there were reminders of Skye, the same waiters, room stewards, and of course, landmarks. They weren't prepared for how emotional it would be.

Zack had been promoted to cruise director.

Morgan and Tammy stopped in to visit Kim; she was still working in the exercise room. Her life with Zack was about to change, she was noticeably pregnant.

"When is the baby due?" Tammy asked, sincerely happy for the couple.

"Four months. Zack was offered a job at the front office. It pays so well that I won't have to work. I can stay home and take care of my little boy. We'll be settling in Florida, near the new headquarters."

"I thought you were going to be missionaries," Morgan commented.

"We are, right here. Skye taught us that each one of us is a missionary wherever we happen to be. Although, maybe someday we'll be missionaries in a far off country, right now we believe God wants us to be here."

Morgan nodded his head, understanding. "Well, congratulations."

"Thank you," her face beamed.

"Make sure you stop by and see us during the cruise," Morgan stated.

"Make sure you stop by and see me." She pointed to Morgan's stomach. "You know, exercise!"

They laughed as Morgan rubbed his belly.

Tammy and Morgan walked the familiar ship together, much of the time in silence. Each of them had private thoughts, memories.

When they came to the lighthouse man, Tammy watched her husband's face sadden. He touched the statue, and a tear fell to the ship's deck.

Thoughts of the past consumed both of them. Nothing could be said, their emotions ran deep.

Walking through the atrium, Morgan's eyes were captured by a sight that took his breath away.

Tammy gasped.

They held each other close.

The replica of the *Isaura* was still on the stand where it had been displayed from the beginning. There were dozens of pictures of Skye tacked to a bulletin board. They were pictures of her interacting with people—waiters, room stewards, and passengers. There was a photo of Skye with her contagious smile, sitting with the captain on the bridge. The wall was covered with photos of people whose lives the little girl had touched.

However, behind it on the wall was a large picture of Skye kissing Jessie, the dolphin. Underneath the giant picture was the caption, "Isaura (Skye) Leontiou."

"Isaura Skye Leontiou?" Morgan said aloud, obviously confused.

At that precise time, Captain Dimitriou had been walking through the lobby and noticed the Hamiltons. He could tell they were upset.

As he neared them, Morgan asked, "Skye's first name was Isaura?"

The captain put his hand on Morgan's shoulder. "Didn't you know that?"

"No, we didn't. We thought the ship was named after some Greek goddess or something," Morgan replied.

"No. The ship was named after much more than a goddess," the captain boasted.

Tammy, still trying to take it all in, asked, "You mean to tell me that this ship was named after our Skye?"

The captain answered honestly, leaving no details out. "Yes, this massive vessel was designed for Skye. Most people don't know about it, but I'm surprised she never told you. Her father sure loved her!" The captain scratched his beard.

Tammy added, "Oh my goodness, that comet was named after her too, wasn't it?"

Captain Dimitriou nodded his head.

"She never told us that either." Morgan shook his head.

"That was Skye. She did things that none of us knew about, and never took credit for any of it." Reflecting on the past, a smile came to the captain's face. "Several times I caught her dragging a suitcase filled with blankets and towels from the ship. The first time I noticed it, she was about eight. In fact, it was the *Isaura's* maiden voyage." The captain rocked back and forth as he told the story.

"I never questioned anything she did. Her father built the ship... how could I? Besides she was only helping others. I asked her what she was doing, and she said, 'From my balcony, I saw some boys sleeping in a field. They looked cold, so I'm bringing them some blankets.' I looked at her for a long minute, and then I reached for the suitcase with one hand, and took her hand with the other. Together we traipsed across the street where three young children were sleeping under a cardboard box. Watching Skye give those children the blankets, towels, and a bunch of chocolates, was one of the most satisfying things I've ever seen."

Captain Dimitriou seemed to drift to another place. "It seemed like only yesterday that she came knocking on the door of the bridge. She'd sit near me at the helm, and pilot the ship. Little did she know that the computer was actually set to steer it. I sure miss that little girl!"

Tammy sniffled. "So do we!"

"Did you know that I was her godfather?" the captain boasted proudly.

"No... we didn't know that either." Tammy sighed.

"That was why we were so close."

The three of them continued to gaze silently at her pictures.

The captain broke the quiet. "Her name sure fit her. She was gone too soon."

Morgan's eyes locked on the captain. "Her name? What do you mean?"

"Isaura... it means breeze. Skye was here and then gone, like a breeze."

"Wow! I can't believe this ship was named after her," Morgan drew a deep breath.

"No Sir, this ship was not only named after her... this ship was built for her. This was her ship, her playground."

"That's why you never scolded her when she was on the bow?" Morgan smiled wryly.

"Mercy no, I wouldn't scold that livewire. How could I tell the owner she could not be there? Besides, she knew what she was doing. She always did. Everything she ever did was to uplift other people. She never thought of herself."

"Funny. Everyone says that same thing." Tammy nodded.

"Well, it's true. The only time I can recall her putting herself first was when Kim asked if she knew of anyone who would like to be her flower girl. Even then, she almost suggested one of the other girls." The captain laughed.

"You're right. You know it's really kind of sad," Morgan added.

"What's that?"

"She always said she was praying for a miracle, but it never happened. I think she truly believed she was going to be healed."

"Don't be so sure of that," the captain said.

"What do you mean?"

"Like I said, she never thought of herself. I'd suspect the miracle she prayed for was not for herself, but for someone else."

For a long time Morgan considered his words.

The captain interrupted his thoughts. "If you'll excuse me, I have a ship to sail."

He faced Tammy. "See you at my table tonight?"

Tammy smiled, nodding.

Tammy and Morgan returned later and pinned a couple of their own pictures on the board.

Morgan displayed the prize picture Skye had made with the two of them dolphin kissing.

Tammy pinned the photo of her and Skye before the Trans-Siberian Orchestra concert, dressed alike in their red Christmas dresses.

As they walked back to their suite, their heart was overflowing with happy memories of their daughter. Memories they would treasure forever. One thing was certain, Skye would never be forgotten.

Like all vacations, this one was over too quickly.

The cruise netted three times more in donations than any other cruise. Many of the donations came from those who worked onboard. Since hearing of Skye's death, they'd collected donations from passengers and also earned extra tips to contribute. All in remembrance of Skye.

Her magic had rubbed off on those who met her.

Upon returning to the clinic, they both plunged into their work. Morgan ran the clinic with love and kindness, while Tammy worked endless hours in the new laboratory trying desperately to find the cure for Batten.

Chapter Thirty-Nine

The dedication of the new playground took place on what would have been Skye's twelfth birthday.

It was already nine months since Skye had died, and the dedication ceremony for her wing was getting ready to start.

Morgan was running late, putting all of the last minute details together, when his secretary, Victoria, stepped in.

"Sir, I need to find Dr. Rozak to give him this fax that just came in. Do you have time to talk with a couple whose daughter has been recently diagnosed with Batten? They were referred by Dr. Tocci in Athens and just arrived on the island."

"I *always* have time for families of girls suffering with Batten. The dedication is in thirty minutes, so I'll have to make it quick. Bring them in, but you run ahead and make sure things are running smoothly with the preparations. Tell Tammy I'll be along shortly."

"Yes, Sir."

Morgan was reviewing his speech when Victoria led in the couple and their six-year-old daughter. Morgan recognized them instantly, and his jaw dropped in disbelief.

"Doctor, this is Markus and Anna Klitou."

The shock of seeing them caused Morgan's face to heat. Within seconds, it was replaced by cold anger. His voice revealed his rage as he spoke to them. "I'm well aware of who they are. Is this some sort of cruel joke? Are you looking for another story, or more lives to destroy?"

Markus sounded nervous. "Dr. Hamilton, I can imagine how you feel toward us, and you are perfectly justified. We feel responsible for what has happened here."

Morgan sliced him with a glare. "You *are* responsible. Your hands are red with the blood of many lives, perhaps more than you'll ever realize."

Anna held their trembling daughter close.

Klitou's lip twitched anxiously. "You're right, probably more than we realize. Our daughter has been very sick for over a year. About a month ago, she was diagnosed with Batten disease. Fate has handed us an ironic

257

blow, one that we as parents must face up to. We recently found out the result of our actions. We're sick about it!"

Morgan didn't know what to think, say, or do. He stood motionless.

"Dr. Hamilton, we come to you begging for help. We don't want a story or a front-page byline. We're not here for ourselves, but for our little girl. Think of us however you want, but our daughter is innocent. We were wrong, we both made mistakes in the past, we know that. We know we deserve your scorn, but will you please help us... will you help her?" The broken father pointed to his child.

Morgan looked at the couple with disdain, but he saw the intense regret, the anguish on their faces. Most of all, he saw a little girl who didn't understand what was going on, and the look of fear on her innocent face.

He remembered Dr. Leontiou's words—*we must be open to helping these families, no matter who they are... give them hope, no matter how faint it is.*

Then he saw a clear vision of Skye's face, and remembered her loving, forgiving spirit.

He looked at the parents, and then back again at their daughter. Just then, he heard Skye's clear voice, "Dad, you *have* to help this little girl. Do this for me... and for Jesus. Remember that Jesus said, *Do this for the least of them... you do it for Me.*"

His heart melted as he stared at the child clinging to her mother and father. A blameless little girl, whose days on earth were numbered. She would only be able to run and play for a short time. Without a cure, she would never experience the love of a husband, or hold her own child.

Morgan's voice grew soft, compassionate. Choked up, he spoke slowly. "I have to go. We're dedicating the new wing in a few minutes. It's a playground made for little girls, like yours."

He looked at the adorable child. Her jet-black hair wrapped around her face. Her big brown eyes showed fear, uncertainty.

He turned his attention to the Klitous. "Mr. and Mrs. Klitou, would you care to have an exclusive interview of the dedication of 'The Skye Wing?'"

Markus Klitou looked at his wife, tears came to his eyes. "Doctor, we would be honored."

Morgan held out his hand.

Markus stared at it for the longest time. The reporter's expression showed his shock, confusion. After all he'd done to sabotage what the doctors were fighting for—their cause—Dr. Hamilton was extending his hand of forgiveness. The grateful father grabbed it readily, and the two men shook hands.

"Come, I don't want to be late for the dedication." Morgan smiled.

Morgan picked up the sweet little girl and began chatting with her, pointing out the sights as they walked to the dedication site.

Her parents followed, holding hands. They smiled at each other, finally having hope. They knew their child would have the best possible care in the world.

"What's your name, Little One?" Morgan asked the girl.

"Venus."

"Ah... Venus, the goddess of love."

"Yes. My daddy calls me his little angel."

"I bet you are. Would you like to see our new playground?"

She nodded excitedly.

Tammy stared at them as they neared the crowd. She couldn't believe her eyes!

Morgan smiled and handed the little girl to her father.

"Something I should know about?" Tammy whispered to her husband.

"It's okay. I'll tell you about it later."

Hundreds of people gathered for the dedication. Dr. Gosset and other doctors and research staff from around the world attended. They were joined by donors, parents, and their children who were fighting the dreaded disease.

It was a bittersweet occasion.

Morgan's face lit up when he saw Mrs. Scott. "I'm so glad you came, Mrs. Scott."

"I would not have missed this for the world. That little girl was the biggest blessing in my life. She was a flower among the thorns. She helped me realize what was important in life."

"Yes... she was certainly an encourager."

Mrs. Scott nodded her head. "I once heard that flowers of today are but seeds of tomorrow."

"That's true, but I tend to look at it a little differently. Seeds planted today become flowers tomorrow. Skye sure planted a lot of seeds."

"She certainly did! Therefore, the flowers will continue to bloom even though she's gone."

"Right here is the perfect example... this incredible playground."

Mrs. Scott smiled. "I was delighted to donate money toward this cause. I just finished talking to your wife. I'm all alone in the States. I have a hard time walking, but I'm good with children. I asked her if I could move here. Volunteer my time, and help out where I'm needed. I promise I won't get in the way. My husband left me very well-off, so you don't have to worry about taking care of me."

Morgan smiled. "I think that would be wonderful. I know of a couple apartments that are open. I'll show them to you later. Right now, I have to go. I have a speech to deliver. Thank you so much for coming."

Morgan walked to the podium. Tammy handed him a microphone, and stood next to him.

"Good morning. We're here to celebrate, remember, and dedicate this new wing. It's a place where our children can play. A place where our children will feel normal."

Morgan glanced up at a row of girls, Skye's friends, all suffering from Batten disease; some in wheelchairs, others had lost their sight, some suffering from dementia.

"This playground was not my dream. I can't take credit for it. This was the dream of a young girl. A bundle of energy who was only on this earth for a short time, but who left an imprint on our lives that will last a lifetime. Her name was Skye."

Morgan's tone was upbeat. "Let me tell you about my daughter, Skye. She was a blue-eyed, blond, little girl who brightened up the darkest room with her smile and outgoing personality. She was never afraid to speak to anyone, or to encourage a person however she could. One of the things I loved about her was the way she used her hands, actually, her entire body, to get a point across."

He continued, "My wife and I recently took some time off from the clinic. We went back to the place where we first met Skye. The place that changed our lives forever. The cruise ship *Isaura*. I've wondered what our lives would have been like if we had not gone on that cruise. What if I had not met that little girl? Where would our lives be now? I can't even imagine the loneliness, the emptiness! I don't have enough time to tell you the many ways Skye enriched our lives, or the things she has taught us about life and love."

Morgan noticed Victoria hand Dr. Rozak a paper. The doctor studied it, and put his hand to his chin. Then, as if he remembered something, he smiled and rushed off.

Dr. Hamilton shuffled his papers to stay with the script. "On that beautiful ship a few months ago, we discovered some things we didn't know about Skye. We didn't know that her given name was 'Isaura.' We didn't know that the giant ship was named after her...let me rephrase that, it was actually built for her, a gift from her father, the late, great Dr. Leontiou, better known as Dr. Leon by his patients. Skye never boasted about it. My goodness, if I had a five hundred million dollar ship built for me... people would know about it!" he chuckled.

He felt a surge of strength to continue. "I'm sure everyone here was impacted by Skye's life. I know her memory will live on. It's seen every day by thousands of people as the ship bearing her name passes by like a breeze. Isaura, in Greek, means *breeze*. Skye's life touched many people, and then she was gone like a refreshing breeze with a lasting effect. Her names fit her, Isaura... Skye." Remembering the day he met her, he added, "Skye... with an e."

Some in the audience snickered. They too, had been introduced to her in the same way.

He continued, "Many times Skye would tell me in that cute voice. 'I think we should have a playground right here.'" His voice cracked. "She pointed to this spot and told me that we needed a place where kids can play and have fun. It had to be made of soft material, so if someone fell they wouldn't be injured. 'It's important in a child's life,' she said. I remember those conversations like they happened yesterday. She was only ten at the time, but she was wise beyond her years. If only we had her thoughts, her ambition, her spunk, her caring attitude, her love."

Just then, a large blue butterfly landed on the microphone. Morgan froze. Then, it fluttered off into the playground area, as the entire audience watched. "There are reminders of Skye everywhere we look. Though she'll always be missed, she will never be forgotten."

Morgan went on, "It's not a coincidence that we had this dedication today, Skye's twelfth birthday. The ten thousand dollars that Skye won with her photo started this fund. She would've wanted that. I wish to thank those of you who have donated generously of your time and resources. The playground will be used. I guarantee that!"

Tammy moved close to the giant curtain behind her husband.

Morgan smiled at the children who were waiting with anticipation.

"Ladies and gentlemen, and all our sweet girls, we dedicate this wing and this playground, to all of the children in this hospital. And I pray that one day soon, we'll find a cure for Batten disease. I present to you... *The Skye Wing.*"

Tammy pulled the cord on a giant curtain unveiling an arched entrance. Over the arch were the bright, bold words, 'Reach for the Skye.' Above the giant letters was a brilliantly-hued rainbow.

On one side of the entrance was a display of pictures Skye had taken, including the award winning photo of Morgan and Skye kissing the dolphins. But, it was the painting on the other side of the arch that captured everyone's attention. It was Skye's painting of her walking with Jesus through the pearly gates into the arms of her mother and father.

At the planned moment in the ceremony, hundreds of birthday balloons were released, racing toward the sky.

Tours of *The Skye Wing* followed the ceremony. The crowds of people were delighted by the beautiful, kid-friendly, indoor/outdoor playground. They were especially excited about the pool. Chairlifts complete with a harness, could safely hold the immobile children in the warm water, allowing them the benefit of water therapy.

As the crowd toured the area, Morgan and Tammy stared at the entrance bearing the inscription of Skye's name.

Their thoughts were interrupted by a small, but sassy voice. "Dude, can you please move... you're blocking progress."

Morgan shifted his focus to an unfamiliar little girl staring up at him. He lowered to one knee. "And what is your name, Little One?"

"Samantha... not Sam, that's a boy's name. What's yours?" She placed her hands on her hips, waiting.

"Morgan."

"Do you work here, Mr. Morgan?"

"It's just Morgan, and yes, I do work here."

"Could you tell the person who owns this place that I think it's awesome?"

Morgan noticed a young woman standing nearby. "Is this your mother?"

"Yes. Isn't she beautiful?"

The woman smiled and waved shyly.

Morgan began to ask the mother the dreaded question. "Does she have—?" He didn't have to finish the sentence.

Her mother nodded her head sadly, acknowledging that her daughter suffered from Batten.

Morgan studied her thoughtfully, and then looked back at the child. "Yes she's beautiful. You look a lot like her. And you're right, this playground is awesome and it belongs to all of the children who live here. Would you like to come with me and explore it?"

"Yep!"

"Then let's go!" Morgan picked the girl up. After introducing himself to the worried mother, Morgan carried her to the playground. She chattered the entire way. Her mom walked next to them.

Tammy smiled, watching the touching moment. *Yes... we have plenty of children. We are blessed beyond all measure.*

Dr. Rozak strode over to her. He was holding a sheet of paper in one hand, a manila envelope in the other. Confusion showed on his face. "Tammy, I just received this report from the physical you had last week. I was shocked to say the least. After I read it, I recalled a certain young lady giving me some instructions. She said that I would know when to give this to you." He paused.

"What are you trying to say, Doctor?"

"Well, I have some news for you, which I would love to tell you about, but—"

The doctor looked at the large envelope and back to Tammy. "Skye told me that when the miracle happened, I'd know. I wasn't sure what she was talking about. She talked all the time about the miracle she was praying for. I always thought she was talking about a miracle for herself. A cure. But I should've known better. Skye always put others first. Aways! Her little video camera is in the envelope. It contains a video, which she made only days before she passed away. She made me leave the room when she recorded it. I'm sorry, but I have to confess that I watched part of it."

He handed the envelope and paper to a stunned Tammy. "Here. I think Skye has an important message for you."

A puzzled look came over her as she removed the camera. "When the miracle happened? What do you mean? Tell me *what*?"

Dr. Rozak winked at her. "It's all in the video. Skye was a remarkable young girl. I believe she has a lot of pull in high places."

She glanced at Morgan who was on the playground laughing with his new friend as they jumped on a bouncy toy.

Tammy turned the camera on. Skye was sitting up in bed. Her expressions were just as she remembered. Just seeing her daughter in the last days brought tears to her eyes.

Skye began, "Let me see. Yeah, it's working. Hi, Mom! This is for Dad too, but I wanted to talk to you first. I always loved calling you Mom."

"I hope you and Dad are doing okay. Since you're watching this, I suspect two things have happened. Dr. Rozak has given you some wonderful news, and I've gone to be with Jesus. Remember the many times that I said I was praying for a miracle? I knew Jesus said my prayers would never return void. I think that means they will never be ignored. When I got to heaven, I was going to make sure Jesus heard my prayer. I was bound and determined to talk to Him personally." Skye was making her well-known hand gestures.

"I would suspect that with this video you're holding another paper. One that says you're going to have a baby! Congratulations!" Skye's eyes twinkled, and—despite the illness and weakness written across her face—her smile was as bright as it had ever been.

Skye clapped her hands excitedly. "I wish I could be there with you when she arrives. Oh yeah, I forgot to tell you. I asked Jesus for a girl. A healthy daughter. I know she'll bring joy and happiness to you and Dad. Give Dad a hug for me, and please tell him how much I love him. I miss you both, but at least, I have no more pain."

Tears came to Skye's eyes. "I never told you about the pain. I wanted to be a big girl, and not make you worry, but the pain was so bad that many times I cried myself to sleep. I fought really hard to keep my mind and eyes working. I knew I could lose them both. I want to thank you for coming into my life and taking such good care of me. I think I can be a handful."

Tammy smiled amidst her tears.

Skye continued, "One day I will greet you both here, but for now, have a great life. And take care of that little baby. My sister! And whenever you feel lonely or sad, remember to look up and reach for the sky."

Skye reached her arms high. "That's where I'll be. Uh oh, I have to go now. Mother and Father are going to take me to the park. We're going to fly our kite. Dad, I guess kites can fly to heaven! I can't wait! Oh, and Mom, thank you for being my mom. I love you and don't worry, be happy!" She blew a kiss.

With trembling hands, Tammy's eyes turned to the paper. Her eyes were so blurry with tears that she couldn't read it. She faced Dr. Rozak. "I can't read this."

The doctor took her hand. "Congratulations, Tammy! You and Morgan are going to have a baby. You're three months pregnant, and past the critical mark. I have no doubt that this baby will be born healthy."

He smiled. "You have a powerful young lady in your corner, praying up a storm."

Noticing how distraught Tammy was, Morgan rushed to her expecting bad news.

All she could do was hand him the doctor's report, and replay the video.

Morgan watched the recording with amazement. He didn't know what to say. *Could it be true? Is it possible?* He let out a loud breath, and shot a questioning look at his wife.

Tammy nodded, confirming that the report was accurate.

They were going to have the baby they dreamed of, the baby they longed for.

Silence hung between them for a moment while the truth settled in.

The expression on Morgan's face changed to pure joy. As the realization swept over him, he embraced his wife with such force that under normal circumstances it may have hurt, but on this day, she didn't even notice.

They finally drew a short distance apart. Morgan looked up at the picture of Skye on the wall. He could almost hear her say, 'I'm going to ask Jesus for a miracle.'"

Morgan glanced at the lettering over the doorway... "Reach for the Skye." A huge grin encompassed his face as he held his happy wife in his arms. He exclaimed, "We have Skye's miracle!"

He kissed his wife passionately, their lips tasting salty from the tears streaming down their faces, but this time they were tears of joy!

The wonderful sound of laughter on the playground interrupted their tender moment.

Morgan closed his eyes. He could almost hear Skye's laughter and see her in heaven. She was running through the park, flying her kite with dozens of butterflies following her. Her loving parents looked on.

Gratefully, he raised his hands toward heaven, reaching for the Skye.

Letter to my Readers

*While **A Quest For Skye** is fiction, Batten disease is not. The children and family members who struggle with this crippling disease can tell you how very real it is. Batten disease is rare; many doctors don't even know about it. It certainly is not on the top of the list for financial support. Only a few people and organizations donate to the cause of Batten disease. It doesn't affect as many children as other well-known diseases, but still it affects someone's child. I urge you to research this disease, see the children online who have been touched by it, and get to know their parents. When you do, you will see how devastating the disease is. Batten sufferers need men and women in this novel like the Leontious and Hamiltons who dedicate their lives and money to search for the cure. Above all, these families suffering from this disease need your prayers. Please read the letter below from one such parent—my friend, Tracy VanHoutan.*

Thank you,

J. L. Rothdiener

Dear Readers,

My name is Tracy VanHoutan and 2 of my 3 children (Noah and Laine) are affected by the Late Infantile form of this devastating disease that first takes away childhood and then takes away the child.

Noah and Laine began their lives as healthy, energetic kids who loved to jump, giggle, and run. They had endless things to say, and were always looking for their next big adventures. They appeared perfectly healthy until they turned three, when they began suffering seizures and gradually lost skills they had once mastered.

Noah now has a feeding tube. He can no longer walk, talk, see the world around him, or control his body. Laine communicates and eats only with extensive assistance. In the past year she has lost the ability to walk independently and is losing her vision slowly. She has become increasingly frustrated as she no longer can keep up with her twin sister, Emily. Meanwhile Emily continues to astonish us by doing new things every day, reminding us how far from "normal" her siblings have come.

Life is a struggle for all of us. But we try to remember the simple blessings that come with the great loss we face. Noah and Laine will be forever simple and sweet. They'll never see the complications of life. They will never have their hearts broken. They will never see their own kids get sick. God will welcome them home early so that they can run, jump, and talk again someday. And they are, and always will be, an inspiration for the countless friends, family, and volunteers whose lives they've touched.

Our family and the entire Batten community would like to thank John for telling this story... our story... in such a special way.

Batten disease or Neuronal Ceroid Lipofuscinosis (or NCL), is named after the British pediatrician who first described it in 1903. Although Batten disease in the past was usually regarded as the juvenile form of NCL, it has now become the term to encompass all forms of NCL. The forms of NCL are classified by age of onset and have the same basic cause, progression, and outcome. However, the forms of NCL are all genetically different.

Over time, affected children suffer mental impairment, worsening seizures, and progressive loss of sight and motor skills. Eventually, children with Batten disease become blind, tube fed, bedridden, and unable to communicate. Presently, it's always fatal. To more easily understand what this disease is, imagine combining Alzheimer's disease with Parkinson's disease, and then have that disease manifest in a child. Batten disease is not contagious, and currently there is no FDA approved treatment or cure.

There are four main types of NCL, including two forms that begin earlier in childhood and a very rare form that strikes adults. The symptoms are similar but they become apparent at different ages and progress at different rates.

Infantile NCL (Santavuori-Haltia disease) begins between about 6 months and 2 years of age and progresses rapidly. Affected children fail to thrive and have abnormally small heads. Also typical are short, sharp muscle contractions called myoclonic jerks. Initial signs of this disorder include delayed psychomotor development with progressive deterioration, other motor disorders, or seizures. The infantile form has the most rapid progression and children live into their mid-childhood years.

Late Infantile NCL (Jansky-Bielschowsky disease or LINCL-Batten disease) begins between ages 2 and 4. Children hit their early milestones and then early signs are loss of muscle coordination (ataxia) and seizures, along with progressive mental deterioration. This form progresses rapidly and ends in death between ages 8 and 12. This is the disease Noah and Laine are living with.

Juvenile NCL (Batten disease) begins between the ages of 5 and 8. The typical early signs are progressive vision loss, seizures, ataxia, or clumsiness. This form progresses less rapidly and ends in death in the late teens or early 20s, although some may live into their 30s.

Adult NCL (Kufs Disease or Parry's Disease) generally begins before the age of 40, causes milder symptoms that progress slowly, and does not cause blindness. Although age of death is variable among affected individuals, this form does shorten life expectancy.

Fewer than 1,000 children in the United States are currently living with Batten disease. Because it's so rare, it receives very little research attention and only a handful of scientists around the world are focused on potential therapies. Compared to other diseases, Batten disease receives only the tiniest fraction of federal and industry funding for research.

If you want to learn more about Noah and Laine, and about Batten disease I have provided a few websites. The first is **www.BDSRA.org**, the website of the Batten Disease Support and Research Association (BDSRA), where I sit on the Board of Directors. The BDSRA is the largest and oldest organization in the world dedicated to scientific research and support of families affected by Batten disease.

And here are few other sites where you can learn more about these special children, and the efforts on their behalf.

www.NoahsHope.com

www.beyondbatten.org

www.hope4bridget.com

www.taylorstale.com

www.drewshope.com

www.helphayden.com

www.ourpromisetonicholas.com

www.blakespurpose.org

A percentage of proceeds from this book will be donated to combating Batten Disease.

About the Author

J. L. Rothdiener was born in Syracuse, New York. Raised in Lakewood Colorado, he and his wife of thirty-eight years now reside in Bolivar, Missouri. They have two sons, and three wonderful grandchildren.

Rothdiener has had a lifelong passion for writing and began submitting articles to magazines and newspapers for publishing at an early age. He believes that God has given him the ability to write stories which can help change lives.